The Rise and Fall of Rocky Love

ALSO BY KATIA LIEF

Last Night (as Karen Ellis)
A Map of the Dark (as Karen Ellis)
The Money Kill
Vanishing Girls
Next Time You See Me
You Are Next
Names of the Dead
Waterbury
Here She Lies
One Cold Night
Seven Minutes to Noon
Five Days in Summer
Love, Sex & the Wrong Bride
Soul Catcher

The Rise and Fall of Rocky Love

A Novel
Katia Lief

"To understand one life, you must swallow the whole world."
—Salman Rushdie, *Midnight's Children*

"I am the work of art. My work is my shadow."
—Justin Green, *New Comics*

For Oliver Lief

excellent boyfriend
tender husband
epic father

Manhattan
1989–1991

Chapter 1

The Beginning of the End

*L*ate summer roses bloom along Park Avenue—red ones—a bright seam running up the wide sunwashed avenue all the way to 89th Street and beyond. Cat crosses Madison and turns on Fifth. She passes under the blue awning, through the polished bronze entrance and into the familiar lobby. Her leather soles click along the marble floor. She smiles at Angel, the doorman, who winks and opens a drawer in his small desk. He hands her a bulky envelope, marked with her name, holding a spare set of keys.

She pushes the elevator button and waits. She wonders if she'll miss Angel. Right now, she feels she will. But even as she steps into the elevator, that sentimental feeling begins to dissipate. As she is whisked up to the penthouse, to her former boss Rocky Love's old digs—uninhabited and on the market—she realizes, really *gets*, that after this she will never come back here again.

A feeling of happiness sweeps through her when she thinks of her secret. *She is pregnant—again.* She has savored this knowledge for over a week, but before she can risk revealing it to anyone, she has to tie up some loose ends. A few hours at her old office, where for the last year she has learned what it really means to be a celebrity assistant, and then she can begin her future.

The living room is drenched in sunshine. Cat stands in front of the wall of windows and looks out. The view from way up here is spectacular, twenty stories high above Central Park. Her view at home, downtown on Sixth Street, is of a two-foot airshaft and the brick side of another building. She has a small mirror propped in the window, facing up, to catch a tiny bit of the sky. The same sky falls right into Rocky's vast uptown window, engorging it with color and light.

What struck Cat at first, when she started working for Rocky and the glitter dazzled her, was the transition home on the subway. The contrast was so stark, going from this penthouse with its luscious golds and lavenders and blue-skied panoramas, into the dark subway tunnels. People begging for food-pennies and drug-dimes below, when above fortunes went for *haute couture* and limousines that traveled between two beautiful, lonely homes.

Rocky could be anywhere in the world she wanted, but eventually no place and no one could comfort her. All that time and energy she put into angling for a comeback she thought would revive her once-brilliant career and rejuvenate her life—only no one would tell her the truth. She was a has-been, the world had moved on without her and it wasn't looking back. The problem was that no one really wanted to hurt her feelings. For all her faults, Rocky was capable of tenderness and humor and it was hard not to care for her when you didn't despise her.

Looking out the window at the inspiring view, Cat feels a stark awareness of how similarly ambivalent she had felt, as a girl, about her mother Janet before she conquered her alcoholism. Now, a year after entering Rocky's sinking-celebrity life, the parallel between these two women—both addicts, of one sort or another, who doled out heartbreak like after-school candy—seems painfully obvious. Her reaction to the familiar emotional toxins should have been predictable: first she would collaborate, then she would rebel. But if anyone had suggested, when she started her job, that as a so-called adult-child-of-an-alcoholic she was *repeating old habits by setting herself up for disappointment in a co-dependent relationship*, she would have told them to take their shrink-speak and stuff it. What she was looking for, she would have said, was a day job so that at night she could pursue her art without worry. The job was never just about paying off the mountain of credit card debt she had accidentally accumulated in her life as an aspiring cartoonist. It was an adventure. And what would be better than working for someone whom, as a teenager, she had idolized?

On her very first day, a warm September morning a year ago, Cat took care to dress professionally so she would make a good impression. She wore a white skirt with a pale yellow-and-blue striped blouse, and French braided her long wheat-blond hair, cinching the bottom with a little blue bow. She had never expected circumstances to converge into this job, but then that's life. You do things you never thought you would, learn things you never particularly wanted to know. Her live-in boyfriend Teddy just couldn't support them both as a freelance art critic, though he had tried valiantly, giving her the gift of time to concentrate on her own work. When she told him her father had said that his friend, the famous Rocky Love, was looking for a new assistant, Teddy nodded his head slowly, unsurprised, and she guessed that her lover and father had already discussed it. That her father and Rocky had had an affair made Cat wonder if it really was a good job or if he just wanted to do his old flame a favor. But the salary would be enough to cover her bills and pay down her credit cards, the hours would be tolerable, she'd be given health insurance, after six months she was promised her first week of paid vacation—and it was a chance to be close to an idol.

She arrived exactly on time that first day and entered the magnificent penthouse in awe. The morning light was pure and brilliant and the living room was like a jewel shimmering atop the sordid city, a crown on a crazy head. Cat was greeted by Annie, the woman who cared for Rocky's seven-year-old son Parker and also ran both homes. (The country house was perched behind a dune in Amagansett, and they fled there every weekend.) Annie was somewhere in her sixties, small and stout, with curly short gray hair and smile lines wrinkle-etched into her face. She dressed in bright white sneakers, pants and pastel sweatshirts which sometimes bore legends such as *have a nice day before some jerk comes along and wrecks it* or *executive cook and parlor maid*.

Annie smiled. "Come on in, honey. What can I getcha? Coffee, tea, some juice?" When Cat hesitated, Annie added, "Rocky's on the phone to France. It'll be a while."

"Okay, coffee. Thanks."

Annie walked in small even steps through the sunken living room, with its lavender couches and golden-framed paintings, into the adjoining dining room. Cat followed.

"Have a seat," Annie said before continuing into the kitchen.

Cat sat at the oval dining table, sun-streaked smoky glass, and waited. A red button on the multi-line wall phone near the kitchen must have been Rocky talking overseas. Annie clearly intended to make Cat feel welcome. They chatted, Cat sipping her coffee and Annie her tea, until they heard the thud of footsteps. The red light was gone. Rocky was coming.

She burst into the dining room with a bright, "Hello!" She was wearing a green silk caftan, her feet were bare and her reddish brown hair was swept back in a ponytail. Her face looked puffy without makeup. When they had last met, for Cat's interview, Rocky was dressed as for TV, lavishly, with a made-up youngish face. Now she looked sleepy, raw—real. Cat could feel a smile stretch across her face as Rocky planted a kiss on her cheek.

"This is going to work so well for both of us." Rocky's voice was smooth and youthful, hopeful, contrary to her fatigue-rimmed eyes. "I can *feel* it."

Cat said, "Me, too." She was too nervous to summon her normal loud voice which probably would have blurted out something like *if I have to have a job this is the one I want so thank you*. This was The Rocky Love, voice of courage and hope. Cat felt lucky to be here.

"Your father was a genius to put us together," Rocky said. "How *is* Mort, by the way? We haven't spoken lately."

Cat was aware that her father's unclassifiable relationship with Rocky petered out soon after Cat's interview. From what he said, Rocky had been undergoing a transformation, and had apparently transformed him out of her life. "A relief," he called the ending of the friendship, advising his daughter to, "Have fun if you take the job—Rocky is like no one I've ever known." It was his only comment about a woman he had dated, or whatever, for months.

"He's fine," Cat said, and left it at that.

"He told me you're an artist."

Cat felt a blossom of gratitude for Rocky's interest in her. "Yes. A cartoonist, actually. I've been working on a comic strip about bisexuality and AIDS."

"It sounds brilliant. You should show it to me one of these days. I'd love to see your work."

"Thanks for asking."

But the way Rocky's smile remained frozen, Cat wasn't sure she meant it, and decided she'd better play that one by ear.

"Well, the day is short." Rocky stood. "Shall we?"

Cat followed Rocky through the living room and down a long hallway. There were six rooms off the hall, two on either side, and two at the very end. Cat's office was the first room on the left. It was bigger than her bedroom downtown, where she and Teddy squeezed themselves into a dark space with just enough room left over to maneuver around the double bed. Here she would have space and light and quiet and a door to shut. An L-shaped desk faced a huge window that overlooked Central Park. There was a computer and a printer, a heavy duty copier, a fax machine, an answering machine and a phone.

"This is our control center," Rocky said. "If you need anything to make yourself more comfortable, ask. You're in charge here. You'll work very much on your own."

Cat had never imagined she would have a room like this to herself and couldn't resist a smile of pleasure.

They proceeded down the hallway. Rocky walked with a swagger, her bare feet pressing into the champagne colored carpet. Cat felt acutely conscious of the history of the woman leading her down the hall. *This was Rocky Love—in person.*

Back when the women's movement had some exciting voices that offered hope to drifting young girls like Cat, Rocky Love's voice was the loudest. The things she said became buttons and posters and television sound-bites. *Don't Call Me Girl!* demanded that people stop infantilizing women. *Slavery Lives at Sixty-nine Cents on the Dollar!* was a battle cry for equal pay. *Choice Is Our Right!* championed and helped win the right to choose abortion. Rocky Love made it her business to broadcast the idea that becoming a woman was a hopeful prospect. Cat remembered wearing a button with one of Rocky's most famous slogans: *The ERA for change is NOW or never!* Well, the Equal Rights Amendment never passed, and the National Organization for Women lost the promise of its early momentum—but Cat still had her button, knowing that sometimes old fashions returned.

Next to Cat's office was the guest room, blue-flowered walls and antique furniture and the same Central Park view. She expected to move consecutively door to door along the hall, but instead Rocky led her back to the beginning, to the door directly across from Cat's office. This was Annie's room, done in shades of cantaloupe, and more antiques. The country inn feeling was adultered only by the view, which on this side of the penthouse was a cityscape of building apexes and valleys at the bottom of which were the city streets. They moved on to the next door, which was Parker's room. One whole wall of shelves was crammed full of toys. A Star Wars mobile hung from the center of the ceiling. A single bed was pressed into the corner. Something was wrong with this room and then Cat realized what it was: there was no mess, no little boy clutter, no residue of last-minute play. She felt mildly uneasy as they moved to the last two rooms, twin doors at the end of the hall leading to what Rocky called her "suite."

She was shown the bedroom first, the door on the right. The walls were painted a deep maroon and spotlights directed your attention to specific areas. A black lacquered table in the corner. Four small Oriental pictures that Cat saw, upon really looking, were blatantly erotic. A big lacywhite bed. Immediately she sensed the contradictions: hard surfaces and soft, sharp edges and smooth, black lacquer and white lace. Next to an antique dresser, upon which sat a red and gold jewelry box and a large bottle of Opium perfume, was an old battered trunk.

Rocky's study was connected to the bedroom by an inner door. This room, in contrast to the darkness of the bedroom, was light and airy, more a room for dreaming than working. The walls were papered in creamy orange swirls. The floor was plush with a fawn colored carpet. On the wall above an antique wooden desk was a large framed poster of a black-and-white photograph advertising a Dutch play—a bride in windswept white and her groom clung together and hurried forward. They were beautiful, urgent. Across the room was a picture window, bursting with another lush park view. Half of one wall was completely covered with photographs, mostly of Rocky.

"This is the Love Wall," she said, with her wide smile and big brown eyes watching Cat's face. Cat stepped up for a closer look. Rocky moved with her, and pointed. "This is me as a child. And here, with my parents on a ship when I was eleven. Here I am when I first hosted *The Mad Wife*. Here, with my first husband Bob Love. Second husband Jason Barthoff. When Parker was born. My boyfriend Tim. Correction, *ex*-boyfriend. *He* turned out to be just another cad, but don't they all?"

Cat tried to follow but got sidetracked by a collage of black-and-white nudes taken when Rocky was young. She must have been forty-five by now, and in these she was barely in her twenties. She had had an earthy beauty; her appeal was not blatant, not covergirl cute, but easygoing and direct. Like her first solo radio show. *The Mad Wife* had a gutsy, honest voice women loved and a sexiness men loved. It had made her famous and, eventually, rich. There she was, as the girl within whom that voice was building up its tenor. Stretched out naked on the sand with her eyes closed. Spread-eagled on a bed looking innocent and terrified. Striding across a room with a happy, surprised expression.

"I don't know why I have those up," Rocky said. "I sued the photographer. He published them without my knowledge, after I was famous. I'm very litigious." She smiled. "I won."

"Who's this?" Cat was struck by a candid black-and-white photo of the same earthy young woman standing with a tall-dark-and-handsome young man. "Were you in love?"

"That's me and my brother, Nathan, after he got back from Vietnam."

But Cat thought the photo showed lovers, not siblings. She looked again. Their eyes were shining and they leaned together with unmistakable intimacy. But *incest*? No way. The sexual politics of *that* would be too dark for an idealist like Rocky Love. Cat told herself that she must have misread the photo. It was the only explanation.

"Where is he now?" Cat asked.

Rocky touched the next picture without answering. "Here's me with Parker."

It was a professional portrait, happy faces pressed together. He was a chubby boy with black hair and a wide smile that was just like Rocky's.

"He's adorable," Cat said, though it was an exaggeration. He looked remarkably average in the picture.

"Isn't he?" Rocky smiled. "Motherhood is about the best thing that can happen to a woman."

Cat didn't know what to say; it was the kind of throwback remark she never would have expected to fall from the lips of Rocky Love. But expectations were made to be broken. It was a disappointment *and* a relief to discover that this woman, famous for her salty social commentary, was soft at the core.

And then Rocky broke the spell. "Motherhood is *great*, as long as you don't have to raise the little bastards yourself!"

Red roses. Cat had doodled a bouquet of five dogs, leashed to the hand of a single dogwalker, sniffing the roses with Park Avenue buildings looming above. It was just a rough idea but she had liked it and taped it to the wall next to her desk. Beneath it is the first four-frame row of the *Man in Tights: Adventures of a Bisexual in the Age of AIDS* comic strip she finished just before coming to work for Rocky. All the cartoons she has done since are too subversive, raw and autobiographical to hang on an office wall.

Legends, she calls this new work, the chronicle of her life in a series of comic strips: Growing up alone-ish in 1970's Manhattan; failing to starve herself to death, but not for lack of effort; abortion (making a choice without ever really deciding); finding and losing and re-defining love; the undertow of being both woman and artist, how the conflicts start early, pull hard and become who you are. These strips grew out of the journal she began writing as a way to keep herself sane during this last challenging year. To her surprise, *Legends*, which she created purely as a personal exploration with no intention ever to show them to any-one—on the assumption that even in 1990 no one would be interested in comic strips about a young woman's inner life—have turned out to be her most persuasive work. She recently received the good news that they will be included in a gallery show of emerging cartoonists, setting the stage for a promising career of her own, should she be so lucky.

And then, of course, there is her secret, which will change her life more than anything else, and which she will keep to herself for now. *Motherhood.* She would raise her own child *and* follow her ambition, which was the ultimate feminist litmus test Rocky not only couldn't master but never even tried.

Cat lays the cartoons from her office wall neatly in a file folder, which she packs into a cardboard box marked CAT-PERSONAL. Then she stoops to the floor to get her purse, in which she has been carrying the disk with the most recent version of Rocky's memoirs ever since she deleted it from the hard drive. She decides that while she is here, she may as well print a copy of the memoirs for John Paglia, Rocky's collaborator and recently her nemesis. He had worked hard at understanding her, certainly harder than she ever had, and when he was through the mirror he held up—and the secrets he revealed—sent her tumbling over the edge.

Cat inserts the disk in the B drive and calls up the directory. Then, one by one, she prints out the chapters of John's formerly authorized, currently unauthorized biographical opus of the roller coaster ride of the life of Rochelle Libbon Love Barthoff: *The Rise and Fall of Rocky Love.*

Everything else, all the office stuff, is going into storage and will have to be inventoried in detail.

It's amazing how time can slip by. A whole year in this room, organizing Rocky. Liking her, even loving her, then learning to pretend to like her, and finally betraying her. Well, they *all* betrayed her, didn't they? There's money in fame, even if it's not your own, and with money comes temptation. Though Cat herself didn't do it for money, nor would she get any. It was really just Rocky's agent and biographer who were poised to make off with extra cash. What she got was a private satisfaction, a sense of her own small powers in a situation in which she had come to feel powerless. Handing over Rocky's secrets to John was wrong, Cat knows that now. Even so, she feels justified by John's own notion that no one betrayed Rocky until long after she had betrayed herself.

The big L-shaped desk is scattered with papers Cat called "miscellaneous" and never really found a place for. But today she must. She has to label and categorize these random left-over memos and clippings and photos and receipts and bills and letters. For a moment she considers stuffing them all into a big file and titling it The End.

And yet, for Cat, this is a beginning. That Rocky's fall has coincided with the start of Cat's rise is an irony that does not escape her. She doesn't yet know how to interpret the fact that some of her recent choices seem antithetical to the ideologies that made Rocky famous. The ideas that inspired Cat as a girl now seem to fly above society's head like untethered helium balloons. She has stood on the ground of her adulthood watching the balloons vanish, discovering that real-life choices are too wordy, complex and uncertain to fit on a button or bumper sticker. She wishes she had the clarity of Rocky's early convictions. But then again, look where it got her: locked up in a psychiatric facility, free-writing a version of her life no one would ever see.

Poor Rocky, Cat thinks. Sitting at the desk, she surveys the mess. There is so much to do. She starts with the easiest—bills. She digs through the paper debris and collects eleven utility and service bills, setting them aside for Rocky's father, Dr. Norman Libbon. He brought her into the world; he can decide what to do now.

The photos from Rocky's childhood can go to Dr. Libbon, too. It seems a shame to pack them up with the publicity glossies of Rocky, all teased and sprayed and skin-stretched and made-up. The old photos from her childhood are black-and-whites of a dreamy girl with wild brown hair, wearing jeans or miniskirts with scanty tie-dyed halter tops. Smiling. Rocky used to smile with so much hope. She had fire in her eyes when she was young; you could tell she intended to conquer the world. And she did, in a funny suicidal kind of way. Some of the childhood photos have been published in books, but the Libbons might appreciate having Rocky's own tattered prints. At one point, she had signed the backs of some of them with her huge round signature, which grew over the years, screaming ME ME ME.

Chapter 2

The Rise and Fall of Rocky Love

an unauthorized life
by Rocky Love with John Paglia

Genesis

*I*n eighteen years as an obstetrician, Dr. Norman Libbon had welcomed hundreds of babies into the world, including four sons of his own. But on April 6, 1947, at ten-o-six in the morning, he had the shock of his life when from between his wife Mabel's legs emerged a tiny pink hand. An electric reaction of surprise passed through the delivery room as Mabel's volcanic scream erupted and the tiny one's shoulders seemed to split her in half. Though she had given birth five times in nine years, each time the scream was just as primal, as if she were being axed down the middle as out came a baby in a gush of blood. As his wife collapsed in a final whack of pain, Dr. Libbon lifted the tiny baby by the ankles and slapped her bottom. The baby turned pink from her backside to her cheeks, and with the first cry that burped from her lips began the colic wailing of months.

Dr. Libbon cradled the goopy crying baby in his arms and bent at the knees to lower himself to bed level. Mabel breathed heavily. Her brown hair was caked with sweat on her forehead. She turned her head to see.

"We have a girl, Mabel," he said. "Can you believe it? Four sons, and now a baby girl."

Mabel smiled, her thirty-year-old face lined with fatigue, and she looked upon her weeping daughter. "Rochelle," she whispered, "don't worry, you'll never want for anything." She strained her neck to kiss the tiny forehead.

"Such a beauty," said Norman of his pink wrinkled babe.

"Well, we have our little princess now. I'd say that's enough children for one lifetime." Mabel beamed love at newborn Rochelle.

Norman leaned into his wife. "You know," he said in a low voice, "she came out *reaching*."

"Me, me, me!" Mabel said, rocking her bawling infant on the back porch, as she watched her sons play softball in the yard. Norman's father, Dr. Lawrence Libbon, had bought this mansion at the turn of the century, when it was already over fifty years old and Brooklyn was an urban outback. The house stood next to the Promenade like a regal eye, keeping watch on the visitors who came to stroll by the side of the river and delight in the glorious silhouette of Manhattan. Curious onlookers would stop to peer into the gigantic windows. The family life of the Libbons was obscured by lace curtains, betraying nothing more than movement and light. In front of the screened back porch was a large yard, beyond which was the cobbled walkway of the Promenade, the river, and the southern end of Manhattan. The Promenade was popular with lovers, no matter what the season; and in the urgent late-September wind, couples clung on benches, then hurried away. Surrounded by her children, Mabel watched the lovers and remembered herself and Norman, twelve years ago, frozen in a moment of her memory.

From the beginning, they had shared a spirit of devotion which was defined for Norman in science, and for Mabel in religion. Raised a Protestant, Norman had disavowed God, and because she loved him, Mabel Rosenberg chose to view his lack of belief more as an open field in which her faith could roam free. She agreed to a quiet wedding at City Hall. They both believed in the ultimate goodness of people, and they were equally serious about the importance of having a large family.

But at the bottom of all that was love. What started in wind under stars—on a bench at the Promenade, watching the dark blue river curl around Manhattan—rooted itself in earth. He presented her with a good solid future. And she cared for him deeply, slowly teasing feelings from him with love. She always listened to his views even when she strongly disagreed, and he dared to hope that she might allow an atheist home.

She led him to believe this, which was deceptive of her; because the day Robert Libbon was born in 1938, Mabel announced that their children would be raised as Jews. Her one concession was that Norman need not directly participate, as long as he didn't obfuscate her efforts. This was the couple's most serious compromise, and to their credit, they lived with it more or less peaceably. As the family grew, and the couple became distracted from each other, Mabel carried their original love like a shutaway jewel, which she took out from time to time to remind her.

"I am an incurable romantic," she would tell her young sons. Robert was nine, Earl was seven, Nathan was five, and Leo was two.

"When's that little zero gonna ever stop crying?" Earl begged his mother. "*When?*"

"Maybe when her brothers learn to treat her like a lady, how's that?" Mabel said with a sharp nod. She knew his complaint was not so much about the crying as about all the attention it gathered to his sister. For five years, before Leo, Earl was a middle child in constant struggle to be remembered. Now, there was another youngest baby to steal his parents away. He had liked it when it was only Robby and him, and their father would play with them on weekends. Now he never did.

"Daddy can make her stop," Earl said, grimacing his squarish face at Rochelle.

He looked so cute in his short pants and dirty sweatshirt and Dodgers cap. His knobby knees were scraped, and his serious face was streaked with mud. Mabel smiled at her little Earl.

"Go on, sweetie, your brothers need you on the ball field."

Earl stood there sulking, until Rochelle's frantic crying had once again stolen their mother's attention—then he dashed back to the game.

Finally, at the age of five months, two weeks and six days, during a storm one Sunday in late September, Rochelle Libbon stopped crying. She smiled, and blinked her eyes, and laughed. Her brothers gathered around the crib, pinched her chubby arms, tickled her under the chin, and pressed their fingertips into her dimples. Without all the noise, they learned to love her.

Teeny four-year-old Rochelle knew how to jump so her petticoats fluttered up and her brown banana curls bounced. She was a cheerleading squad of one, adamant in her adorableness, a girl with a mission. She had four handsome, popular brothers who needed to understand that of all the females in the world—women and girls, large and small, round and narrow, loud and quiet—she, Rochelle, was the most important to love. She performed for them: at the table, before bed, on the way to school, on the sidelines of their afternoon games. Robby, who as the oldest was the most important to woo, smiled, waved, even blushed, but otherwise didn't pay much attention. Earl flatly ignored her. Leo, the youngest boy, wavered between joining the baseball team and the cheerleading squad and, never making up his mind, stood at the sidelines and watched.

It was Nathan who most felt the power of young Rochelle. By the age of nine, he was the most handsome and sensitive of the good looking Libbon boys. His thick brown hair was traced with gold which glittered in the sun when he moved. Rochelle thought his soft brown eyes were dreamy. His slender rounded nose was slightly arrogant, and he used it to make a point when he needed to. In contrast, his lips were full, naturally pouting for kisses. He knew he would be a doctor when he grew up: they all would, except Rochelle, whom their mother was training to be a doctor's wife. Nathan's idea was to spend his youth dreaming, before it was too late, and he wasted no time with frivolities such as sports. He stretched out on the ground with a book, alongside the baseball diamond where the other boys and their friends played, and watched his sister campaign for attention. Despite appearances, Nathan spent more time gazing up into his baby sister's skirt than at the page. And Rochelle knew it.

"Na-than!" she giggled, and he turned a page and pretended to read. Nathan's imaginings, which would come to mark his life, began there on the miniature baseball diamond behind the big house on Columbia Heights. His loving gaze silently taught Rochelle how to move, to kick, to call out her appreciation of the opposite sex. Without realizing it—because after all she was too young to know—she followed him like a mentor: learning, absorbing, taking his cues.

Rochelle was a boy's girl, geared to trust and to please. Mabel, who felt she had been blessed with a daughter and should reap the benefits of a special friendship, observed Rochelle's intense loyalty to her brothers and father, and strove to impart a female point of view.

In her campaign to align female with female in an otherwise male home, Mabel displayed a blue and white flowered apron she had sewed especially for Rochelle. There were ruffles around the edges. *Ruffles.* Nathan laughed, and so did seven-year-old Rochelle. Mabel forced a smile and waved the apron like a flag. "Darling, wouldn't you like to help Mommy in the kitchen sometimes?"

Leo shyly approached the apron. "I'll help," he said, touching the ruffle. "Can I try it on?"

"Aprons are for girls, Doctor Leo," said Mabel. "Your wife will have her own apron."

Leo looked aggrieved. He stood by that apron, demurely sullen, and tried to suppress a blush that rose from his neatly ironed collar up his slender neck and blazed into his narrow face.

"Okay, Mom," he said.

"Rochelle, darling, would you like to help Mommy make dinner tonight?"

Rochelle shrugged. She looked to Nathan, who slightly curled his bottom lip: their secret sign for *no*. The *yes* sign was quickly flared nostrils.

"I have homework, Mommy," Rochelle said.

"Nathan will help you with your homework later. Come, spend some time with Mama in the kitchen. Learn from me before I die."

Mabel's most lethal bullet: "Before I die." That meant she really wanted you to obey. It meant if you didn't, she'd tell Doctor Norman. And he would order the sacrifice of some important pleasure, like dessert for a week, or the monthly movie.

"Yes, Mommy, okay."

So Rochelle put on the apron, transforming her from a poetically inclined cheerleader to a stupidlooking ruffly baby-doll. Robby and Earl collapsed in hysterics. Nathan shook his head, suppressing laughter. Poor Leo burned with jealousy.

This was the day Rochelle first observed the making of a True Jewish Blintz.

"Into the batter you pour everything you know," Mabel said. "Art, literature, music. Everything. Into the batter. Mix—around, around, around—slowly, with strength, with grace, like a dancer. Pour the batter onto the griddle one ladle at a time. These are your children, and each should be perfect. Brown and flip, brown and flip, brown and flip. You are an acrobat. Here we are sunbathing, laying each perfect pancake like a towel on the sand, carefully, side by side. Now, my Rochelle, for the filling! The filling we have prepared in advance, of course. Cheese filling, only a little sweet with honey, and our personal touch of nutmeg and vanilla just to confuse the boys a little. Ah, there we go. One big spoon each pancake. And now we fold our little babies into their blankets, one corner at a time, with love. This, Rochelle Libbon, *this* is a True Jewish Blintz! It will be one of your most powerful tools as a woman. Learn it, and never divulge the secret. The best way to marry a doctor is first to master the blintz."

Another tool of the trade was clothes. "You are a bird and these are your feathers," Mabel instructed thirteen-year-old Rochelle. They studied the children's clothing department at Saks Fifth Avenue, where Mabel taught her daughter about fabrics, styles, colors, prices. "You buy what you like, but also what suits your needs." Mabel flung above the rack polka dotted dresses and tight slacks with back zippers, saying, "Rochelle, darling, how about this?" Her response was an inevitable, "No, Mommy, *no*." Rochelle couldn't understand all the flashy clothes her mother chose for her, since Mabel herself wore strictly conservative dresses.

One day, offended by the suggestion of completely matching accessories for a red dress that Rochelle hated anyway, she shot the question to her mother: "Why don't *you* wear it if you like it so much?"

The answer was a resigned, "You're still young. Me, I have different fish to fry. There comes a time for an older woman to turn her mind to other things."

Other things. Rochelle had it figured out: her mother was having an affair because her father was hardly ever home. She imagined the scene: Mabel in her tailored pink suit and little pink hat with its beige net veil, whizzing up in a mirrored elevator to the penthouse love nest. Her lover was rich, of course, and the secret apartment was severe with leather and chrome. A vast window took in the Empire State Building, the tallest building in the world, lit from bottom to top. The city flickered in a mass of red and blue and green and white lights. The apartment had a large bathroom with a deep tub and a double sink. Rochelle never pictured a kitchen; a lovers' hideaway didn't need one. She watched her mother burst from the elevator and run down the hall. The front door sprung open. And there he was: The Rich Lover, standing in front of the picture window. He wore a light gray suit with a blue tie, his steely gray hair was slicked back, his eyes were as blue as sapphires blazing *love* and Mabel rushed into his arms. As the lovers spun around, Rochelle caught sight of a medical bag on a chair. Aha! Mabel's secret lover was a doctor, too! Not that it was such a big surprise; what else could one expect from Mrs. Catch 'Em With a Blintz?

Rochelle was wrong about her mother, though—as most children are. Mabel was devoted to her family. And despite his frequent absences, Norman appreciated his wife. He watched from the distance of his demanding profession as she was contoured by the winds of their children. At times he thought her job was harder than his; and other times he felt so burdened and tired, he wished they could trade places. For all the joy he was privy to as he welcomed babies into the world, his sadness lay in not knowing any of them. Including his own children. He had delivered all of them, and while he saw them most every day, he didn't understand what drove them, or who they were.

Robby was already in medical school at Columbia, on the brink of marriage to his high school sweetheart, Natalie. Earl was at Ohio State University on a football scholarship, acing pre-med, dating girls. He wrote long, loving letters to his father, describing his life, begging for approval without ever asking. Norman sometimes answered with short notes jotted in doctor's scrawl on his prescription pad: "Go get 'em, son." "Too busy to write at length, but thinking of you." "Congratulations on all those A's!" "Your mother hopes you'll be with us for Passover." Leo was in the tenth grade, excelling in art and not science, embarked upon an after-school private tutorial program to prepare him for pre-med. And Nathan was in his junior year of high school, editor of *The Bohemian*, his all-boys school's newspaper into which he bootlegged a column by his sister, secretly published under the byline "Rodney Parker."

Rochelle was determined that the last person she'd ever marry was a doctor. And she'd never just be someone's wife. She had better things in store. Writing as Rodney Parker freed her from the antipromise of the fate professed by her mother. And furthermore, Rochelle decided, she would shed her Jewish half as soon as possible. She would take a pseudonym and do something amazing.

Nathan told her about Collette, who began her career writing erotic juvenile novels under her husband's name, Willie. He took the money and the credit, until she came out of the closet, then everyone knew. Collette. Rochelle. Rochette. Collelle. She was convinced of the inevitability of what she believed to be her destiny: greatness. Inside her beat a rare and great heart, definitely not a Mrs. Doctor.

Rodney Parker's "Advice for Boys" column was immediately popular. Some letters requested information about sports injuries. Rochelle got the information from Robby and Earl, and printed the answers. Other letters asked about parents, which was one of Rochelle's specialties. "Whatever you do," she wrote, "obey, but keep clear on what *you* know is right for you. Be firm in what you believe, just don't let Mom and Dad know it!" The most popular letters were the secret ones: anonymous requests for Rodney's advice about how to date girls. Rochelle told them: "If you know a girl likes you, ask her out to dinner at a nice restaurant, even if it costs all your savings. If you're not sure if she likes you, write a short note; if you never hear from her, assume the worst. When you meet a girl at her house, always bring a gift. Flowers are nice, or perfume, or chocolate. Dress well and be clean. Wear cologne but only if it's exotic. Always escort your date by taxi, never subway, even if you have to borrow money from your parents. Never ask a girl to pay." When asked for advice about sex, Rochelle wrote: "No means no and Yes means yes. If a girl wants it, she'll let you know. If she doesn't, try someone else."

The Advice for Boys column was publicly ridiculed and secretly read. Letters to Rodney collected in Nathan's makeshift office in the library, and he brought them home to Rochelle, who read every one. She learned more about boys from the letters to Rodney than she had living in a house full of males all her life; for the first time, she got a glimpse of their inner thoughts. She didn't realize that much of the advice she doled out came straight from Mabel, but with a twist. Rochelle wanted boys to treat girls well out of respect, not just because one of them might end up their wife. She wanted boys to learn to expect nothing of girls except what girls expected of themselves. She wanted boys to desire girls, and not be too shy to let them know. And she wanted boys to be generous, not because of a moral prerogative, but because she liked to receive gifts and assumed it was their duty to give them to her.

One day the strangest letter so far arrived, and Rochelle didn't know how to answer it. It said "Dear Rodney, I love you. You are so sensitive and deep. Your insight knows no bounds. No one knows how to treat girls better than you. You must be a good friend and lover. I wish I knew what you looked like. Will you print your picture? L."

Some poor girl had gone and fallen in love with Rodney! Rochelle felt guilty for the first time about the deception. What a strange feeling to be loved by a girl; it had never occurred to her that she could elicit such powerful feelings in someone of her own sex. She would have liked to have put the girl out of her misery, but didn't know how to answer without revealing the hoax. So she took the letter to Nathan, and asked his advice.

Since Robby and Earl had gone away to school, Nathan and Leo no longer shared a room. Nathan had taken over the older boys' room and redecorated according to his own tastes. In place of pennants and footballs and posters of star athletes, were photos of Walt Whitman, Ezra Pound, Hemingway, Thomas Wolfe, Yeats. Rochelle called it the Male Hero Wall. He had not taken her dare to include pictures of Collette, Jane Austen, or the Brontës.

She knocked on his door.

"Enter," he said. He was sitting at his desk in the near dark, with an open book illuminated by a small lamp. He had grown tall but still had a lanky teenage build. His hair was cut very short, and he was beginning to shave his reddish beard, which he had let grow stubbly. For added poetic effect, he carried a cigarette between his lips, but never lit it.

She came in flapping the letter. "Some *girl* has the hots for me."

"Let me see that." He grabbed it from her. "Turn on the overhead, why don't you."

Flooded with light, the filth of Nathan's room really hit her. She crossed the floor, avoiding mines of garbage or dirty clothes, and tossed herself onto his bed. She stretched out long, closed her eyes, and tried to feel the blood coursing through her veins. She saw darkness inside her closed lids, black laced with red, and blue dots, and green stripes.

"Nathan?" she whispered.

"Shh," he said, "I'm reading." But really he was watching her.

Rochelle at the age of fifteen was blossoming, but not into the flower Mabel had tried to cultivate. Mabel wanted her only daughter to be small and compact, lithe, with good muscle tone; she wanted her daughter to have manageable hair; she wanted her daughter to be effortlessly beautiful; and she wanted her daughter to dress like a lady. Were Mabel to have her way, Daughter's destiny would further Mother's own; Rochelle would learn all Mabel's lessons in a crash course, and graduate to bigger and better things. But Rochelle the adolescent was a stubborn weed, growing strong and wily into the wind, not with it. In her secret soul she cultivated madness, dreams of a life not of her parents' stable prosperous world but of lunacy and adventure. Rochelle had even grown too tall, with loose muscles hanging on a strong frame. Her breasts were larger than was respectable (but boys appreciated them) and she liked to flaunt them in her brothers' T-shirts, which she wore without a bra. She bought her clothes a size too small, wearing tight T-shirts over crisp jeans cuffed above the ankle. She polished her fingernails and toenails with the most vivid colors she could find: red, orange, yellow, green, black. She refused to wear face makeup, because Mabel wanted her to. And since

Mabel would have liked her to tame her weedy brown hair with curlers and spray, Rochelle let it go wild.

Rebels, after all, are born before revolutions.

It was the beginning of a war, which Rochelle perpetuated in the oblivion of her innocence, and which Mabel fought with conviction. "Our children will be respectable members of society if it kills me!" she told Norman, who remembered that tiny pink hand *reaching*.

Stretched out on her side, Rochelle propped herself up on bent elbow and wiggled into comfort. Nathan enjoyed watching her as much as she enjoyed settling her body into his bed.

"So Nath," she said. "What do you think? I have a *girl*friend."

Nathan swung his long legs up onto the desk. He read the letter again. "Where does it say a girl wrote it? All it says is that it's from L, and L loves you. It's a boys' school, remember."

"You think a boy wrote it?"

Nathan shrugged. "Could be. Why not? Haven't you ever heard of a fruit?" Nathan smiled. "You've got a boyfriend. I'm jealous."

"Jealous enough?"

He walked slowly to the bed, watching Rochelle—who watched back—smiling his cynical sexy James Dean smile. He stretched himself over Rochelle, body on body, a perfect fit. "I'm tempted," he said, "really tempted."

"You're tempting me."

They laughed. Nathan sat up, his back against the wall, his legs flung over hers so their bodies crossed.

"Let's draw him out," Nathan said.

"Who?"

"Your boyfriend, the fruit."

L became "Lover" and Rochelle replied publicly. She had to; the author of the letter had not given a return address. So as not to embarrass L. into hiding, she wrote with the assumption s/he was a girl. "Dear Lover, We at *The Bohemian* are happy to know girls read the paper, too. Your letter was charming. I was personally touched. Maybe we can meet. But first, would you write a letter for the column? Rodney."

Rodney's letter to "Lover" caused a sensation at Nathan's school. A girl writing in? Everyone's sister became suspect; who else was likely to have seen the paper? Nathan wisely mimeographed extra copies of the next issue—in which Lover's letter was expected to appear—and as soon as stacks of the issue were distributed to classrooms, they disappeared.

"Dear Rodney, Thank you for the kindness of your answer. You are very considerate—you know what I mean. I *would* like to meet you in person. Can we arrange a private meeting? L"

"Dear Lover, You are a gentle soul, and would make any man a good wife. Yes I will meet you. But only if you specify place and time in your next letter to *The Bohemian*. Signed, Rodney."

"Dear Rodney, I am so embarrassed, but since you insist, I will comply. The following instructions are in code: ofsosobh nitntfoa efterl tupol ers ed na y. I hope you can decipher this and that your readers will be gentlemen enough not to try. L."

Nathan and Rochelle cracked the code late at night, under his covers, with a flashlight. The intrigue was unnecessary, but it was exciting—side by side in their flannels, like lovers, but not.

"It's so easy," Nathan said. "One fifteen saturday on steps of boro hall."

As she walked to Boro Hall on a sunny early afternoon late in April—in her tight cuffed jeans and red V-necked sweater, hair flying wild—Rochelle felt both excitement and guilt. L, whoever s/he may turn out to be, was a sad soul, and deep in her better heart Rochelle would have liked to have spared him or her. But she also felt thrilled at the possibility and scope of ridicule she could weave around this person.

Stately Boro Hall with its wide steps and pillars had never been visited by so many teenage boys at one time. They were everywhere: across the street, behind the pillars, pacing at the very foot of the steps at either side. Rochelle was not surprised; everyone had been expected to crack the code. Poor L. But what fun! Rochelle glanced around for Nathan, spotted him across the street in a phone booth, and proceeded up the steps.

She sat in the very center. It was one-fifteen. The boys were thrilled; they thought she was L. They thought she was the lovesick girl in search of Rodney's true identity. She looked around for another girl, someone off to the side who would never climb the stairs now that Rochelle was sitting there. But there were only boys, tens of them, waiting. A feeling of intense pleasure filled her as she gathered all their attention.

Then, down at the foot of the steps, Leo appeared, all scrubbed and nervous and thin. He was watching her, just standing there and staring as if trying to understand what to do next. At first she thought he had come along with the other boys to see, but then she realized that Leo didn't know the secret. He didn't know that she was Rodney. Maybe he thought she was the girl who wrote the love letters. No—it was suddenly clear to her—he didn't think that. If he had come to watch, he wouldn't have been standing there as if he had been about to climb, and he wouldn't have been holding that pink carnation. Her insides twisted as she understood that *her brother Leo was L.*

She needed to console him, so she waved. He paled, waved back, then dropped the flower and crossed the street. Rochelle looked at Nathan, whose expression said that he, too, was stunned but had understood.

They decided they had to help Leo. Not to change him, but to let him know it was okay. He was their brother and they wouldn't deliberately hurt him any more than they already accidentally had. He holed up in his room all afternoon until dinner, and they waited for the meal that always began at seven, when he would have to face them.

The dining room occupied the ground floor corner room, whose tall windows, draped in lace, overlooked the Promenade. The large round table that had accommodated the family of seven for twenty years was set tonight for the remaining five: Norman, Mabel, Nathan, Leo and Rochelle. Mabel used her blue and white everyday china for family dinners, and while the table was set casually by her standards, it was opulent with gleaming oak, blue linen napkins, sterling candlesticks of various lengths, red tulips arranged in a low bowl, and platters of boiled chicken, blintzes, challah, vegetables steamed in spicy broth, new potatoes sautéed in garlic. It was Saturday dinner, the end of Sabbath, so dessert would be a bakery cake, probably chocolate. Norman had called to say he'd be half an hour late from the hospital, and as Mabel used the time to advance the after dinner process by cleaning what she could now, Nathan and Rochelle lounged on the living room couch, reading Chinese love poems. Nathan read, in a whisper:

I stand and watch The moonlight creep Through the great gate Across the court. I cannot sleep!

A stir in the night! It is you, my lord, Come to my arms at last?

Ah! 'Tis but the shadow Of dancing flowers, High on the garden wall.— And still I watch And wait!

"Beautiful," Rochelle sighed. She lifted her face to see Leo slip like a wisp of smoke into the dining room. "We have to tell him it's okay," she whispered to Nathan.

"No, we can't say anything. We just have to let him know."

The front door creaked open and Norman walked in.

"Evening, children!" He hung his hat on the round wooden globe that punctuated the bottom of the banister where it curled to its closure. He had developed a middle-aged paunch, and his hairline had receded so far that the front half of his head was totally bald, leaving the back of his head covered with tight gray curls.

Rochelle got up to kiss him. "Hi, Pop."

"Pop!" Norman chuckled. Despite Mabel's warnings, in private, of the dangerous direction in which their daughter was certainly headed, Norman adored Rochelle. Without his having put any real effort into it, she had come to reflect his point of view more than his wife's. Rochelle's renegade spirit charged Norman with a youthful energy he himself had once felt. He secretly approved of his daughter. Not, though, his third son, and on this point he and Mabel concurred.

Nathan should conform, they thought; no one liked a laze-about poet man.

"Where's Leo?" Norman asked.

"At the table," Nathan said.

"What do you say we join him?"

Leo was sitting alone at the table. He looked away when his brother and sister entered the room. Rochelle felt his humiliation, and smiled warmly at him, almost too warmly to seem sincere. Nathan lightly patted his younger brother's shoulder, and sat by his side. They did not speak directly to him, but around him: of school, and friends, and future. Norman and Mabel noticed nothing unusual; they were too used to the tribulations of adolescence to find meaning in discomfort. As cool and easy as Nathan and Rochelle strove to be, Leo remained miserable.

Finally, Rochelle saved him. She said, "And this afternoon, it was *wild*. I've been writing love letters to Nathan's paper and today I went to meet Rodney."

"Love letters?" Mabel said.

And Norman: "Who is this Rodney?"

"He never appeared," Rochelle said. "I don't know."

"Love letters?" Mabel repeated.

"Just for fun," Rochelle said. "You know, to entertain the troops."

Nathan laughed. "People loved it, Mom and Dad. I printed more copies than ever. It was like a continuing epistolary drama, with Rochelle writing letters to Rodney under a pseudonym."

"Who is Rodney," Norman asked.

"I can't tell you, Dad," Nathan said. "As a journalist I have to protect the anonymity of my source."

"Well, I think it's cruel," said Mabel.

"Why, Mom?" Rochelle said. "It was fun."

"Fun? To ridicule this poor Rodney? Fun?"

Rochelle shrugged. "I didn't really ridicule him, Mom. I just wrote that I loved him."

"Which is even worse!"

"It's no big deal. Now everyone knows it was me."

Leo's expression melted into a smile as he realized the gift his siblings were offering. "It doesn't really matter," he said, "if it was only a joke."

Late that night, Leo knocked on Nathan's door. Rochelle was with him, sitting in a corner, blinking a flashlight on and off while Nathan sat crosslegged on the bed and moved his arms balletically in the lightdarklight of the makeshift strobe.

"Who?" said Nathan.

"It's *me*."

"Enter."

They continued their performance for Leo, who watched from the doorway.

"Close the door, we need total darkness," Rochelle said.

Leo shut the door. "What are you doing?"

"Pretending," Nathan said.

"Pretending what?"

"We're not sure," Rochelle said, and she and Nathan cracked up laughing.

His cheeks flush with humiliation, Leo turned to leave.

"Wait." Nathan jumped off the bed, flipped the light switch and the room popped into focus. Leo was in his blue terry bathrobe. His thin legs were covered with dark curly fuzz. "Leo, stay."

"I just wanted to say—" Leo began.

"Never explain and never complain." Nathan laughed, and Rochelle laughed, but Leo wasn't ready to relax even with them; their strange twinship was impenetrable and always had been. He sat stiffly on the edge of his big brother's bed, feeling like a reluctantly invited guest.

"Who is Rodney, anyway?" Leo finally asked.

Rochelle smiled. "Me."

* * *

As the Rodney Parker enterprise soared to its zenith in the Libbon home, and as her children detached from her influence, cleaving instead to each other, Mabel began to think something would have to change. Rochelle and Nathan were too close—they seemed to look at each other with, well, *desire*—and Mabel's fertile imagination feared the worst. Exactly what the change needed to be came to her late one Wednesday afternoon as she lifted the blades of her hand-held mixer out of a dark brown devil's food cake batter.

Nathan had to go.

She ejected the blades, tapped them against the side of the bowl and twirled them above her hand to prevent batter from dripping onto the floor as she carried them to the sink. He was a bad influence on Rochelle. He could go away to boarding school for his senior year.

Before dinner, she summoned Norman into the kitchen, closed the door, and informed him of her decision.

"But dear," he said, "do you really think that's necessary?"

"I've thought it through and I know it's the best decision."

"For who? Not for Nathan."

"For everyone." She walked across the room, opened the refrigerator door and withdrew a bowl of salad she had prepared earlier.

Norman shook his head. "Mabel, in a year he'll be leaving for college."

"It needs to be done now. Before something terrible happens."

"Terrible? How?"

She looked at him and raised her eyebrows.

"Oh, Mabel, that's ridiculous!"

"Nothing is impossible, Norman. Your daughter was born hand-first. I bet you thought *that* could never happen."

Norman paused, thinking it over. What if his wife was right? It wasn't as if, in the history of the world, siblings never

... he couldn't even think it. If she *was* right, and they failed to act because of his hesitation, then he would be responsible.

"I suppose you have a school in mind?"

"San Diego Boys Academy." She vigorously shook a bottle of salad dressing and dripped some onto the salad.

"Mabel!"

"It's a fine school, dear."

"It's practically a military academy!"

"It emphasizes discipline. It is not a military academy."

"I think you should let the idea go. Nathan won't like it."

"I already called the school and they're willing to accept a late application. They think he'll make a good candidate. It's the perfect idea for Nathan, whether he likes it or not. And it will give me some time to help Rochelle become a little more refined before she leaves for college."

"I don't like it."

"Norman, in all the years I have devoted to raising our children, have I ever done anything that wasn't in their best interests?"

"Well, no."

"How can you think I would ever misguide my own children?"

"Of course you wouldn't, dear."

"You'll need to tell him tonight."

"Me?"

"It's a father's job."

And so, after the family had finished their dessert of chocolate cake, after they had pushed their plates to the edges of the place mats and scraped backwards in their chairs, after Mabel had risen and begun to clear the table, Norman looked at Nathan. A child's face ripening in maleness, hormones raging beneath a surface of pimples and whiskers, Adam's apple pronounced in the thin neck, body tall and lank from fast growth. He was drumming the table with a spoon and knife, and Rochelle was bouncing in her seat to his rhythm. Maybe Mabel was right.

Leo was the first to ask to be excused. Norman nodded. All three teenagers stood and began to leave.

"Nathan, hold on a minute."

Nathan paused in the doorway and turned around.

"Have a seat, let's talk."

"About what?"

Norman gestured toward the chair. Nathan sat.

"Can I stay, too?" Rochelle asked.

"This is private."

"Please?"

"What's going on?" Nathan asked.

"Rochelle, please give us some privacy."

She glared at her father and threw a quick kiss to Nathan before stomping up the stairs.

Norman observed his son—leaning back in his chair, arms crossed over his chest, eyes staring solidly ahead—and for a moment surrendered to a deep feeling of love. Nathan was his *child*. He couldn't do this. Then Mabel swung through the door, leaned over the table to snatch away the butter dish, and dug a sharp glance at her faltering husband. Norman leaned forward, cleared his throat, but still couldn't speak. Instead of returning to the kitchen with the butter dish, Mabel sat down at the table.

"Your father and I have something to say to you, Nathan."

"Your mother and I ..." Norman's voice sounded thin. He cleared his throat again. "Your mother and I have decided that you will be going away to school in the fall."

"What?"

"We've found an excellent school we think you'd do well to attend in preparation for college."

"College? That's like two years away!"

"Less than that," Mabel corrected. "Norman?"

"We feel it would be a good idea if you spent your senior year—"

"I'm not going."

"I'm afraid your mother and I have decided—"

"Forget it."

Nathan stood. Norman stood. For the first time, Norman saw that he and his son had reached the same height.

"I don't want to go away, Dad."

"We often don't want to do what's best."

"Why is it best?"

"We feel—"

"Whose decision is this? Yours? Or *yours*?" Nathan faced his mother. "You put him up to this, didn't you?"

"Your father is the head of this household." Mabel stood up and carried the butter dish to the kitchen.

"Dad, are you telling me this is your idea?"

Norman received the blazing eyes of his third son, the middle spoke of his progeny, a boy he dearly loved. And he lied, "Yes, it is."

Nathan left for California in the fall of 1962. The Libbons received tuition bills along with notes from the principal, attached to Nathan's report cards, suggesting that he could do better if he tried. By spring, they received a letter informing them that Nathan would need to attend summer school in order to graduate. Before their deposit check had even reached the school, Nathan had run away to Berkeley.

Nathan wrote only to Rochelle, describing his adventures hanging out with Beatniks reading poetry in coffee houses and staying up all night smoking wacky weed. She begged her parents to send her to California for a visit, and they refused. Rochelle and Nathan corresponded like unrequited lovers, in long tense letters. From the safe distance of three thousand miles, Nathan revealed the flip side of his love for her, the lust side of the coin. "I want to marry you," he wrote in one letter. And she replied, "Yes." They both knew that, if a visit had been allowed, their yearning for each other would have crossed every boundary.

Home was intolerable without Nathan. And with Leo preparing for early admittance to the University of Pennsylvania the following year, Rochelle was in despair. The thought of being left alone with her mother, who would only become more ferocious in her attempts to sculpt her, was terrifying. So she escaped into her school, joining every plausible activity: Speakers Corner, Literary Ladies, Art Circle. Anything nondomestic. At night she studied alone in her room. She did so well in her classes that, by the time she graduated, she had earned prizes and a scholarship to the college of her choice.

Norman was proud, but Mabel was worried. What kind of a wife would this girl make? "I'm gonna be a famous writer!" Rochelle proclaimed. And Mabel shrieked, "Rochelle, calm down, *now!*"

Chapter 3
Celebrity Smile

First thing in the morning, as always, Cat meets with Rocky in her office to begin their day. She perches on a footstool with a pad of paper balanced on her knees and a pen ready to write. Rocky sits across from her, crosslegged on the couch, in a pool of sunshine that would have been enough to blind Cat. But Rocky soaks it in, never so much as shielding her eyes. It is the start of Cat's third week on the job and some things have come to be expected. For example, the day will revolve around the list they make now, together.

"Call back those pushy people who wanted me to talk at that boring thing," Rocky says.

"And tell them?"

"I'm unable to speak, but I'm happy to make a donation. Send a hundred dollars."

Cat jots it down. *No city parks fundraiser.*

"They should be paying *me*."

Cat almost notes that, too, then stops herself.

"Talk isn't cheap."

"I guess your usual speaking fee would eat up too much of their budget."

"Call Charlie." Her manager. A man Cat has already spoken with numerous times though she has yet to meet him in person. "Tell him I'm thinking about our conversation. Tell him I think I like the idea. Tell him I'll let him know."

"Okay."

"Ask Annie to make sure she has Parker's class curriculum meeting marked in her calendar. It's some time next week. Tell her I can't make it."

"Got it."

"Call back the assistant to that editor at Vanity Fair and tell them I'll do the interview, but they'll have to book a hotel room. I'm tired of journalists criticizing my interior design. Cat, stop writing down everything I say. Just tell them to get the room."

"Sorry."

"It's okay, you're still new to this. You'll learn how to separate the flotsam from the jetsam."

"I'll try."

"Don't worry, you will. Next. Call Connie and tell her I love her."

Cat pauses, then writes it down, unsure exactly how she'll make such a call.

"She's having a bad time with her boyfriend. He won't leave his wife. Connie's feeling impatient, but hell, she's only waited ten years!" Rocky's laughter bursts out then quickly dies. "I probably shouldn't have told you all that. Scratch that off your list. I'll call her myself."

Cat crosses it off, relieved.

"Almost done." Rocky pulls apart her crossed legs and drops one of her feet onto Cat's pad. Her toenails are craggy and yellowed. Cat forces herself not to push the foot off her lap. "I can't seem to get rid of this fungus. It's contagious, I think."

"Do you want me to find you a podiatrist?"

"Why else would I be showing you my toes?"

Rocky removes her foot and Cat makes a note.

"Nail polish doesn't even cover it anymore. It just makes my toenails feel like they can't breathe."

"Is it on your fingernails, too?" Cat asks.

"Just my toes."

"Oh, I thought maybe that was why you did your nails." Over the past weekend, Rocky had her long fingernails squared at the tips and painted bright red. Up until now, Cat has only seen Rocky's fingers decorated by a changing assortment of rings.

"You noticed." Rocky splays her hands in front of her, examining her manicure. "I went with Connie to her salon. It was insanely expensive. Do you like it?"

"I guess so." A safe *un*answer. She likes it well enough, but not on Rocky Love.

"You know, I've always been hated for my sexuality," Rocky says, as if her manicure is a call to arms. Cat almost buys the logic—she *wants* this bright gesture of femininity to be a show of strength and not just another mating call—but it doesn't feel completely stable.

"It looks nice," Cat says.

"Bullshit." Rocky leans forward, her eyes sparkling. "Tell me what you really think."

The invitation to share her mind surprises and delights Cat. "It's just that I thought feminists don't wear nail polish."

"Says who?"

"I don't know. I guess I thought it was too silly for someone, you know, *like you*."

"I guess you thought wrong."

"I guess I did. Wait a minute, is this conversation okay? I don't mean to offend you. The nails themselves are very *pretty*. Maybe *I* should get a manicure."

"Maybe you should." The grin: wide and dazzling. "Men love bright objects, you know. You'll want to hold on to that cute boyfriend of yours."

Cat can't tell if that last comment is meant seriously or as a joke.

"You're probably right about most men," Cat says. "But Teddy once told me that he thinks makeup on women is cheap."

"Oh, I know I'm right. About *all* men." Rocky shifts on the couch, coming closer, and Cat can smell her boss's perfume. Musky. Seductive. "Let me tell you a little story. When I was in college, my friend Lizzie had two close friends, both guys. They were *just friends* until one day, on impulse, Lizzie got herself a makeover at a department store and came back to school looking pretty gaudy. We all thought it was funny. But the next day, she told me that both her *just friends* had separately tried to seduce her. So you tell me. Maybe Teddy likes makeup more than he'll admit."

"Maybe." Cat's pen moves down the edge of her list, doodling a starburst inside a three-dimensional cube, balanced in the palm of a hand. Obviously Rocky has never met a man like Teddy—brilliant, loving, deep, authentic, honest, fun, and sexy to boot. A man capable to seeing a woman as an equal human being. A man capable of real friendship with his lover. From what Cat has gleaned so far, all of Rocky's relationships with men have been train wrecks.

"Just think about it," Rocky says.

"I will." Cat stands, clipping her pen onto the pad of paper. "I should get started on all this if you want it done today."

"Don't you want to know what happened with Lizzie?"

"Sure."

"She slept with the cutest one, but he couldn't get it up. Then she slept with the other one, who stopped talking to her the next day. So there you have it. You're damned if you do, and you're damned if you don't."

"But if she hadn't gotten the makeover," Cat can't resist pointing out, "and hadn't slept with those guys, then maybe they'd still be friends."

"Maybe," Rocky says. "Maybe not. But fucking each other was a helluva lot more fun than pretending they didn't want to."

Cat settles into her office and gets to work. She has found that sometimes Rocky's energy inspires her, but other times it has the opposite effect, leaving her depleted. This is one of those times, and she feels happy to be alone with her thoughts, the hours and a set of tangible goals.

Later that day, after crossing items off the list, going out to lunch, and returning to cross off some more, Rocky comes into the office cradling a stack of papers. Cat swivels to face her desk and sits upright, having been gazing out the window at the brightening hues of autumn in Central Park.

"Call Charlie," Rocky says. "I've made a decision. I'm going to do it. I'm going to write my memoirs." She drops the pages onto Cat's desk. "This is the beginning of Chapter One. Can you type it up today? It's brilliant and I'm dying to see it printed out."

"That *is* exciting."

"You'll be part of it, helping with everything except the writing itself." Rocky clasps her hands, bright fingertips buckling over each other into a fancy double fist. "I love projects, don't you?"

Cat nods, thinking how busy this will make her, on top of everything else. But she'd rather be busy than bored.

"And add this to your list: Find me a photographer. I'll need an author photo."

"Will do."

"Ask Charlie. He should be able to give you some names."

As soon as Rocky is gone, Cat begins to type. She is learning to hit the right letters without looking at the keyboard. Now that Rocky's going to write a book, she figures she'll become an expert typist when all is said and done. One of these days, she'll borrow Annie's kitchen timer and clock her actual speed so she can track her progress.

Two months go by; Rocky's memoirs grow; and finally, Cat meets Rocky's manager, Charlie Webb, in person. Fiftyish, shortish and pot-bellied, he is nothing like what she imagined. But isn't that always the case when you've known someone solely on the phone? What is left of his graying hair flies freely around his head. Wearing round wire-rimmed glasses and a casual suit, he is dumpy and faded, yet he has a natural charisma that defies his looks and Cat decides that she likes him more in person, for the paradox, than she did when all she had was the smooth voice and the fast words.

Rocky is running late, as usual, and so Charlie hovers in Cat's office, making calls on the second phone and occasionally turning to her to speak.

"I just want to know one thing," he says. "Is Rocky off the stuff?"

Cat has ascertained that Rocky had a problem with drugs in the past. "I think so."

"Good. Gotta keep her clean. She gets nuts, you don't know, it's bad. Five years ago it wasn't so hard selling someone who wasn't clean and sober. But now? Forget it. Shit's *out*."

Cat nods and smiles.

"Just tell me one thing. These memoirs. She's actually sitting down and writing them? Rocky the rocket?"

"Yup."

"And you read everything?"

"I'm typing it." What she cannot bear to tell him, but wonders if he's already figured out, is that the memoirs are anything but coherent prose. Rocky can't write to save her life.

Rocky walks in, wearing a designer sweatsuit. She has been working out in her study with her personal trainer. She pauses a moment, apparently unnerved to see her agent and assistant in a tête à tête. Then Rocky proffers what Cat has come to recognize as one of her specialties, the *celebrity smile*—wide and quick, all teeth.

Charlie bolts over to his top client with a kiss. She bends to offer her cheek.

"How do you feel about perfume?" he asks her.

"You're giving me a present?"

"I'm talking endorsement opportunity."

"Jesus."

"It's a perfume for intelligent-women-of-a-certain-age kind of thing. They want an original libber."

"Tell them to call Margaret Sanger."

"But honey—"

"Perfume, Charlie?"

"Well, you did the fur. Anyways, that should have been a quick call. That's not why I came over. I'm in the neighborhood and I realize I haven't feasted my eyes on my Rocky for too long, that's all."

"You're solid, that's why I adore you."

"Someone's gotta anchor the sail."

"A metaphor, Charlie?" She laughs. "Your thoughts are beginning to cohere in your old age."

"Don't push," he says. "So, Rocky, when do I get to see these famous memoirs?"

"Soon."

"It can't be too soon. Remember, I've got my nose in the air."

"Don't worry, darling. This will sell itself."

"You know this in your gut?"

"My gut just did a hundred sit-ups."

"Cute."

"I'll messenger you a copy tomorrow, okay? You'll see for yourself."

"I can copy it right now," Cat says. "It'll just take a minute, there are only about twenty pages."

Rocky glares at her. Cat faces the computer and opens a file she doesn't need. Charlie looks at his watch and abruptly stands, saying, "I gotta be somewhere ten minutes ago," then kisses Rocky and is gone.

Rocky rifles distractedly through some papers on the desk. Then she focuses a stern look on Cat. "Never offer to give someone a copy of something unless I tell you to. It doesn't matter what it is."

"Sorry, I just thought—"

"Don't. Don't think. You are not the decision maker, I am."

Cat clamps her lips and sits back in her chair. This is the first time Rocky has used that tone of voice with her. That dismissive, castigatory, get-in-line tone. That unedited tone that instantly reduces Cat from woman to girl.

Rocky leaves without offering an apology, instantly changing the terms between them. They had been friendly, if not exactly friends. Now Cat isn't so sure.

It is five o'clock, a whole hour to go before the end of the day. Cat lifts her hands to cradle her face. If there is a name for this heavy feeling, she doesn't know it, but she recognizes it well. It is the feeling of blind defeat that has riddled the stem of her life. The feeling of helplessness when your beloved big brother rebels too hard and is sent away before you're finished worshiping him. The feeling of loneliness when you're eight years old and you find your mother passed out drunk (again) on the couch when you get home from school. The feeling of danger when you're twelve and your father spends most of his time working or *out* and you're alone with a woman you love-and-hate, a woman who hardly notices you. The feeling of out-of-proportion desire when you grow up and every man who smiles at you looks like an island in a storm. The feeling of foolishness when you take a job for security and your boss reduces you to utter *in*security with the tone of her voice. Because you expected more of this job and of *her*, and when this feeling hits you, you are reminded of how stupid you were to expect anything at all.

Cat's emotions rise higher than her head and she needs to find the horizon line, to focus, to stay calm at work. Beside the new computer file she just opened, she types in her initials, CRG. Then she double-clicks the file, opening a blank page, and begins her *own* memoirs. Even as she does it, she recognizes it as a desperate impulse. But she needs, *right now*, to find the vibrant thread of her *self*. A thread that is too easily lost.

The Legend of My Birth

It seems as if all my life things have happened in pairs, starting with the moment of my birth. The story goes like this.

It was November 22, 1963. Janet went into labor while watching a television announcer say that John F. Kennedy had been shot in Dallas, and Cat was born at the moment a nurse ran into the delivery room to cry, "President Kennedy is dead!"

The doctor stood there holding the tiny baby who screamed and screamed, and the nurses were like statues. Everyone was frozen, except the baby, who shivered and cried. Janet strained to see the baby. She counted two arms and two legs, one head, eyes ears nose mouth all in place, ten fingers and ten tiny toes. Janet was stunned from childbirth, knocked out, dragged down, exhausted, yet a wave of euphoria swept through her. Her long brown hair was stuck to the side of her face. She wished someone would comfort her, or at least hand over her new baby. One nurse was crying. The baby was crying. Finally, Janet said, "May I please have my baby?"

Everyone awoke. The doctor carefully handed the baby to a nurse, who solemnly showed her to Janet. The baby had a tiny face with squeezed shut eyes. Her tiny fists shivered by her shoulders.

"We'll clean her up," the nurse said. "You rest."

Janet fell asleep and woke two hours later. Mort's parents were there, loyal and involved as always. Rose and Ben Gold weren't even her own parents, but they cared more. Janet's parents had never even met Eddie, her first child, who was already ten. Now, two hours after giving birth to her second child, Janet wondered if maybe her parents had been right—too extreme, certainly, in their reaction—but right perhaps in rejecting Morton Gold as their son-in-law. He had been as unreliable as they had predicted. When she had told him to leave, eight months ago, to "go live with that flit downtown!" she didn't think he really would. Especially since she was pregnant.

Ben Gold was a stocky handsome man of sixty who took pride in his appearance of affluence. He always wore a suit, even on the weekends. She knew from Mort that his father had been unfaithful to his wife. Janet assumed Rose didn't know, unless she had decided to live with it. She had been protective of Janet these last eight months, a violent critic of her son's adultery. Maybe Rose clung to her security for fear of slipping back to the old days, when she and Ben had grown up and met on the Lower East Side, poor immigrant working children. Rose still looked like an Eastern European Jew: short and heavy, with blue-tinted gray hair and a utilitarian way of wearing her expensive clothes. She was a woman who meant business. Janet suspected Rose had made a career of possessing her husband, and in a funny way respected that even though Janet herself did not feel capable of such deliberate blindness and unspoken forgiveness. Rose could have survived alone but chose not to. Janet could not survive alone but had cast off the man who had vowed to protect her.

"What a gorgeous baby she is, that one!" Rose huddled by the side of Janet's bed. She had brought homemade rugelach which filled a coffee can on the nightstand. "She has every single digit," said Rose, "I counted. Do you know she weighs only six pounds? Less than six pounds and you have an underweight baby, they incubate."

"Don't frighten her, Rose," Ben said. "The baby's perfectly healthy. Two healthy children—"

"—is worth more than you realize," Rose said.

"More important than money—" Ben said.

"—or even marriage."

Janet had always appreciated Rose's acceptance of the love that propelled her to marry Mort. They had known each other three months at the time, were students, and Janet was five weeks pregnant. So they married, it was as simple as that. Rose was supportive of them from the beginning and Ben wasn't far behind. It was her own parents, John and Ellen, the Superior Phillipses, the oil-rich Golden Mile couple, who refused to acknowledge the marriage. Janet understood then that she had been an investment and marrying a musician and a Jew was defaulting on that investment. She was a stock gone bust. So she named her son Edward Avery, after her paternal grandfather Avery Edward Phillips, who was a failure and a drunk and deep-

ly hated by his son. She sent her parents a birth announcement: Edward Avery Gold, born July 6, 1953, at Beth Israel Hospital in New York City. *She had not spoken with them for ten years. But she would send them another announcement: Catharine Rose Gold, born November 22, 1963, at Mount Sinai Hospital, New York City.*

On Thanksgiving Day, Ben took the limousine to pick up Janet and Catharine and bring them the thirty blocks downtown to the Park Avenue maze they called home. Ben joked, "I once counted twelve rooms, but who knows?" They had been kind enough to situate Janet and Eddie—and now Catharine—at the far end of the apartment, where they could have some privacy. Rose said, "You are welcome here, remember that," and had never made Janet feel otherwise. Rose treated Janet like another daughter, a tall sharp-nosed WASP daughter, the kind she would have called a shiksa *if she saw her on the street.*

Janet stood in the creamy marble hallway, her arms full of Catharine, while Ben unlocked the door. She felt like she'd gone out shopping. Funny, the difference ten years made. With Eddie, she had felt like she was coming home from war.

The front door swung open. Eddie was standing there, waiting. He looked confused.

Ben said, "Here we are! Where's Rosie?" and disappeared down the long hall to the left.

Janet thought Eddie looked tall, that this four-foot ten-inch manboy could hardly be the baby she birthed ten years ago. The time had flashed by so fast. Eddie had golden hair that hugged his head like a tightly curled rug. It was neither her hair nor Mort's but Eddie's own. He was so much his own person, a separate entity, and it amazed her. Rose had made him dress up for Thanksgiving in a navy blue suit and brown tie. His soft brown eyes, shaded by tender lashes, looked pleadingly at Janet.

"Mommy, can I change my clothes?"

"How about a kiss?" She approached him carefully with the baby. He smirked and forced himself to kiss Janet on the cheek. Then, like a boy at a social embarrassed by the presence of a girl,

he glanced at his sister for the first time and stared, mortified. Then he looked at his mother.

"What's her name?"

"Catharine."

He peered into the folds of the blanket, at the little pink face that peeked through. "I'm Eddie," he said, "your big brother, so you better listen to me." He blew her a kiss then looked up at Janet. "Can I take off this stupid monkey suit, Mommy, please?"

"After dinner," she said.

"Please?"

"Keep it on for Grandma, honey, okay?"

Eddie skulked off dramatically. Janet pushed the front door closed with her hip. She was surprised that Rose had not appeared yet; she must have been in the kitchen, far at the other end of the apartment, supervising the big meal. Janet was glad for this unexpected moment of privacy. It gave her a chance to settle in. She needed to collect herself, to poise herself somehow so that the darkness she felt inside did not show.

She was wearing the purple-flowered maternity dress she had packed in her overnight bag, and felt ugly. She didn't know where this little baby had come from. They were just flukes, anyway, she thought as she carried the restless bundle down the long hallway to her room. It had nothing to do with her, or Mort, or either of their wishes. Pregnancy was just a forceful act of nature, the arbitrary continuation of the human race. Why, women even bore children from rape. How to explain that to your children, or even to yourself? How to go on living with the needy fruit of a haphazard seed?

Her room had been neatened since she rushed off three days ago. The bed was made, the clothes she had thrown over the chair next to the dresser were all put away, the shoes she'd strewn around the floor by the closet were also gone. A vase of white roses, dozens of them, sat on the round glass table by her bed. A tiny card was propped next to the vase.

A white cradle with eyelet ruffles stood against the wall near the bed. Janet herself would have chosen something sim-

pler and cheaper. Ten years with Mort had taught her austerity. But Rose had insisted on this cradle and Janet was grateful. At least the new baby wouldn't have to sleep in a dresser drawer, like Eddie did, courtesy of Mort's struggling career. He was still struggling. Only now he had a twenty-year-old girl to struggle with him, a girl too young to understand how meaningless that kind of struggle really was. Janet took the baby to the bathroom, hoisted her up to let the blanket fall off, and carefully set her down on the changing table. She removed the dirty diaper from this tiny soft baby who seemed to have appeared out of nowhere, from nothing, cleaned her up and wrapped her in a fresh diaper.

"How's that?" Janet cooed.

The baby blinked her eyes.

"Hungry?" Janet lifted her up with slow, careful hands. She settled into an upholstered antique chair and unbuttoned the top of her dress. One large breast tumbled out of her bra. The baby's mouth latched onto the nipple and sucked.

Eddie wandered in, his tie loose but still technically on, one shirttail hanging out of his pants. He stood in front of Janet. "What're you doing?"

"Nursing the baby."

"But she's ..." He stared at his mother's swollen breast.

"How do you think you ate when you were born?"

"You mean she's eating you?"

"She's drinking the milk from my breast, just like I explained to you before. Look." Janet released the other breast and squeezed her nipple between two fingers. Cloudy milk dribbled out.

"Yuck."

Janet laughed.

"Daddy's here," Eddie said. "He said did you see the flowers." He walked over to the vase of roses, picked up the card and read aloud: "Dearest Janet and Catharine, I love you both, Daddy Mort. Hey, what about me?"

Janet stared at Eddie with no thought of him at all, or even of baby Catharine in her arms sucking hard at her breast. "He's here, now?"

"Yeah, he's out there smoking cigars with Grandpa."

Janet wished the baby would stop feeding so she could put her down and go find Rose.

"Go get Grandma, honey. I want to see her."

Eddie went off and in a few minutes Rose came in, her fancy holiday clothes covered by a stained apron.

"Oy, sweetie, when did you come in? I'm in the kitchen with the chestnut stuffing and Eddie comes in with the suit I bought him at Saks such a mess and he says to me, Grandma, he says, Mommy's been home for hours and she wants to see you! For hours! And so how is my little bubbeleh?" She folded at the knees to inspect the baby, paying no attention to Janet's huge breast.

"I got here about twenty minutes ago," Janet said. "I changed Catharine and just started feeding her."

"This place," Rose said, "it's too big. No one knows who comes and goes. So? How do you feel today?"

"Rose? Eddie said Mort's here."

Rose's squarish face pulled in like a dehydrated prune. She nodded quickly, once. "That he is. I suppose it's some kind of reflex action, him coming here on Thanksgiving."

Rose was only too happy to take up the gauntlet of betrayed wife for Janet, even against her own son. But deep down, Janet wondered, wouldn't she have liked to see Mort happy?

"Do you think he came to see the baby?" Janet asked.

"What do I think? I think he came for a free meal, that's what I think. Who knows? Maybe he had some pangs of regret." Rose shrugged dramatically. "So! You? What do you want? You want I should send him away?"

"No," Janet said quickly. "But don't let him back here. I want to put the baby down and clean myself up. He'll have to see me before he sees her."

"Good thinking," Rose said. "In the meantime, I'll make sure that boy of Mort's tucks in his shirt."

That's how it was with Rose: wayward sons belonged to their fathers, and obedient daughters to their mothers.

After a while, Catharine relaxed her grip on Janet's breast and lay her little head down. Janet paced for a few minutes until the baby emitted a tiny burp, then wrapped her in a soft white blanket and set her carefully, like fragile glass, in the center of the cradle. The baby sighed, and slept.

Now it was Janet's turn. She washed at the sink, powdered and perfumed herself, and looked for something to wear. She chose an electric blue and orange print dress, with short sleeves and a square neckline, and put it on. Mort particularly disliked this dress. She clipped her hair into a long ponytail that dangled between her shoulder blades, then applied a touch of makeup. She decided at the last minute to take the extra time to polish her nails orange-red.

She left her door slightly ajar, in case the baby cried, and walked quietly down the hall which was lined with photographs of the Gold family she had seen so many times she no longer noticed them.

At the end of the hall, the apartment flowered into the communal living quarters. Down another hall to the right was the kitchen and dining room, and to the left were the foyer and front door, book-lined reception room and enormous living room. Janet could hear the low rumbling of male voices and smell the thick woodsy odor of cigars. She heard Rose's squawky laughter.

As Janet entered the living room, she quickly took in the relatives who had come for the annual feast: Ethel, the oldest Gold, and her husband Jon Wasserstein; Warren, Mort's brother, a widower, was here with his teenage daughter Emily; and Becky, the youngest Gold, who had divorced her husband at the age of twenty-three, gone to law school at Columbia, and at twenty-eight was the first woman associate at a prestigious law firm in midtown. This was the whole family. Ben's and Rose's parents had all died, Ben had no siblings, and Rose's only relative in America was her cousin Katinka Lehman who had lived with them in their early marriage and whose twin sons, George and Henry Lehman, had reputedly been fathered by Ben.

Eddie stood next to Emily, his cousin. When Janet walked into the room, Emily said, "Hi Aunt Janet!" and everyone turned. Mort watched her carefully, to detect her mood before doing or saying anything.

"Doesn't she look wonderful?" Rose said loudly, and glanced at Mort.

"Even in the hospital," said Ben, "after the birth, she was beautiful!"

Becky rose and came over to hug Janet. "Hiya kid," Becky said. She was Janet's favorite. When Becky married at the age of nineteen and within the first year realized it had been a mistake, it was Janet who urged her to leave. Becky soared beyond Janet, who at that time had been a young new mother, happily married. Now Becky was happy. She was small and blond, a little on the heavy side but still attractive. Janet envied her—if only she too had had her marital downfall early instead of too late, after children.

Becky put an arm around Janet's waist and they walked across the room, over the enormous Oriental carpet, past two cozy enclaves of sofas and chairs, to the main formal area arranged with antiques and glassed-in bookcases housing Ben's collection of first editions.

Mort was seated on the salmon-pink feather-filled couch. He wore a brown corduroy suit, a pale yellow shirt and a Western tie. His thick brown hair had grown slightly long, curling down behind his ears. Janet yearned to suggest he cut it, then wondered if he had worn it long today on purpose, to involve her in his inability to care for himself, to indicate to her that his new woman was not caring well for him. His round, ruddy face opened to her in appeal.

"You really look good, Janet," he said.

She turned away. After greeting everyone individually and accepting their congratulations, she sat across the room, with Becky, on an embroidered divan. Janet listened as the relatives discussed the assassination of the president with tones of anger, confusion and remorse. Her depression had melted naturally into the communal state of shock, and only now did she begin to fully realize what had happened.

After a few minutes, Mort got up and came over. He stood in front of her and asked, "How are you?"

Becky looked at Janet, patted her knee and left. Mort sat down.

Janet said, "I'm fine."

"But after the baby, I mean. Are you feeling all right?"

She recalled her depression after Eddie was born. Yes, she was feeling darkness invade her now, too. But it was her darkness, not a hiding place for strangers, deserters.

"I feel fine," she said.

"So, how is she, the baby?"

Janet couldn't help smiling. "Catharine is wonderful."

"I'd like to see her."

Now Janet looked at him fully. How many times had she seen his face inches away, full of panic, of holding-on as he approached orgasm? Somehow that face had gotten into her, invaded her, filled her hips with boys and girls was a line she recalled from an e.e. cummings poem, she couldn't remember which. This was the man who had given her her children, whether she wanted them or not. The man who had left her pregnant, broke, alone.

She didn't answer him. When she looked up, she saw Rose watching them.

It was Eddie who broke the silence, strutting over in his suit and tie. He walked right between his father's legs, leaned heavily into one thigh and looped a small arm over Mort's neck.

"Did ya see her yet?" he asked.

"Not yet."

"She looks just like me, I mean when I was her age," Eddie said.

"No kidding!"

"Except she's a girl and all."

"She must be very good looking, then," Mort said.

Eddie smiled. "Catherine's a dumb name, don't you think?"

Mort shrugged heavily. "Oh, I don't know. I think your mommy found a good name."

"But can we call her something else?"

Mort thought. "How about Kitty?"

"Oh, no!" Janet said. She had not meant to involve herself in this conversation, as if they were a family. She quickly retreated, but Mort took up her small thread.

"No, no, not Kitty, you're right."

"How 'bout Cat?" Eddie said. "Kitty Cat. But just Cat? I mean, she's so teensy and all."

"Cat," Mort nodded. "Cat Gold."

Janet thought it sounded too easy, but wouldn't say so. She sat silently, like a shadow, and pretended indifference.

"Want me to show her to you?" Eddie said.

Mort turned to Janet. "Is that all right?"

"She's sleeping now. It'll have to wait."

The dinner table, which was long enough to seat twenty-five, was covered with Rose's best lace cloth. The silver candlesticks had been specially polished, along with the good silverware. Rose's best china—which she had bought as a gift for herself ten years after her marriage to Ben—was laid out in full regalia at one end of the table where the family sat for Thanksgiving dinner. Ben was at the head of the table, Rose at his right, Janet next to Rose, Eddie next to Janet, and Mort all the way at the end where, gratefully, Janet could not see him.

But she could hear him, talking, and his deep voice stirred memories in her body, somewhere in the cave of her chest where she had loved him. Echoes of her past feelings resonated, disturbing her. She knew, just knew, that if she let him he would stay. She had two children now, no job, no skills, no money of her own. How long could she go on living off her in-laws?

Janet was surprised by her appetite. She ate everything offered: turkey, chestnut stuffing, sweet potatoes, cranberry sauce, challah bread with sweet butter, Brussels sprouts, salad, pumpkin pie and coffee. From time to time she noticed Mort straining forward to see her. Her appetite must have pleased him because, just as she had cleared her plate, he leaned forward, caught her eye and said, "Good work!"

They were still at the table when the baby's cries were heard faintly from way down the hall. Janet responded as if a cord had tugged her center; she rose and hurried away. Eddie jumped up and followed. And so did Mort.

Eddie moved with Janet like a shadow as she hovered over the cradle, gently peeled back the blanket and undid the top snap of Cat's fuzzy pink suit. The baby eyes fluttered.

"Why's she spitting?" Eddie said.

"That's just drool. You did that too."

Eddie was mildly indignant, but said nothing. His father was hovering over the cradle now, too, and he wanted to see what was going to happen.

Mort's face bloomed into a huge smile. "I don't believe it!" he said. Janet lifted the baby from the cradle and held her against her shoulder. Mort and Eddie followed their females across the room. Janet sat to nurse Cat, then hesitated. Mort.

But he didn't recognize her discomfort and pulled up another chair to sit near them. Eddie hopped onto Mort's knee.

"She's a real beauty," Mort said. "I'd like to hold her."

"Well, maybe just for a second before feeding."

Janet stood and brought Cat to him. Eddie got up from Mort's lap and Mort rose halfway to meet Janet as she lowered the baby into his cradled arms.

"Me next," said Eddie.

Janet thought he was asking for some attention so she went to hug him, but he squirmed away.

"No, I want to hold her."

For an instant she felt rejected, then realized that his acceptance of the new baby was a gift. So she sat back down and waited.

Mort cooed over Cat, touching her tiny face with his hairy stocky forefinger, holding her tiny hand in his large fleshy palm. "Catharine Rose Gold," he whispered to his baby, "that's your name. I'm Morton Gold, your father. I helped make you."

Eddie, hovering over Mort's shoulder, looked at Cat and said, "And remember me, your big brother? Eddie's the name. You have to listen to me. Don't forget that."

Every afternoon, Parker comes home from second grade, has a snack, does his homework and watches TV. He never has a friend over. One day, on impulse,

Cat brings him one of her old Marvel comics. She has hundreds and as collectors' items they actually have some value. But the real value, she knows, is their link to the imagination. She recalls how happily she had burrowed into the bright worlds of the comics, with their clear-cut conflicts and dramatic resolutions, nothing like the murky emotional life of her family in which the proverbial elephant—her mother's drinking—overshadowed everything and was never discussed. She understands how a child can be loved and yet ignored, and when she hands Parker the old comic book his smile is ample compensation.

They squeeze together into the comfy guest chair opposite Cat's desk and page by page she leads this sweet boy on a tour of an alternate universe. The intensity of his concentration thrills her. When they reach the last page, she asks, "Want to draw with me?"

"Yes!"

They spread out on the office floor with paper and colored pencils.

"What should I draw?" he asks.

"Anything you want."

He stares at the blank page, chubby fingers gripping a purple pencil.

"Okay," she says, "give me an idea. I'll get us started."

"If I were a crystal ball."

"You mean if you *had* a crystal ball?"

"No, if I *were* a crystal ball. What would happen then? Do that one."

Cat free associates, jotting as she thinks. "If I were a crystal ball … there would be no poverty, no pollution, no violence in the entire future of the whole wide world … there would be no need for money … there would be no disappointment, no pain, no dust…."

Parker calls out: "No parents!"

"There would be no mothers, no fathers, no grandparents. In the future there would be just us kids and we'd be magic and our powers would be as big as the biggest chocolate chips in the whole wide world forever."

Parker's round face glows in smile. He leans over the paper on which Cat has sketched a little boy in a spaceship soaring amongst stars and planets.

"That's me!" he says. "Put a sun on one side and three moons on top."

Cat giggles and begins to sketch a dazzling sun to the left.

"Now *you* do one," she says.

"Tell me an idea," he commands.

"This apartment turns into a sail boat."

His purple pencil gets busy, then he throws the purple down for green, orange, blue. She leans in closer, admiring his work, when Annie comes in.

"Hey, kiddo, outta here. The lady's got work to do."

"*Please?*" Parker pulls one side of his mouth into a deep dimple.

"Oh, honey," Annie says, towering over him in her pale blue sweatshirt that says *take it or leave it*. "Come on, you can have a snack."

"He's not bothering me," Cat says. "We're having fun."

Parker beams at Annie.

Annie shakes her head. "He's got homework to do."

"Yuck."

Cat laughs. "Hey, at least you don't have eight hours of homework every day, like me."

Parker stares at her as the thought of *so much homework* sinks in.

"But isn't it *fun* working for Mommy?"

Annie says, "Yeah, it's a barrel of laughs, now get outta here."

Parker gathers his pencils, paper and the Marvel in heavy disappointment. Then he walks over to Cat, back at her desk, and gives her back the comic book.

"No," she says. "That's for you."

The luscious smile returns and he hands her his drawing as a gift.

"Thanks! I'll put it right here on the wall."

"Can I have yours?" he asks.

"If you don't take it I'll be very sad."

He kisses her cheek, she tickles him and he bursts into cacophonous giggles ... which stop abruptly at the sound of the penthouse's front door opening and smacking shut. A cascade of footsteps and voices approach the office. Annie grabs Parker's hand before he has a chance to collect his comic book and Cat's drawing. Quickly, Cat gathers the afternoon's phone messages into a neat pile.

The office door swings open and there is Rocky in her fur coat, carrying a shiny white shopping bag with LL stamped in big purple script on both sides. Her face is pinkish from the winter chill. Directly behind her is another woman in a fur coat with a matching fur hat. The woman is short and all the fur makes her look like an animal, a cute chubby Koala bear, an effect ruined by sunglasses and heavy red lipstick.

"Hey, Connie, how are ya?" Annie asks, as she leads Parker out.

"Stuffed. How are you, Annie?"

"A little tired, but you know. Well, you girls are busy. I'll just get Parker started on his homework."

Rocky watches Annie and Parker go—not even acknowledging her child, Cat notices with a pang—then drops the shopping bag on the desk, strips off her coat and flings it over the footstool. Connie lumbers over to the armchair and nearly falls into it. "I shouldn't do lunch anymore. It's too exhausting."

Rocky stands at the desk and looks through the day's mail. "Connie saved my life," she tells Cat. "Without Connie, I'd be a basket case today."

Connie removes her fur hat and shakes out her short blond hair. "It's hot under there."

"Any calls?" Rocky asks.

Cat hands her the pile of phone messages. Rocky reads through them quickly until she comes to one, a message from Charlie, at which she stares. *Needs to talk to you about the memoirs. Wants you to meet with John Paglia.*

"Connie," Rocky says, her eyes still glued to the message slip. "You know John Paglia, don't you?"

"I used to see him around. Dark hair, kinda cute, kinda funny. Worked on that soap. What was it called?"

"*Rising Tides*. He's a TV writer. Why would Charlie want me to meet with him about my memoirs?"

"He left the network before I did," Connie says. "I think he was freelancing around."

To Cat, Rocky says, "Give me five minutes then get Charlie on the phone." She plucks a piece of paper from the desk, a lined sheet scribbled with notes Cat has written to herself as reminders, balls it up and tosses it into the trash can under the desk. Then she notices the whimsical drawings and the comic book, which she picks up, declaring, "Lowbrow *crap*." The Marvel hits the bottom of the can, on top of Cat's crumpled To Do list, with a *thwunk*. Cat cannot bring herself to look down at the discarded treasures at her feet. Instead, she keeps focused on Rocky's face. *Too much makeup glopped over wrinkles. Age spots. Tiny bulges of fat beneath her eyes.*

Rocky hands Cat the drawings. "Doesn't Annie have some place she keeps Parker's *stuff*?"

"I'll give them to her," Cat says, holding the drawings so they hover above the desk, not sullying the surface where so-called *real* work is done.

"John Paglia," she hums, shakes her head and looks at Connie. "Coming? I've got some calls."

"Honey, I love you, but I've got better things to do than sit around watching you talk on the phone." Connie hoists herself out of the chair and pulls the hat back on her head. "Call me after your date. I want to know how it went."

"I hate blind dates."

"You'll love Larry. He might seem a little eccentric at first but he's a great guy and I've known him *forever*—before he was famous. Did you know he's won three Tonys for his work on Broadway?"

"Is he really so bad you need to tell me that?"

"Just give him a chance."

"I'll call you."

They touch cheeks and part ways, Connie heading to the front door and Rocky to her suite. Cat swivels around and digs through the trash for the comic book and her notes, which she unballs and flattens on the desk. She dials Charlie and puts the call through to Rocky. The button for line-one burns red for twenty minutes with whatever plans they are hatching. One thing Cat has grown sure of during her time here is that Rocky will never be able to write her memoirs without help. A soap opera writer. *Perfect.* Charlie Webb must be a genius to think of a *soap opera writer* to tell the story of a fallen star whose life seems more cartoon-ish than any cartoon Cat has ever drawn. More cartoonish than any of the heroic quests in a classic comic book. *Lowbrow crap.* Rocky doesn't even know what she's talking about, Cat thinks, slipping the comic book into a large envelope on which she sketches a little boy beneath *Parker* in riotous bubble-lettering.

Annie stands in the kitchen, watching the kettle on the ring of blue gas flames. Everything has been ready for a good half-hour, but as usual, when Rocky's guests arrived she had just stepped into the shower. If she were Annie's daughter, she would catch hell. Sometimes Annie feels like giving it to her anyway.

"A watched pot doesn't boil, or something like that," Charlie says. He is standing in the kitchen doorway, hands shoved into his pockets, smiling.

"You know, I've wondered, did people ever call you Chuck?"

"Sometimes when I was a kid, but I don't know. Chuck Chucky Upchuck. I don't know, it doesn't hit me right."

"How about Charles?"

"Nah, I'm not much of a Charles, either. Charles is too serious, and Chuck is too—"

"I know what you mean."

Charlie looks at his watch, then veers back into the dining room. Annie follows him to the doorway and watches as he circles the dining room table, inspecting its bounty. Shrimp salad, turkey breast, sliced tomatoes, crusty French bread and a salad of apples, oranges, pineapple, raspberries and kiwi. For lunches she always uses the black and white zigzag china from Rocky's first marriage to Dr. Bobby Love. For dinners she uses the floral Wedgwood from Rocky's marriage to

Jason Barthoff, Esq. Charlie looks at his watch again. "She's now twenty minutes late."

John Paglia stands by the window, absorbed by the dramatic view. He turns to Charlie. "Is she always this late?"

"Always."

John nods and shrugs his shoulders. He glances through the window again then turns to smile at Annie.

She smiles back. He's a nice young man, polite, and he reminds her of someone but she can't think of who. He's not exactly tall so much as large, big boned, well fed. His dark brown hair is neatly trimmed, as if he just came from the barber. He looks boyishly uncomfortable in a tie and jacket, and though he is wearing blue jeans, they are pressed. Finally, it hits her. She snaps her fingers and says, "You remind me of Orson Welles when he was just starting out. Oh, what a nice looking man he was before he put on the weight."

"I'm flattered!" John smiles, a big unselfconscious smile, and Annie sees that he is not just polite and nice looking, but friendly too. "There's no way you could possibly know this, but Orson Welles was my spiritual mentor when I was a kid, I mean, he was this amazing genius, and he was in charge of his own destiny, he wanted to make movies so he did it, he got out there and he did it and he did it brilliantly. I mean, back then, you had Hollywood and it was full of stars, but Welles, he was the northern lights."

"That's good," Charlie says. "The sky's full of stars, but this guy, he's the northern lights. You should write that down, you should use that somewhere."

John whips a pen and a small spiral notebook out of his jacket pocket, and jots it down.

"Well," Annie says, "I guess I hit a nerve or something." She can hear the kettle rattling on the stove. "Would you boys like some tea while you wait?"

"Thanks," John says. "Why not?" He pulls out a chair and sits at one of the place settings. Charlie sits beside him. From inside the kitchen, Annie can hear them chattering about Rocky's memoirs. She hears John's enthusiasm pouring out in every direction, and then finally when he says something about a "rise and fall story," Charlie stops him. "Listen, whatever you do, don't you say that to her. She doesn't see it that way. Fall? What fall? This is a rise story, understand?"

Annie pours boiling water over the basket of loose tea suspended in the teapot, then carries it to the table and puts it on a trivet. "Rocky's not the kind of person you can set your watch by, is she?"

Rocky appears, dressed in black from head to toe, with a black turban wound around her head. Charlie and the writer are already installed at her table. She hates lunch meetings; and the nerve, sitting down before she arrived.

"So good to meet you," she greets John. "I understand we were at the TV studio at the same time."

"My office was just down the hall," John says. "I used to see you walking by. You came in one day, I don't know if you remember—"

"I do vaguely remember your face." A lie.

"You remember me? Wow."

"Wow, nothing," Charlie says. "You were the best writer they ever had on *Rising Tides.*"

She joins them at the table and begins to pass around the dishes of food.

"You flatter me," John says. "There was a lot of talent on that show in the early days, a lot of people made it great."

"Seventeen Emmys in the six years John wrote the show," Charlie says to Rocky. "It was the best daytime drama on the air."

"I never watched it," she says. "I never had the time."

"Of course you didn't," Charlie says. "People like you don't watch TV in the day, you're too busy being who you are, am I right?"

"You are right, as usual."

Charlie finishes erecting a triple-decker turkey sandwich. He places his hands around it and lifts it an inch above his plate. "Rocky, I have a great feeling about this. What you are is a great personality with a great life, you have lived a fascinating and brilliant existence, you have everything it takes. But what you're not, the one thing you're not, is a writer. This I think you know, in your gut, am I right?" He lifts the sandwich and jams one corner into his mouth.

"Did you know I wrote a novel when I was in college?" she says.

"Really!" John leans forward, his face shining with energy. He flips open the little pad he has placed beside his lunch, and holds a clear plastic pen above a blank sheet. "When did it come out? Who published it? How did it do? My God, what was it called?"

"*Poetsong.* You know, it was a brilliant novel, better than my columns, but it was never published."

"Oh?"

"One editor saw it, at Scribner's, a really pathetic man, an alcoholic. Actually I may have shown it to a few other editors, I can't recall, but in the end I decided to keep it to myself."

Suddenly the years reel in and she is a young woman again, full of pride at her accomplishment, her brilliance, her novel. She can still feel each rejection, each jolt testing her confidence, raising the obstacle higher until she could no longer see beyond it. They were idiots and fools, those editors, telling her *no*, telling *her* no. She won't set herself up for that again. She is smarter now, a grown woman with resources. This time she will position herself to fly right over obstacles before they appear.

"You know something, Charlie, you're right. I always knew I wasn't a writer. I always knew I needed a larger stage, as it were. I'm just not someone who has the time to write, that's why the immediacy of radio and television is so, well, perfect for me." She shines a smile at John, who, she notes, receives it with an adoring gaze.

"Am I right, then?" Charlie asks.

"Of course you're right. I never expected to write my memoirs without a collaborator, I was just priming the pump."

"You're too smart, babe, and do I love you." Charlie reaches out to squeeze her arm. "Lemme tell you something else. Lemme tell you why John is the perfect guy for the job."

"Why doesn't John tell me?"

"That's what I was gonna say," Charlie says.

"Exactly my feeling," John says, "that you should hear about me from me. Who am I? Who is this guy sitting in your dining room, anyway? I'll tell you who I am. Rocky—can I call you that?"

"It's my name."

"Rocky, I may be your biggest fan. That's the truth. I'm old enough to know who you are and young enough to know you're the role model for every woman I've ever loved. It's true. I knew that before I started working for the network. But once I was there, wow, I really understood the power of TV, how it's the happening place, it's where our real idols come to life, it's where you go to find out what's happening. You're TV, I'm TV. So now we have to ask ourselves, why a book? Good question! I'll tell you why a book. Because a book you do once, it's a one-time punch, and it's a loaded punch. In a book you get to the Rocky underneath the gorgeous woman, you get to break out the whole story, tell about where greatness comes from, and everyone wants to know this. This is probably the biggest question people ask today: Where do celebrities come from? What makes a celebrity? Why them? Why not me? Why am I such a putz when this person is a celebrity? That is why a book."

"Exactly," Charlie says. "Honey, do you know the market out there for a book like this? The kind of book John can write for you? A book that says fame, TV, wow, punch, grab you by the throat? Not one of those wordy books full of wind blowing on cornstalks. We're talking about a book with a ready-made market, a real money-maker."

"A book about me."

"A book about you, done with that Rocky edge, with that TV kind of edge that nobody can do better than John Paglia, seventeen Emmys for *Rising Tides*. Honey, you tell me."

"You've repackaged the idea for me, Charlie. It's very good."

"That's my job, putting you in the right package."

Rocky nods, her eyes resting on John. He is an attractive man, enthusiastic and adoring, and he seems to understand the perfect angle as she herself had not. They're right, of course, to package the memoirs in a television spirit. She had been way off the mark in thinking she could try it on her own.

"Okay," she says, "let's do it."

"Good!" Charlie takes a swig of diet soda. "I'll do the contract."

"I have to lay it on the line," John says. "I'll only do this for a credit and a percentage."

"But don't ghostwriters get a flat fee?" Rocky asks.

John flips shut his pad and drops it into his jacket pocket. He sits back in his chair. "Sorry, but I don't ghost. My understanding was that I would co-write."

"Co-write, Rocky," Charlie says. "That's the big thing these days. Ghostwriters, they're a dime-a-dozen, any college dropout can ghostwrite a book for cheap. All the celebrities get their books done by co-writers these days. Now, John, what you want is a small percentage, am I right? You're not asking for a lot, and Rocky gets all the publicity when the book comes out, you take a back seat."

"Absolutely," John says.

"How much?" Rocky asks.

"Twenty percent," John says.

"Of everything?"

"Everything."

"Now that may be pushing it," Charlie says. "Everything is a lot, that's all advances and royalties for hardcover, softcover, North American rights, and subsidiary rights, media and foreign subs—you've got a small fortune right there alone."

"Five percent of hardcover sales," Rocky says. "Period."

"Ten percent of hard and soft," John says. "And five percent of film and electronic media options."

"No," Rocky says. "Charlie?"

"Okay, here's what's a good deal for you both. Rocky, you want John's help making this book what it needs to be, then you gotta give him something. And John, you're good, you're the best, but let's face it, it's Rocky's life and it's her name, without her there is no book. So here's a good deal for both of you. Fifteen percent of advances on hard and soft, ten percent of advances on sub rights, all royalties going to Rocky."

John shakes his head. "That's setting me up as a writer-for-hire and you know it. Listen, I want to do this, I love this project, so how about this as a compromise. I'll take ten percent on hard and soft, advances and royalties both, and I'll let you get away with five percent on all sub rights, electronic, film and foreign sales."

"Where did you learn this?" Rocky asks. "Who's your agent? Shouldn't he be doing this?"

"I'm my own agent. It's easier that way."

"That depends," Charlie says. "Celebrities as big as Rocky Love cannot go it alone, big mistake, no way."

"That's right," Rocky says. "Charlie protects me. What do you think, Charlie? Is that a good deal?"

"I'll tell you what. We agree the project's a go, we finish our lunch, we change the subject, we go home and we sleep on it. Tomorrow, we finish the deal."

By the following week, contracts are signed, sealed and delivered, and John Paglia is standing in Cat's office next to Rocky, holding a bottle of champagne.

"You," Rocky says to Cat, "are going to keep typing up my pages, which you will then fax to John."

"I'll use conversations and interviews, along with Rocky's free associations to help build the official version of the memoirs," John says.

"Well, they're not exactly free associations."

Cat knows better by now than to add her two cents, which would be to say that the sheets Rocky scrawls out are indeed not free associations, but worse— they are self-congratulatory ramblings.

"Free associations," John says with verve, "but not in that sense, Rocky, not in the sense of disconnected thoughts. Free association is the heart of true writing. Writing the truth. Getting at the heart. Let's call it free writing, self discovery, discovery of the self through a freely written inner dialogue that shines the light on the path you need to follow to get to the heart of the real story."

Cat bolts from the room, down the hall and to the bathroom, where she lets out a hiss of laughter. This guy is just amazing, she loves this guy. She had not realized how satisfying it would be to watch someone manipulate Rocky. Yet at the same time Cat feels a sizzle of guilt. Whatever Rocky is now, she was once a trailblazing feminist who took personal risks exposing hypocrisy. She spoke up when most people were afraid to challenge the status quo. Rocky Love once inspired other women to expect more from the world—to *demand* it. Even if she has softened over time and maybe even abandoned the battle, doesn't she still deserve respect? Shouldn't Cat, as her assistant, serve and protect the *idea* of Rocky Love, regardless of her personal feelings? Sobered, she flushes the toilet and returns to her office. Rocky is seated in the leather armchair and John is hunched on the ottoman, leaning eagerly toward her as if fascinated.

"Sorry. I suddenly had to *go.*" Cat takes her post at her desk.

"You drink too much water," Rocky says.

"Yet one wants to flush the kidneys," John says.

"I guess I just have a small bladder," Cat says. "So, John, I should take your fax number."

He reels it off, then asks, "Do you have a modem?"

"I don't think so. Do we, Rocky?"

"I have no idea."

John gets up and comes around to join Cat at the desk, where he starts jabbing at keys until he is at the DOS screen. He types in codes which cause other codes to scroll quickly down. Finally, he says, "No, I thought there could be an internal modem, but no dice. If you get one, I can install it for you, then we can electronically transmit our documents back and forth. I mean, hey, it's 1989."

"That sounds *so* exciting," Rocky says. John looks at her, clearly on the verge of agreeing, then he sees her lips tilt into a sarcastic half smile. He rolls his eyes and backs away from the computer.

"You mean," Cat says, "that we could just zap each other and skip all the other steps, save trees and everything?"

John shrugs. "But it isn't really necessary."

"I don't think we need to fill the computer up with all that hocus pocus," Rocky says. "We have a copier and a fax machine, that's good enough."

"Right," John says. "When I have a chapter finished, I'll get the disk to you, Cat, and then you can print it out here. If Rocky has minor changes, you can make them directly. In the end, I'll blue pencil the final draft and you can enter the changes. So that's how we'll do it. You'll fax me her pages, and then you'll work directly off a copy of my disk."

"Okay," Cat says, a little disappointed. She has heard good things about modems.

"Forget about all that stuff," Rocky says. "Let's celebrate! Cat, buzz Annie and ask her to bring in four champagne glasses and a can of diet soda."

In minutes, Annie arrives with four tulip glasses upside down on a tray, along with Rocky's sobriety soda. John pops the cork across the room and champagne fizzes into a glass Annie holds up just in time.

Rocky toasts, "To our brilliant future!" and the four of them happily drink.

The relay of rough drafts begins, with Rocky writing her pages and John writing his chapters which arrive on three-inch diskettes in the mail. Months whiz by as Cat types and faxes and prints and corrects. As the book takes shape, it becomes clear that they are writing two different stories. One is a free writing extravaganza, a pouring out of self-discovery, an embarrassing spiral of redundancy and fully blossomed narcissism. The other is a TV movie of the week, a rise and fall story in which the rise is spectacular with an edge of destiny, and the fall is foreshadowed at every turn.

Chapter 4

The Rise and Fall of Rocky Love

Evolution

*I*t was 1965, and Rochelle Libbon was eighteen and ripe for independence when she finally left Brooklyn, and home, for college.

The moment she stepped foot on Bennington's stone and ivy campus, she was ecstatic: Mabel couldn't monitor her in Vermont. The old, leafy campus felt like a foreign country to her, so distant was its culture from the city's. But she gradually adapted, and the lush trees and hills and sweet air came to seem as normal as dark tunnels, grit and the ammonia smell of urine on concrete.

Her roommate was a smart black girl with a shaved head, who wore round tortoiseshell glasses and big silver hoop earrings. Her name was Ann Jameson but she called herself Reebah. She was serious and kind and they got along well from the beginning. Reebah started a group called the Bennington Black Brigade, which met every Wednesday night in their room. The purpose was to raise consciousness, and she invited Rochelle to sit in. Why not? Rochelle believed in consciousness-raising as much as the next person; and be-sides, it was her room. But after the first meeting, she decided her skin was too phosphorescent white for the group's dark anger, so she signed up with the school literary magazine, *The Benningtonian*, which also met on Wednesday nights.

The editor was Scott McNeil, a skinny brown-haired Irish boy who would have resembled a Libbon brother if his nose hadn't been so straight and pointy. He was a lone wolf at a girls' school that was on the brink of becoming officially co-ed. Actually, there were three other boys enrolled that year, and during the week they had all those girls to themselves. On weekends competition stiffened when boys from Williams College came to call, but the benefits of being a resident male were undisputable. Until Rochelle came along in his senior year, Scott had managed to date around without going steady.

When Rochelle walked into the classroom/office of *The Benningtonian*— bosomy in a tight black T-shirt and a denim miniskirt squeezing her hips—Scott leaned back in his chair, clasped his hands over his stomach and tilted back his head the better to look down his long nose at her. Rochelle knew enough about boys to see that he was attracted to her. And she knew enough about society to understand that men didn't take attractive women seriously. She decided he would take *her* seriously; she would just have to show him how. He had the sharp handsome look of a young Fitzgerald, and Rochelle thought he could be her first real lover. She saw them sitting on the grass reading Shakespeare to each other, and Dickens, and Yeats, and Whitman, and the Brownings. She smiled. He cleared his throat and grimaced. But he was staring at her breasts, so she thought he'd be easy to break down.

She leaned against the scratched wooden desk, behind which he seemed to feel so important, and picked up a copy of the magazine.

"What are you, a weekly?"

He snorted. "Bi-monthly."

"I can write a column for you," she told him. She whipped out a manila envelope containing her Rodney Parker clips. Scott rifled through them.

"You can be an editorial assistant," he said.

"I *write*."

"The kids at Bennington don't need advice."

"Wanna bet?"

"Forget it."

"I'm not giving you an advice column, anyway. I'm giving you a narrative that's gonna set this fucking school on its ear."

Scott broke into a wide, crooked-toothed smile. It was the *fucking*. "What exactly do you propose?"

"You'll see," she said. "Just leave one page empty and I'll fill it in."

Scott put on his black beret and took her out for coffee. The night trolleyed by in heated conversation. He called her dirty names like "liberationist" and "suffragist bitch" and "commie lesbo" and she called him a "fuckfaced chauvinist pig" and "virgin schoolboy" and they laughed their heads off and when the sun rose they were shocked at the hour and hurried to his room and went to bed. Actually, Rochelle was the virgin. She gave herself to Scott with fanfare.

"This was destined," she said, pulling off her miniskirt and dragging her T-shirt over her head with such enthusiasm that her breasts jiggled wildly.

"Wow!" He watched her from the bed, where he sat, legs crossed, fully dressed.

"Aren't you—" But before she could say *going to get undressed*, he leapt up and disrobed. Naked, he was a pale stalk, hairless, and with a teenage boy's ready-to-go erection.

He folded down the red woolen blanket and starched white sheet on his single bed, and said, "After you, *demoiselle*."

Rochelle's breasts blushed, which amazed Scott, who recited some poetry to them with his face pressed into her cleavage. "Juliet," he sighed, and kissed her with a tense, flicking tongue. He lost his erection at the crucial moment, and she comforted him. They rocked like old lovers, not first-time kids, lovers who had read more than done. When the sex finally occurred, Scott lost control and Rochelle lost her virginity so fast they hardly know what had hit them.

He rolled over like an exhausted stud. "Ah, that was great."

"It was wonderful."

She was thinking that Rochelle McNeil would look pretty good on a novel, and he was distractedly twirling his finger in her pubic hair, when she lifted her leg to scratch an itch and he saw the bloodstain on the sheet.

"A virgin," he said. "Wow!"

The Benningtonian gained a column called "Brotherly Love," which Rochelle filled with juiced-up versions of her and Nathan's correspondence. Nathan liked the idea so much that his letters started sounding more like erotic tracts than notes to his sister Rochelle. But that was okay, the students liked it, and so did editor/poet/lover/friend Scott. Nothing got people's ear faster than SEX. And there was just about nothing sexier than the erotic meanderings of a lost soul deadbeat dropout post-Beatnik poet to his little sister.

Nathan was fulfilling their parents' worst fears; it did not look like he'd ever be a doctor. He was living so far on the edge that even Rochelle was afraid he was going to fall off. For some reason that Nathan kept a mystery, he left Berkeley and gave Rochelle a mailing address care of one Tanya Jones in Haight-Ashbury. Now he was sleeping in the back of a bar, not drinking particularly much— Nathan never liked alcohol—but smoking weed galore and living off the pittance he earned selling hand-scrawled poems to passersby in the street. The next thing Rochelle heard, Nathan was burning his draft card in a big bonfire in San Francisco. A few girls threw their bras into the fire and a revolution started. Rochelle would have liked to have joined it, but she was much more comfortable observing and reporting.

She wrote about her brother's seamy, exciting, illegal, revolutionary California happenings with such verve that, when a straight-A senior packed her knapsack with a few necessities and hitchhiked west, the school tried to stop the column. Scott geared into action and convinced the school's weekly newspaper, *The Lion*, to print the headline BENNINGTONIAN INVOKES FIRST AMENDMENT TO BLOCK SCHOOL CENSORSHIP. An article by Scott McNeil detailed the situation. The administration fought. *The Lion* printed more pro-first amendment articles. A Burlington paper reported on the disturbance. And by the time *The Boston Globe* ran its piece, the whole East Coast knew about it. The *Globe* ran a series on the changing ideological climate on American campuses, focusing one section on the Bennington scandal, and interviewing Rochelle whom they termed "the precocious freshman." The series was syndicated nationally.

Rochelle, at the age of eighteen, glowed in the limelight. She appeared on television in an orange tie-dyed turtleneck and tight faded hiphugger jeans, with her thick brown shoulder-length hair flying like crazed electric wires around her head, and Reebah and her gang picketing vehemently behind her in their psychedelic African dashikis. Mabel called to say, "You're killing us, Rochelle Libbon!" and hung up—confirming Rochelle's suspicion that she was on the right track.

Rochelle got a diaphragm and unofficially moved into Scott's room. She cleaned it up and draped colorful Indian spreads over his battered wooden furniture. She hung a poster of the Brontë sisters and put peacock feathers in a big bronze vase at the foot of the bed. They made love in the missionary position because it hadn't occurred to either of them yet that, even though it was the only legal position, it wasn't the only possible one. Living together was a forbidden concept, especially at school, and Reebah covered for her roommate whenever necessary. Scott gave Rochelle his high school ring, which she wore around her neck in the cleavage of her substantial bosom. Together, they rewrote history. At least for a while.

Scott moved "Brotherly Love" to the front of *The Benningtonian* with an announcement: BENNINGTONIAN DISCOVERS NATIONAL TREASURE: THE NEWLY SYNDICATED *BROTHERLY LOVE*. Rochelle's column appeared in the human interest slots of newspapers around the country. The adult world considered it an amusing sample of American juvenilia. But when Nathan was drafted and chose war over jail, "Brotherly Love" took a turn for the serious. Tales of Vietnam transformed the frolicking mood of the column to one of fearful, confused questioning. Rochelle used her blunt, sexy style to tell Nathan's stories of sudden fireworks on dark infested rivers, of bodies oozing blood, of bayonet-stuffed babies and raped mothers and ravaged villages and

American boys with pricks in their arms and, instead of red stripes and white stars in their eyes, death.

Leo was excluded from the draft for homosexuality. He was perplexed as to how the Army could tell. He lived alone in a studio apartment on the Upper West Side of Manhattan, and worked as a paralegal in a midtown law firm. Granted, he spent his spare time sculpting miniature male lovers in clay; but no one knew, not even Rochelle or Nathan. He dressed conservatively and had a slim mustache. From time to time he took a woman out to dinner. He had no close male friends. But that's what the Army said—homosexual—and the official tag challenged more than insulted him.

Robby was also exempted from the service, because he was the married father of twin daughters—Leslie and Lisa—and also because he had been appointed Associate Director of Psychiatry at Stanford University.

Earl was single, and though he hadn't finished his medical degree, seven months after Nathan was drafted, he decided he had no good reason to stay at home and watch. But before enlisting he told Norman, who offered a parental, if distracted, pat on the back. Tall strong eager Earl Libbon made it through boot camp with honors and went to Vietnam to fight. And he fought. And after three weeks, there was an accident, and a veil of darkness fell as if someone had snapped off the light.

The news came on a Tuesday evening. Rochelle and Scott were studying in the room they shared, when there was a knock on the door. Scott jumped up to answer it.

It was Reebah, looking anxious. "Your dad called."

"Is something wrong?" Rochelle pushed her book aside and sat up on the bed.

"He said it was an emergency. He said to call as soon as you could."

Rochelle went to the pay phone in the hallway and called home collect. Mabel answered and responded to her daughter's voice with a moan of despair. There was a long pause before her father came on the line. "Rock, I'm sorry."

"What happened? Mom's hysterical."

"Honey, it's Earl. He fell on a land mine. We had a visit from the Army this afternoon." Norman's voice was heavy with sorrow.

"You mean he's dead? Earl's dead?"

In the background, she heard her mother wail, "Why my Earl? Why him and not—"

"No!" Rochelle slammed down the receiver. Scott and Reebah were hovering nearby. When Rochelle began to slump, they caught her and brought her back to the room.

Earl's sudden death put a halt to time, which up until then had been flying forward. Every moment had been filled with energetic purpose. But now, everything seemed to stop. Earl's death ended Earl, an unthinkable concept, yet absolute. He was *gone*. After that, every casualty reported in the news felt personal to Rochelle—she wasn't alone. Accumulated, all the deaths stunned the American consciousness, glacially shifting the country's perception of patriotism. Rochelle's anger exploded into heightened awareness and action—and fear for Nathan, who was still over there.

When she showed up for Earl's funeral in Brooklyn in a purple and yellow shirtdress, cradling a bouquet of white roses, her protest was misunderstood. Mabel, dressed appropriately in black, snapped, "Show some respect for the dead!" Norman tried to calm his wife with a hand on her shoulder. She jerked away—forward, toward Rochelle—and said, "Do you think this whole world revolves around *you*?"

"No, Mom, I don't. *I miss Earl*. I won't bury him. I won't forget him. He shouldn't have died."

"But he is dead. *He is dead*." Mabel collapsed into Robby's and Natalie's arms, and wept inconsolably for her obliterated son.

Leo stood solemnly with Rochelle, tears streaming down their faces. Kneeling, they stuck the roses one by one into the fresh brown earth of Earl's grave. Norman joined them, and Rochelle gave him the last flower, which he planted with his tired red-rimmed eyes full of tears.

Nathan wrote to Rochelle with the crazy good news that he had had a half-Vietnamese son, called Sun, with a sweet South Vietnamese woman called Le Ly. Rochelle wrote up the news, but before it had a chance to go to press she received the next letter. A Vietcong soldier had buried Sun alive. In her passion, Le Ly killed the soldier by first castrating him with a pair of garden shears and then slowly slicing him down the middle. She was immediately captured and taken by the other side as a prisoner of war. Nathan was sure she was dead, or if not dead, destroyed. Rochelle was shattered by Nathan's news. She pulled the article; she couldn't bring herself to expose that much reality. Nathan! He wrote to her, "Oh marry me sister marry me!"

And then his letters stopped coming.

The country was contrite over Nathan Libbon's silence. He had come to represent the unknown soldier, everybody's boy, the American son. Rochelle received hundreds of letters asking for news of her brother. She created a form response explaining that he had been sent farther east on a secret mission and would write as soon as he could.

Nathan disappeared in the secret mission of his loster-than-ever soul, and Rochelle joined the antiwar movement, writing and shouting and marching as if her life depended on it—or Nathan's. It was already too much to have lost Earl to the war, but if there was any chance of bringing Nathan home alive, she had to try. She was a girl, woman, sister driven by love. Rochelle found herself searching for Nathan in the distant pictures on the television screen, which was a pageant of violence and suffering. She knew he could be dead. Readers wrote to ask her why we were in the war. She published an article titled "I Don't Know!" which began, "It seems that our capacity for violence has caused a national amnesia. We must try to remember. We must STOP THE WAR."

Too much had happened to remain unchanged. The whole country was erupting in anger, needing revolution, demanding peacelovehappiness, the right to vote, equal pay. Without Nathan's tales of war to funnel into her column, "Brotherly Love" broadened to take on the world. Rochelle spoke her mind, guided by her readers' reactions. Her columns were not so much informed by fact as passion. She was almost twenty, a feminist, a liberal, a tie-dyed shouting writing antiwar activist. She felt the glow of power like a sun trapped in her rib cage, boiling her up, pushing her out. She had a voice, and it was loud, and she believed it was her duty to use it.

In light of all this, Scott's literary aspirations began to seem small. His plan was to spend two years in Iowa, getting his graduate degree at the University's Writing Workshop, then try for a job at *The New Yorker*. He wanted her to apply to the Workshop when her time came; he said he'd wait for her in Iowa. But she didn't want to dicker around with highbrow lit magazines; she wanted to converse directly with the masses.

The moment the dean moved Scott's black tassel from right to left, Rochelle decided it was over. She sat in the audience on the sunny lawn, hot and bored along with all the other family and friends of the graduates. Scott's parents were somewhere here, and she was supposed to meet them after the ceremony, but she decided to leave instead. When people stood to applaud, Rochelle, camouflaged in her white cotton springtime dress and flat white shoes, unknitted herself from the crowd. She vowed to write him an epic poem in lieu of saying goodbye.

Reebah had gone to Georgia to work in the civil rights movement. Their room was empty but for the one suitcase Rochelle had packed to tide her over for a few days before going home; most of her things had been sent ahead of her. The plan had been that she would drive to New York with Scott and his parents later that afternoon, and spend a few days with them before he left for his summer job in Iowa. But she felt a hollowness inside, an echo of loneliness, a strange unspecified *wanting*; and her urge was to search. She wasn't sure for what, exactly; maybe for an explanation, or maybe for Nathan, or maybe just for some adventure. She definitely didn't want to go home, and in a flash, as she owned up to her true feelings, she decided to take a trip instead. She had her passport with her, and plenty of cash left from her columns, and if she hurried she could still make the bank in town. There had been talk of some pretty wild things happening in a mountain of caves on Crete, and she decided that Greece would be as good a place to go as any.

She called the consulate to see if she needed a visa; she didn't. Then she booked herself onto a flight from Burlington to Logan airport in Boston, with a connection to a flight leaving for Athens. There were only two seats left in economy class, and she reserved one. She would say she was a writer if anyone asked, and that she came from Manhattan, and was twenty-five years old (not almost twenty) and had been divorced.

She teased her hair, put on some light pink lipstick and, still in the white dress, headed to town by cab.

She had made small trips on her own before, but never such a long one. She had had no idea the immensity of anxiety that was possible so high and fast in the air. Bright clouds and black sky, then straight into a pink and purple sunrise and the distant uneven grid of Europe below. She squeezed shut her eyes and pressed back into her seat.

The man next to her leaned over and said, "Would you like a drink?"

She was so nervous, she hadn't taken a really good look at him. Now she did. He was a muscular man in khaki shorts and a red shirt. His arms and legs were covered with curly black hair. The thick black hair on his head was straight and wiry and swirled into an ecstatic cowlick. His eyes were smallish, alert, bright blue. Straddled between his squarish leather-sandaled feet was a black camera bag.

"I'll take a Tequila Sunrise," she said.

He waved for the stewardess and ordered the same for himself.

"On vacation?" he asked.

She looked him straight in the eye, and said, "No, I'm here to do a story on some caves."

"The caves of Matala? That's where I'm headed, on assignment for *Life*. You?"

She gathered her forces and said, "UPI."

"Ah, syndication. I've thought of working for the wire, but this thing fell into my lap." He lowered his table for the drinks. "I'm Tad Crawford."

"Tad?"

He looked into his pinkish orange drink. "Thaddeus."

"Funny name." She laughed. "I'm Rochelle Libbon." And now he laughed. But somehow she didn't think it was so funny.

By the time the plane taxied into Athens, in the blazing early afternoon, Rochelle was drunk. Having decided to spend the night in Athens and travel together to Matala the next day, Tad maneuvered Rochelle to the old quarter of the city at the foot of the Parthenon. He parked her at a cafe, ordered her a black coffee, and went looking for a hotel.

They ended up in the Hotel Phadre, in a hot stuffy room with a balcony overlooking a small park filled with flowers and mismatched decorative pillars, reminders of the city's antiquity. The inside of the room was sparsely furnished and vaguely dirty. Tad sat on one of the twin beds. Rochelle lay down on the other and groaned.

"How old did you say you were?" he asked.

"Twenty-five. I wish we had a better room."

"Double bed."

"*Clean.* Are you broke or something?"

"Rochelle Libbon!" His face lit up. "Wait a minute, I've read your stuff." And he moved to her bed and touched her shoulder. "What ever happened to your brother, anyway?"

"I've got to get out of this dress." She rolled over and sat. "Unzip it, please."

As the zipper came down, one strong warm hand slid around to her breast.

"How old are *you*?" she asked.

"Twenty-nine."

"I think you're older."

"I think you're younger."

His body was nothing like Scott's. Tad was muscular, tight, experienced. Most of his body was covered with soft black hair. She realized now that her relationship with Scott had been lustless; she knew this because suddenly she felt charged with sheer sexual desire, and it was a new feeling. Just as Tad was about to roll onto her, she pushed him aside and dashed to the bathroom with her diaphragm. It took a few minutes to insert it correctly. When she came out, striding naked across the room, he snapped her picture repeatedly.

"Hey, why did you do that?" Despite her complaints, though, the attention thrilled her. She lay on one of the beds and gazed into his lens as he continued to shoot.

Matala was three hours from Iraklion in a rented car. Tad drove like a lunatic, speeding along deserted roads, through fields of olive trees, rushing up steep single-lane mountain roads and racing down. There were no barriers on the curvy roads, just a sheer drop down through blue sky into green ocean. Goats perched fearlessly on rocks that jutted out from the edges.

The village of Matala was simple and quiet, with a few small hotels and lantern-lit tavernas off the beach. Nude sunbathers were bronzed from head to toe. Whitewashed buildings were vined with red flowers and gardens were wild with purple and yellow. Rochelle found the place enchanting, and Tad seemed to fine *her* enchanting, so she figured she'd stick with him until she got bored or left Greece, whichever came first. Anyway, a woman was better off traveling with a man ... at least that was what Mabel had always said. They booked themselves into Nikos Hotel, where they got a large clean room with a double bed and a good stiff breeze. Then they went to find the caves.

Facing the ocean, to the right of the beach, was a mountainside pocked with hundreds of caves like gaping toothless mouths. Tad, strung with cameras, navigated them up the craggy mountainside to the first tier of caves. Rochelle was right behind him, in her red and white polka dot bathing suit top and frayed cutoffs.

As he shot the exterior, she went inside, and was startled to find someone living there. Sitting on a stone cot carved into the wall of the cave was a skinny man with hair to his waist and a long grizzly beard. He was wearing a necklace of dried seeds, his eyes were closed, and he was humming.

"There's someone in there!"

Tad went in and minutes later emerged with a smile. "The guy's an American! He told me there are people living in a lot of the caves. Let's go meet them. Where's your pad? Aren't you working?"

"I work from memory. My stuff's on the creative side."

They climbed from tier to tier, calling into caves and talking to whomever was willing. In one cave lived a family of three: a man and a woman wearing dirty white cotton robes, both with long hair, and a tiny naked baby with a multicolor braided headband on her fuzzy head. He had been a salesman and she a housewife, and they had come to Matala to visit and never left. Everyone had a story. Many were Americans who had fled the war.

Rochelle and Tad were so excited about the caves that when they got back down to the beach they stripped and ran into the water. They came together and made love right there, neck-deep in ocean. After, she stretched naked on the sand to dry in the hot sun. Her mind had begun to drift, when she heard the familiar clickclickclick and opened her eyes to find Tad leaning over her with his camera.

He wanted to take pictures of them in bed together, he said; and though Rochelle felt uneasy about it, she refused to shrink from an experience. So they returned to the room and he arranged his Leica camera on a tripod at the foot of the bed. He ran a long wire with a little plunger on the end, to Rochelle.

"Here," he said, "press the release at the right moment."

She held the release in her hand, terrified. She didn't know when the right moment was. And this time, he frightened her; he was too intense, somehow it was not *her* he was about to have sex with, but anyone. She didn't know how to say no to him, lying in bed naked with the camera pointed between her legs, so she played along like a disenfranchised body. He straddled her and plunged in, turned her around, slid under her so she could ride him, whispering "Click, now, *now*," and exploding into her and resting in a sweat and then starting again.

Tad Crawford, she decided, was not for her. So she packed before sunrise, left him sleeping alone in bed, and took the rental car back to Iraklion.

She arrived in New York in the evening. When she walked into the Columbia Heights house, four days late, Norman looked up from the newspaper and said, "There you are! We expected you'd want to spend a few extra days with your friend, but honey, next time *please* call." Mabel, however, was not as cool as Norman; she was icy, and wouldn't speak to her daughter for hours. Rochelle was happy to be left alone. She had scared herself by running to Greece like that, and ending up in bed with a pornographer, and then running, of all places, home.

When Rochelle returned to school in the fall, she had a single room and papered the walls and ceiling with tin foil. She melted candles onto every level surface, lit them, took out a pad and a pen and wrote. Not the column, though; this time, she put her pen to fiction. In the spirit of Thomas Wolfe, she wrote of a poetic young man in search of past, present and future. The time was never specified, and the hero contemplated instead of lived and in the end was an antihero who had undone himself by not doing anything. She eked the pages out slowly, and by early spring had an impressively long manuscript in need of typing.

When she arrived home for the summer, she first showed Norman and Mabel her year-end academic reports, all excellent, then took Norman aside and showed him the manuscript. She assured him of its brilliance, and without reading it he concurred. She said she was going to get it published, and he offered to have it professionally typed for her. With a hug and kiss and "Thanks, Dad!" *Poetsong* was readied for submission.

Rochelle personally escorted the bulky manuscript to the esteemed editorial-ship at Scribner's. She didn't know exactly who she was looking for, but she'd know when she found him. She assumed it would be a man. Wearing a tight black turtleneck, an orange and green herringbone miniskirt and thigh-high boots, her hair wound into a knot at the back of her neck, she entered the Scribner's bookshop, asked a saleswoman for Editorial and was directed to a staircase at the back of the store. The saleswoman grinned at the busty girl with the conspicuous manuscript; she had seen this breed before. Rochelle, too young and arrogant to recognize her own stereotype, assumed herself to be an original, and without thanking the saleswoman she marched away.

At the top of the stairs was an elevator, which she took to the fifth floor. The door opened onto a green-carpeted reception area with an unattended desk. She turned down a long hallway lined with bookcases on one side and glass walls partitioning offices on the other. A few unoccupied offices along, she found a clean-cut man of about thirty bent over a manuscript. He wore a pair of round wire-rimmed glasses low on the bridge of his nose. His door was halfway open. Just as she was about to knock, his eyes wandered to her, then glanced at his wristwatch.

"Come in," he said.

Whom had he been expecting? She didn't care. She smiled, walked in, sat down, crossed her legs and rested the manuscript on her bare thigh.

He leaned over his desk and shook her hand, which she extended, without reaching, forcing him to lean even farther. An expression of perturbance crossed his face, as he said, "Sam Roderick. And you are ... I'm sorry, I'm no good with names."

"Rochelle Libbon."

His eyebrows scrunched; clearly the name rang no bells at all. Seated, he leaned back, steepled his fingers, gazed upon her, waited. Then: "What's your experience?"

So he thought she had come for a job. She gave him a minute to catch her smile, really absorb it, before saying, "Here." She heaved *Poetsong* onto his desk.

"I don't understand."

Rochelle leaned forward, grouping her breasts into one impressive mound, and said, "It's a novel. I wrote it."

His eyes flickered from her breasts to the manuscript, and he ahh-ed recognition of what had just happened. At that moment, a smartly dressed young woman appeared in the doorway and introduced herself as "Sue Harrison, here to interview for the assistant's position."

Sam Roderick nodded. He turned to Rochelle and said, "Are you by any chance—?"

"No," she said, "I'm strictly a writer. Will you read it? My phone number's on the cover page."

"Yes, of course. Thanks for dropping it by."

Three weeks later she gave up waiting to hear from him and called his office. He said he had just "taken a look at it" and before he had a chance to say anything else, she convinced him to meet with her again in his office. They made an appointment for Friday at five o'clock.

After lunch on Friday, Rochelle put on her jeans and a T-shirt, told Mabel that she was going to meet a friend in Central Park (thus the big shoulder bag, "For a picnic," she explained), and made a beeline for Bonwits. She bought herself a tight black minidress, black fishnet stockings and black sandals with little pointy heels. She stashed her old clothes in the shoulder bag, and proceeded to Scribner's.

Friday at nearly five on Fifth Avenue was a crazed rush, with masses of people pressing downtown and masses pressing uptown. Rochelle strolled. It was a gorgeous day and she was on her way to triumph. She felt good, great, beautiful, and knew she was exuding it, because so many of the men who passed took a second look. She knew, at the age of twenty-one in her little black dress and fishnets, that she had *it*.The *thing*. The natural aura of sex. She swished through the hazy late afternoon, cool and slow, enjoying every minute. She was sure this must have been some kind of passage: literary or female, she had yet to discover.

On Friday afternoons, publishing slowed to a halt in the middle of the day, and most of the editorial staff at Scribner's had already left. But Sam Roderick's light was on; she could see it shining into the hall. She liked that. He was wait-ing—for *her*.

She knocked on the door, and asked, "Am I late?"

Hunched over a manuscript, he looked up suddenly, as if surprised to see her. But he said, "No," casually, and smiled. "You look very nice. Have a seat."

Rochelle sat across from the desk. She smiled and crossed her legs, letting her hem slip up her thigh.

"I've read *Poetsong*."

Here it came, the *yes it's a masterpiece and let's publish it immediately*.He cleared his throat, hesitating. "Actually, it's been a long week. Can we talk about this over a drink?"

"Okay." She stood.

He opened his desk drawer and withdrew a quart of whiskey. She sat down again.

"I only have one glass, unfortunately." He poured an inch of whiskey into the glass and handed it to her. "Excuse me," he said, and took a swig directly from the bottle.

"I liked Jack in *Poetsong*." He peered at her thoughtfully and she noticed the tiny wrinkles just blooming around his brown eyes. "There's an awful lot that's good in that novel." He took another swig.

Rochelle sipped her whiskey and it burned all the way down her throat into her stomach. She took another sip, this one bigger.

"So—you liked it?"

"Let me just ask you something, if you don't mind."

"Ask away."

He cleared his throat and straightened his back. "Would you by any chance be interested in going out with me?"

"I don't know. Maybe. Would you by any chance want to publish my novel?"

"I *want* to want to." His back slumped and he forced a smile, showing his age. Older than thirty, she now thought. Maybe even forty.

"Meaning?"

He capped the whiskey bottle and stowed it back in the drawer. Then he reached over to click off his desk lamp, and stood up. "To be honest, Miss Lib-bon, I'm already overcommitted. My list is full for the next two years. I'm just not in a position to take on another book."

BULLSHIT was what Rochelle titled her comeback article in *The Benningtonian*. After seventeen more rejections of *Poetsong* by publishing houses, she had returned to her old beat, only older now and tougher and louder. She realized where she had gone wrong: she was a woman and had written about a man. What did she know about anything but herself? So she wrote out her raw thoughts and printed them. The syndication wire picked her up again. Vietnam raged and America boiled and finally, finally Nathan wrote to her.

Well, actually, he drew. There were no words on the page, just a picture of a bomb exploding on a tropical horizon. She knew it was from him, not just because of the postmark, but because she recognized the lines, the unsteady hand that drew them. During the course of the next two years, through and beyond her graduation (with honors), she received Nathan's drawings and told no one. Some were pencil sketches but a few were in full color. Shattered earth. An exploding sun. A man made entirely of intertwined blue veins with a red missile for a head.

Chapter 5

Don't Step on My Blue Suede Shoes

"A first kiss is never as dignified as in your fantasies." Rocky holds the receiver of Cat's office phone lightly to her ear, laughing at whatever Larry has said in response.

Cat sits at the computer, pretending not to listen.

"You're a wet kisser, darling. All tongue." That laugh, wild and high.

Cat stiffens. Her typing speeds up; she can do over sixty words-per-minute now.

"Six o'clock." Rocky hangs up and says to Cat, "Larry's picking me up *here*. Can you believe, in all these months, he's never seen my *home*?"

"Before you go," Cat says, as Rocky moves dreamily toward to the office door, "could we take a minute to discuss something?"

"Larry's madly in love with me. Connie was a genius to introduce us."

"I'd like to take a week of vacation soon, if it's okay with you. It *has* been almost six months, when we agreed I could—"

"I'll never be a white bride again. Maybe this time I'll wear ... red!"

"I'd just like to take a little time—"

"Sleep a little late tomorrow, darling." Rocky, at the door, turns around. "If Annie doesn't have enough money to pick up my cleaning, give her something from petty cash. And someone should tip the delivery person from Lamar." She is expecting the delivery of a two-thousand dollar dress she plans to wear tonight.

Cat swallows what has become a familiar lump of frustration. "Petty cash is almost empty."

"Someone will have to go to the bank."

"I'll go during my lunch hour," Cat says, capitalizing on the opportunity to underscore the sacrifice of her time. She flaps the calendar open to the first week in April. "Could we please discuss the dates for my vacation?"

"*I* need a vacation."

"I've looked at your schedule and it's pretty light in April. So this seems like a good week for me to be away."

Rocky sighs. "Where are you planning to go?"

"Teddy and I can't make any definite plans until we know the dates."

Rocky's mouth pinches at the corners. She returns to the desk to look at the open calendar. "Okay, that looks fine. Mark it in my personal calendar, too."

"Thank you!" Cat feels a trill of elation at her small victory. She has her mind set on a week of inn-hopping in New England, and Teddy already said he'd take the time off whenever she could arrange her own schedule. "Also, Rocky, while I'm looking at the calendar, you never told me what to do about that celebrity auction. It's coming up and they keep calling me."

"I'll think of something to donate."

"Okay, I'll stave them off. Oh, and Rocky, John called. He needs to set up another interview."

"Find some time next week. Call him back for me, will you?"

The rest of the day passes quickly. When the doorbell rings just after six o'clock, Cat is in the dining room saying goodnight to Annie, lingering in the hope of catching a glimpse of Larry Drumm, celebrated playwright, in person.

Rocky comes running down the hall, calling, "I'll get it!" She's wearing the new red minidress with sheer black stockings and spiky black pumps.

Annie whispers what is obvious to Cat. "She's too heavy for a dress like that."

Rocky stands by the wall mirror next to the front door and gazes at herself. "How do I look?"

"Beautiful!" Annie says.

"I look sexy in red, don't I?"

The bell rings again.

Rocky opens the door to a small, squat man with the tight-skinned gleam of someone who has been overhauled by plastic surgeons. A thin web of brown hair fails to hide the pinkish circles of hair plugs. His body looks lumpy in some places and lean in others, as if from botched liposuction. Cat can hardly believe her eyes. She has seen photos of Larry Drumm in magazines, and he looked nothing like the plasticy gnome standing in the doorway.

Towering over him in her heels, Rocky coos, "You look so handsome," and touches a red-enameled fingernail to a gold button on his navy blazer.

"That dress," he says in a nasal monotone that hardly reveals his meaning, but it's definitely not a compliment.

"It's new." She stands back so he can get a better look.

He turns his attention instead to the living room, with its hot colors and skyline view. "Looks like a ritzy whorehouse."

She laughs.

He smiles a tight non-smile, an *uns*mile that is worse than a frown.

"We have a reservation for six-thirty," Rocky reminds him, "so—"

He turns and walks out, not waiting for Rocky to finish her sentence, or acknowledging Cat or Annie, who hover in plain sight. Rocky grabs her coat and follows.

All the way home, Cat thinks about Larry Drumm. His plays are supposed to be funny, witty, quick, and maybe they are. Maybe in the theater his sensibility is effective. But just looking at him in person tells a different story. The man has faked himself nearly out of existence with all that plastic surgery. So much effort and he isn't even beautiful. *These* people are beautiful, Cat thinks, looking at the unaltered graying sagging *real* people riding home at the end of the day. Bodies have slowed down, as all head up and down and across town toward whatever well-earned comforts await them. She thinks of Teddy and her day's exhaustion begins to wane.

She ascends the subway at Astor Place and passes the big tilted cube, someone's outsized abstract sculpture which moves slowly with any subtle breeze. Walking along St. Marks Place in the purplish twilight, among the bums and addicts and homeless and artists, she feels a surge of love for her corner of this city. Not Rocky's glamorous Upper East Side corner, or the Upper West Side corner of her childhood, but *her* corner, downtown.

At Second Avenue, she stops to buy a bouquet of flowers, pink-speckled tiger lilies that the Korean salesman wraps in a cone of paper printed in green army camouflage. She cradles them in her arms and goes home, eager to tell Teddy the good news that they can now plan their long-awaited vacation.

The moment she walks through the front door, directly into the kitchen, she is enveloped in the rich aromas of Teddy's cooking. A large soup pot on the stove is sending up steam. She walks over to it and looks in: Teddy's homemade marinara sauce full of basil and mushrooms and onions and garlic. She gives it a stir with the long wooden spoon he has left on the counter.

"Teddy?"

"In here."

The rest of the apartment is dark except for the light in Teddy's small study, the third room in their railroad. He is seated at his desk, reading a library book. Cat walks in, flicking on lights as she goes, and stops in front of him. She hands him the bouquet. "Flowers for my Teddy bear."

"Well well." He flutters his eyelids in mock female delight, his beautiful pale eyelids fatigued from hours of reading. She knows he studies intensely during the day when she's gone, and can see him relaxing upon her return, opening, becoming not Ted the scholar but Teddy her lover, her best friend.

"I've got a week off, the first week in April!"

"Hey, great! So we'll do Vermont?"

"Vermont, New Hampshire, whatever. I can't wait."

"That's good news."

He fills a vase with water and arranges the flowers. His hair is thick and curly, the color of clover honey which is rich and dark and bright. Cat thinks his face has a kind of Renaissance look: high forehead, long straight pointy nose with finely chiseled nostrils, a wide mouth with a thin top lip and pouty bottom lip, and cool bluegray eyes. She stands behind him and wraps her arms around his middle. Considerably shorter than he is, she stretches up to kiss him.

"Ah, this is nice," he says.

"I love you, Teddy."

"And I love you." They kiss.

"Aren't you hungry?" he asks.

"Not yet."

They move to the bedroom and undress each other. The familiarity of their naked skin is luscious as they roll together, body into body. At the moment of dare, Teddy withdraws and sits back, concentrating on conserving his excitement. Cat jumps up and runs to the bathroom, where she inserts her diaphragm. It's a dangerous habit, starting unprotected then stopping at the edge.

Dinner is penne with the red sauce that has cooked to perfection over a long afternoon, and salad with Teddy's homemade mustard-dill vinaigrette. Everything is delicious, as always.

"I'll buy a book of bed and breakfasts tomorrow." Cat reaches for a piece of Italian bread.

"I can look for something in the library," he says. "It'll be free."

"But out of date. I'll buy the book. We'll split the trip."

"Sounds good. There's more pasta, want some?"

"No thanks, I'm full."

He crosses the kitchen and refills his plate.

"So." He sits back down with his second mountain of penne. "Vacation."

"Vacation's going to be great," Cat says. "We really need it."

"We do. It'll be nice to just hang out together. One week, huh? When's your *next* vacation?"

"I don't know. Summer, I guess."

"I've been thinking." Teddy leans forward, resting his chin in the palm of one hand. "Why don't you use some vacation time to do some of your *own* work? Get back to cartooning. That was the plan when you took this job, wasn't it?"

"I know," she says, sensing the looming shadow of disappointment she feels with herself every time she thinks of how little she's accomplished since starting her *real* job which is starting to feel more and more *un*real. "I want to. I *need* to."

"You could always do some drawing on the weekends, you know. Or at night."

"That's easier said than done. There's stuff to do on the weekends. And I'm so tired after work. And when would I spend time with you?"

"Don't use me as an excuse."

"That was a little harsh."

"I didn't mean it to be. What I'm saying is that it's time to get back to work. We love each other ... that's not going to change. But we both have to reach for the whole balance now."

"Teddy, are you feeling like you're not getting enough accomplished because of me?"

"No, I'm doing what I need to do. But you're not." He pauses, then adds, "I'm worried that someday you'll resent me if you look back and realize you stopped cartooning when we met."

"I didn't stop when we met. I stopped when I went to work full-time." Her tone is more defensive than she'd intended. And she's splitting hairs. With or without Teddy, sooner or later she would have ended up facing this very dilemma. "I guess I could try to carve out some time."

"I think you should. Your work's really interesting."

The compliment nearly levitates her off her chair. "Thanks, but I've got a long way to go before I show it to—"

"Cat, your work is good. Don't be such a *perfectionist*." He spits out the word like a hard seed and stands up. "I know what you need—*incentive*. Come on, we're going out." He tosses his napkin onto the table and pushes back his chair.

"Now?"

"Right now."

"Where?"

"You'll see."

They walk along Second Avenue, bundled up against the early-March chill. As they cross the street, Teddy stops and claps his hands together. "I'm going to introduce you to Isabel."

"Who?"

"Isabel Rodriguez, she edits *Freak*."

"That weird magazine?"

"She prints cartoons."

"I haven't drawn a cartoon for five months. Forget it, Teddy."

"Exactly. You're drying up, sweetie. If she doesn't light a fire under you, no one will."

"This isn't the right time to show my work."

"It's the perfect time. Come on, let's go see if she's home."

"You mean *right now*?"

"Why not?"

He takes her hand and pulls her along St. Mark's Place until they reach a crumbling stoop next to Zen Sushi. One of the bells is labeled with an icy lettered *freak*. Teddy rings.

A window thumps open and a woman with spiky, bleached-white hair looks out. She is wearing red lipstick, and calls down, "Who the fuck is there?"

"It's me!" Teddy calls up.

One corner of Isabel's mouth curls. Her gaze lands on Cat. Then she nods once, goes back inside and closes the window. A few moments later the door buzzes open.

They climb to the second floor. The stairs are filthy and peels of paint seem to drip off the ceiling. The same lettering as on the bell downstairs labels her door, only bigger: FREAK. Teddy knocks and the door swings open.

Cat is surprised at how small and delicate Isabel appears. Hanging out of the window, she seemed tough, even a little scary. Well, she *is* a little scary, standing there with her spiky bleached hair and fire-engine red lips and black kimono and leopard slippers. But up close there is too much surface defense, as if she is trying to protect something breakable. Cat smiles and waits to be introduced.

Teddy and Isabel lean toward each other and touch cheeks.

"This," Teddy says, "is Catharine Gold."

"Come on in." Isabel walks across the room and flips off the TV. Then she turns around and looks at Teddy. "Long time."

Teddy sits on one of her wooden chairs and Cat stands next to him. Isabel sits on the couch, which is haphazardly covered with a zebra print cloth. She reaches for her pack of Camels on the battered wooden coffee table, slides one out and lights it.

"How long *has* it been?" she asks Teddy.

He rolls back his eyes in thought, looks at Cat, smiles.

They were lovers. Suddenly, Cat *knows* it. She swallows an impulse to bolt, along with spike of resentment that Teddy had the audacity to bring her here. What was he thinking?

Isabel nods. Her eyes wander away. She says, "So."

"Listen, Izzy," Teddy says, plunging right in. "Cat has some cartoons to show you. She's good."

Isabel forces a flatline smile. Then she shrugs. "All right. Let's see 'em."

"They're at home," Cat says, feeling helpless, somehow *betrayed* in a way she can't quite put her finger on.

"I just wanted to stop by to introduce you. She'll bring the cartoons over tomorrow evening."

Isabel shakes her head. "Tomorrow's no good. Gotta meet with the printer at six. Thursday morning, late, like around noon."

"No good," Teddy says, knowing Cat's workaday schedule limits her to nights and weekends. "How about Saturday?"

Isabel shrugs; evidently, that means okay. The deal is done, and they leave with as little fanfare and as much awkwardness as when they arrived.

Cat and Teddy are silent all the way home, she hot with anger, he bright with some inexplicable pride. But as the hours slip by, Cat decides Teddy is only trying to help. He loves her. He wants her to be happy. And he must know as well as she does that, once the bloom of their romance fades, her happiness will rely as much on her work as on him. She spends the next few nights trying not to worry about what Teddy's and Isabel's relationship had once been, or how terrifyingly vulnerable she will feel showing her cartoons to a stranger, an *editor*-stranger, and focuses instead on which cartoons to bring to the meeting.

Teddy says, "Just bring your best work," and Cat says, "But what *is* my best work?" and Teddy says, "You know what your best work is, Cat, don't get stupid on me now."

Stupid! But he's *right*. She has entered a kind of frenzied confusion at the thought of facing Isabel with her work. It is only *Freak*, she tells herself, an insignificant offbeat journal that probably no one even reads. And it is only some paranoid punk chick who is probably more afraid of Cat than Cat is of her. But still, her nervousness builds as Saturday arrives.

Having assumed that Teddy planned to go over with her, she is surprised when he doesn't make any move to get ready to come along. He sits hunched over his desk in the still posture that has become familiar, and tells her he is studying.

"Can't you take a break?"

He leans back in his chair and looks at her. "Sweetie, *go*."

"Teddy—"

"You don't need me to hold your hand."

"I don't know why you started this."

"Go!"

She grabs her folder and marches out.

But she isn't really angry at Teddy anymore. She has solved her irritation with the gradual understanding that he really *is* trying to help, not humiliate, her. He made a connection for her—everyone says you need connections to get anywhere—and he only expects her to take advantage of it. She knows what he is doing: daring her to strike a balance between practicality and aspiration, to *walk the walk*, and handing her a moment for action. So he and Isabel used to be lovers. So what? *She publishes cartoons.*

She marches up the crumbling stoop and rings the bell. This time, Isabel doesn't pop out of the window to look, she simply buzzes Cat up.

The front door is cracked open, and when Cat knocks, Isabel calls, "Come in."

She is sitting at a desk, which is really just a plank of wood resting on two rickety sawhorses. The desk is piled with papers and books. Two Rolodexes and a telephone totter on top of piles. Isabel wears tight faded bluejeans, a black turtleneck, and a pair of black thick-rimmed glasses. She has on the same leopard slippers as the other night and her lips are just as sizzling red, redder even in the bright winter daylight.

As Cat walks in, the phone rings, and Isabel speaks quickly and bossily with the caller. She hangs up without a goodbye.

"So let's see," she says.

Cat hands over the folder, which Isabel lays on a heap of papers and briskly opens. She lights a cigarette and smokes deeply as she turns over the cartoons one by one. There is no expression on her face. Cat doesn't like it. Not one bit. She feels violated, invaded, judged.

Isabel flips back to the beginning, separates out two individual cartoons and squashes out her cigarette in an overflowing ashtray.

"I can't pay you," she says.

"You like them?"

"Yeah, not bad. Where else do you publish?"

"Nowhere."

That tight smile reappears on Isabel's face. "You work full-time?"

"Well, just lately. I used to mostly just do this."

"Trust fund run out or something?"

"No," Cat says, swallowing a sense of shame she doesn't deserve. If Isabel thinks she's a dilettante, why take the cartoons? "I worked part-time, and Teddy helped me for a while."

"So I guess it must be love."

"Guess so," Cat says. And she knows that not only have Teddy and Isabel slept together, but she was in love with him.

The prospect of having two of her cartoons published—if only in *Freak*, and by a woman who is jealous of her and possibly holds a grudge—is more satisfying than Cat had imagined. It is at once an exciting and vulnerable feeling to know that her cartoons, her *art*, will soon be seen by others. This small accomplishment propels her through a blizzard of similar days. She feels a new wave of inspiration, which at times sweeps over her at the office when she is supposed to be concentrating on All Things Rocky.

When the inspiration is strong enough she gives in to it, pushes aside her piles of work, sets a blank sheet of paper on her desk and begins to draw. But she finds that her subjects have changed. Now, instead of siphoning stories of other people's lives from newspapers, she finds plenty of material in her own life. A drawing juxtaposing a busty big-haired celebrity boss and mousy secretary comes out especially well, and without planning to, she features the two pseudo-women in a comic strip she calls *Max & Min: 2 Sides to Every Woman*.

On one such morning, minutes into a detailed frame featuring a close-up of the inside of the celebrity's wide-open mouth, Cat realizes that John Paglia has been standing next to her desk, observing her. A jolt of surprise passes through her like an electric shock. She covers the drawing with a blank page.

"You draw?" he says.

"I had a few spare minutes. I'm really not supposed to be doing this here. Sorry."

"Don't worry, I won't tell her. You're an artist?"

"Cartoonist."

"Same thing, right?"

"Are you here to see Rocky? Because she's out for the morning."

"I'm just dropping off a disk." He tears at the Velcro of a large outer pocket of his blue down jacket, reaches in and pulls out a disk. He places it on the desk. "What's your cartoon about?"

"Don't know yet," she lies. She knows exactly what it's about—the unbeautiful inside of a greedy celebrity and her prime feed: the people around her. "I just felt like doing it. I guess I'm *free drawing*." Her smile is exaggerated, to remind him of the silliness of his own term.

"Touché. I know I was laying it on thick, but it really is a good idea."

"I guess so."

"Which?" he asks. "Laying it on thick or free writing?"

"Both. But you have to do that with Rocky, she needs tons of affirmation."

"Well, I'm used to the star mentality from my days on *Rising Tides*. Everyone's a prima donna on the soaps, you get used to it."

"So you don't really believe all that stuff about free writing?"

"Actually, I do believe it. I started out as a fiction writer, you know, in college. I thought I was going to be the next Hemingway."

"Who doesn't?"

"And you were going to be the next Gary Trudeau, right?"

"I still am," Cat says, surprising herself.

He lets loose an enormous smile. "Of course. So anyway." They laugh together. "I used to practice free writing to get my juices flowing before I sat down to write the Great American

Novel which I never wrote in the end, then eventually I just did free writing as therapy. It's amazing how well it works. I used to sit in my office at the network, in fact, just like you are now, stealing a few minutes."

"So you really won't turn me in?"

"Not a chance. I'm a freelancer, I know my place."

"Well, you sure know how to work Rocky, I have to hand it to you. And to be honest, this book of hers has been keeping her busy, which means she doesn't hang around in here so much, which means I'm less harassed. So thanks."

"We should talk some time, I mean about Rocky. I should interview you. What do you say?"

"Me?"

"Well, I've been interviewing other people in her life, and you're a people in her life, right?"

"I guess I am. You should talk to Annie, too."

"I will. I'll take you to lunch or something, but we shouldn't talk here." He winks.

"Deal."

"So, how serious are you about your cartoons?"

"Serious, I guess. I'm getting two published soon in this little journal I'm sure you never heard of."

"Called?"

"*Freak.*"

"I think I've seen it. Isn't it one of those ultra hip magazines they have down at the St. Marks Bookstore? I used to lurk around down there when I felt like a piece of human garbage, like I was selling out everything I ever thought was true about myself. I used to stand there and leaf through all those underground journals because they're the polar opposite of soap operas. But the truth is I never bought one. I never even read one. In the end, I'd just go home and watch TV."

"I don't think anyone reads them, but it's my first credit, so I'm happy."

"You should be, those things are stepping stones. You live down there?"

"Sixth Street. I live with my boyfriend. You?"

"Upper West Side with Maria, my dog, and the leftovers my ex-wife called 'solid furniture' when she moved out with all the good stuff." He smirks. "I should get going, I've got an appointment to have a corn removed from my toe."

Cat laughs.

"I do! What's so funny?"

"Sorry, it was just the way you said it. You have a wicked sense of humor, don't you, buried under that salesman thing you do?"

"Salesman thing?" That smile, big and toothy and unembarrassed. "No, you're right. But you have to have a sense of humor in this biz."

"I've been wondering, is this your first celebrity bio?"

"It's the first one I've actually put down on paper, but when I was at the network I wrote those diva bios in my head twenty-four hours a day. They ran through my mind like movies."

"TV movies?"

"TV movies-of-the-week, multipart, the whole shebang."

A few weeks later, Teddy comes home with an armful of *Freaks* and a big bouquet of lilies.

"Here it is!" He drops the magazines onto the kitchen table. "You're on pages seven and ten."

Cat flips right to her cartoons. "I don't believe it! Do you think anyone will see them?"

Teddy shrugs. "Sure."

"You must have spent a fortune on these. Isabel said she could only give me two free copies."

His face is pink from the chilly early spring. He yanks off his jacket and tosses it over the back of a chair. "It cost me nothing. Except the flowers—I paid for them. But Izzy gave me all these free."

"Izzy?"

He unzips his jacket. "I guess I've got charisma and you've got talent."

"When did you see her?"

"Just now, on the street. I bumped into her and went up for a beer. I asked for some extra copies and she gave me these."

"She just gave them to you? She doesn't seem like the most generous person in the world, she's—"

"Are you're getting your period or something?"

"What's that supposed to mean?"

"Just let it go. She gave me these and that's the end of the story."

"You're wrong, by the way," Cat says. "I'm not upset because I'm getting my period, though I am expecting it any minute, but that's not the point—and while we're on the topic, I hate it when you default to that. It's Isabel, there's something about her that disturbs me, and I just don't see—"

"Let's just drop it, okay?"

Cat doesn't like the feeling that's pulsing between her ribs. Suspicion, or jealousy, she isn't sure, but it's something new. She decides she better get to know Isabel, befriend her, wedge herself between them before they get too close again.

So on Saturday morning, her period now three days late, Cat shoves five cartoons into her folder and goes over to Isabel's, who, she has come to learn, rarely goes out before two o'clock.

This time, Cat stands right behind her as she goes over the cartoons.

"Okay, this one." Isabel pulls one out. "The others you can still work on." She closes the file and hands it to Cat.

Cat smiles. "Busy for lunch?"

"Today?"

"The sushi place downstairs has a lunch special."

"I don't usually go out for lunch."

"My treat."

"Well, I guess I could. It'll be tax deductible, you know, 'cause it's a working lunch."

They go downstairs and share a tiny square table shoved against the wall of Zen Sushi.

"Thanks for giving Teddy all those copies of *Freak*, that was nice of you." Cat bites half a California roll.

Isabel pinches in one side of her mouth and Cat sees that she has a deep dimple. "Yeah, well, I'm not going to make a habit of it. He's a little hard to say no to, you know? I was sort of in a rush when he came over."

Is this what Cat was looking for, a rift in their stories? Teddy told her they had bumped into each other on the street.

"Well, thanks," Cat says. "I'm sending them to my family. They love Teddy. They all think it's really great he introduced me to you, and *Freak*, I mean."

"Great," Isabel says.

"Teddy's behind me."

"The thing is," Isabel peers cautiously at Cat. "About Teddy, I mean. The thing is he's a man."

"I know that."

"I like men," Isabel says, "but I wouldn't trust one, and I wouldn't depend on one."

"Why not?"

"How old are you?"

"Twenty-five."

"I'm thirty-one. I used to be dumb, too. Everyone was, I guess."

"Dumb?"

"Listen, you gotta live your own way. All I'm saying is we all make the same mistake early. We lose ourselves just to love someone. It's a luxury, love. You gotta pay for it. And the price can be too high. The thing about feminism people forget is that it's not just about day care and sharing the vacuuming. Jeez, look around. How many men do I know who moonlight as rapists?"

"Rapists?"

Isabel shakes her head quickly. "Not *literally*. I'm talking about violence, you know, all kinds of violence. I mean, it can be something invisible like knocking down self-esteem." Isabel stares at Cat, and Cat stares back, confused, helpless, excited. "I mean," Isabel says, "I fuck men, I even like them, and damned if I don't fall in love again. But I'll tell you *no* man ever stood behind me who didn't stab me in the back."

"What about women? Don't women betray you sometimes?"

Isabel's nostrils flare. "Yeah, sure, sometimes."

"I think maybe you're seeing things too black-and-white."

"Listen, all I'm saying to you is *that's the way it is*. Don't get *fooled*, is what I'm saying. Don't lose your *self*."

Cat feels ashamed and she doesn't know why. She doesn't understand what Isabel is talking about, not really, though she wants to.

"I'm not telling you to turn away from Teddy. I'm only saying we *all* have to watch our backs, on the streets, and at home too. Even at home."

But at home, Cat wants to say but can't think of how to explain it so Isabel will believe her, *at home is where I'm loved*. What she says is, "I think I can trust Teddy."

"'Course you can. At least, you have to. All I'm saying is there are pros and cons to everything, even love, and don't think you're gonna get off without the cons."

The waiter whizzes by and drops their bill on the table. Cat hoists her purse up from where she has slung it across the back of her chair and takes out fifteen dollars. She puts the money on top of the bill and weighs it down with the salt shaker.

Isabel pushes her empty plate away and leans forward. "I've been through all this with Teddy, and he even *agrees*."

"What do you mean? Been through what?"

"I've told him how it is for us, you know, for women. It's no great revelation. He's a smart man, he knows, but...."

Isabel hesitates, and Cat says, "What?"

"Nothing, never mind, I'm just blabbing." Isabel smiles, a broad friendly smile that strikes Cat as strange for someone who is so guarded and solemn. "If I couldn't be honest, like, if I didn't make a *commitment* to saying what I *think* whether I'm right or wrong, then I never would have started *Freak*. You know?"

"Yeah, I think I understand that."

They leave the restaurant and stand out on the street in the cold overcast early afternoon. Isabel's threadbare black coat hangs open.

"Thanks for lunch," Isabel says.

Cat shrugs. "No problem."

"Sorry if I upset you. But listen, maybe it isn't so bad to get upset about things every now and then, right?"

"Right."

"Good cartoon. Come around when you have some more." Isabel walks slowly up the stoop and lets herself into the building with her key.

Cat isn't exactly sure what Isabel was getting at, but she obviously doesn't trust Teddy. Her vague warnings feel like insults. Her words hurt, poke wounds Cat hadn't even noticed were there. And now, walking along, skimming the surfaces of Isabel's words and not wanting to go deeper but wanting to, needing to, hoping never to, but understanding that she will have to, she reaches home without noticing her surroundings. She had completely miscalculated the danger Isabel poses. Cat doesn't understand Isabel at all, yet Isabel claims to understand her. And how, Cat wonders, how has she gotten through to Isabel with her cartoons? What is her own work saying that *Freak* understands and she herself does not?

When Cat gets home she finds Teddy in the kitchen mixing up a batch of tuna. "Hey there, pussycat. Hungry?"

Cat shakes her head. "Went out to lunch."

"Alone?"

"With Isabel. I brought her more cartoons."

"Izzy went out for lunch? Did she take the cartoons?"

"One."

He mounds tuna on a slice of bread and covers it with another slice, then cuts the sandwich diagonally. "She's a killer, huh?"

On Monday morning, Cat rushes in to work ten minutes late and goes straight to the bathroom with her bag from the drug store. She takes out the early pregnancy test and reads the directions. As instructed, she holds the little plastic wand in her stream of urine, then prepares to wait the full four minutes for a result: a pink circle for positive, a blank window for negative. But in less than a minute the bright pink bull's-eye appears.

Pregnant.

She goes to her office, feeling as if she suddenly inhabits a different world. She sits down, and only after a moment does she notice that on top of her desk is a pair of Rocky's shoes, neon blue pumps. Strangely, in Cat's daze, their presence does not seem unusual.

Maybe she could talk to Rocky? She's a smart, mature woman, despite her faults. And she was a pioneer 20th century feminist; she has given talks on issues like single motherhood and the option of abortion. Cat gets up, walks down the hall to Rocky's study and knocks on the door.

"Come in," Rocky says.

"Do you have a second?"

"I have many seconds." Rocky leans back in her chair, where she has been writing pages of her memoir. Yellow sheets covered in loopy writing are scattered across her desktop. "I have hours and years. I have a *lifetime.*"

"What I mean is, Rocky ... I'd like to talk."

"Sure." She swivels in her chair to present her full attention. Cat sits opposite, on the couch, and tells her about her pregnancy.

"And I just don't know what to do," Cat finishes. "I feel really torn. How will I support a baby all on my own?"

"You can't," Rocky says. "That's the conundrum we face. Day care sucks, it's too expensive. Men can't be counted on. And if we have our unwanted babies, their needs suffocate us."

Listening to Rocky's well-intentioned advice, Cat realizes that she is talking to a woman who *is* a single mother and yet doesn't have a clue what a woman like Cat, someone with an average life, faces. As Rocky goes on, Cat wishes she hadn't sought Rocky's counsel because it isn't helping. It *can't* help when the conversation is carried out over such a vast divide.

"End it," Rocky says, regaining Cat's attention. "Abort it. Liberate yourself. That's what we fought for back in seventy-three."

"I'll think about it," Cat says. "Thanks, Rocky."

"Any time." Rocky smiles. "By the way, I left you my shoes. I think they gave me the fungus. You can give them to the charity auction people."

It sounds so wrong that Cat can't answer at first, then manages: "But if they gave you the fungus, maybe you should throw them away."

"They're expensive shoes, and they were mine. Someone might buy them."

"Well, okay."

"I want to dictate a letter to go with them."

Cat nods. She finds a pen and a pad of paper on the desk, and sits down next to Rocky. She can feel her heart rapidly sinking. She can't do this now, can't send out infectious shoes to people in need. Can't take dictation. She needs to *think*.It was a dumb idea to even consider trying to talk to Rocky about her own problems. Rocky Love, that inspirational icon, no longer exists—and maybe never did.

Rocky begins to dictate: "*Don't step on my blue suede shoes* was always a favorite song of mine, and even though these blue shoes aren't suede, they are donated to your important cause with true feeling. For these are my favorite shoes, and only with sorrow do I part with them."

C h a p t e r 6

The Rise and Fall of Rocky Love

Brother Love

After graduation, Rochelle went straight to Manhattan. She had honed her style, sharpened her wit and broadened the horizons of her critical social observations. She was gifted with confidence, and lucky to have been encouraged, and it never occurred to her not to develop herself. The question now was: develop herself into what, and how?

She thought of writing more articles, but she yearned for something bigger, broader. Nathan was gone. *Poetsong* had failed. There was a globe of energy trapped inside her and she knew there was a key, a special key that would let it out—then nothing would stop her.

In the meantime, Norman offered to subsidize her until she figured things out. Mabel tried to pin him down to a time limit, believing that if life wasn't made too comfortable for her, Rochelle would smarten up and find a husband. But Norman argued that he wanted his baby to be happy, and refused to qualify his offer of support. Rochelle accepted the offer. She had never supported herself; she hadn't been raised to it, and didn't know how.

She enrolled in three classes: psychology, essay writing, and acting. And every Sunday evening, she took the subway to Brooklyn and had dinner with Norman and Mabel at home.

She would arrive in bellbottoms and turtlenecks, minidresses with thigh-high suede boots, long hair ironed straight and parted in the middle, giant hoop earrings, thick-heeled psychedelic shoes, hiphuggers with wide belts and peace symbol buckles, tight black knitted maxidresses, white lipstick, fake eyelashes, phony nails, or in tattered jeans and a T-shirt and no makeup at all.

Mabel couldn't seem to decide what was worse: the wild styles or the no-makeup-at-all. "See these grays?" She indicated her salt and pepper hair, which in fact looked quite distinguished. "*You* gave them to me. Rochelle baby why don't you settle down and find a nice boy? You're not getting any younger."

Norman carved a roast chicken as if deaf to his wife's pleas. His eyes flicked to Rochelle just long enough to catch her reaction.

"I'm not too old for today," Rochelle said. "Really, Mom, getting married isn't necessary anymore. A lot of people just live together."

"Live together? What do you mean by *live together*?"

Norman was also shaken, and Rochelle regretted it now.

"Who lives together out of wedlock but hippies and prostitutes?" Mabel said.

"Rochelle isn't living with anyone," Norman said. "If she's going to live with anyone before she marries, it will be with a nice young girl like herself. Look at Leo." Leo tensed. There he sat, every Sunday, prim and quiet in his hiphuggers and crazy-printed polyester shirts, with his oversized mustache neatly clipped and combed. "Leo lives with a nice boy and they double date."

"Leo is a good boy," Mabel agreed.

Leo and Rochelle would take the subway uptown together after these meals. Leo never explicitly described his relationship with Chip, but Rochelle knew. They double dated together: Leo and Chip, and Rochelle and one of her men friends.

"I don't know why I go every Sunday," Leo said. The train was scattered with Sunday evening travelers. Leo and Rochelle sat side by side, swaying with the metallic to-and-fro, talking above the clatter. The subway was prolific with graffiti. As Leo made his weekly anguished remarks about home-and-mother, Rochelle took a blue pen from her huge brown leather purse and wrote on the wall behind them: LOVE.

"Why did you do that?"

"I don't know," she said. Something filled her up, a sudden feeling. "It just came to me."

They got out at 79th Street and walked slowly up Broadway in the cool autumn night.

"I don't know exactly what she means by marriage," Rochelle said.

Leo laughed. "Oh, I do. She means tucking yourself away with a neat label so she can stop worrying. It has nothing to do with the real you or what you really want."

"Or the real you."

"Definitely not the real me. I'm beyond her comprehension."

"Sundays, yuck," Rochelle said. "I only go for Dad."

"It keeps your checks coming. I wish I were a girl." They both knew that Norman would never have considered supporting one of the boys.

They kissed cheeks at the corner of 82nd Street. Rochelle turned in to West End, and Leo continued uptown on Broadway.

Rochelle lived in a one-bedroom apartment on the fifth floor of a huge old pre-war building on West End Avenue. The walls and ceilings of the common hall had been painted a wild aquamarine fantasy by her neighbor, a photographer, who must have slept all day because he seemed to receive visitors all through the night. She was never really surprised by whom or what she found waiting in the fishtank hallway.

The elevator door scrolled open and she stepped into the blue-green swirl, digging in her purse for her keys. She sensed someone, and looked up. A man in jeans and a denim shirt with mother of pearl snaps leaned against the wall. He had long brown hair and brand new desert boots. His brass belt buckle was a quarter moon. A long fat duffel bag rested on the floor by his feet. His face was hollow, his skin a leathery tan, his eyes brown and vacant, the lines of his face intimately familiar.

"Happy birthday," he said.

"My birthday isn't until April."

"It's *my* birthday, sister."

He was right, she had almost forgotten. Tomorrow Nathan would be twenty-eight.

But he looked more like thirty-eight, and she stared at his lined face and looked for her young sweet poetbrother, her late-night under-the-sheets Brooklynbrother, the one she had so deeply loved.

"Knock knock," he said.

A smile broke over her face. "Who's there?"

"I am, goddammit. Aren't you going to let me in?"

She found her keys and unlocked the door. But before she opened it, she turned to him. "I want a hello kiss first."

"I'll kiss you later. Right now I have to pee."

"Down the hall, through the bedroom, on the left." She moved aside and he dashed in like an invading spirit. He had already invaded her. She had been waiting for this for years.

She didn't know exactly what to do with herself. *Nathan.* So she boiled some water for tea. She recalled that he used to like Earl Gray; they used to drink it on cold afternoons together. She took some butter cookies in their paper accordion cups and arranged them on a plate.

She could hear him moving around the living room, opening things, peeking, sneaking, spying. It gave her a thrill; she wanted him to know her, to smell her secrets, to taste the ways she'd changed.

"What is this shit?" he shouted.

She carried a platter with the tea and cookies and laid it on the table. He was standing by a small table next to the couch, holding a wicker ball with a blue ribbon tied around it.

"It's potpourri."

"It stinks."

"Where've you been, Nathan?"

He carefully replaced the wicker ball and looked at her for a minute. Thinking. Deciding what to tell her, and how much.

He sat across from her at the table, picked up a spoon and stirred his tea. Up close, his face was like a walnut, dark and veiny, the hard surface shielding a rich, soft meat.

"They had me in the loony bin." He smiled.

Rochelle could believe he had been in a place for crazies, but not that he was crazy himself.

"Did you do it to get out of the war?"

"Maybe. Maybe not. But I'll tell you why I didn't let you know where I was. Partly because you'd try to help me. And partly because the way you would have tried to help me would have been by printing it, telling the whole world, and I didn't need that. I wanted to be left alone."

"What about now?"

"I guess I'm all right because they released me, gave me a one-way ticket home, honorable discharge." He smirked.

"How long were you there?"

He rolled his eyes back in mock-thinking. "Oh, about three, four years I guess."

Rochelle was stunned. *Three or four years* and she had been searching for him among the dead bodies on TV.

"You sure grew up, Rock." That smile. "Tea and biscuits on a tray. Dig it! Just like Mabel."

Rochelle sighed, sucking back the scream she wanted to throw at him for that.

"I suppose you know Earl died," she said.

His bloodshot once-brown now-empty eyes froze on her. Either he really hadn't known or he was just giving her the pleasure of shocking him, playing big brother, letting her get back for the remark about Mabel.

"That was almost five years ago," she said, driving the nail all the way in. "In the war."

"His number came up?"

She shook her head. "He enlisted. He did really well but it didn't take long for him to get killed."

"He was stupid for going. It's worse than hell over there. I'd rather go to hell."

Nathan slept on the couch night after night, without ever giving her details about the last four years or filling her in on his plans for the future, if he had any. He said she'd print what he said and it was safer to say nothing. "I don't write those articles anymore," she told him, but he did not seem to hear. She reminded him that he had once liked her publicizing his secret thoughts. He said he never really liked it, it just gave him a kind of thrill.

In the mornings he would sit at the table, drinking coffee and thinking. He refused to speak before noon. Rochelle never really adapted to this; his air-tight silence made her uncomfortable. She would sit with him for a while, and when she couldn't take it anymore she would retreat to her bedroom desk to write in her journal. And what she discovered, pouring herself out more privately than ever onto a blank white page, was frightening.

She felt she was in love with him. And she dreaded the day he would leave.

Some time in the early afternoon, he would go out. She thought he might have been looking for work, but he never told her what he did exactly. Maybe he just walked. He returned home in the evening and they would eat together.

She thought he thought he was in love with her, too.

And that that was why he decided to leave.

She didn't know when the actual decision was made, or exactly how, but one night she saw that his duffel bag was zippered and lumpy-full.

She'd been out at Sunday dinner in Brooklyn, bottling in— week after week after week—the sensational fact of Nathan's visit. She had rushed back as usual, bursting with family talk, when she saw him sitting on the couch with his bag at his feet.

"What's this?"

"Time to hit the road." His hair was brushed back into a ponytail and he looked so much calmer and lighter than when he had first arrived. He looked more like her-old-Nathan and she loved him.

"You can't go." She dropped her purse on the table and sat beside him on the couch.

"It's time to move on."

"No, it isn't."

He sighed.

"Why?"

He rubbed his fingers together. "Feel it? Feel the electricity in the air?"

"Yes, I feel it."

His large veined hand stroked her wiry hair. "Little sister," he said, softly, "you've got some good things in you to do. Not me. I only have this feeling."

"Stay with it, then, Nath."

He shook his head. "Can't. It'll eat me."

"Stay here and write. You're a poet. I'll help you get your work published."

"I'm not a poet! Rock, look at me. What do you see when you look at me?"

"I love you, Nathan."

"No, I said tell me what you *see*."

"Nathan."

"Go on. Don't stop there."

"What happened to you in the war?"

"I got wounded," he said, pointing to his head.

"You're different but you're the same." She started to cry. "I don't like that long hair!"

He snorted laughter then his face bloomed into a smile. "Go ahead, cut it off." He had a dare look in his eyes, a flicker from childhood.

She went to the bedroom and got the good, sharp scissors, the ones reserved for sewing. "Come to the bathroom," she told him, and he got up and calmly joined her. "Take your shirt off."

He looked right into her eyes as he methodically unbuttoned his shirt, the front first, then the cuffs. He pulled it out of his jeans, took it off, and tossed it over the edge of the tub. She hadn't seen his chest for almost ten years. They had been swimming one summer at a friend's parents' country house and Rochelle had asked if she could touch his hairy chest. He'd said yes, but she didn't do it, and that was the last time he'd even partially disrobed in front of her. Until now. Now, the hair was curlier and his chest had thick sinewy muscles. His wine-red nipples were erect from the chilly air and his abdomen was tight as a fist. Her own nipples hardened and an inner pulse sent shivers through her.

"Sit," she told him. He sat on the toilet seat and she wrapped him up to the neck in a towel. She pulled off the elastic band and his hair fanned out. Then she wet and combed his hair so it fell heavily down his back, poised the scissors just below his right ear, and slowly closed them. A six-inch blanket of wet hair fell with each swipe of the blades. She ran the comb through each time before cutting. And with each snip she moved closer, until her breasts grazed his skin each time she shifted her angle.

It took an hour and as she cut and layered and looked and evened-out-the-sides, she allowed herself to feel her true feelings and decided that just for this moment she would give herself to what she really wanted. Had wanted all along. *Nathan.* She could feel the pulse of his long-ago plea to *marry me sister oh marry me*. Her answer had always been *yes*. Only distance had stopped the inevitable.

As if reeling in similar thoughts, he released the towel, which scattered snippets of hair as it fell around his waist. He raised both hands and gently placed them over her breasts.

"Is this what you want?" he asked.

"Don't you want it, too?"

He moved his hands slowly and lightly as if grazing velvet. This was the first time she had been touched with love, real love. She had always known this was how it would feel. Heat rushed through her body. She could tell, by looking at him—at the color that animated his eyes, at the familiar contour of his face brought into relief by shorter hair—and by feeling the determination of his movements, that he would not stop himself this time.

They fitted like a root twining into earth. There was no give, no take, just sheer supplication, a movement like air, water pouring into itself. Their love in flesh felt more like an expansion than a joining. Rochelle knew this would be their only sexual meeting, and he must have known too, because they did it several times through the night. They pounded themselves in an animal fever, and pretended not to look, and would remember every moment of this forever, Rochelle with fascination and Nathan with profound regret.

In the morning, Nathan sat at the table in silence. He had one cup of coffee. He picked up his duffel bag and started to leave.

"Nathan?" she said, as he opened the door. She was crying. He stopped and looked over at her and nodded, cool to her anguish because his was worse, more permanent.

Then he left.

Chapter 7
Freak

The dark evening shimmers with flurries—a surprise late-winter storm—and Cat and Teddy take their usual nightly walk. She wishes she could share his enchantment with the 3-D fog of light snow filling the air, but ever since she found out she was pregnant she's been too preoccupied to think of anything else.

"Come on." He takes her mittened hand into his gloved hand and tugs her into a run.

She can feel herself slipsliding. "Stop, I'll fall."

"You won't fall. Courage!"

He swings her around a corner.

"Stop!"

He slides quickly, dragging her.

"Let's stop for some cocoa," she says.

"That costs money."

"Teddy, Teddy, *stop*. I'm pregnant."

He keeps running for a few moments but she can feel the slowdown, an imminent release of their hands as if he wants to let go of her and keep on running.

They come to a stop in front of a tenement guarded by six snow-capped garbage cans. Teddy continues to look straight ahead. Then, slowly, he turns to her. His face is bright red and his lashes glitter with soft snowflakes.

"How did that happen?"

She feels like laughing, she is so nervous, so scared. "Didn't your mother ever tell you—"

"Don't be sarcastic, Cat. I thought we use a diaphragm."

"They're not foolproof."

"Don't you get it inspected or something?"

"Inspected?" She has never had her diaphragm checked or replaced, but has wondered recently if the rubber didn't look a little dried out.

"What are you going to do?" he asks.

"*Me*?"

"This is no place for children." His gesture opens to the garbage cans, the quiet street, the snow-sleeping night. "I would love to have children some day. But I'm a graduate student. I won't have my degree for another five years."

"Teddy ... it happened. It isn't just *my* problem. It's *our* problem. And why does it have to be a *problem*, anyway?"

He sighs. A car passes. And in the shifting shadows of the headlights, she sees something close down in his face. He doesn't want this. Not now, or not with her—she can't tell.

"We should sleep on this, at least," Cat says, sensing him drift away from her, as if someone snipped their cord. "Shouldn't we?"

He nods, and then he is silent. Achingly, completely *silent*.

At home, Cat goes right to bed and Teddy stays up. She can hear him moving around the living room. It is chilly in bed, even in her flannel nightgown, and she huddles under the blankets. She feels guilty for having gotten pregnant, and for suggesting an extra burden to Teddy before he's ready. But she also feels little flickers of happiness, of hope, of *wanting* it. *It*. She reminds herself that it's just a knot of cells in her womb. It isn't even really a person. Yet she feels a yearning for that little cell-clump. If she does nothing, it will simply grow and one day emerge from her body, indisputable. She knows it will change her life. But Teddy ... she *loves* him and wants him, too. The thought of having to choose between them is impossible.

In the morning, she finds him sitting on the edge of the bed. From the rumpled sheets on his side, it looks as if he came in eventually and slept next to her. That's something, at least. She opens her eyes and for a moment feels happy, like it's a regular morning. She stretches and smiles. Then she remembers and quickly sinks.

"I've been thinking." His voice is gentle and as he speaks his forefinger moves a strand of hair across her forehead. "I'll do what I can to help if you decide to go through with it. But I have to be honest, Cat. No guarantees."

She says, "Fine," but doesn't mean it. She lies there and her feeling that it is *not* fine quickly escalates. He has impregnated her and in that moment they were equal. Now, because her body carries the seed, she has become dangerously unequal. Why has *all* the burden of risk and responsibility—and the choice— landed on her?

Teddy gets dressed and bundles himself up for the winter morning. He packs his briefcase and knapsack for long hours of studying elsewhere. "I'm going to the library," he says. "I have some research to do." He pecks her on the cheek. "Are you okay?"

"Fine." Her new drumbeat. *I am fine. I will be fine. Everything is fine.*

She feels paralyzed by confusion. If she has an abortion, will she be able to forgive him—or herself? If she doesn't have an abortion, will it drive him away? Only one thing is clear: it will be a matter of having and keeping it, or not having it at all. She would not be capable of bringing a baby to term, giving birth and then relinquishing it forever. Even now, she feels stirrings of fascination and love.

She needs to talk to a woman who would understand and immediately realizes her mistake. It was never going to be Rocky. Alone in the chilly apartment, she dials her mother.

Janet makes them herbal tea and dumps a box of shortbread cookies onto a big plate. She has put on weight and her hair is now cut short. Cat thinks her mother looks healthier and prettier than when she was a skinny drunk. Janet carries a tray to the living room and sets it on the coffee table, where,

Cat notices, a copy of *Freak* is displayed along with the latest *New Yorker, Atlantic Monthly* and book of Helga drawings.

"I had dinner with Eddie and Penny last week," Janet says. "They'd love to see you."

"I'll call them."

"How's Teddy?"

Cat shrugs.

Janet nods, clearing the way for Cat to explain this sudden visit. But she is silent. So Janet says, "What's new in the world of cartoons?"

"Actually, Mom, I'm pregnant."

Her mother is still, except for her eyes, which blink. "Well," she says, "let's talk."

"I don't know what to do."

Janet smiles. "Whoever does?"

"I mean, I know what I *want* to do. But there's a practical side, *reality*, and it seems to be the problem."

"Having a baby is *not* a romantic thing," Janet says. "It is a practical matter. It's very expensive, and it's a good idea if your relationship is stable. I suppose in a way that's what marriage is for, to clear up issues of responsibility before they get tested. At least in theory."

Cat knows well that her parents' relationship broke all the theoretical rules of marriage, and Janet's heart, again and again.

"Your father and I got married because I was pregnant with Eddie," Janet says.

"I know, Mom."

"It was not a good idea."

"I know that, too."

"Not that I regretted having Eddie, but we were too young and it was difficult. Mort was not prepared to be a husband and father. But I loved him and I *wanted* Eddie. I was a very privileged child and didn't understand hardship or what it meant to work or make sacrifices, so when my father cut me off I didn't blink an eye. It seemed very romantic at the time.

My father, your grandfather, is a real stiff, and I think he was wrong, but so be it. *He* is an ACOA, too, you know."

Adult Child of an Alcoholic. Ever since Janet first admitted her own role in the family dysfunction, Cat has been unable to hear the acronym without feeling doomed: ACOA, MIA, DOA, RIP.

"Yes, Mom, you've told me all about Grandpa Phillips and his father, Avery Phillips, the fall-down-drunk." Cat raises a finger to swipe an errant strand of hair from her eye. All this family history weighs so heavily. She needs to know what to do *now*.

"So, there we were, Mort and I, twenty-one years old with a baby. Oh my God, to think back on that now! Well, we lived frugally. It was not easy. It was very hard and I was lonely. He wasn't monogamous. When I was pregnant with you, ten years later—and I was worn out by our small closed life—"

"Mom, I know the story. You kicked Daddy out for being unfaithful when you were pregnant. Then you had me."

"That's *part* of the story. I suppose this is a good time to tell you the rest." Janet pauses to take Cat's hand gently between hers. "I want to clear up one thing right now, Cat, before I go on. I *never* regretted having you, either."

"What are you saying, Mom?"

A weight seems to fall on Janet's expression, pulling it down, adding shadows and years. She does not take her eyes off Cat as she speaks. "My darling, I tried to have an abortion. It was scheduled, but the doctor was arrested. It was illegal in those days, you know. It was a very dangerous procedure and most people didn't do it. It was risky. But I was desperate, *desperate*. I already had one child and I didn't know what to do with *him*. Well, Eddie was a great boy, a lot of fun. But I was scared."

"You mean you wanted to abort me?"

"At the time I felt I had no choice."

Cat sits there, taking in the bits of information her brain is able to process, the rest of it flying above her head. She always knew that she was, technically, a mistake, part of the tumult of her parents' marriage. But never before had she considered herself to be that dark, dreaded notion: *unwanted*.

"I'm going to tell you everything, because you're a woman now and you need to know." Janet looks into her beloved daughter's eyes, and Cat looks back, into her mother's: sky blue, faded and tired. "When the abortion fell through, I tried to abort myself. With a hanger. Just like the stories you hear about now, about what used to happen. Well, that was the reality then. If a woman is desperate, she will try anything. And I did."

"But what *happened*?" she asks, gesturing with her free hand as if to say *Why am I here*?

"Luckily," Janet says, "I failed. I didn't abort myself—"

"You mean me you didn't abort *me*."

"That's right. I didn't abort *you*, and I didn't puncture my uterus, which is amazing. I bled a lot, though, and I thought I'd aborted … you. But after some time I realized the pregnancy was continuing. So, Ben and Rose took me in and I lived with them until after you were born. They were very generous, but I could never feel quite comfortable living with Mort's parents under the circumstances."

"Then Daddy came back."

"Right. That was another mistake. It added sixteen more years of pain before we finally got divorced."

"What was the first mistake? Having me, or not aborting me?"

"Getting pregnant in the first place," Janet says softly, spilling a liquid truth that doesn't collect neatly but dissipates into a cloud that infiltrates every part of Cat like invisible poison gas. "Once you're pregnant, if you aren't ready, there is no perfect choice."

Cat sits silently, her mother's hands warm on her skin. She does not feel ready for this confession, and suspects she never really will. It's the kind of information she wishes she didn't possess and will never be able to forget. And she cannot begin to understand how to process it in light of her own pregnancy now.

"It's not an easy decision, sweetheart. I can't help you with it. But I'll support you in whatever you decide. The trouble is...." Janet shakes her head resignedly. "Money. I just don't have the resources to help you financially. And I'm sure your father doesn't, either."

"I know, Mom. I don't expect you guys to help with money." She hears herself sounding so rational, while inside she is pinging with anguish, wishing someone would come along and serve up the perfect solution. She can imagine how relieved her mother must have felt, twenty-five years ago, when Grandpa Mort and Grandma Rose came along with a safety net. And, later, how that net had trapped her into a life for which she was unprepared.

"What about Teddy?" Janet asks. "I take it he isn't enthusiastic."

"He's leaving it up to me."

Janet lifts and lowers her head in an exaggerated nod. "That's too bad. But in a way, darling, it *is* your decision, because you are pregnant, not him, and no matter what promises a man makes it doesn't mean he'll keep them."

"But isn't it better to start off with good intentions? I mean, if he was happy about it, I wouldn't be so confused."

"Maybe, maybe not. *If, if, if.* Unfortunately, you have got to look at what your situation *is.*"

"He said 'no guarantees,' Mom. That's what he said. It's up to me."

"I hate to say it, Cat honey, but he's right, in a brutal kind of way. It shouldn't be like that, but it is. The decision you have to make is terrible. *Impossible.* But not making one would be a decision by default, wouldn't it?" Janet smiles sadly, her eyes growing wet. She leans over to hold her daughter, patting the young back that now heaves with sobs. After a while, during a pause in the crying, she adds a final bit of advice: "It might help not to lump them together, Teddy and this pregnancy. Think of them as two separate things and figure out, one at a time, what feels right and what makes sense. Heart and head. Listen to both. And then project forward to imagine your life in every possible scenario. Being a single mother, Cat, will change everything about your life, if that's what it comes to."

Every day, the embryo develops, forms into something closer to a baby. And now, every day, Cat feels sicker and sicker, edging to the moment when she will start vomiting as part of her daily routine. There isn't time to decide. She wishes she could suspend herself and take a year. Wait. Be reasonable. But her body won't let her.

At home one evening, she stands by Teddy's desk and delivers the only decision she has been able to make so far.

"I don't want to go away with you," she says. "I want to spend my week off alone, thinking."

"Okay."

Okay. No argument. Not even a discussion about the hard-earned deposits to all those inns and the rental car, all that money they'll lose. But why—*why* should she have expected more at this point?

"I need to think."

"I understand," he says. But how can he?

"I'd like to take the week off from work and spend it here by myself. I don't think that's too much to ask."

"So you want me to leave."

"I think it would help me to have some time alone."

"And then?"

"I don't know."

Within an hour, he is gone.

All the lights in Teddy's study are off except the blue back-screen of his computer. She can hear an echo of the energetic voice of John Paglia talking and talking about *getting to the heart of the truth of the real story*, like a sales pitch to the inner mind. What heart? What truth? What real story? Who am I and why am I here and what should I do now? Cat poises her fingers on the keyboard and begins to type.

The Legend of My Transformation

Once I was a cartoonist, an artist, living happily inside my mind. Then I fell in love. Got a job. Got pregnant. And now I spend all my time figuring out how to survive.

I used to walk around just looking for ideas. I would wait until I heard that click-click *inside my mind, then I would stop and begin to pay attention. It could be anything—an old Chinese man handing a flyer for a tanning center to a black woman— and that became a cartoon. Ideas came from everywhere.*

Sometimes I would buy a stack of newspapers, all of them, including the trashiest ones, and go to the park and read. The Star *and* The Enquirer *were full of fascinating and hilarious true stories: shoe size determines life span, Elvis seen panhandling on Dallas street, extraterrestrial mows neighbor's lawn, man who 'can't' impregnates wife with thought waves. All these stories became cartoons. From* The Post, *I got one of my favorite ideas: the story of a young actor who lived a double life, as gigolo to a rich older man, and boyfriend to a sweet Midwestern girl. I turned it into a comic strip*: Man in Tights: Adventures of a Bisexual in the Age of AIDS. *I sat at the kitchen counter, drawing doodling and plotting each frame. As the strip grew, I started spending whole days and nights inside. After a while I would force myself to take long walks just to keep my sanity.*

It was a wonderful time.

As a child I studied, collected, consumed Marvel *comics. Now, an adult, I dug deeper. I spent hours in bookstores and comics specialty stores looking for the work of the masters— Will Eisner, Robert Crumb, Harvey Kurtzman, Art Spiegelman, the Hernandez brothers—until I started to wonder where all the women were. So I looked, and I found them: Trina Robbins, Cat Yronwode, M.C. Lord, Mary Wilshire, Wendy Pini, and there were more. There were so many cartoonists and so many magazines:* Zap, MAD, Spirit, Love & Rockets, RAW, Weirdo, Elfquest,

Pork Roast. And there were publishers just for comics: Rip Off Press, Last Gasp, Kitchen Sink, New Wave Comics. But I wasn't ready for them yet. First I needed to polish my work.

To survive, I worked part-time for a woman who made and sold jewelry out of her home. I would sit with her, stringing beads and listening to music, or take the work home with me. The pay was miserable but the flexibility was ideal. I never told her about what I thought of as my secret ambitions and I never showed anyone my cartoons. I thought of them as forming, half-baked, unready. Plus there was the problem of me not taking myself seriously. Always waiting for the day to make my move—to submit work—and never doing it. I loved my work but feared it had no value, and worse, I worried that, as soon as I showed it, the experts would confirm my fears. And then what would I be left with? Without cartoons, I would have, think, feel, dream, desire nothing.

I was content, believe it or not, with my secret work, my paltry job, my tiny apartment, my band of like-minded aspiring-artist friends.

Then one scorching day in July, after a long morning sketching at the kitchen counter, I went out to take a walk and get some pizza for lunch. I walked and walked until I reached Famous Ray's on 11th Street.

I bought a slice and a root beer and carried them to a corner table and sat down. I was still thinking about cartoons, that the thing about cartooning was that it looked easy but it was hard, you had to get the whole wide world in there just to make your point, for it to click, and if it wasn't exact, perfect, on the mark, then it was nothing at all.

That's what I was thinking when in walked Teddy.

I noticed him right away. He seemed arrogant yet unself-conscious, swinging open the door and lurching in as if pushed by the heat. He had this cocky look on his face like he wanted to go back out and give the weather a piece of his mind. He was wearing baggy white shorts—half-pants, really, that reached all the way to his knees—and brown leather shoes with no socks.

His calves were long and muscular, sexy, I thought. He wore a gray T-shirt that said RED on the front and SOX on the back.

He got his pizza—two slices flopping over the sides of the paper plate—and carried it to a table near mine. I took a first bite of my slice and the cheese stretched into a long string which I had to struggle to get under control. But my mouth was full of too-hot pizza and the cheese wouldn't break, it was like putty.

He looked at me. "Some weather, huh? Have you ever seen such a hot day?" He pretended to wait for an answer. Of course I was annoyed. Then he said, "Uh, cat got your tongue?" For a moment I thought he was referring to me by name and it confused me enough to look at him squarely—cheese still dangling between my mouth and the slice of pizza in my hand. He puckered the sides of his mouth, making a kind of chipmunk face, and said, "You look like some kind of pizza-producing silkworm. Sorry to say."

I finally managed to break the tenacious string of cheese, draw in what dangled from my mouth (I did feel like a silkworm, in a way) and coil the rest onto the slice. He continued to watch me.

"Sorry," he said again. But this time it really sounded like an apology.

"Let's see you eat that," I said.

He tucked a napkin into the neck of his T-shirt, cleared his throat, picked up a plastic fork and knife, cut the tip off one slice and placed it carefully into his mouth. He chewed slowly, then swallowed. "A new invention, the fork and knife."

I sunk my teeth into my slice.

He said, "I noticed you're not wearing a wedding ring."

I glanced at my left hand, as if to confirm his observation, and said, "So?"

"So, what if I wanted to ask you out, and seeing that you don't have the social grace to use utensils, decided I'd be better off not taking the risk? Appearances count, you know."

I half-grinned, shook my head, bit my pizza again. He was a jerk but I kind of liked him.

He continued: "It's a theoretical argument. I'm posing a simple question based on a premise that a man and a woman, out for pizza, separately, might just possibly look across a string of cheese and skip right into that fourth dimension they call love." He was laughing by now, trying to suppress it but it leaked like fumes from behind his face.

"Who are you?" I asked.

"Theodore Morton Foster the third. And you?"

"Catharine Rose Gold the first."

He didn't ask for my number but gave me his card. I thought it was pretty strange that a graduate student had a formal business card. I waited a week before calling him. His machine answered with the message: "Teddy Foster's Deconstruction Hotline. Please inlay your voice pattern on the magnetic tape following the tonal moment."

I said, "This is Cat Gold calling you, I think," and left my number. He returned the call within minutes, and invited me over for dinner that very night.

He picked me up at my apartment on Barrow Street and walked me east to his place on Sixth Street. He lived in a third floor walkup. You entered right into the kitchen, which was small and cluttered, and a series of doorless doorways led you through the living/dining room, to the tiny study crammed with books and piles of papers, and then the bedroom.

He had prepared what he called "the dining nook" by setting the small round table with his mismatched thrift store china, silverware and cloth napkins. A candelabrum with five long white candles was too big for the table but gave it a romantic look.

Teddy made pasta that first night, angel hair primavera, stringbeans sautéed in olive oil with garlic and shallots, and salad with vinaigrette. I was amazed at his cooking skills. I myself had not mastered food as an art. I was hungry and he fed me. How could I not fall in love?

He was funny and charming through dinner, took care of the whole meal, even washed the dishes. It turned out he was a first year doctoral student at NYU, studying deconstructionism *in postmodern American painting. In another year, he would begin his thesis. He supported himself with a combination of loans and freelance articles for art magazines, which paid well enough that if he pressed himself and wrote more of them, he could be "almost solvent," he said, and clinked my wine glass which he'd filled with white wine.*

After dinner was done and cleaned up and put away, we sat next to each other on his gunmetal-blue couch, which had a slash in one of the cushions. We talked and I lay a hand on his bluejeaned knee and he wove an arm around my back and I pressed a shoulder into his blue cotton shirt and he reached his face down and the words stopped. Our first kisses were long and gentle. Not much later, he moved over me in his bed, kissing me sweetly, making love to me with perfect cocoon-like warmth. In the morning, the feeling was still there for both of us. We didn't want to leave each other, even for a minute. He was nothing like past boyfriends who couldn't wait to carve out their space. Teddy enjoyed our blossoming love as much as I did. We stayed together minute to minute, hour to hour, day to day, week to week, as the feeling deepened. After a while it seemed stupid paying two rents and I moved in all my things.

"I'm ready for my second act!" Rocky laughs and tosses back her head. Oprah claps her hands and the audience joins her. "If not my third!"

"Who's counting?" Oprah asks, and the audience erupts in cheers. "We women need to think *transformation!*"

"*Absolutely!*" Smiling, Rocky pumps her famous fist in the air and the audience goes wild.

"*You go girl!*" Oprah says to riotous applause.

"I might just use *that* as the title for my memoir!"

Cat sits on the floor of Annie's bedroom with Parker in her lap. Annie perches on the end of her bed, lips tight. When the television screen goes to commercial, the women glance at each other but neither speaks. Cat is stuck on Oprah's *you go girl*, or more specifically Rocky's embrace of it. When did these influential people stop being women and start being girls? *Don't Call Me Girl* had been one of Cat's favorite childhood slogans, particularly when she *was* a girl, and she had enjoyed the expectation that she would grow into a strong and able woman. It made her feel powerful and forward-moving. Now, this—*you go girl*—sounds so silly and misguided. It's okay coming from Oprah. But a proto-feminist like Rocky Love? And as the title for her memoir? *No way*.

"Mommy looks different on TV." Parker shifts in Cat's lap and she wraps her arms around him for balance. She has grown to love this little boy.

"They put extra makeup on her and gave her a hairdo," Annie says, as if that explains the phoniness of Rocky's TV performance.

"And on TV," Cat adds, "everyone acts extra happy, especially on a talk show." When he grows up, Cat thinks, Parker will figure out his mother on his own, poor thing. She runs a hand up and down his soft arm and then, without warning, tickles him to the floor. He curls into a ball, laughing. Cat kneels over him, trying to find his hidden underarms. And then Oprah and Rocky are back on screen and Parker jumps into Cat's lap.

"So, Rocky, you're writing your memoirs. *Very* exciting! Any plans for a new radio or TV show?"

"Yes! As a matter of fact, I've got a television show in production right now."

"Uh oh!" Oprah says. "Sounds like competition!"

Laughter and friendly boos from the audience.

"Who could compete with you?" Rocky says. "Don't worry, we're *sisters*. I've got your back!"

Oprah leans over and Rocky receives her in a hug. The audience goes wild.

"That true?" Annie asks Cat. "About a new show?"

Cat shakes her head, not wanting to speak for fear of letting Parker hear the sarcasm that will certainly leak through her tone.

"We'll be in production by the fall," Rocky flat-out lies to the legions of viewers. "As soon as the book is finished. I plan to produce it myself to make sure it's done right."

"You know what they say," Oprah says. "If you want a job done well, do it yourself."

"That's right. Sometimes I think it's pointless having *any-one* on staff. I end up handling *so much* myself."

Oprah looks directly at the screen and speaks, seemingly to Cat and Annie: "Ooh, watch out! This girl's on a roll!"

"Women have trouble asking for help," Rocky says. "And when we do, we're too competent to be satisfied with the help we get. It's a catch-22."

To stop herself from barking out a comment to Annie—*that woman is so full of shit* is what comes to mind—Cat presses her nose into Parker's velvety hair. His shampoo smells sweet, like bubblegum. The smell prompts a wave of nausea. Morning sickness has been coming all day long, every day, and getting consistently stronger, though she has not yet thrown up. She breathes deeply and closes her eyes, trying to will away the sensation. But this time it doesn't work. She doesn't want Annie to know about her pregnancy because it will break her heart to hear of Cat's conflict. Annie has five children of her own and lost one young, a blow from which she has never really recovered.

Cat gently nudges Parker off her lap, saying, "I have to go to the bathroom." He springs up and goes to Annie, who shifts back onto the bed and settles him into her own lap. Cat crosses the room to the door as casually as possible while her insides threaten a volcanic explosion. This is the worst she has felt. *If only it could be for something*, she thinks, as she rushes down the hall to the bathroom. She shuts and locks the door. Hinges over the toilet. And her insides unfurl without mercy.

The Rise and Fall of Rocky Love

Wanting

*H*oliday bulbs flashed and twinkled in the gray winter light as they drove down the FDR in Bobby's midnight blue Mercedes convertible. Destination: Brooklyn. Bobby maneuvered them swiftly around slower, clunkier cars. Rochelle watched him: his large, finely boned hands on the leather steering wheel, his brown skin melting into the red crew-necked cashmere sweater he had bought just for this meeting, his Italian leather loafer calmly pressing the gas petal, his brown eyes sliding across the road, watching, controlling, protecting them. He wore his hair short and tight; no outsized Afros for him. His license plates read LOVE-MD.

A diamond engagement ring glistened on Rochelle's finger like a trophy or a dare. So far, on the phone, Mabel had been ecstatic. But she hadn't heard all the details yet—or *seen* them—and Rochelle could hardly wait. She watched Manhattan blur by as they approached the Brooklyn Bridge with its swooping strands of white lights. She was going home to leave it, to sever herself from it for good.

"I admit I feel no small amount of trepidation," Bobby said in his rich, deep voice. He swerved the car into the exit for the bridge. Rochelle let the momentum pull her into him. She grasped his thigh and squeezed.

"Don't worry," she said, "my parents are going to love you."

The sun went down quickly, and by the time they reached the Heights it was dark. Bobby was lean and dignified next to buxom Rochelle. She rang the bell and the door swung open almost immediately.

Mabel's welcome smile froze on her face. She stood there in her ruffly flowered dress and stared at Bobby.

Rochelle beamed her triumph. "This is Dr. Love."

Alerted by his wife's silence and the long pause by the door, Norman dashed over with a ready-for-anything greeting. Rochelle was just as aware of the wave of surprise that passed over her father's face when he saw the color of Bobby's skin as his openheartedness when he said, "Hello!" and vigorously shook Bobby's hand. He was like a ship captain in a storm, guiding everyone into the living room, forging against the torrents of disappointment surging from his wife.

"Sit, sit," Norman said.

Bobby sat on the couch and Rochelle snuggled up next to him. Mabel's furious gaze rested momentarily on her husband, who threw back his own look, a *be friendly or die* look that sent her to the kitchen for the tray of hors d'oeuvres she had fussed over all afternoon. She brought it out in a state of disarray: caviar spilling off crackers, cream cheese smeared on the edge of the silver tray, a fin-ger-pocked bowl of dip. Looking mildly vindicated, she offered the tray to Bobby, who gamely chose a broken cracker with brie hanging off the side.

Norman poured the premixed martinis, seated himself in his armchair and leaned toward Bobby. "So, you're a medical doctor?"

"Gynecologist," Bobby said.

"I was his patient," Rochelle said.

Mabel left the room.

"What hospital are you affiliated with?"

"New York Hospital. And I have a private practice."

"Park Avenue, Daddy."

Norman's eyebrows arched deliberately.

Bobby's expression was serious. Rochelle recognized the look: calm, ready, waiting. It was a paternal look and it really turned her on. She pressed against him and he moved away, forward, toward Norman.

Bobby said, "I'm sorry if I've disappointed you and your wife, and I know I have, but the fact is I love your daughter and there's no scientific reason not to. It troubles society, yes. But you know something? I have troubled society since the day I got a scholarship to Harvard, I have troubled society by hanging out my shingle on Park Avenue, I have troubled society by owning a good home on a good block in one of the best neighborhoods in the city. But I can tell you that I have not troubled society as much as society has troubled me. Frankly, sir, I am not grateful for Rochelle because she's white, I'm grateful because she's a fine woman and she loves me. I would sooner have fallen in love with a woman of color. But facts remain. I hope you can live with it. If you think it will be hard for you, rest assured that it will be doubly hard for us."

Norman nodded. "I can only respect that."

Bobby smiled, showing his beautiful bleached whites. Rochelle planted a kiss on the back of his hand.

Mabel served dinner with such extreme indifference that an outsider might have thought she was hired help. Rochelle could see her father's frustration. She could hear them later, alone:

So he's got everything but the right skin, so what? He'll be a good provider.

Provider, blech! Any man can be a provider. He's a Negro if you didn't notice, not to mention he isn't Jewish either.

Bobby Love was Rochelle's dream man, because he satisfied all the basic status quos, except one, and that one was big enough to permanently enrage her mother.

The wedding took place at the end of January in the Love brownstone on 84th Street between Park and Madison Avenues, a huge old place with four floors of charm, original detail, and a landscaped garden. The decorator had filled it with bachelor colors of maroon, beige, burnt orange and gold. Rochelle planned to redecorate as soon as she got access to a joint account.

Over a hundred well wishers, and Mabel, packed into the house in true seventies fashion, wearing jeans or gowns, passing joints to friends, stealing kisses from strangers. The house was filled with flowers and Rochelle had sprayed every room with Shalimar. She felt beautiful today, a goddess in a white leather minidress, hair coiled and laced with baby's breath, elevated to nearly Bobby's height on platform shoes with four-inch heels. She carried a bouquet of yellow and white miniature orchids.

Leo was her bride's maid, in a creamy felt suit and wide white tie. Mabel stood off to the side in a black dress streaked with vivid yellow lightning bolts and observed the ceremony with an expression of disdain that thrilled Rochelle. Norman ignored his sulking wife and focused instead on the ceremony, as his only daughter was married by a Justice of the Peace in a magenta Nehru shirt and jeans beneath a chuppa of iridescent silver cloth. Norman and Bobby wore matching yarmulkes, courtesy of Rochelle, which irritated her mother even more profoundly, which made Rochelle even happier. The marriage vows were lengthy and romantic. After, Rochelle laughed wildly and the newlyweds kissed to loud applause.

By evening a white limousine had parked itself outside the brownstone. Rochelle ran upstairs to change and Bobby followed calmly. Fifteen minutes later they descended in travel clothes: Bobby in crisp bluejeans and a yellow sweater, Rochelle in a baggy white pantsuit covered with tiny purple stars. They hugged and kissed friends and family on their way out the door.

Bobby got into the back of the limo and Rochelle stood on the curb for the last act of bridedom. She scanned the small group who had followed them outside and poised her wedding bouquet to toss, concentrating on her task as if doling out a divine directive; she was, after all, designating a future bride.

Seeing her mother standing on the stoop with such grim determination in her bolts-of-lightning dress, Rochelle felt a stab of remorse. The thought to throw Mabel the bouquet flashed in her mind, then quickly faded. She had a better idea. Leo was standing on the sidewalk next to Chip—two clean looking men with big mustaches and matching brown suede shoes—and she couldn't resist. Bobby was already in the limo and the door was gaping for her. With a wide grin and an obvious wink, she threw the bouquet right to Leo. The group cheered and laughed. Leo turned red and in his excitement he handed the bouquet to Chip. They kissed.

As Rochelle slid into the limo next to Bobby, she could hear the residue of her mother's voice, "What did I do wrong?"

Bobby's long brown body was stretched neatly down one side of the honeymoon bed. Next to him, Rochelle sprawled. They agreed that their inconsistencies were charming: his body's smooth perfection, her body's cavalier disorganization; his formality, her recklessness; his coolness, her heat.

He leaned on his elbows and sucked on her earlobe and whispered, "I want you pregnant."

She said, "Yes, let's think about that."

"Let's not think, let's just do it."

"I'll have to finish out the cycle of my pills, then wait a while for my system to clear out."

He was a doctor and knew she was right. "Then finish the cycle and stop."

She kissed him hard and bit his lower lip and he got excited and they started to make love. Waves of panic rolled through her; she hadn't even thought about having a baby so soon. She was a married woman now; she hadn't really thought about that, either. She was a doctor's wife; what would *that* mean? The panic swelled and so did he. She could tell he thought he was making her wildly excited. In fact, she was in the beginning throes of an anxiety that would become a kind of second career.

Bobby was so solid and reliable that, as time went on, she began to feel unhinged inside. She sat in her top floor study, her wiry hair pinned haphazardly on top of her head, a red silk caftan draped comfortably over her morning-naked body, feeling free of any real responsibility yet wanting more out of life. She was twenty-four years old and had reached the end of the road, having married a doctor and become a doctor's wife. Once the bold statement of their interracial marriage faded, she realized she had bought the standard package. She didn't want a baby now. She wanted to do something, be something, have an identity of her own. She was aware that she possessed an extraordinary confidence, as well as a tendency to abandon her focus for sensual pleasure. Eating, sleeping, sex. But her mind was strong; she *knew* she was responsible for her own destiny. The more she thought about having a baby, the more she knew she had to make a conscious decision, a choice, about the direction of her life. She wondered if she could find the answer with the help of an analyst. She would ask Bobby what he thought of the idea; after all, he would have to pay.

"Why?" Bobby asked over dinner at the huge oval table she had bought with his money and which he hated. The thick glass, tinted a smoky gray, shouted pretension, *look at me I'm rich, I have this funny table.* Bobby would have preferred something in wood, a long table suitable for a serious man with a family. But where was his family? He'd been waiting, hoping; and nothing. Now she wanted to go into analysis, a long process with dubious potential for results.

"I need it," she said. "I don't know why. I'll know once I've gotten further into myself."

Bobby shook his head. "Fine, if that's what you want."

Dr. Carr's office was just across town on the west side. Rochelle crossed the sidewalk, her red dress ablaze in the summer heat, and a cab screeched to a halt by the curb. She swung open the door and got in. She loved this, loved the way the world responded to her. It was a different sensation than she had in college, when people read her column, admired her courage and said she had a good mind. This was more primal, a bodysensation, a basic physical force. Her *it* was gaining power, tuning her mind in to different frequencies. Sex and love and marriage had altered her. She still loved Nathan and now she was a wife and before babies she wanted something else, something else. She decided on this for her focus in analysis today: *wanting*.

She loved the drive through Central Park—she loved this city—brilliant sun flicking on tiny green leaves, a forest of sparkling coins. Manhattan was exciting and alive and she wanted to conquer it, own it. *Wanted*. But how?

Dr. Carr worked on the ground floor of a brownstone and lived on the floor above. Downstairs, two rooms were joined by a soundproofed double door: the first room was a waiting area, and the second room was the lounge-cum-office where he worked. He sat in his brown leathereen Lazy Boy armchair and nodded and listened to Rochelle, who reclined on an old green plaid couch. An industrial fan swept air across the room, rippling the red fabric of her dress against her skin. The doctor was wearing baggy old jeans and a denim shirt. His long gray hair stood out in frazzled wires.

He said, "You're self-conscious with me. Are you feeling disturbed by something here?"

His voice was tight like the sound of a slap on a drum. A *drumslap* voice, she thought, and decided she must remember that. He had droopy blue eyes and his fingernails needed a cleaning and a trim. Something about him made her nervous, excited her; she loved sitting on his dirty couch watching him listen to her, being his only focus for an hour.

"There's something I want," she said, clenching a fist in the air. "*Want*."

"Yes?"

Rochelle had a great big smile and used it to coax and charm. She tried one on now. The doctor's face was sober. She said, "I don't know exactly what, but I want something more in my life."

When he smiled, lines fanned across his cheeks. "That seems normal to me."

Normal? That sounded like a challenge. Who wanted to be *normal*? "I'm materially comfortable. I'm married. But there's something else I need. *Want*. I'm aching inside," she said, "here." She pressed a manicured hand between her breasts. "There's something I want right *here*."

Dr. Carr smiled. "Yes, I see."

Her adrenaline pumped at his smile, his *I see*, his *yes*.

"I want you to try something," he said. "I want you to detach yourself from words. We learn to use words to classify, identify, analyze, judge. Here, we want to get to the level *below* the words. For this, I want you to try images. Visual images."

"But I can't draw."

"But you can see. If you can see images, you can draw them. When we dream, our minds use visual images to symbolize our deep feelings and anxieties and conflicts. Stop thinking in words. Let these dream images surface. See them. Follow the lines. See where they take you. Maybe we can find out what it is you're looking for."

The hour was up. "Next week, same time?"

He nodded.

She sat at her desk in the mornings and fantasized about sex with Dr. Carr on the plaid couch, no talk, just bodies crashing, then at the end of the hour getting up and walking out. It was a familiar feeling, a strong attraction unrequitable for the forbidding boundaries that separated doctor and patient. But she had married her gynecologist, and she had made love with her brother. Boundaries did not deter her. She thought about Nathan, and their adolescent yearning for one another, the deafening crescendo of consummation. She could never speak of this to anyone; it was one of the last remaining taboos. Yet its memory haunted her. She was a woman who knew what she wanted when she saw it, and reached for it, and took it.

What did she want, really *want*, now?

She put her pencil to her pad and drew a large shadowy question mark, a tall dark bent figure hovering above an even darker planet, a lone hunchback unicyclist, a narrow man searching his naval for balance. The image absorbed her and her eyes followed her hand as it moved the charcoal to illuminate an eye in the figure, and the suggestion of an arm. And the question mark became a man's body twisting. Then the line ruptured into a mouth, an open mouth, a scream. And then she knew what she was drawing, who: Nathan. *He* was who she wanted, who she loved.

Having found her shadow man, she couldn't abandon him until she had explored him fully. He was erratic and unpredictable, and she followed him, first on the page and then out onto the streets. The visual image, which began as a spark in her imagination, extended first into the charcoal line on paper and then into a path, an imperative, which she obeyed.

Bobby was worried the first day she told him that she had spent the afternoon wandering the streets guided by an inner vision. She did not mention the can of spray paint she had bought at a hardware store, on whim, and tucked into her purse. He was worried but he accepted it, because it was 1971 and people did things like that, primal screams and fetal regressions and psychodrama and psychedelic explorations of the inner self and got lost even there. Rochelle returned home every evening, and as long as she knew where home was, he was happy for now to let her wander unquestioned. He knew that to attempt to separate this woman from her inner forces would be to lose his wife.

And so she wandered. It was early spring, and chilly. One evening, in the ashy twilight, she withdrew the can of red spray paint from her purse and without knowing the direction of her line began to draw it. It was long and shaky, a path to nowhere—or somewhere—and she followed. It snaked along blocks, bending down at curbs and rising jagged on steps. She was down below Houston Street where no one thought twice about an artist following impulse in public, where common ground was a found surface, a communal canvas.

As she moved loosely and slowly, dragging the bright paint-line behind her, she came upon a purple footstep. And then another. And another and another and another, right left right left right. They were the large purple prints of a man walking, striding purposefully southeast. She made a red loop around the first step, then followed, zigzagging her line unevenly alongside the purple feet.

She followed for seven blocks and came, finally, to a rectangular garden wedged between two dilapidated buildings. The purple feet entered the garden on a stone path, then ended. The garden was long and grassy, bordered with buttery daffodils. Vines of would-be roses climbed a trellis that leaned against the brick wall in the back. A square patch of earth had been tilled and was ready to be planted.

Rochelle wondered what would be planted there. She wondered where the person who had made the purple footprints was. She wanted to meet him, and realized that if he noticed her red line as she had noticed his purple feet, he would want to meet her too. So she went to the last stone in the path, which ended in the middle of the garden, and sprayed a loose red circle around the final footprint.

She returned the next day, and for three days following. On the fifth day, in the early afternoon, he was there: a lanky man with long graying hair, shirtless, in denim overalls, with traces of purple paint on his workboots. He was bending by the square patch of soil, digging with a hand trowel. A string of dark squarish numbers was tattooed on his left forearm— so, he was a Holocaust survivor. He looked like he was in his forties. A young pregnant woman in a soiled white dress and a green sweater squatted beside him. She slipped her hand under the strap of his overalls and he leaned to kiss her cheek.

Rochelle stood on the sidewalk, looking into the garden, holding her can of red spray paint. The couple didn't notice her. She never went back.

The next day, she bought a pre-stretched jessoed canvas and some paints, and began to recreate the garden and the purple man and his young pregnant woman. She did not forget the numbers on his arm, and painted them in jet black so you couldn't miss them among the blaze of daffodils. There were certain things everyone had to remember, to be reminded of; life and death; survival. In that garden there was no real right or wrong. In that garden, there was forgiveness. There had to be. Suddenly, guilt fountained up through her and she felt overwhelmed. She lay down her paint brush and stood back from the canvas. There was something inside her that wanted out, a monster feeling, something large and strong and ugly.

The red line that led to the purple footsteps that led to the garden that led to the survivor and his procreating lover had led to this: the knowledge that she was unable to be satisfied with her own good life. She was not a counter of blessings. With the shock of her marriage in the past, with its risk played out, with only the platitudes of motherhood before her—the honeymoon was *over*.

Chapter 9

Guaranteed Loss

*C*at is awake before the alarm. It is Saturday, the eighth day of the solitary week that replaced her vacation. She has not heard from Teddy, nor has she called him. *One word*, she has thought all week like a mantra, *one word* could tip her decision. His silence has said it all.

She gathers her robe around her, goes to the bathroom and starts the shower. The water flows in hard crinkly streams and she stands under it, wondering if she will regret her decision. Either way, whether she goes through with it or backs out, she will be set in an irreversible direction. She tilts back under the shower and lets it soak her long hair. *If only I could stop time*, she thinks, *at least indefinitely postpone the decision*. But she can't. As her mother pointed out, postponement would be decision by default. She squirts shampoo on her hair and lathers it up. She starts to cry and lifts her face into the stream.

By the time Cat's taxi arrives at the clinic, it has started to rain. To the right of the entrance stands a youngish man in a yellow slicker, his hood pulled way up, shadowing his face. As she approaches the front door, the man rushes up and shoves a pamphlet in front of her, saying, "Murderer!" She recoils, partly because she is shocked by the man's crude self-righteousness, but also because deep down she *does* feel she is killing something alive. Yet she knows why she has made her decision and stands by it. Single motherhood will consume every hope she ever had for her life, the tiny bridges she has built toward a future will crumble, she will become an island and, she fears, like her own mother she will find a way to desert her child emotionally or physically or both.

She raises a hand like a shield against the man and proceeds into the building.

At the front desk the receptionist takes information and money, then directs Cat to a waiting room lined with posters of sunsets and mountains. Couples, all young, mostly minorities, wait silently. One young woman is accompanied by a female friend and another, like Cat, is alone. She feels nauseous. Confused. Overwhelmed.

A woman with a clipboard comes in through swinging doors and calls, "Catharine Gold?"

Cat follows the woman through the lobby and into another waiting room where six women fill out forms.

Age: twenty-five. Color: white. Marital status: single. Those are the facts. Under *Remarks* she writes: "I am not sure I want to do this yet it is just this indecision that makes me think I should. It seems to me that if I'm going to make a mistake, better to make this one than the other. Why ruin someone else's life?" Her gushing embarrasses her; why should they care about her confusion? If she got herself this far—to the clinic, filling out this form—then she must know what she wants. She crosses out her remarks with hard repeated lines and redundant curlicues.

After a while, a counselor comes into the room with a lecture about contraceptives. Cat feels like a fool. She wishes she were brave and strong and clear enough to walk out of the clinic, that she had the strength and vision of a heroine who does whatever she wants. Her mind is cacophonous with wishes, hopes and realities. In all her uncertainty she is sure of just one thing: She will be unable to manage single motherhood—not the economics and not the responsibility—alone.

The counselor pokes her finger into the rubber shield of a diaphragm until it stretches to its limit. "Hold it up to the light," she instructs, "and check for holes. Even the tiniest pinprick and sperm can get through." Cat pictures a devilish shovel-shaped sperm beating the rest through the pin-sized hole in the diaphragm, rushing for the egg and digging itself in. For a second she thinks it might make a cartoon, then realizes it would only be funny to her, then thinks that even she would not find it funny in a normal state of mind. Then, suddenly, she sees *it. Him*. She thinks it is a boy. She knows she shouldn't name him, but she does anyway: Peter. He has brown hair and big brown eyes, and his birthday would be some time in late November.

Her name is called again by a plump Hispanic woman with a clipboard.

As instructed, Cat changes into paper slippers and a paper robe that opens at the back. She carries her clothes in a plastic bag and waits in another room. Some of the women from the previous room are there, also in paper robes and slippers. It feels warm and strange to be enclosed in one small room with six other pregnant women. It strikes her that, all through the process, no patient has uttered a single word to another. She knows it's because they don't have to; they have all come to the same conclusion: to end it, terminate, abort. Yet despite their decisions, for now they are all still pregnant. Cat wonders if they, too, are savoring the last moments. Within hours—for some, minutes—they will be literally wounded inside. That's something the counselor explained: the uterus will be an open wound, susceptible to infection. They are to take antibiotics for four days and strictly avoid sex for two weeks. They can expect a period within two months.

Cat is called once again by a woman with a clipboard—another woman, another clipboard—and is directed down the hall to what looks like an examination room. In the middle of the small room is a padded table covered with a long strip of white paper. There are two metal stirrups at the end. She hoists herself up and sits between them.

The door opens and the nurse, an efficient black woman, gently tells her to lie back and place her feet in the stirrups. Then comes the anesthetist, a tall middle-aged white man who takes his post beside her and turns knobs on a machine. He says to Cat, "First time, young lady?" and it takes a moment for her to realize that his question is not meant to be answered, that it is a derogatory comment aimed at her as if she is nothing but a reckless, promiscuous girl. He turns away from her and readies his equipment. In the same moment, the doctor arrives, an East Indian woman who instructs Cat in sharp tones on the advisability of contraceptives. It sounds like she is reading rights before an arrest, and Cat's guilt comes surging up like a fountain, drenching her. The doctor briskly washes her hands and pulls on tight rubber gloves. The rest happens fast: the anesthetist pressing a mask over her lower face, the doctor pushing something metal into her, and her last thought—*it is not too late to change my mind.*

The next thing she knows, someone is shaking her shoulder. She feels drowsy. Two women stand by her bed and one of them tells her to get up. She is in the recovery room. It is done, over, gone. She pushes herself up, realizes she is wearing a big diaper, and lies back down. Silently, lids shut tight, she sends pleas for understanding out to her baby, and apologies for nearly loving him, for tempting him toward life then denying him. For naming him. She should have left him unimagined and let him go.

The intercom buzzes and Rocky's voice says, "Cat? Cat?"

"Yes?"

"How are you? How was your vacation?"

"Okay, considering."

"So you went through with the abortion."

"I did."

"How are you feeling?"

"Fine."

"Really?"

"Okay, no. I feel like crap."

"Welcome to womanhood." Rocky's laugh crackles over the intercom. "Oh, I almost forgot. Teddy called."

Cat's heart jumps a little. She has been wondering when, and if, he will finally try to reach her. "What time?"

"Not today. It was before you left for vacation."

"*Before*?"

"I'm a lousy secretary. Annie was out and I shouldn't have answered the phone." Another hollow laugh. "I figured he'd try to call you at home."

"He didn't."

"Then it couldn't have been too important, right?"

"Unless he expected me to call him back, and thinks I just didn't want to talk to him. Things haven't been good between us."

"If it makes you feel any better, I had a *terrible* weekend. Larry was supposed to come out to the house and he canceled. I was alone the whole time."

Alone. What about Annie? Parker? Why does Rocky consider herself alone in the company of her own child?

"Well, we've got a million things to do," Rocky says. "Is the computer on?"

"Yes," Cat says, and Rocky begins to dictate. Cat's fingers type but her mind absorbs nothing, it's too frantic processing Rocky's casual lapse. *Teddy called.* Crushed emotions jostle hopelessly toward some kind of coherent understanding. There is something hard trying to get out, trying to define itself, to make itself known. As Rocky's voice drones on—this voice that once raised the feminist banner, this famous voice now diminished by electronic disembodiment—and as Cat's fingers sail across the keyboard, her mind grinds away at trying to understand something that feels unfathomable. She may never know why Teddy called her, and why he didn't call again, or what might have happened if they had spoken. But even if she did know, if she *could* know, it's too late to change things now. She is propelled forward by the cruelty of her mixed emotions, the sense that she made a mistake, the sense that she *didn't* make a mistake, and the wishful thinking that someone—Teddy? Rocky?—possessed a secret that might have changed the decision she thought through long and hard. She feels totally, utterly confused.

Typing as the famous, oblivious voice dictates through the intercom, Cat thinks she might really hate Rocky now for that single omission of information that might have tipped the balance. That failure to deliver a message that might have changed the course of Cat's life. Or not. The problem is, now she will never know.

But she blames Teddy, too, for only calling once. Which returns her to her original thought process, weeks ago. "No guarantees," he said.

So he had called her. So big deal. *Why didn't he try harder?*

Finally, after the long morning of serving Rocky's needs—her absurd, self-centered needs—Cat breaks free for a lunchtime walk outside. She chooses Park Avenue because it is wide and mostly residential, has more space and more air and more sky. At one point, she turns her head and there is a baby being strolled past, and suddenly she is overwhelmed by a pure feeling of loss. It's like this baby knows, like it's thinking *hey it could have been me*! It's like it somehow knows that Cat herself was almost aborted, that her life in a way is a black hole, something mysterious, almost not meant to be. She feels she walks a fine line between life and emptiness, that if she veers a little too far off-center she'll tumble into some crazy dark void and cease to exist in 3-D.

Become a cartoon.

Back at her desk with a tuna sandwich by her elbow, she draws a woman, naked and spread-eagled on a table, heels raised in stirrups, and the hole between her legs is a window on the universe. Everything happens inside her core: birth, death, peace, love, laughter, war, abandonment, sorrow, betrayal, yearning, boredom, ideas, plans, starbursts of inspiration, knots of frustration. She contains, literally embodies, a mansion of intent: a copy machine and a printed page, a dark room and a light bulb, a sky and an airplane, a bowl of soup and a spoon. She is compartmentalized with rooms in which possibilities are endless, some are realized and others never discovered.

The days slide by, and all the while Cat is aware that Teddy is out there waiting for her to summon him back. But after a week she still isn't ready, and she is beginning to realize that she will not be ready for a good long time. She decides she should at least call and tell him this.

On Saturday morning, she takes the note he left with his contact information and sits at his desk by the phone. It is exactly one week after the abortion, three weeks since he has been gone. She dials. A man answers, Cat asks for Teddy, he is retrieved.

"Teddy, it's me."

"Hey! How've you been? How are you feeling? I almost called you so many times, but you told me you'd call when you were ready so I figured I should wait. And here you are—calling."

"I would have called you back," she says, "but Rocky never gave me your message."

"Oh, that. It wasn't any big deal. I just wanted you to know I was going away for a few days, in case you needed me. I visited my parents. I checked messages a lot so I knew you didn't call. And I was wondering how you were feeling."

"I would have had a lot to say," she tells him, feeling utterly deflated to hear his casual explanation of that sorely missed phone message.

"Did you—?"

"Yes. I had the abortion."

"I'm sorry. I really am."

She can't think of what to say. Sorry for whom? Himself? Her? Their baby-not-to-be? She can feel in their conversation that something else between them has been lost. Innocence.

Trust. And she knows in a heartbeat that they will not be able to pick up where they left off.

"We need to talk," she says after a moment.

"I know."

"Will you meet me at Four Brothers at noon?"

"Why don't I just come home?" *Home*. The way he says it makes her feel so sad. "It would be quieter."

"I'd rather not, please."

When she arrives at the diner, he is already waiting, a finished cup of coffee on the table in front of him. He half rises to kiss her cheek.

"How do you feel?"

"Fine." She shrugs. "It doesn't matter, anyway. I had the worst cramps of my entire life on Thursday night. But I'm fine."

"I should have been there. You should have called me."

"I thought about it, but—" She shakes her head.

"What's been going through my mind," he leans forward, face distraught, "is how much I *love* you. Period. And how I'm hoping you'll give me another chance."

"Teddy, I thought we could bounce back after this. I can see how upset you are now, but I keep wondering why you weren't upset a few weeks ago, when it would have counted."

"I *was* upset a few weeks ago."

"But you didn't show it, not really. You pretty much abandoned me to the problem. Problem—why was it automatically a problem? We never even discussed it, really. You just tossed the flaming ball at me and slid away to let me feel all the pain."

"I felt pain, too."

That startles her. "What *did* you feel, Teddy?"

"I don't know. I'm not sure. I've been thinking about it. The baby...."

"How can you let yourself think about it *now*? That's too easy. You can't make any choices in retrospect. They're all made."

"All of them? What about us?"

"Teddy, you gave me a disclaimer then you kept quiet and let me figure out that I have zero resources to have a baby all on my own. It would have meant moving back in with my mother, or going on welfare, something completely ridiculous and life-destroying in a different way."

"You have a good job, Cat."

"I have benefits and a paycheck, but I have to show up. I have to show up every day, just like you'd have to for a kid. You can't be in two places at once."

"I would have been there for you, if you'd decided to keep it."

"Why are you telling me that *now*?"

"I don't know."

"Why didn't you tell me that three weeks ago? Two weeks ago? *One* week ago? Why didn't you call me again when I didn't call you back? Why didn't you tell me you were thinking about the baby? Why didn't you tell me you wanted to talk about it? Why didn't you stop me?"

"I don't know."

Cat notices a waitress hover a moment with menus, then drift away. Teddy's eyes are downcast into the empty porcelain cup that is stained like old teeth with a film of coffee.

"I'm going to find another apartment as soon as I can," she says.

"No, you don't have to."

"It's your place. You should move back in. I just need a little time."

"Nick said I can rent his spare room; he needed someone anyway. So you don't have to move. I want you to keep the apartment. If I could just leave some of my stuff there for a while—if you don't mind."

His eyes now scan her face, as if memorizing it. She has only seen his forehead this pinched with tension once before, and that was the morning after she told him she was pregnant.

"I wish I could go back and—" he began.

"Well you *can't*. You can't seize the day when the day is over. You just can't do that. You're so smart, but I never knew how weak you are. It's my fault, too, because I misread you. I thought you had more vision for us. I didn't realize how limited your view of *me* was."

"It isn't. It wasn't."

"I feel *so* angry at you, Teddy. I just cannot get beyond that feeling. I can't understand why you were unable to have any faith in us, why your first reaction was to retreat, how you could just step right out of us the minute I really needed you for the first time."

Teddy's gaze wanders out the plate glass window to the street of people. "I'm sorry," he says, but he doesn't look at her when he says it, and she feels abandoned once again.

"Did you need to come over and get some of your things?"

"Another time." His eyes are still elsewhere, anywhere but on her.

Cat walks home alone, heavy with the singularly awful burden that is the ending of something you love.

Back in the apartment at mid-day it seems like the dead of night and the hours ahead feel hollow, devoid of any possible satisfactions. Now that she has banished him, she begins to wonder if he will come back anyway, if any minute now she will hear the turn of his key in the lock.

No, it's final. She must learn to fill the time herself, as she used to.

She goes to his desk, turns on his computer, summons a blank page.

The Legend of How I Drove My Brother Away

It felt like Halloween to me: all the people marching around, and my costume. I hoped there was some candy involved. I wondered about that, since Eddie hadn't given me a bag.

"Where'm I gonna put it?" I asked him.

He pulled me along by my little five-year-old hand. "Put what?"

"The candy."

"I dunno what you're talking about. Come on." He bent down, grabbed me under the arms and hoisted me way up into the air, settling me down on his shoulders. I liked it way up there! People around us said how cute and someone even said he looks young to be a father. Eddie, at fifteen, had grown to almost his full height. His dark golden hair had grown unchecked into a mop that settled on his shoulders. Fuzz sprouted from his upper lip and chin. Mom wanted him to shave it but he refused; he was a man and this was his beard. He wore hiphugger bellbottoms with a wide leather belt, and an orange and yellow tie-dyed T-shirt. He had made one for me, too, and I had it on now, which was probably why that guy thought he was my father. I was wearing tiny bluejeans and dirty white sneakers. He had given me his tear-drop-shaped peace medallion to wear around my neck. I had insisted on wearing my favorite hot-pink smiley button right next to it. My long hair kept flying around in the wind so it was hard to see all the action.

Eddie was still in high school, and our parents didn't want him up here rabblerousing at Columbia University, but he had heard there was going to be a big demonstration going on today and hadn't wanted to miss out. I usually stayed at home with Mom and all the other little kids that messed the place up every day just because she had to run a daycare out of the apartment, but Eddie thought I should be in on the action, too. So he said, *"Mom, I wanna take Cat out to the park, okay? She said she wanted to build like a sandcastle or something in the sandbox, and today's my only chance."* Mom said sure and Eddie grabbed me and we ran.

Huge crowds of students filled the Morningside Heights campus, packed so tight you couldn't get into the library if you tried. They wanted to take over the school and Eddie thought that was a great idea. Then they started chanting stuff about the war. *"END THE WAR IN VIETNAM"* and *"NO NO NO I WON'T GO"* and *"BURN BURN BURN."* Someone got a fire going and people tossed in their draft cards. Eddie was too young to have one but he wanted to join in, so he took his library card from his billfold and threw it into the flames, yelling, "BURN BURN BURN" along with the rest.

"Burn witch!" I shouted. "Yeah!" I had no idea what was going on but I was having a good time anyway. I loved it when Eddie took me out.

Once, he took me ice skating in Central Park when we were supposed to take a taxi to Grandma's and Grandpa's across town. We got in big trouble for that, but Eddie, through the bedroom door behind which he was confined, said, "It was worth it anyway!" and I wholeheartedly agreed. Another time, Mom gave Eddie ten dollars to buy some milk for the daycare kids, and instead he bought us doubledip ice cream cones and gave the rest of the money to a beggar on the street. But the best time, the most fun of all, was when we went to visit our father at the piano store where he worked and Eddie pretended he was the piano player in Three Dog Night and went wild and our father almost lost his job, or so he said.

Mom stayed home with me every night. Dad had a brass quartet that rehearsed twice a week at a friend's downtown. Sometimes they had emergency rehearsals and Dad was out more often. Eddie came and went. Sometimes he returned home muted, distant, his eyes like balls of foggy glass.

One Saturday morning, he wandered bleary-eyed from his room—the walls of which he had painted black and hung with Day-Glo posters of rock stars and underwater life—and flopped into a kitchen chair. Mom was just getting me my breakfast of cereal and a glass of chocolate milk. Dad was making coffee. Eddie wore only boxer shorts. He slumped over the table, his face in one hand, his hair a concoction of curls.

"Morning, Eddie," Mom yawned.

"Coffee?" Dad offered him. They had been trying to treat him like a grownup, just to make him feel good. It wasn't working.

"Listen, you guys," Eddie said. "I've been thinking of going to Canada."

"What?" Mom said. She stared at him, holding a carton of orange juice suspended above an empty glass.

"Well, it's that or jail," Eddie said.

"Ah," said Dad, "the war."

"The war," Mom echoed.

"What's jail?" I asked.

"It's where they send criminals," Mom explained.

"What's—"

"Bad people," Dad said.

I looked at Eddie, stunned.

"The way I see it," Eddie said, "is I ought to get out of here before my number comes up."

"But you're only fifteen," Mom said. "They can't draft you for another three years, and maybe the war will be over by then."

"It probably will be," said Dad.

"Well, I don't wanna take that chance," Eddie said. "I hate the war! I won't go!"

"No no no!" I shouted. "I won't go!"

Mom cringed and grabbed her head with her hands; she always had a headache in the morning.

"Burn witch burn!" I shouted.

"Quiet, willya?" Eddie said.

I grinned.

Mom placed a glass of orange juice in front of Eddie, and sat down. "Listen, honey, we understand you're worried about the war, but it will end, and for now the best thing to do is wait."

"If it's not over by the time you're eighteen," Dad said, "well, maybe we'll all go to Canada."

"I'll go!" I said.

"Oh yeah?" Eddie said. "I thought you just said you won't go."

I banged my fists on the table and shouted, "No no no, I won't go!"

"There's no time to wait," Eddie said.

"You're restless," Mom said. "Don't worry so much."

After that, Mom and Dad urged him to find a hobby to help keep his mind off the war, and so he did. He said I could help if I wanted to and I didn't hesitate to say yes. And so, one warm *afternoon, Eddie took me upstairs to the roof to help him plant a garden. He filled a cardboard box with dirt and poked dozens of fingerholes. Then he took a little bag of seeds and poured them into the palm of his hand. He dropped a few seeds in each hole and covered them with dirt. My job was to sprinkle his garden with handfuls of water. He made me promise not to tell.*

A month later, he led me upstairs to show me an amazing sight.

The plants were so tall! I stood in front of them, pigtails sprouting out of my head like cornstalks, five years old and innocent. "Pretty flowers," I said. "Can I pick some?"

"No way, Jose. And don't tell Mom and Dad, okay?"

"Why?"

"Because they're magic flowers and grownups don't believe in magic. Okay?"

I had already noticed this sad, sorry fact. All Mom and Dad ever did was work, talk, eat, drink, sleep and yell.

Eddie reached into his jeans pocket and pulled out a dollar bill. "Here," he said, pressing the bill into my little hand, "this is for you."

I didn't know how I would spend a whole dollar, and so treasured it until I decided what to do with it. The dollar had many hiding places over the next weeks: in my pillow case, under my biggest green-haired Troll doll, in my favorite storybook, in the toe of my black patent-leather Mary Jane shoes that didn't fit anymore. Finally, one day, I saw what I wanted in the window of a toy store on Broadway: a little perfumed doll in an egg-shaped clear plastic case. I wanted that doll more than anything. But it cost almost two dollars. I'd need some more cash.

How to get that doll became a secret quest for me, secret because I couldn't let my parents know about the dollar. Then one day I saw my chance. Daddy wasn't home for dinner yet, Eddie was still out, and Mommy was fast asleep on the couch with a kind of sour smell to her. So I snuck into her purse.

I didn't know how to count a dollar's worth of the metal money in the little pouch, but I knew that one of those green papers equaled a dollar. So I took one of those. Now I had two dollars and could get the little doll! I would have to ask Eddie to help. I stashed my money in the panties of my Talking Angela doll.

Later that night, from my bed, I heard everybody shouting and didn't know why and was afraid they knew about the dollar. Dad, Mom and Eddie were all arguing. I listened carefully. Then I heard Eddie say, "I didn't take anything from you!" and then Mom said, "But it's gone, where did it go? Who else would go into my purse?"

I had to save him. I knew it was wrong and I shouldn't have done it but they wouldn't punish me as badly as they would punish him. So I slid out of bed in my flannel feetsy pajamas with the little blue sheep jumping over fences, got my Talking Angela doll from the wicker chair in the corner where she guarded me as I slept, and headed into battle.

They were in the living room, standing up, facing each other. Eddie was angled toward the door, like he was ready to bolt. I had seen him exit home in a flash and I couldn't let that happen. I loved him so much, we were a team, and if he left I would be all alone. I had to tell them, now. They all stopped shouting and looked at me as I shuffled quickly between them and held Talking Angela up to Mom.

"Here, Mommy."

"Sweetheart, what are you doing out of bed?"

"Mommy," I said, "here."

"Is your dolly sick?"

I shook my head.

"I put it in her panties."

Eddie started shaking his head and flapping his arms around like he was conducting an orchestra. "Hey, wait a minute, was it you?"

I looked at him and nodded.

Mom looked into Talking Angela's white cotton panties and pulled out the twenty dollar bill. "Here it is."

"You see?" Eddie said. "I didn't take your friggin' money!"

"Sweetheart," Mom said, "I'm so sorry."

Dad lifted me into his arms and I settled my head on his shoulder.

"Kitty Cat," Dad said. "What are we going to do with you?"

"Throw her in a pot of boiling oil!" Eddie said, and stalked angrily off.

"No!" I cried. "Please, Daddy, don't!"

Mom stroked my hair. "Honey, why did you take this money from my purse?"

"I needed another dollar for the doll."

"What doll?"

"The Perfume Babydoll."

Mom held up the bill, and said, "You took twenty dollars from my purse. Do you understand that?"

I shook my head. "I needed another dollar."

"Another dollar? Did you already have one?"

I nodded.

"From my purse?"

I shook my head.

"From my wallet?" Dad asked.

I shook my head.

"Well," Mom said, "where did you get the first dollar, then?"

I looked from Mom to Dad and considered my options. It seemed I had taken a lot of money by mistake, and if I wanted to reduce my punishment I would have to tell them the truth. So I said, "From Eddie, from his garden."

"Eddie gave you the first dollar?" Mom said.

And Dad said, "What garden?"

I pointed to the ceiling. "The one up there. It's got flowers and he gave me a dollar not to tell." I cringed, and buried my face in Dad's neck.

"Okay," Dad said, gently placing me on the floor. "So, let's see, we have a five year old stealing money from her mother's purse, and a fifteen year old with a secret garden. Eddie, come in here, now!"

Eddie came back into the room. I wouldn't look at him.

"Yeah?" he said.

"We hear you're interested in horticulture," Dad said.

"What the f—is that?"

Mom said, "Sweetheart, what are you growing on the roof?"

Eddie shrugged, and said, "Ya know."

"A new crossbreed," Dad said. "Ya No. Why, we'd love to see it."

"Thanks a lot, small fry!" Eddie said. Then, to our parents, "Okay, bust me, see if I care."

Mom took me back to bed while Dad followed Eddie out of the apartment and up the back stairwell to the roof.

Eddie wouldn't talk to me all summer long, except to say things like I can't trust even you *and* all women are the same. *On his sixteenth birthday, I gave him a shiny three-ring looseleaf binder with a unicorn running down a rainbow. He'd need it, because they were sending him away to school.*

I figured that going away to school *meant he wouldn't be living at home anymore, because he had to pack up a lot of his things. I thought he was going away because of me, because I took that money and told about his garden. Since now he wouldn't be my friend, the suspicion that it was all my fault was confirmed. He wasn't allowed out with his friends, so he moped around a lot. Sometimes I followed him through the apartment, just to show him I was willing to be his ally again whenever he was ready. He told me to* get lost *and* beat it *and* scram pest. *I didn't think he really meant it, until the day he went. And when he was really gone, the apartment seemed empty and I felt a lonely space inside me where he had forgotten to put his goodbye.*

The silence is full of voices at first, random words from random conversations that have lodged like musical refrains in Cat's mind, memories turning to echoes. Teddy is gone. He is gone and gone and gone. That his things still fill the corners of the apartment gives her a strange dreamlike feeling and at fleeting moments she wonders if it really happened. Is he really gone?

The days and weeks pass slowly. The month of April fades and with it go the last chills of winter. As she turns the corner into May, the voices begin to fade as well.

And then the smells begin. Garlic and onions sautéing in olive oil, chicken roasting, basil stewing in a vat of boiling tomatoes, flecks of ground pepper drifting in the air. When Teddy left, so did his meals. As the final residues of his cooking fade, like a ghost being sucked through each crack in the walls, the air becomes dry and empty. And then, gradually, new smells infiltrate—curries, cardamom, rose water—from the Indian restaurants on the block. She wants them vanquished; she wants the *old* smells back.

Miraculously, in mourning their absence, the old aromas begin to return, looming like shadows thrown across her sensory memory. The feeling of loss and yearning finally drives her to the bookshelf, where she takes down Teddy's worn paperback of *The Silver Palate Cookbook*. There is a party at Eddie and Penny's over the weekend, a perfect opportunity to cook. She goes straight to the chapter called *Dazzlers*. Herbed Caviar Roulade. She likes the sound of that.

Penny has laid out a buffet: a big golden turkey, loaves of rye and pumpernickel, cold pasta salad, spinach salad, raw carrots, cauliflower, broccoli and radishes arranged around a yogurt dip, and piles of cookies. Arranged on one of Penny's nice serving platters, Cat's roulade makes an impressive addition.

"Beautiful," Penny observes.

Eddie adds, "Fancy. Where'd you get it?" His arms are filled with coats, the most identifiable of which is Grandma Rose's heirloom fur.

"I made them, dummy."

"You? Cook?" He smiles, winks, and proceeds toward his bedroom with the coats.

Cat follows him. The high-ceilinged bedroom is typical of the huge old pre-war buildings on the Upper West Side. On the wall above the bed is a giant grape painted purple, a gift from one of their artist friends. They surround themselves with people of good conscience, as they themselves are, to a fault. Eddie works as a legal aid lawyer, forgoing wealth, and pretty-petite-Penny risks a subway ride to the South Bronx every day where she is a social worker.

Eddie has thickened with age, and Cat thinks he has grown handsomer than ever. The lines on his face, the slight toughening of his skin, dignify him. There is a trace of gray in his curly golden hair.

"Is this party for a reason?" she asks.

"What do you mean?"

"I saw all that champagne in the fridge."

"Look at you," he says, trying to change the subject. "Little sister in a dress, I don't believe it. When did you grow up, anyway?"

She puts her hands on the waist of her blue dress, beams her best smile at him, shrugs her shoulders. "Guess you weren't looking," she says. "So, come on, what's the occasion?"

"You'll see. It's a surprise."

"You're getting married," she says.

He cracks a smile, takes her arm and coaxes her out of the room.

"That's it," she says. "You and Penny are finally engaged."

As he veers her back into the party, he whispers, "Keep quiet, kid, and don't think you've got it completely right."

"I won't say a word," she promises, and goes off to find her mother.

Janet has been talking with Mrs. Havermeyer, Penny's mother, who is tugged away toward the food by her husband just as Cat approaches. Janet has had her short hair highlighted. She is wearing red lipstick, big silver earrings and a white sweaterdress. Cat thinks her mother looks like a veteran newscaster or lady executive. Funny. The overwhelming

Jewish influence in their family has tended to make Cat forget that her mother is a WASP grown in rich conservative soil.

"Don't you look lovely," Janet says. "Is everything all right?"

Cat shrugs. "I'm adjusting."

"You're a survivor, sweetheart. You always have been."

"Think so?"

"I know so. You survived *me*."

Cat reaches out to stroke her mother's shoulder. Janet's hand floats up to take her daughter's with a gentle squeeze.

"I should be comforting you," Janet says. "Not the other way around."

Mort strides up with such a big smile on his face that Cat knows he is nervous about seeing Janet. After constant separations and reconciliations, their divorce was finalized three years ago.

"Hi Dad."

He kisses Cat's cheek. "Hi Kit Cat. How's work? Rocky treating you okay?"

"I guess so," she answers, not knowing where to begin and not wanting to right now, at a party. One day she will corner her father about just how well he knew Rocky Love before sending his daughter into the lair.

"Hello, Janet." Mort nods and smiles.

"Mort," Janet says.

They stand before each other awkwardly, until Janet gets a mischievous glint in her eyes. She leans toward him and says, "Your parents seem to have shrunk."

He snorts a laugh, then whispers, "They're both over eighty."

"Eighty!" Cat says. "They're really getting up there." Janet shushes her, but it's too late. Rose has overheard mention of her age.

"You," she says, with a sweeping gesture that encompasses all three of them. She walks to them in quick tight steps. She *has* shrunk. Her skinny legs are bumpy under heavy beige leggings. She has had her hair coifed into a helmet of brown waves. She is a real little old lady and looks it, carries it like a dare, because anyone who knows Rose Gold *knows* she is to be reckoned with until the day she dies. She uses a cane now, which she stabs into the floor every other step. When she reaches them, she lifts both arms—the cane dangling from one hand—and tries to get them all into one hug.

"Daalinks!" she says, pursing her wrinkly lips.

Each pecks her cheek in turn.

"Who's discussing an old lady's age, eh? You think I didn't hear you?"

"You're not old, Mom," Mort says.

"I *am* old." Humor gleams in her eyes. She slaps her own face and says, "I have earned this, don't forget."

"It's so good to see you, Rose," Janet says.

"You look marvelous, darling."

"I feel good."

"And this bum, my son, he couldn't be patient."

Mort cringes, and Cat says, "Oh, grandma, *don't.*"

"Oy, so now the babies are giving orders?"

"Rose," Janet says, "have you eaten?"

"I don't eat buffet anymore."

Janet takes her arm. "Come on, let's get some food. I'm starved."

Rose says, "You don't look starved to me, but anyway." And off they go toward the dining room.

Grandpa Ben joins Cat and Mort, trailing yogurt dip from a piece of broccoli. "Look at what she feeds me these days," he says. "What am I, a rabbit?" He waves the broccoli in the air and a drop of dip sails onto the shoulder of Cat's dress. "Don't worry, I'll buy you another dress. Anything you want, my angel."

"That's okay, gramps. I'll get it cleaned. Did you try my Herbed Caviar Roulade? I made it myself."

"It sounds deadly. If Rose finds me eating caviar she'll kill me. Where is it?" He heads off toward the buffet table.

Then from across the room comes the pop of a cork. Eddie holds up a bottle of champagne gushing with bubbles. Penny, next to him, holds out a glass and he pours.

"Toast!" Eddie says. "Everybody, grab a glass."

Elaine, Penny's younger sister, circulates quickly with a tray of champagne glasses. Eddie fills glasses, then pops another bottle and fills more.

"Quiet everyone!" Penny calls.

Cat stands with Janet, holding their obligatory glasses of champagne. Janet has not had a drink in two years.

Eddie clears his voice. He takes Penny's hand.

"Here it comes," Cat says. Janet looks at her. Cat whispers, "They're getting...."

"We have an announcement to make," Eddie says. "Now, the way we see it, we've spared both families a lot of trouble—"

"—and expense," Penny adds.

"That's right. We've lived together for a long time, and for us marriage is mainly a formality. So ..." he looks at Penny, "we were married yesterday at City Hall."

Rose shouts, "Oy!" Her cane shoots out at a Japanese screen in the corner, which buckles. Penny runs to the screen behind which, on a small table, had been their wedding cake.

Isabel looks at Cat's cartoon of a squashed wedding cake surrounded by happy, laughing relatives, while off to the side stands a stiff, mannequin-like bride sliced vertically in half. One side of her cross-section shows rooms, each busy with a project or equation. The other side shows a tangle of veins sprouting from an oversized heart, connected to a swollen womb.

Isabel's face is impassive as she studies the cartoon, and Cat thinks that maybe you can't leave a cartoon ambiguous like a story or a movie. That maybe without a punchline, a point, a clear quick idea, a cartoon will never work, and her experiment has failed, and now, now Isabel is going to cut her down with one of her terrible sharp judgments, and it will be awful, a final failure as she sinks into her lonely singlehood and will probably be too preoccupied with dating and work to cartoon ever again. So now it is over, finished, an empty dream, years of her life dissolving into one moment of....

"It's different," Isabel says, dropping the page onto her messy desk. "Interpretive. For me it's about how a woman's brain is trapped inside her body. How her uterus betrays her potential, and how society condones that." She smiles, her wan face spreading as her bright red lips stretch into humor. "Maybe I'll do a special wedding issue." She laughs, one loud burst. "Yeah, yeah, with a lot of happy photos and a piece on battered wives and a box with divorce statistics and then maybe something on child brides in India. Something like that. And if I can find someone who's been happily married forever then I'll ask them to do a piece, too. Good fucking work, Gold." Isabel's lips tighten and she looks at Cat seriously. "You feeling okay now?"

"Sorry?" *Does Isabel know about the abortion?*

"I had three," Isabel says. "The first one's the worst."

"I won't have another one," Cat says sharply, hating that Isabel knows. That Teddy, obviously, told her.

"One was Teddy's," Isabel says. "The last one."

Cat stares at Isabel, at her tiny body clad in black, at her bleached-blond boy's haircut, at her cherry red lips, at her cool blue eyes. She doesn't like Isabel, she decides; in fact, she despises her. But still, she feels drawn to hear what Isabel has to say.

"When?" Cat says.

"It ended when he met you." Her face is calm, deadly—Teddy called her a *killer* and she is, she is, *she is*. "He was in love with you, you know," Isabel adds.

Cat nods to say *yes I know* and in her mind is a sudden fight over whether to leave the cartoon for *Freak* or take it back. The phone rings and Isabel is lost to another conversation. Cat doesn't wait, doesn't take back the cartoon, doesn't say good-bye—she just leaves while she has the courage.

But by the time she gets home, she knows what she has to do. She has to fully root Teddy out of her life, her mind, her *heart*, which means vanquishing Isabel, which means getting back her cartoon. She made a mistake thinking she could continue their editorial relationship after breaking up with Teddy. It was never a very professional relationship, anyway; it was always infused by him, by his cloudy motivation for connecting them, by his words and convictions which would spring from Isabel's lips, like ammunition, when Cat was least expecting it. She does not want to see Isabel again, does not want her cartoons in *Freak*, does not want to hear the woman's voice. So she sits down and writes a letter asking for the return of her cartoon, not worrying about the fact that she has never published anything anywhere else and has no other prospects. If her work's really any good, she'll find another venue. If not ... well, she'll cross that bridge when she gets there.

"Love never lasts," Rocky says. She sits in the armchair in Cat's office, leaning back into the soft white leather. "I've learned that the hard way. Don't worry, you'll survive."

Cat listens to the clichés as they stream from Rocky's bright red lips. Having just returned from an outing, she is dressed up and made up, offering advice that reeks as much as her perfume. Annie, it seems, has filled Rocky in on the basics of Cat's breakup with Teddy. Ever since she returned from her so-called vacation, and realized how irrelevant Rocky considers her troubles—with her cheery banter about abortions and broken hearts, and her inability to put a simple phone message through—she has lost any desire to talk to Rocky in a real way. Or to listen. She doesn't want to hear Rocky's spiel anymore. She is *at work*. This is her *job*. Period.

"Men are only good for one thing," Rocky says.

Cat turns to the computer and types a list that begins *type this list*.

"The first betrayal is the worst. Trust me, it gets easier. When my first husband left me, I was stunned. I lied to the network; I told them we were still married. Women were still stigmatized by divorce back then." Rocky shrugs. "Now it seems absurd. I've left them, they've left me. At least I have plenty of money. Anyway, there's only one man I ever really loved." Rocky shifts her weight forward so she is sitting on the edge of the armchair. "John's sexy, in his own way, don't you think?"

"John Paglia?"

"He's in love with me, you know."

"I didn't realize that." Cat suppresses an urge to laugh, her first in many weeks, and for that alone she is grateful to Rocky, whose listening is too shallow to influence Cat's broken heart. *Rocky Love*, Cat thinks; what an ironic last name. Lust is more like it—or maybe *stone*. Yet she believes Rocky when she says there was once a man she really loved, and wonders who the lucky devil was.

C h a p t e r 10

The Rise and Fall of Rocky Love

Tripping on Fame

"Consciousness raising?" Rochelle said. "I don't know." "You stirred people up with the articles you wrote back in school," Reebah said. "We need someone with a strong voice, a good presence. You know, smart and sexy and—"

"White?"

"Black and white. You and me. A coupla chicks beefin' *loud* and *live* on the air." Reebah's face lit up when she laughed, her dark face glowed, her smile was electric. She had worked hard down south, promoting consciousness for civil rights, and now she was back east determined to raise some ire on the radio. The local public station wanted a weekly show about activism. They wanted a format that would cover black and white and black-and-white and women and the war. One of the producers, Arnie Kahn, had met Reebah in Georgia and recruited her to host his show which he was calling "Live Talk."

"I already told them about you and they're interested. This is an opportunity, Rock. We could *do* something with this. I don't want to see you shut down into this, you know, *married woman* cop-out thing." An indignant tone in Reebah's voice tapped Rochelle's vein of defiance. She had married a doctor, after all, and become a doctor's wife. The question remained to what degree she would *be* a doctor's wife. She knew she couldn't follow her mother's prescription too exactly. She knew, in the twist of that moment, that she would agree to do the show.

"Live Talk" was set to air on a Saturday afternoon. Rochelle and Reebah, twenty-five years old, sat together at the console, attached to headsets which gripped Reebah's massive Afro and sat tightly on Rochelle's frizzy auburn hair. Rochelle wore hiphugger bellbottoms and a tight ribbed orange turtleneck. Reebah wore an ankle-length red dashiki. Neither wore makeup. They sat side by side on swivel chairs, backs straight, knees touching, eyes on Arnie Kahn in the control booth. He was a dark, bearded man, a contrast to his wife Susan who was slender and light. They worked together as co-producers, and though Arnie had conceived of "Live Talk" it was Susan who had pitched and sold it to the station's executive director.

Susan slipped into the room and showed Arnie something on a clipboard. He read it and nodded. She handed the clipboard to the announcer, George, who sat hunched in front of a microphone, watching the clock. A red light above the glass separating them from Arnie and Susan turned on. They were on the air.

George's deep voice said: "Hello, we're back. Get ready for something really special. We've got a new show and we know you're gonna like it. Say hello to Reebah Jameson and Rocky Love. They got it and now you got it—half an hour of talk and whatever—here they are, our very own—Mad Girls."

First there was silence on the air. Then, Reebah's voice asking, "Girls?"

And Rochelle's voice: "Women!"

And they were off at a gallop, talking to each other, with each other, at each other, verbally picketing every injustice that came to mind. That half hour slot became a riot of laughter and anger, *a coupla chicks beefin'* about racism and sexism and rallying against the war. Two women talking, strongly, smartly, about everything. Discrimination. Pollution. Female orgasm. Fantasy. Pay equity. Everything.

On the one year anniversary of *Mad Women* and the launch of the show's national syndication, the network threw a party at Studio 54. Everyone who was anyone was there.

Mabel faced her daughter in the mink coat Norman had given her for their thirty-fifth wedding anniversary. A photographer approached, lifting his camera, and Rochelle laughed and struck a pose in her black beaded maxidress. She flicked back her long hair. Flash. Knowing that Reebah was somewhere across the room, contending with her own family and the same greedy press, gave Rochelle courage. The mad women were on to something and they both knew it, and the fact that some were vehemently against their message was only testament of its power.

"Mom, I wish you would relax," Rochelle said when the photographer had departed.

"I don't know why I'm here." Mabel looked at Norman.

"She's our daughter," Norman said.

Mabel's face went burning red. "And I am your wife."

Bobby calmly asked Mabel, "Have you read the press on the show, Mom? People are really relating to the openness of Rocky and Reebah."

"So now you're calling her Rocky too? I could vomit. I listened once to that show, enough to hear it's nothing but trash. Norman?"

Norman slowly shook his head. "No, this is Rock's night. Just one more hour, you can do that, can't you?"

"Mom, please," Rochelle said, then *flash* she smiled for a camera.

"Yes," Mabel said, "I could stay, but I'll tell you something, I choose not to."

As Mabel left—a small angry mink blending into the crowd—Rochelle could feel Norman's wish to leave with her. But he didn't; he stayed with Rochelle and Bobby. He stayed to meet her producers and Reebah's family and every techie connected with the show. He even greeted Leo's new beau, John, who was dressed like a cowboy in studded leather and a ten gallon hat.

By the end of the evening, Rochelle was high on wine and the realization that she was a star. She felt that her father was proud of her, and was happy about that; but then he said a funny thing. He was leaving, hovering by the entrance in his gray coat. She leaned over to kiss him goodnight. He hugged her very tightly, and said, "Rocky, don't let this sudden fame hurt you."

She didn't understand it; how could it hurt her? What could go wrong?

Rochelle's mad woman was Rodney Parker in drag: a man in a woman's body working the world like a crowd of suckers. Using, cajoling, telling the truth, then not giving much of a damn about it. The mad women spotted hypocrisy then played it for all it was worth. They were loved and hated, inevitably.

Their new fame was a paradox. They were lauded for creating live talk heroines as heroic as heroes created by men in the great white male venues, and they were ridiculed for being two women, one black and one white, who were helping to catapult other women from the role of straight man in the joke of daily life, to Riddler, Joker. For perpetuating, on the air, the idea that women could play the game by their own rules and not men's. For saying *I want, give me*, then taking. For discussing recipes and penises in the same five minutes.

The mad women said things that *good* women didn't say. Most female listeners thrilled to their courage. Male listeners vacillated between thinking they were hot babes and angry bitches. And then of course there were those who understood it was just live radio. But what got everyone about the mad women, what no one could deny, was that they were smart. They whipped you awake by hitting bone. And all they were doing was speaking their minds.

Rocky Love. ROCKY LOVE. Rochelle loved her new persona; it thrilled her, empowered her. She became enthralled by the sound of her own voice. She never knew what she was going to say until she'd said it. And it was right ... at least on the air. At home, it was a different story.

Bobby was a man. Black or white, a man. With Reebah the color mix was dynamite, it worked, because more than anything they were women. At home, more than anything, Bobby and Rochelle were husband and wife.

Bobby worked long hours, both in his office seeing private patients and at the hospital. Often he received calls in the middle of the night and would rush to the hospital to deliver a new life. He never spoke to her when those calls came, he would dress in silence and leave. This was worse than demanding children from her; this wrenching silence pressured her more than words. With each birth, Rochelle's guilt rose, followed quickly by resistance. Bobby's desire for family, though mostly unspoken these days, worked directly counter to her urge for freedom and sometimes, she thought, flight.

Then one day her marital ambivalence bubbled up on the air. Without thinking, Rochelle said, "Married women work twice as hard as single women, and let's face it, our free time is never really *free.*" She saw the look on Susan Kahn's face: standing behind the glass partition, studying notes on her clipboard, she looked up suddenly, startled, like a soldier whose camouflage had been discovered. Susan quickly shook her head.

Rochelle said, on the air, "Ask someone if they believe in animal rights. The answer? Yes! Ask that same person if a woman deserves to have rights. The answer? Maybe. How about a married woman? *He* rules, she obeys, there's your answer. If you don't do what he wants, you'll suffer."

Rochelle felt excitement speed through her. Behind the glass, Susan wilted onto a stool. Arnie rushed into the room and was speaking to her. There was a flurry of flashing red lights on the telephone.

Reebah took the floor: "Hey, maybe Rocky's got something. I'm a single woman, and yeah I kinda like it, you know? I own myself. I do what I want. And speaking of rights, Rocky, how about abortion rights? The sexual revolution ain't no revolution until we have the right to choose what happens inside our own bodies. Legalize abortion! Write to your congress person! Get a voice in D.C. Roe's going to the Supreme Court soon and they have got to know what we think."

As Reebah read phone numbers and addresses into the microphone, Rochelle stared into Susan's eyes, through the glass, smiling. Arnie was on the phone behind her, talking animatedly, going from one call to another.

Finally, Susan smiled back.

Six months later, Reebah published a book called *The Choice* examining the history of abortion in America and arguing for a congressional action in favor of legalization. Roe v. Wade was headed for the Supreme Court and Reebah's book became a focal point in the media, bolstering the argument for free choice. She hit the lecture circuit with force, talking to women and men about human rights, civil rights, women's rights. Reebah Jameson became a household name, a black woman with a voice, using it. She returned as much as possible to do the show on Saturdays. But when she couldn't, Rochelle worked alone, focusing on what she called "the marriage net" and taking calls from listeners.

After a while, Arnie and Susan decided to spin off another show. They would drop the plural from *Mad Women* and Reebah would carry the show alone, live, from wherever she was. Rochelle would launch a new show on Monday mornings, an hour format: half an hour of Rocky Love talking, and half an hour of listener calls.

And so was born the *Mad Wife*.

Bobby lay beside Rochelle, neat and straight down the bed in his cream silk pajamas. She rolled next to him and he calmly, routinely, put his arm around her shoulders. She kissed him and his lips did not respond.

"Let's make love," she whispered in his ear, slipping her fingers under the neck of his pajamas. His luscious skin felt softer than the silk.

He was silent, still.

The tip of his tongue traced his outer ear, then slipped inside.

"Stop it, please."

She leaned back on her elbow. He had never refused her before. *No* man had. "What's wrong?"

He looked at her with the stern expression of a doctor delivering an unwanted diagnosis. "You don't want a husband, Rocky, you want an antagonist. You use me like you used your mother to bounce yourself off into the world. It isn't working for me right now. You may not realize it, but every time you push yourself *off* you push me *away*."

"Away?"

"Emotionally," he said.

"Are you leaving me?"

"No, I think you're leaving me. You've distanced me with your show. You know that, don't you? You do know that."

"*You* know that what I say on the air isn't all true, Bobby."

He looked incredulous. "Of course it is."

"The stuff I say is about women's lives. *Other* women's lives, not *mine*. It has nothing to do with *you*."

"Maybe you're only fooling yourself," he said, and rolled over to face the wall.

He hadn't asked her for a baby since the *Mad Wife* was launched. It struck her now that he was leaving her slowly, gradually, like sand slipping off the castle until it was just a lump on the beach. She didn't *want* to be a lumpwoman on the beach alone. She wanted him, she wanted Bobby, she wanted Dr. Love at his office all day and Mr. Love at her table in the evening and Bobby Love in her bed every night. She wanted him for the stable center of her life so she could swing wildly without fear. And she wanted him not to mind it. Was that really too much to ask?

Rochelle swiveled to face her desk. Behind her, two large windows met in a corner like an open book. Her view was mainly industrial, with the Hudson River snaking by the New Jersey shoreline. The television studios were housed in a former warehouse space, far west in midtown, but the executive suites were as plush as the view was grim. Charlie Webb, her agent, had negotiated this prize corner office in her contract with the network. He always said you had to get what you could during the negotiations, because once they had you, you were theirs.

Rocky Love, Live aired as a daily morning show targeted at married women. Charlie alone knew that Rochelle had only recently signed her divorce papers. She had intended to tell her producer, but Charlie shook his head and shut her office door and shook his head some more for dramatic effect. Rochelle leaned her elbows on her desk and said, "Why not?"

Charlie was a small man, a good eight inches shorter than Rochelle, who was relatively tall for a woman. But Charlie was the kind of short man who didn't look short until you stood next to him. He didn't notice his height so didn't project any insecurity about it. He stood in front of her door, legs planted wide, arms folded, shaking his head. He wore a brown and white checkered suit, an electric blue shirt with long pointy collars, and a wide tie. His brown shoes were squarish at the toe and had chunky heels. He was very stylish.

He said, in a loud whisper, "Rocky, honey, you tell them your husband left you and you're *pfft* around here."

"It was a mutual separation."

"Whatever. But between you and me, he wanted out, am I right? And what's worse, to network honchos, is that you left the home. You left the home, Rocky, do you hear what I'm saying to you? No, don't tell them anything. Just keep it like I told you, *you and your husband, you moved.* Change of address, that's all. Say yes, baby, keep the contract alive."

Rochelle said, "Maybe I'll frame the divorce paper and hang it on the wall."

"Honey!"

Rochelle laughed. "You're a kick, Charlie."

"But are you listening to me? Are you hearing me? That's all I want to know."

"I hear you. But it's bullshit, you know that, right?"

"Gotta face the realities." He took a step forward. "So listen, did you find out? You know?"

"Suzanne?"

"Did you ask her?"

Rochelle leaned back in her purple and black striped chair. "I'm not sure you're her type."

"You didn't even ask?"

"She's young."

"What, so I'm ten, eleven years older."

"She's sort of an intellectual, Charlie. Not your type."

"She's my type, believe me, I know my type when I see it. Ask her or I option out."

"You slimebag. You need me more than I need you."

"You're finally learning how to think, honey. Ask her. On what you're paying her, she could use the free meal."

Though they were close in age—Suzanne was twenty-eight and Rochelle was almost thirty-one—their circumstances polarized them and naturally precluded friendship. Suzanne was smart and ambitious and intended to work hard and build a career. Rochelle was smart and ambitious and wanted everything *now* and got it or walked away. Suzanne's doggedness worked in an assistant; Rochelle, however, would never want to actually be that way herself. She dealt with Suzanne in the same way she dealt with everyone else: with directness, warmth, and an expectation that she would have her way. She would not, though, push any woman to date a man against her will.

After Charlie left, Rochelle waited a few minutes then went to Suzanne's desk, clustered in the hallway outside her office along with the other assistants' desks. She was on the phone, booking a guest for the show. Rochelle lifted her hip onto the desk and waited.

Suzanne was an athletic young woman with olive skin and silky black hair. Often, as today, she wore loose Indian dresses and flat leather shoes to work. She had a healthy, wholesome look, not beautiful, barely attractive. Rochelle heard a little Mabel-voice calling up from the depths of her mind, wondering if the girl's looks wouldn't be improved with a little makeup. She pushed the thought away.

Hanging up the phone, Suzanne said, "That man asked me what my breast size is!"

"Dr. Carlotta?"

"He should be sued."

"He will be, after the show." She laughed. "Did he agree to do it?"

Suzanne said, "Yup," and made a notation on a list in front of her.

"Plastic surgeons are desperate for breast implant customers now that thin is in," Rochelle said. "So, speaking of the war between the sexes, I want to bounce something off you."

Suzanne swiveled to face Rochelle. "Shoot."

"Charlie Webb."

Suzanne's face arched in smile. "What a strange man."

"Would you go out with him?"

"Are you doing a show on creepy guys or something? Am I research?"

"No, this is real life. Sorry, Suze, but he wants to take you out on a date."

Suzanne stared at Rochelle for a moment, before asking, "Is this an imperative? I mean, are you telling me—"

Rochelle snapped her head back and forth. "Never. He wanted me to ask. I'm asking. Do what you want."

"I'll pass, then."

Rochelle leaned towards Suzanne, and asked, "Just out of curiosity, would you have done it if I said I wanted you to?"

Suzanne thought a moment. "Unfortunately, probably, yes."

Rochelle slid off the desk. "Never do that," she said. "But I'm glad I asked. Anyway, Suze, I think you made the right decision." They giggled together and for a moment they were two young women united. Then Rochelle abruptly returned to her office, sidetracked into thoughts of women and men and power and love and dating and wondered, swiveling to absorb her view of the river, just how far she could push the limits of her power, if she tried.

Rochelle lifted her face to a powder puff and held her breath. She didn't like to inhale the murky powder, and made a habit of washing her face immediately after the show was finished. She saw her own hairdresser and chose her own clothes, but the television network insisted she let the in-house makeup artist, Arlene, do her face before each show.

Arlene had a tendency to be heavy-handed, though, and after she plucked out too much of Rochelle's eyebrows one time, she was not allowed near her face with tweezers. Rochelle then did a show on body image: fat, height, breast size, body hair. The show was called "Loving Yourself" and challenged the Twiggy look which was the rage at the time, prompting women to starve themselves to the bone, perpetuating a nationwide anorexia. In protest, Rocky Love took to flaunting her heavy breasts and untoned muscles and hairy eyebrows. For the body image show in particular, she refused to wear any makeup, despite her producer's argument that she would lose viewers by neglecting her appearance. She gained viewers, and had that week's winning ratings framed and posted on her office wall.

Hanging next to her proof of that success was a framed mock-diploma reading "Class of '72" in calligraphy, with a gold seal in the lower left corner. This was a gift from Reebah, who had helped to champion the Equal Employment Opportunity Act and celebrated its passing by honoring all the women she knew who breezed up toward a suddenly heightened glass ceiling. Rochelle was one of them. She was lucky enough to have been her sexy opinionated self at a time when society was beginning to give noisy women credence, power, space to move and run. From the minute she had opened her mouth on the radio, Rochelle became a prototype, without even meaning to; she was just being herself. Her sexual rawness translated well from radio to television. They gave her a large wardrobe budget in addition to a hefty salary with good benefits, and let her spiff herself up while holding the belief that none of this would ever change her.

She liked to arrive in the office early, to prepare for the show which aired at nine-thirty. She figured the programming people had deliberately scheduled the show at a time when most husbands were out of the house. Why infuriate half the viewing public? Let the nonworking wives hunker down by the tube, after breakfast, and get revved up for the day with a dose of Rocky Love. It was good timing for everyone: the ratings were high, women got what they wanted, men weren't bothered, and everyone got to glory in the appearance of rocking the status quo without rocking it at all. She was a safe, opportunistic star. Charlie had positioned her that way. She managed to keep the balance between Charlie's "realities" and the real ones, until one evening, in a most unlikely place, she found herself broadsided by her past.

She sat in a clear Plexiglas chair, covered to the neck in a hot pink nylon cloth emblazoned at the neck with Lisa Long's scripted LL logo. It had been a tough day, and Lisa herself had stayed late to do Rochelle's hair, an honor bestowed only upon star customers. The slender Chinese woman whizzed behind Rochelle with scissors, comb and spray. These days, she wore her hair trimmed to the shoulder, hennaed and straightened. She enjoyed watching the kinks and curls disappear, and loved the feel of the firm steady tug of Lisa's comb massaging her scalp. She was just curving into alpha when Lisa said, "You have such beautiful hair, it's so thick and curly. Why don't you let it go natural like when you were a girl?"

"When was I a girl?" Rochelle said.

"In the pictures. You were so earthy, so sexy."

"Pictures?"

"In *Playboy*, the new issue. Haven't you seen it?"

"No." Rochelle's adrenaline started pumping.

"We have it. Wait, I'll show you." Lisa walked off and returned a minute later with the magazine. She quickly flipped through the pages. "Here. That's you."

The familiar images stunned Rochelle: herself, young and carefree, striding naked across a room; herself, young and busty, stretched naked on the sand; herself, young and innocent, spread-eagled on a bed. A short piece described "A Brief Encounter with a Mad Woman" and bore the byline Tad Crawford.

Rochelle turned bright red and shot from her chair like a rogue missile, heading for the pay phone on the wall.

When she was told that her attorney was on vacation, she demanded his secretary reach him in St. Croix. The woman sounded a little testy when she told Rochelle that she would have to consult with his partner, who specialized in libel suits.

Rochelle taxied directly to the offices of Barthoff & Singer and marched past the receptionist like the Queen of Mod in her denim pantsuit and purple suede boots with chunky four-inch heels. She wore her diamond engagement ring from Bobby on the middle finger of her right hand, which clutched the rolled-up *Playboy*.

A tall man in brown slacks, a tweed jacket, yellow shirt and burgundy knit tie came down the hall with his arm already reaching for a handshake. He had brown hair that curled down below his earlobes and a neat brown beard. He wore gold-rimmed aviator glasses.

"Rocky Love?" His voice was deep and creamy like double chocolate ice cream.

"Jason Barthoff?"

They shook.

"Thank you *so* much for staying to see me," she said.

"I was working late anyway." He directed her into his corner office. He sat casually on the edge of his desk, one hip hiked up and the opposite leg stretched long like a dancer's, showing his pink and yellow argyle sock. "May I see the photos?"

She handed him the magazine and he opened it to the dog-eared page, which he scanned thoughtfully, nodding, licking at his mustache.

He's cute, she thought, glancing around the office for evidence of marriage— rings, family photos—and finding none.

"Actually," she said, "I'm feeling too upset to keep my dinner engagement. May I use your secretary's phone?"

"Dial nine for a line out."

She shut his office door and lifted the phone receiver, dialed her home number and listened to it ring for a while. Then she hung up.

"Everything all right?" Jason asked when she returned to his office.

Rochelle sighed. "Poor man, he's madly in love with me. But it's so new, and my divorce isn't even final." She laughed and Jason grinned. He handed her the magazine.

"They're lovely photos," he said. "You haven't changed much in ten years, I see."

Rochelle could feel the blush rising from her breasts up to her face. "I was so young then," she said. "And stupid. When he started taking a lot of pictures, it disturbed me and I left. It didn't occur to me to take the film."

"It would have saved you some trouble now. Crete?"

"Matala was a beautiful village, but what an awful man."

"It'll be a simple matter," he said, "if you didn't sign a release. We'll file an action against Crawford and *Playboy* and they'll do half our work for us. If he's an independent contractor they won't defend him, they'll cut him loose to defend himself. They'll never use him again which is just a little extra icing on the cake. You never signed anything?"

Rochelle said, "I didn't sign anything. I'm not even sure it's *me* in those pictures."

"Oh?"

She knew she was pushing it too far; it had just been so tempting to say that. "It is me," she said. "But I hate to think about that miserable time in my life."

"We've all made mistakes."

"But if you're a public figure, they don't let you forget it."

"Want me to nail him?"

"Would you?"

"I'd love to."

Jason Barthoff was a man possessed, and she knew it, and he went after Crawford with a passion he would rather have applied to his client, and she let him. They spoke on the phone so frequently that when Suzanne buzzed to introduce the caller, she merely said, "Jase," and hung up.

The network, meanwhile, recovered from its shock after a mind-numbing meeting with Charlie Webb, who felt he had no option but to go for broke and convince them to accept Rochelle's idea of doing a show on the magazine article. The network executives didn't know if they were committing suicide or if it was a brilliant idea. They opted to listen to Charlie.

Rochelle did the show. It was a hit.

Jason Barthoff was right about *Playboy*: they disowned Crawford and even supplied his home address. When Rochelle's lawsuit reached the press, it frightened him into action.

He showed up one night, just past seven, as Rochelle was getting ready to go out to dinner with Leo and his new boyfriend, Rich. She had showered and stepped into her green leather dress with a tight bodice and full skirt, had just slid one dangling strand of opals into her pierced lobe and was about to insert the other one, when the intercom buzzed. She assumed it was the boys, early, so she ran to the intercom and buzzed them up. She got the second earring in on her way to the bathroom, where she bent over, gave her hair a few whacks from beneath, and flipped up to standing. She quickly powdered her face, blackened her lashes and reddened her lips.

The doorbell rang.

She flung open the door singing, "Hi!" and then stopped. It wasn't Leo, it was someone else.

She didn't recognize Tad Crawford for a few minutes, but when it hit her, memory reeled in ten years and there she was, in bed with this very same stranger.

He looked basically the same, but older—the same tight body and thick black hair, the same darkish olive skin, the same black eyes and square jaw. His hair was very short now and stood straight on his head like a brush in the center of which was a spiral cowlick. She recalled in an instant her attraction to him back then. But he had betrayed her, and that thought sent the door slamming shut.

He pounded on the door. "I want to talk to you! Open up for a minute, I just want to talk to you!"

"Talk to my lawyer!"

"I did! I'm settling with you. I want to apologize, Rochelle Libbon. Hey, you said you were twenty-five."

She laughed, remembering. He had been intense, too sexual for her inexperience to appreciate. But now, she thought, now she would relish him.

Rochelle unlocked the door and opened it a crack. "I shouldn't talk to you," she said. "You did a rotten thing."

"I'm sorry. But listen, my picture's been in the papers, too, and so has my girlfriend's. We're suffering over this. Don't think it won't be a while before I work in New York again."

"If ever."

He was wearing a black leather jacket and jeans, and his dark beard was unshaven. He looked tired and angry.

She said, "I'm expecting someone."

"You have to admit, the photographs are good."

"They're interesting."

"I'll sell you the negatives."

"Do you have them?"

He patted his rear pocket. "Right here."

"You never had an assignment for *Life*."

"Yeah I did. They bought my pictures of the caves, used two of them. But you, lady, you didn't have any assignment.

"You believed me."

"What, are you going to a St. Paddy's parade or some-thing?"

"I happen to look good in green."

"Didn't say you look bad. I know they're real." His nostrils flared. "Yeah, I remember them."

He meant her breasts, and she knew it. No fewer than three men had asked her if her breasts had been enlarged with silicone.

"Real as ever," she said.

"Well, I liked you, really," he said. "I'm sorry I did that piece. I was low on money. I panicked. I made a mistake and I'm sorry."

"Do you really mean that?"

"Yes, believe it or not, I do."

"I want to see those negatives."

She invited him in and they drank Scotch. When she thought his defenses were sufficiently down, she reached behind him for the milky paper packet of negatives which were sticking out of his back pocket.

He caught her hand. "Not so fast, lady."

"My brother's coming," she said. "Can I have the negatives, please?"

"You gave me some problems by taking that rental car, you know."

Yes, she remembered now; she had taken off in the rental car while he was still asleep in the hotel.

"You know, my girlfriend can't stand your show. She thinks you're slutty. I'd have to agree."

"Oh, fuck you." She grabbed for the negatives.

He was so very sexual and she had been celibate since Bobby and she was making Jason wait until the case was over and she was, well, *horny*, that was what the mad wife would have said. Somewhere deep down inside her, Rochelle Libbon

Love *was* the mad wife, it was inevitable. Maybe Tad Crawford had helped get that closet crazy lady started, and now he was going to tap her again.

It was insane, Rochelle knew that, even as it was happening. She could hear the chorus of her family in the deepest seed of her mind as Tad lowered his jeans and raised the skirt of her green leather dress and she very willingly let him. Mabel crowed *you whore you have shamed me in front of the world now* and Leo watched thinking he wanted this too and Norman said *honey don't let fame hurt you* and Bobby said *I want you pregnant now* and Nathan said *marrymeohmarrymesister.*

C h a p t e r 11
Brotherly Love

Rocky sails down the hall in her new eight-hundred-dollar billowy oversized molten-silver shirt. Her collar is unbuttoned to the cleavage, where black lace hugs her large bosom. She wears black stretch pants and no shoes, just fire-orange polish on her toes. She loves the woolly feel of her carpet. As she passes the office, she sees Cat hovering by the copy machine.

"Rocky!"

She turns back into the office. "Yes?"

"Didn't you want a copy of the manuscript for the meeting?"

"Did I?"

"You asked me before. Here it is." Cat hands over a stack of neat white pages bound by a rubber band.

The girl is always reminding her of things she never said, giving her things she never requested, confirming appointments she never made. Yet, somehow, things manage to fall into place, which is what an assistant is supposed to do, after all: anticipate her needs.

"Thank you." Rocky takes the manuscript. "Has Larry called?"

"Not today."

"Will you get him on the phone, please?"

"But Rocky, John's waiting in the dining room. You're already late for the meeting."

"I know that. Never mind. If Larry calls, put him through. Hold any other calls."

Cat nods and at the last minute punctuates it with a smile. *Lipstick*, that's what the girl needs to help her looks. *Ever since she broke up with her boyfriend, she hasn't even made an effort to attract a new man. Good thing she took my advice and had that abortion. It would have looked bad for me if I fired her just because she was pregnant, but what choice would I have had? Everyone knows that single mothers are unreliable workers.* Rocky rubs her lips together to smooth out the *Passion Bud*,a new color she bought yesterday at Bendels, and heads to the dining room, carrying the neatly typed manuscript.

Annie has laid out her standard luncheon table, china circa Bobby Love. Indispensable Annie; she's been with Rocky how many years now? Six, seven. Her service is as perfectly understated and reliable as a good restaurant, where you know what to expect and it will always be satisfactory if not excellent.

"Thank you, Annie, it looks beautiful." Rocky smiles warmly at Annie and then broadens her smile as she turns it on John, who is seated at one of the two place settings. She drops the manuscript on the table next to her place and moves toward him.

He stands, always the gentleman, to receive her friendly kiss. She lingers a moment to make sure he has a chance to inhale her perfume, Liz Taylor's *Diamonds*, also purchased yesterday. The trick, however, is not to linger indefinitely, to pull away just at the moment of longing. She steps back, feeling her silver shirt undulate on her powdered skin. He is staring at her, blushing. Bingo. She knew it: he wants her, bad.

"Please, John, sit. I have a lovely lunch for you."

He sits down and begins to serve himself. She sits beside him, and waits. When he's through, she spoons a dollop of cottage cheese onto her plate, then covers it in fruit salad.

"Counting calories?" he asks through a mouthful of roast beef sandwich.

"Do I need to?"

"Absolutely not, that's why I ask."

"I watch my weight." Which, according to her bathroom scale, has been steadily escalating for the past few years. But controlling it would mean dieting, and she can't see how she could find the time.

John sets down his half-eaten sandwich and turns his attention squarely on her. "Rocky, before we get started, I'd like to know what you think of my work so far."

"Your work? Your work is perfect. I like your sense of humor. You make my life sound like an adventure."

"I see it as an adventure, a flight to the pinnacle. I'm glad that comes through."

"I like the sound of that, *a flight to the pinnacle*. Could that be our title?"

"Possibly. I was also thinking of something more straightforward, like *The Rocky Love Story*. Love Story, that's your hook. See what I mean?"

"That's a possibility, I suppose." But she doesn't like it, it sounds too simple, as if it neatly encapsulates a story which has already begun, evolved, and ended— past tense. "We'll find the right title later, we don't need to decide that now."

"Of course not, the title can wait."

"And so, John, *qu'esque tu veux avec moi?*"

"Sorry. I took Spanish in school."

She laughs. "Silly boy, it's nothing. What shall we do today?"

He takes his tiny tape recorder out of his pocket and sets it on the table between them. "Any time you're ready, I thought we could talk about how you got started in radio, your first big break, when you turned the corner from obscurity to—"

"Well, I was never actually obscure, you know."

"I realize that, what I meant was before you became a star."

"My columns were syndicated, I was well known when I was still in college."

"Absolutely."

"*The Mad Wife*, though, made me a celebrity."

"That's where we are now, that's what I need to know about."

"It's the most exciting part, isn't it?"

"The *most* exciting part. I can't wait to hear about it— whenever you're ready."

She knows what he's trying to tell her, and she knows that he's too professional to blatantly admit how much he yearns for her. She knows she will need to make the first move. So she slips her hands beneath the table cloth and slides it over his knee and slowly up along his thigh. He immediately begins to blush again. How *cute.*

"I'm ready," she says.

When Cat returns from her lunch break, she is surprised to find Rocky and John still at the table, still talking. He has his little tape recorder propped between them and he's leaning way back in his chair, while she is leaning forward, speaking into the machine. Cat tiptoes through the dining room and into the kitchen to leave some money on the counter for Annie, having been to the bank for petty cash. When she moves back through the dining room, she is aware of John's eyes on her. She turns to look at him and catches a tiny, crooked smile. Rocky, lost in telling her story, doesn't notice.

About twenty minutes later she sees a flash of silver bolt past her office— Rocky, no doubt, returning to her room. Then John appears at her door. His face is bright red. "I need your advice," he says, "if you have a minute."

"Sure." She gestures him inside.

He shuts the door behind him and turns to face her. Hesitating, he steps closer, paces back toward the door, returns to pass her desk, sits on the ottoman and buries his face in his hands.

"Uh oh," she says. "What happened?"

"Rocky is.... She seems to be.... I don't know how to say this."

Cat breaks into a smile. "Has she proposed yet?"

"She told you?"

"More or less. I hate to say this, but she thinks every man is madly in love with her."

"She put her hand on my leg. I nearly peed in my pants."

"I take it you controlled yourself."

"I pretended I had an itch. I moved back in my chair and scratched my butt." He shrugs. "I think she thought the itch was real. She just kept on flirting the whole time. I left my chair where it was, I just kept my distance."

"She won't back off, you know."

"She might, now. When I was leaving, she just stood there like some kind of teenager posted on the front porch, waiting for her kiss. I didn't know what to do. I mean, she's my boss essentially. I need this gig, this is an important project for me. I'm getting a royalty, you know?"

"So what did you do?"

"First I kissed her, but just a little peck on the cheek. Then I lied. I didn't have time to really think it through. I told her I was gay."

Cat bursts out laughing. "Well, that was courageous. Most men would rather die than say that."

"I'm not really gay, though."

"I'm sure you're not, but it wouldn't bother me if you were."

"But I'm not."

"I know you're not."

"But now she thinks I am."

"At least you're off the hook."

"It's just that now she'll tell people I'm gay."

"Forget it. She probably won't think much about it. She doesn't bother with people she can't use in some way. There's got to be something in it for her, like money or sex, otherwise you practically don't exist for her."

"What about you? You don't give her either, do you?" He smiles.

"No way. But I'm one of her slaves, she needs me, so she tries to be nice to me though she doesn't always succeed. Frankly, I don't even know why I'm still working here."

John digs into his pocket and takes out his tape recorder. "This is risky, but I like where we're going here. Do you mind?"

"It's not a good idea," Cat says cautiously. "I mean, see this answering machine? A person could access it and listen to whatever went on in this room."

"Does she?"

"I'm sure she doesn't know how, but she could do it, it could be done. What I'm trying to say is I'm not ready to lose my job yet. I have a credit card bill *this big*." She lifts her hands as if holding a beach ball.

"Okay, then how about after work? You probably have to get home, though. Are you the dinner person?"

"Dinner person?"

"My wife—ex-wife—and I used to have jobs. She made dinner and I did the dishes."

"Oh, well, I was the dishes person, but we broke up. It's been about a month. I don't know why I thought you knew."

"I'm sorry. It was mutual?"

"I'm not sure. I initiated it."

"That's better for you. It's worse to be the one who gets kicked out. My wife, she left me. It was bad. It's much better if you do the leaving."

Cat shrugs her shoulders, truncating the conversation; she can't explain her feelings, fraught as they are with contradictions.

John leans back. "Okay, so you don't have to get home for dinner. What if I take you out to dinner? I'll take you somewhere nice, if you'll agree to do the interview."

She hesitates. "So long as it's not a date."

"Not a date, absolutely not a date. Believe me, I don't date. Remember—I'm gay!"

She laughs. "Okay, I'll do it."

"I'll even come down to your neighborhood, how's that?"

"Very accommodating, but I'm not impressed. If you want me to talk, you *have* to make me happy, right?"

"Absolutely right."

As the afternoon passes, Cat anticipates her dinner with John. There is plenty she could tell him, dirt she could easily dish up, and it would all go into the memoirs. Or she could be discreet. Rocky hasn't done anything specifically to hurt her—not deliberately, anyway. Even the neglected pre-abortion phone message from Teddy was probably nothing. *Probably*. Except that nothing is really *nothing*. Cat knows as well as anyone that the biggest decisions can turn on a dime. What if she *had* called Teddy back that day? What if they had talked? Decided to see each other? *What might have changed*? For the past month, Cat has struggled to soldier on, despite the difficult emotional fallout from her abortion. It was the hardest choice of her life, probably the right choice, but more difficult than she would have imagined. Rocky, meanwhile, has been downright cold about it, devoid of sensitivity or under-standing, leading Cat to realize that this woman who fought for women's right to choose had no real idea what she was fighting for. It has grown impossible not to resent this woman and her daily litany of absurd demands.

The more Cat thinks about it, the more she realizes that she does not particularly wish to protect Rocky from her own self-aggrandizing other-annihilating personality, nor does she wish to be caught exposing it. Her impulse falls somewhere in between. She has her own life to worry about, and she isn't so deeply interested in Rocky's life that she'd want to actually betray her. Or is she? As soon as she thinks it, she wonders: betrayal of what? The myth of the famous Rocky Love? A myth spun out like a puff of cotton candy, replacing the substance of the real woman. Who *is* the real woman, Cat wonders as she shuts down the office for the evening. Rocky Love? Or Rochelle Libbon? Or neither? Or both?

What she can do for John, she decides, is put him in touch with the people who can help him find out: Rocky's husbands, lovers, lawyers, accountants and friends. Anyone and every-one Rocky herself has not already handed over. John can talk to them and puzzle it together himself.

They meet in the garden of a French restaurant on Tenth Street, just east of First Avenue, a pocket of overpriced elegance on a typically derelict East Village block. John's tape recorder stands like a centerpiece on the table, propped between the salt and pepper shakers.

"Let's start with the basics, details, like how long exactly have you been with Rocky?"

Cat notices that the voice John projects when the tape recorder is listening is deeper and mellower than when he's off stage. Yet he engages in this level of presentation, of pretending, without artifice; he's a natural, even when he's faking. In the candlelit twilight, his natural ability to connect cannily with each moment is immensely charming.

"About eight months."

"And what word would you use to describe the experience so far, generally?" He makes a rounded gesture with his hands as if to create an empty space for her to fill.

She has to think about it. One word. "Inconsistent, I guess."

"What do you mean by inconsistent?"

"You know, she *changes*. She's hot and cold. Smart and dumb. Sweet and mean." Cat reaches out and switches off the tape recorder. "John, off the record, you know she's out of her mind, don't you?"

"Of course. She was a loon back at the network. She's worse now, though. That's why this is a rise and fall story."

"Does she know that? That it's a rise and *fall* story?"

"I doubt it, but if she were halfway in touch with reality she'd realize it."

"And she wouldn't let you write a book."

"Exactly. Which is why I haven't shown her anything close to what the final draft will be."

"What about Charlie? Does he know what you're doing?"

"I think he does, but he doesn't ask; that way he doesn't have to lie to her. He must know. He also has to know that this could make her—and him, and me—a lot of money. People love feasting on the remains of celebrities."

"I feel kind of bad, though," Cat says, "because on the one hand she's paranoid about people betraying her, and it seems crazy, but then there really is a kind of conspiracy, isn't there?"

"If there is, then she laid the plans for it. And if I wasn't writing the book, it would be someone else. If it wasn't Charlie, it would be some other agent. If it wasn't you in the position to know what you know, telling me what you can, it would just be someone else. See? This isn't about us, it's about her. She wrote her own story, I'm only gathering it into words. Ready?"

Cat sees exactly what he means, and he's right. Rocky's life is her own creation; the rest of them have simply been swept into its current. Who is she, Cat, to withhold the facts? In that instant, her resolve to watch from the sidelines evaporates and she's in the game. He clicks the tape recorder back on.

"Rocky can be kind, warm, generous," Cat says directly at the microphone, "but she's self-absorbed to a fault. And the way she lies, it's borderline evil."

"Evil?"

"Well, kind of, in the sense that because she's so famous she doesn't really have to account for herself. And because she's rich she doesn't have to answer to anyone. Money is power, right? But fame is insanity if you don't hold yourself in reality, and trust me, she's *not* in reality. Personally I think she got too famous too fast. She has her own set of rules and she doesn't even know it. She has no idea that she uses people, or hurts people. And when someone's hurting her, she doesn't necessarily see that, either. It's creepy. She believes what she wants, regardless, and acts accordingly."

"So you see her as a narcissist?" John asks.

"I guess so. In a nutshell, yes. And because she's a so-called celebrity, she's allowed to get away with it. But in a funny way it's not all her fault, because everyone colludes with her, we goad her into it. We make people celebrities and we give them all these magical attributes and powers and after a while they come to believe they really deserve it. So in a way they're only doing what we want. They're doing their job."

"So you don't think she should be held accountable?"

"No, I think she should be. I think she has to be. I just think that we all help her to be the way she is, even though she possessed all the raw material to be that way."

"So she was born that way, and her fame just gave her the fertile ground for her narcissism to blossom?"

"You're really stuck on this narcissism thing, aren't you?"

He turns off the tape recorder. "I think that might be the key. I've been doing some reading on it and it fits her like a glove. Narcissists self-reference all the time. They put themselves in the middle of every situation. Everyone they come in contact with is seen solely through their own point-of-view. They expect their needs to be served at all times. And what you said about having her own rules? Well, that's textbook. They perceive the general rules as being not for them, but for everyone else. They really do think they're more special than the rest of us."

"But think about it, John, isn't that how she had the guts to do what she's done? I mean, she has this amazing charisma. She can stand in front of a TV camera, lying her pants off, acting like she's talking to her oldest friend. It's phenomenal. She does that at home, too. She treats us like we're her audience, with a kind of patronizing warmth, and then she gets on the phone and I hear her contradicting things she just told us. I mean, she lies to people, she really lies, and she has no idea she's doing it. It's like every time she says something she's saying it to a different audience, and she can invent a new reality and no one will know. I bet she always took license. I think being famous made it worse, but it's also what made her famous."

"Will you say that last part again?" He switches the tape recorder back on.

"Being famous made it worse, but it's also what made her famous. But the fame is what's driving her crazy, because she lost it, and it became her identity."

"A vicious cycle."

"You probably want details from me, right? Descriptions of real situations."

"Sure, but this is helping, too. You've got an interesting perspective on her character. It's good. I can use it."

A waitress comes over to take their orders. They have nearly finished their bottle of wine.

The dinner is delicious—when it finally arrives—worth the wait since the wait was full of the kind of talk that seems to put things in perspective. Q: Why is Rocky so narcissistic and deluded? A: It was her character from birth, intensified by fame. Q: Why is her life at once so full and so empty? A: Her glass is neither half-full nor half-empty, but too porous to hold mass. Q: Do they need to feel guilty for talking about her like this? A: No, because she is fulfilling her own promise, she is her own message, and they are nothing but the messengers.

After dinner, Cat feels warmly satisfied. Betrayal, like gossip, turns out to be good cheap fun. And John is an absorbing companion, the kind of man you might not fall in love with but whom you could grow to love. He is even attractive in this dim light, with wine soaking her brain.

"Want to go to my place for dessert?" she asks. "I made a linzertorte the other day."

"You made a linzertorte?"

She laughs; it does sound a little funny. "I did."

"I thought *he* was the cook."

"He was, but now I am."

"Are you sure you want me in your abode? What if I try to seduce you or something?"

She shrugs her shoulders. "Do you want to come over or not? I can make coffee."

"Do you have fresh brewed decaf?"

"Yup."

"Okay, you're on."

They walk down First Avenue and turn west up St. Mark's Place. Both sides of the street bustle with cheap restaurants, antique clothing stores and the overflowing booths of outdoor merchants. When they cross Second Avenue, Cat notices Zen Sushi and instantly recalls her lunch with Isabel. Her eyes flit left and up, to Isabel's window, which is dark. She remembers her cartoon, the one Isabel never sent back—she never even responded to Cat's letter—and feels a pinch of frustration. Just as she begins to will herself to push the memories and the feelings away, to return to her pleasant evening with John, Teddy and Isabel enter her frame of vision.

They walk together, past Zen Sushi, moving slowly in a vapor of intimacy. Cat stands still and concentrates on clamping down a chaos of emotion. She is peripherally aware of John stopping, turning, saying her name, watching her. She ignores him. Her attention is fixated on Teddy and Isabel, leaning into each other to link arms for a moment before walking up her front stoop. They disappear into her building. Cat stands there, watching, until Isabel's living room light comes on. And she stands there, staring at the yellow rectangle in the dirty white building, just staring.

"Uh oh," John says. He is right beside her now, sharing her cylinder of space—protecting her, she feels. "Was that the dinner person?"

She nods.

"With an uninvited guest, I take it."

Cat takes a deep breath and reels herself back to John. She looks at him, at his interested, attentive face ready to receive her confusion or pain or anger or whatever she needs to release. For a moment she feels that old comradeship of coupledom, that instantaneous buffer of constant availability. But he isn't hers and she isn't his, and she doesn't want him like that, anyway. The wine-haze evaporates from her brain as the insolent lights of St. Mark's Place awaken her.

They walk forward. "That was Isabel," Cat says, "the editor of *Freak*. Teddy introduced us. I didn't realize—"

"Say no more. Life sucks. Come with me." He holds an arm firmly around her waist and speeds her up the block, as if to remove her from enemy territory. He stops at a Korean market brimming with flowers, everything from tulips to African daisies, and disappears around the corner. Just watching him in action makes her feel a little better. When he reappears, he is cradling a bouquet of white roses wrapped in a cone of Mylar.

She says, "Thank you," before he even manages to deliver the bouquet into her arms. "Thank you," she says again. She lowers her face into the fragrant buds and begins to cry. His arms are around her instantly, and he just stands there, the perfect patient friend.

Finally, when she is calm enough, John takes her home. They say goodnight at her door with an understanding that a friendship has just begun to take form, a friendship better than romance, something simple and heartfelt and completely devoid of expectation. No linzertorte seductions tonight.

She goes straight to bed and lies awake for hours. When her body begins to ache from sleeplessness, she gets up to take a couple of aspirin. Then she lies back down again in the dark. Her mind is like a machine, grinding the same questions over and over, wearing down their surfaces, never finding answers.

Should she have given him another chance? Would things have improved between them? Was she wrong to insist Teddy leave? But his ambivalence, his half-baked commitment to her, was an unbearable slow-drip torture. *Could* she have endured it? Or did she do the right thing by demanding emotional fidelity from him? Was it even in her control? Why didn't he try harder to convince her they could work it out? Why didn't he *insist* they try? Had he wanted to be released from her?

Was it Isabel all along?

Was he already seeing Isabel before he moved out? Were they sleeping together? Even before Cat became pregnant?

Or maybe, Cat thinks—in a first for her, and it comes as a kind of revelation— *maybe, for once, I stood up for myself.*

Maybe for once she responded appropriately by sensing that something was wrong and stomping down her foot and saying *No, forget it, I have my limits.* Between Teddy at home— *Get a job* and *Be a serious cartoonist* and *Whatever you do don't expect too much of me, it's a tough juggle but you'll figure out how*—and Rocky at work—*coffee and copies and don't-think—*

round-the-clock someone's been telling her who and how to be. And she's been doing it, keeping still in a storm just like when she was a kid, careful not to upset an already dangerous imbalance.

Well, she thinks, awake in the middle of the night, maybe it's time to rock some boats. Or to let them rock themselves, stand back and see what happens.

"You're late," Rocky says. She is wearing her bathrobe and her face is puffy from sleep.

Cat looks at her watch. "Just a few minutes."

"You're late."

"I'm sorry." Cat tosses her purse on the floor, sits in her chair and folds her arms over her chest.

"You look different."

"Is something wrong, Rocky?"

"You shouldn't wear makeup, it doesn't suit you." Rocky shifts her weight to one hip, then the other.

"I didn't sleep," Cat begins to say, "and I thought I looked—"

"I've been waiting for you. I need you to get David on the phone."

"It's only five past ten, Rocky."

Rocky glares.

Cat spins around, flips through her Rolodex and dials. She puts the call through and Rocky takes it standing in front of her desk. When another call comes in, Cat has to run to the kitchen to answer it. By the time she gets there, the caller has hung up.

Annie is at the table, reading the newspaper and finishing her morning tea.

"What's with her today?" Cat asks.

"She tried calling Yves last night and he wasn't home. She left him a message and waited up half the night and he never called back."

"She left him a message at home? He's married!"

Annie shrugs. "She doesn't care."

"What about Larry? And did you happen to know that she's trying to seduce John Paglia?"

"She has no shame."

"She's such a—"

"Shush, honey. Take it easy, she might hear you."

"So what?" Cat deflates into one of the dining room chairs.

"You can't let her bother you when she gets crazy. Just wait and let it pass. Or decide it's time to get out."

The phone rings again. Cat rises to answer it. There is a long silence into which Cat asks, "Hello? Hello?"

Finally, just when she is about to hang up, a man's voice speaks. "Rock."

She snaps into her automatic answer. "No, this is her assistant, she's on another line. Can I give her a message?"

More silence.

"Hello?"

"Tell her I called."

"And you are ...?"

"Tell her it's her brother. Say her brother's trying to call her."

"She has your number?"

"I can't be reached." He hangs up.

When Cat passes on the message, Rocky says, "Which brother, for God's sake? I have three brothers. Which one?"

"I don't know, he didn't say."

"Why didn't you ask him?"

"Rocky, whatever's bothering you today, it's not my fault. I have my own problems and I'm not dumping them on you, am I?"

Rocky stares at her. "Your job is to help me, not the other way around. Do you understand that?"

"Yes, I understand that. I have always understood that. I'm sorry I didn't get his name, but he didn't give me a chance. He said he couldn't be reached and then he hung up. It was out of my hands."

* * *

Rocky marches down the hallway toward her study. If on better days Cat wasn't so good, then she would have been fired for that display of insolence. But she's got things under control, and there's too much to do now to make a transition to a new assistant. She's been a little too willful lately and that will have to stop. Ever since her boyfriend left her, she's obviously been jealous of Rocky's natural ability to attract men. The way she looked at John when she traipsed through the dining room during their lunch meeting yesterday—it could have melted butter.

She sits on her velvet couch with her cordless phone and dials.

"Leo!"

"Hey, Rock, how're you doing?"

"Did you just call me?"

"Nope. Why?"

"My secretary told me my brother called but she failed to mention which one."

"Ah, well, must have been Robby. Tell him hello for me, and send a kiss to Natalie and the kids."

"Sure. How are you?"

"Fine, but running out the door. Dinner soon?"

"Leo, when you're on your way out the door, you should screen your calls, but I'm glad you answered mine. Dinner soon. Ciao."

It is still early morning in California, and so she finds Robby at home, just out of the shower.

"Hello, brother, when your message said you couldn't be reached, I thought it was an awfully blatant metaphor to fall from the lips of a psychiatrist."

"I didn't leave a message."

"No? It wasn't Leo, either. But it was a message from my brother, it said that he couldn't be reached. Oh God, I'm starting to get a really weird feeling in the pit of my stomach."

"Nathan."

"But it's been so many years. Why would he be calling me now?"

"Rocky, he's been in New York for a few months."

"You've been in touch with him?"

"Not since he left California."

"Did you see him?"

"Listen, it's kind of delicate, but Nathan came to me for help. It was unorthodox, but he needed help and he said he wouldn't go to another doctor. And he had no money. I couldn't say no."

"How did he live? I don't understand."

"Natalie gave him some cash a few times; he wouldn't take it from me. It's a father thing. He kept calling me Dr. Robert, you know, like when we were kids. He's a mess, Rock. Be really careful not to misunderstand that."

"Nathan doesn't frighten me," she says. "He *needs* us. I hope he calls again."

"He's holding things inside that are explosive."

Nathan's body, his beautiful strong graceful sexual body, appears in her mind. She feels first stimulated, then ashamed, then guilty. "What did he tell you?"

"Not much, he mainly talked about Dad. He's tremendously angry about being sent away to school; he interprets it as a rejection from the family. He's still feeling bitter about it. I was already gone when that happened so it's hard for me to judge."

"I remember it. Nathan and Daddy had a *terrible* fight. Mom stayed out of it, but you know how she is; she kind of stood in the background and silently goaded Daddy on. Nathan didn't want to go. Then when he left, that was it, he was gone. Mom and Daddy never heard from him again." She pauses before delivering the next bit of information. "But I did, in New York. He stayed with me."

"Yes, he told me."

"He did?"

"He mentioned it. I take it he didn't stay long."

"About a month."

There is a silence for a moment, and Rocky is seized with fear that Robby knows about her forbidden night with Nathan. It was the most incredible experience of her life, a final taboo to break, a thrilling roller coaster ride for body and soul. But that is not how Dr. Robert Libbon, psychiatrist and big brother, would describe it. *Incest* would be the word he'd use. No, Rocky thinks, it was *love*. Nathan left in a rush the next morning, leaving her alone with the sensation that her heart had been ripped out, leaving her with a loneliness she has never been able to fill. It was her joy and her *secret* to fall in love with her brother. And her tragedy, and his, that he reacted with confusion, silence and flight. They haven't seen each other since. *Incest*. That cold, clinical, condemnatory word that has lurked in the back of her mind now slices into her consciousness. She pushes it away, rejecting judgment for truth, *her* truth, and listens carefully to the nuances in Robby's voice.

"You know, Nathan doesn't really say what he's thinking. He doesn't fill in the blanks. He just acts out his anger, which of course is dangerous behavior." He speaks with such conversational calm that she becomes convinced he has not been made privy to her secret, or read her thoughts, and she is flooded with relief.

"What should we do?" she asks.

"If he calls again, talk to him. I don't think he'd hurt anyone, the danger is really to himself."

"All right, I will. I'll try and help him if I can."

"Keep me posted."

"I will. Love to Natalie and the kids."

"You bet. Be good, sister."

"No way."

They share a chuckle before hanging up. She lays back and runs her hand across her breasts, remembering Nathan.

Chapter 12
The Rise and Fall of Rocky Love

Self-Reinvention

"*I* got married!"

"What?" Mabel said. "All by yourself?"

"I'm so happy, Mom. I wanted to tell you right away."

"Norman, pick up the other extension, it's your daughter, she has something to tell you."

"Rocky?"

"Hi Daddy. Guess what?"

"She says she got married again."

"To who?"

"To *what* we should ask."

"I didn't want to introduce you until I was sure."

"So, are you sure now?"

"He's Jewish, Mom, and he's a lawyer."

"Rocky, congratulations."

"Thanks, Daddy."

"What, he doesn't watch television? He never saw your show?"

"I'm taking a leave from the show, Mom."

"What's this?"

"Leave from the show?"

"But you *are* the show. Now I'm confused."

"I'll explain when I see you. Don't worry, everything's okay, I'm happy."

"Baby, what's his name, your husband?"

"Jason Barthoff."

"The lawyer who sued the bastard photographer for you?"

"I could whip that dirty photographer into a blintz! But what I want to know is what you were doing in Greece when you were twenty years old."

"Leave her alone, Mabel, our daughter is an accomplished woman now."

"Mom, Dad, come for dinner at our place. I already called Leo and he's coming. Robby's got a conference in New York that week and Natalie and the kids are joining him. It'll be a family reunion. Next Sunday, can you?"

"Of course we can."

"We'll have to check our calendar."

"We'll be there."

"We'll see."

Jason and Rochelle Love Barthoff lived in a three thousand square foot loft on Broome Street in SoHo. Jason had been on the Upper West Side, Rochelle had been on the Upper East Side, and moving down here had accomplished two things: it merged their homes, and suited their downgraded financial status which resulted from Rochelle's hiatus from television.

Charlie had fought for her—she had heard voices flying behind closed doors (he had thought they would remain calm if she stayed out of the room)—but the network men would not absorb the blow of what was perceived as adultery then understood to be a secret divorce and remarriage. Women who changed husbands were unfit role models for the viewing public. It was suggested that Rochelle take a leave of absence from the show. Charlie called it, "Murder, not suicide, baby. Murder. You're a fighter. You're gonna fight this one!" But to his surprise, she agreed to leave. She had hit against the network's limits with the *Playboy* incident and survived; another blow could devastate her. She had her reasons for backing off while her reputation was still basically intact. After all, she was Rocky Love, not Doris Day; the network would forgive her this alleged transgression as soon as they realized that the public already had. She would quit, temporarily, while she was still ahead, before the next ill wind swept the plain. Once all was calm in the land, again, she would return—heroic and welcomed.

The Love-Barthoff loft began as a huge open space with half-wall barriers for kitchen, bedroom and bathroom. Aside from the most basic fixtures—toilet and showerstall in the bathroom, sink, stove, and refrigerator in the kitchen—they had their living space transformed into a maze of open spaces and a few very private ones, with a high tech kitchen, three bathrooms and a maid's room. The front door opened onto a massive living room with huge windows and two skylights. Rochelle's overstuffed pastel furniture was interspersed with Jason's beige and white leather, and a few antiques bought by what Rochelle called "the joint estate." Exotic indoor trees loomed by the windows, and flowering cactuses dotted the sills. Jason loved plants. Rochelle's growing collection of erotic Oriental art, framed in gold-painted wood, decorated the white walls.

When they were settled into their new home, they decided to throw a house-warming party, which would also serve to introduce Jason to the Libbons.

"Will your family like me?" he asked.

She looked at her eager husband. How could they not like him with his curly brown hair, neatly trimmed beard, crisp white shirt, adorable blue suspenders and playful red bow tie? With his law degree, his kindness and his authority? And at last, her mother could claim triumph in the Jewish half of Rochelle's rogue soul.

"Perfect man," she said. "How about me?"

She was wearing a black mohair sweater-dress with a big red circle in the middle, a Zen bull's-eye, blazing sun.

"Beautiful."

She fluffed her hair with her fingers crammed with rings. Her hair had gone wild again, as in her youth, but she had kept the henna highlights and Lisa Long had styled it into a glamorous curly mop.

She said, "Mom'll throw barbs at you, so just expect it. She thinks I'm a slut."

Jason hugged Rochelle. "You're no slut, you're my wife."

She found his lips in his beard, like a rose blossom tucked into bramble. They kissed.

Within half an hour, everyone had arrived except Norman and Mabel. When they finally appeared, Mabel stood in the doorway in her mink coat, her arms dangling at her sides, one hand trailing a boxy black purse. "Ehem," she cleared her throat, announcing her arrival.

"Mom!" Rochelle greeted her. "Why don't you come in?"

"What's the rush?"

Norman walked past his wife, who had rooted herself in the doorway. He kissed Rochelle and shook his new son-in-law's hand.

"Welcome to our home," Jason said.

"Welcome to our family," Norman said.

Norman crossed the living room to greet Robby and Leo, who were seated across a low glass coffee table. Natalie, Robby's wife, came out of the bathroom with little Norman, a miniperson in denim overalls. He dashed straight to his grandma Mabel. She lifted him up and he nuzzled his face in her mink before squirming out of her arms and running off.

Robby and Natalie laughed. They had grown into a comfortable early mid-dle-age together, and had come to resemble each other as really close couples tend to. Robby's tall dark sturdy build had softened, with a dusting of gray in his hair and a paunch. And Natalie, who had always been the more innocuous of the pair, had become stronger and more self-assured. At the time little Norman, their third child, had been conceived—a "surprise," they said, not a "mistake"—she had been applying to graduate schools in psychology. But with news of a new baby, she shifted gears back to the idea that her family would be the center of her life for a while longer. It was as if she was patiently waiting for the next onion skin to slough off so she could finally discover her obscured potential. Leslie and Lisa, twelve-year-old identical bookends, sat together on the couch.

Jason took Norman's coat. Norman's salt-and-pepper hair had lost most of its pepper, and his face looked waxen and a little sad.

"I hear they don't even let old women into nice apartments like this," Norman said to Jason.

"Over fifty, it's against the law."

"Well," Norman said, "that's more food for us."

"So, I'm taking my time, so what? I'm invited to my only daughter's home to meet her husband—neither of which I've ever laid eyes on before—and I want to take it in slowly. I don't want any shocks. Why should an old woman open herself to disappointment?"

"Would you like something to drink, Mrs. Libbon?" Jason asked.

"What time is it?"

"Six-thirty."

"Then I'll have a little sherry."

Mabel fixated on a drawing of a man and a woman explicitly copulating amidst yards of flowing Oriental robes. She said, "My drink, please, then I'll die," and lunged into the room.

She headed for Leo, who was standing by one of the windows, and stretched up to kiss him. "My baby," she said. She pinched his check so his face distorted and his mustache arched like a caterpillar stretching its back.

"Let me take your coat, Mom."

She sighed, and in a movement of deflation, the mink coat slid off. Leo caught it.

"Just throw it on our bed," Jason said.

Our bed. Mabel looked at him, really took him in with her shrewd mother's *I've been around for a while so don't take me for a fool* look. "So," she said, "you're my son-in-law?"

Jason approached her with a small glass of sherry. "I have the honor, yes." He handed her the drink.

She smelled it before sipping.

"Don't worry, it isn't poisoned."

"You haven't been in prison? Well, *that's* good news."

"Of course I haven't been in prison." Jason raised his voice, unaware of what everyone else knew: Mabel was not hard of hearing; she was treating him to her signature so-called *welcome*. "I'm an attorney. I have a practice in midtown."

"My last son-in-law had a practice on Park Avenue. So? You're Jewish?"

"I am."

"Your parents?"

"They live in Connecticut. My father was an investor, but he retired last year."

"An inventor?"

"Investor."

"What did he invent?"

Rochelle rushed over with a tray of raw carrots, broccoli and cauliflower arranged in petals around a crystal bowl of sour cream dip. "I made this dip myself," she said.

Mabel took a carrot stick and plunged it into the dip. "Not bad."

Leo joined them, and took a stalk of broccoli, which he ate plain.

Mabel's eyes focused on the red circle on Rochelle's sweater. Then the eyes traveled to the breasts, the face, the hands. Mabel looked right at Rochelle and nodded. "Stay off the salt," she said. "When are you due?"

Rochelle blushed.

Leo said, "Really?"

Jason said, "August third."

"Congratulations," Mabel said to Jason. "So long as it looks a little like you, you shouldn't worry."

* * *

Parker Love Barthoff was born earlier than expected, on July 5th, weighing in at eight pounds and three ounces. Everyone agreed he looked like Rochelle but with Jason's eyes and nose except for the very tip, where it curled down like Rochelle's. His head was covered in downy black hair which swirled into a tiny cowlick at the back.

Parker's room in the loft was decorated with mobiles, stenciled bears and ducks trotting across the walls, sky blue curtains that joined to reveal a hugely smiling clown face, and hundreds of stuffed animals and toys that had poured in from friends, colleagues of Jason's and fans of Rochelle's.

She loved motherhood, loved this little baby who looked like her, loved the extra attention he gathered to their lives. For the first few months, Rochelle reveled in the novelty of motherhood and managed to bond with her baby despite an army of household help.

At the helm of the domestic corps was Nancy McGuire, a born-and-bred New Englander with professional training in childcare. She was plump, maternal, trustworthy and consistently even-tempered, with a flush in her face as if perpetually embarrassed. That she dressed in corduroy skirts, flat shoes and cotton man-tailored blouses suited Rochelle perfectly, as the last thing she wanted was a feminine female—competition—living in her home. Nancy's short brown hair was barbered, not styled. There was nothing vain about Nancy McGuire. She selflessly cared for the family and the household, supervising cleaners, caterers and delivery people as they came and went.

Nancy lived with them in the loft during the week, and bundled Parker up every Friday for the three hour trip to their country house in Amagansett, Long Island—a big old wooden beach house beaten gray by years of sun and salt air. Nancy moved their lives smoothly in and out of both residences, keeping kitchens stocked, laundry sorted, baby fed and clean. She was off every second weekend and never complained about not having enough time to herself.

Rochelle grew acutely aware of how much her life had changed. Less than a decade ago, newly married to Bobby, her days had been slow and empty. Her restlessness and the ensuing search had led her in loops to here, to now. Though she was still young, she was old enough to look back and see clearly the highs of her ups and how the lows of her downs always propelled her up again. In three decades she had been Rochelle Libbon and Rodney Parker and Rocky Love. She was a wife (again) and a mother. She had accomplished so much—more than most people ever did—and now it was time to begin again, to swing up, to reinvent herself bigger and better than ever. She knew, as a fact, that she was capable of having everything: her wonderful husband, her beautiful child, and a new wave of success. She felt as confident as ever as she set herself in motion.

She began by setting up an office in the loft. It was a bright room, compact, with an L-shaped desk built against the wall, shiny new file cabinets, and her favorite purple and black striped chair. Framed awards hung on the walls as reminders and motivators. New ideas started bubbling up—and one caught hold.

Rochelle had thought it would take longer to find the route to her comeback, but here it was, in a nutshell: A new show called *Mother Love* for working women who had forfeited career for family. The idea hounded her until she had to work on it; she needed to be in the world, much as she loved her new family. But she would have to work hard to engineer her return to shore through hostile waters. The network's reaction to her divorce from Bobby had been severe ... but nothing a good publicist couldn't soften, especially now that she was a mother. Rochelle hired one, and the spin began.

While doing interviews, and posing with Parker for photo shoots, she also spent time outlining her concept for the new show. She had never before produced a show herself, and she was surprised at how time-consuming it was to develop an idea. The research alone ate up months. She hired a new assistant, Betsy, who was able to help with rudimentary secretarial duties but turned out to be weak in more demanding areas. Too busy to start a new search for a more competent assistant, Rochelle decided to make do. The Rocky Love machine was back in action.

She spoke frequently with Charlie, who would do the final pitch to the network. He advised her that it would bolster her chances if she could stir the waters of "the motherhood in society thing" and suggested she try the lecture circuit.

Her first appearance was on a panel sponsored by the National Organization for Women to discuss the "Promise of the Eighties" for working women with families. So many of the working women of the seventies had had children that the question of how to do both—work and mother—was high on the list of the public agenda. The discussion took place at Columbia University and Rochelle was one of five women to sit on the panel. Women and men crowded the audience and there were many questions. The press came. Clearly, motherhood had become politicized, and Rochelle knew that once she had enough exposure, the network would sign her up.

Her next stop was Washington, D.C. to address "Working Motherhood" at a lecture sponsored by Women for Equal Access, the lobbying organization Reebah had gone to Washington to direct. Rochelle was eager to see her old friend; it had been years, and much had happened in both their lives since the notoriety of *Mad Women* catapulted them off in different directions.

Reebah had become an established voice in the women's movement, *The Choice* had become a landmark book and her two subsequent books had continued to define the feminist horizon socially, ethically, legally. Reebah had a vision for the betterment of all people. She had told Rochelle, on the phone, that her next book was to be a biography of a black poet who had lived in poverty and raised six children alone. She said that this life of a black woman artist would reach more people and tell a truth more baldly and effectively than her previous books which were academically oriented. She said she saw society backsliding on issues of women and people of color, and that she felt a responsibility to turn up the volume on her voice.

On the airplane, heading south to D.C., Rochelle had the idea to bring Reebah on as co-host of *Mother Love*. It struck her as perfect, a neatly wrapped coup for the network, a shoe-in to the top of the ratings.

She hurried along the corridors at Dulles airport, excited, searching for Reebah as she headed toward the baggage area. As Rochelle waited for her suitcase to loop toward her, she saw a man in a black suit, standing by a group of people, holding a sign with her name on it—R. Barthoff—and searching faces blankly for a response. Reebah must have sent him, and had been thoughtful enough to give her married name. If the sign had said Rocky Love, people would have chased her for autographs; not that she would have minded the attention, but it was more dignified to pretend not to care. When a passing woman did a double-take, Rochelle smiled, fluffed her hair and turned away

The hired driver took Rochelle to an office building with instructions that she should go to the fifteenth floor. The elevator door opened to a drab hallway with a small roster on the wall on which the room number for Women for Equal Access—WEA—was listed.

As soon as she turned the corner, she heard the hum of activity from the WEA office. The door was slightly ajar. She pushed it open and found a room with two women and a young man working at old metal desks crammed together. She heard Reebah's voice coming through a door to the left.

One of the young women looked up and smiled. "Hi, you must be Reebah's friend."

Rochelle nodded. She was aware that the woman had not recognized her, or had pretended not to. She reminded herself that not everyone watched television.

"Reeb's in there." The young woman lifted her chin toward the open door. Rochelle followed the sound of Reebah's voice, rich and energetic, into the inner office.

Reebah sat behind a large wooden desk, an old government issue clunker. She was on the phone, listening, and when she saw Rochelle in the doorway she smiled hugely and waved her in.

Rochelle sat in a chair opposite the desk and took in the beautiful sight of her old friend. Her face had a new round shape and she seemed slightly heavier. Her skin appeared softer, less glistening, than in the past. She had cut her hair so now it rose only an inch or so from her head. She was wearing a loose red dress and gold hoop earrings. As always, she wore no makeup. In contrast, Rochelle was suddenly aware of her own highly arranged appearance. Over the years, as her pockets deepened and she learned she had something called an *image*, she had gradually come to preen her looks. The wiry mass of hair had given way to the softer curls of a permanent and the metallic red hue of a henna rinse. Her fingernails had been manicured professionally, ever since her television days, and she selected colors to complement a wardrobe that was expensive and more complicated than ever. Accessories now matched. Shoes were discarded when noticeably scuffed. She looked as successful and comfortable as she was. Yet Reebah—who was at least as successful and well known as Rochelle, though in a different milieu—carried her beauty from within, as always. And as always, Rochelle was impressed by her old friend's strength, her straightforward acceptance of herself. In a way, Reebah was the woman Rochelle had always talked about on the air when she described the goal we could all reach through knowing ourselves: the goal of self-love and acceptance, confidence, intelligence, strength and accomplishment.

Reebah hung up the phone. "Rocky!" She pushed herself away from the desk and stood, and Rochelle could see now that her friend was four or five months pregnant.

They came toward each other around the desk and hugged. Then Rochelle put her hand on Reebah's belly and said, "Why didn't you tell me?"

"Thought I'd surprise you. Anyway, I didn't want to get into the whole story on the phone."

Rochelle nodded. Of course. Reebah wasn't married.

"Sorry I couldn't meet you, something came up and I had to deal with it."

"You've got them working late tonight."

"Oh, we work late every night, it's an uphill run. Come on, let's get outta here, I want to take you home."

Home was a large, comfortably furnished apartment off Dupont Circle. Reebah set about making pasta, a fresh tomato sauce and salad. Rochelle sat at the counter and sipped a glass of white wine.

"The father is a wonderful man," Reebah explained. "He's kind and he's successful and I love him. But I don't want to marry him. He'd take me over, I can see that in him, and I know I could never abide a possessive man. So, I thought it over and decided I wanted to have this child and I wanted to be single. I made the decision that I would have both. It's my way. I feel good about it. And let's face it, I've done well, I can afford it. I'm going to be the greatest single mother on earth and this kid's daddy is going to be there. He already is."

"It never occurred to me," Rochelle said, "to do it alone."

"You were already married."

"No, actually, I was pregnant when I married Jason."

"Well, I guess it's my turn to break some rules, huh?"

"Tell me about your work," Rochelle said.

Reebah stirred the sauce. "You know, I love it, but I can see that things have really changed. It's like the gains we made in the early seventies are stuck. I'm on the phone a lot, talking to a little of everyone, and I read a lot and my staff reads a lot, and we see a trend in the other direction. Backward. It's scary."

"But you're still at it. I'm proud of you, Reebah."

"Well, thanks. And look at you, turning out a lot *nicer* than anyone expected."

"I think that's about the worst thing anyone ever said about me."

"No offense, honey, but you're lookin' awfully good."

"I have an image to keep up, remember?" Rochelle laughed.

"Right. TV."

"You know, Reeb, on the flight down, I had a great idea for the show I'm developing. I told you about it on the phone."

"I remember. *Mother Love*."

"Picture it: you and me, co-hosting, like in the *Mad Women* days but now, older, wiser. And your having a baby is perfect."

Reebah shakes her head. "There are two reasons I can think of right now that it would not work."

"That was quick."

"Just listen, Rocky. First, no television network would have a single mother, a black single mother, hosting a whitebread morning show. And second, to be honest, I really think it's a mistake to focus on the motherhood issues. I mean, one of the problems for women has been getting lost in motherhood. It took some doing to start getting women out into the work force and feeling comfortable admitting we liked it. It was a bitch getting abortion legalized again. And we haven't exactly got the Equal Rights Amendment fixed in place yet. That stuff's real important to me. I couldn't lead women back to the kitchen any more than I could lead my people back to the cotton fields. It would be a mistake. I'm more interested now in getting legislation passed to close the pay gap than getting stuck on day care. Day care's important, but pay equity is more at the heart of a woman's ability to pay for that day care for her child when she's out earning that equal dollar."

Rochelle sipped her wine. She felt, surprisingly, lectured. "Well, you don't need to lobby me."

Reebah's eyes slid to look at Rochelle, sitting on the stool. "Are you sure? I mean, when you thought up this new show, why didn't any of this occur to you?"

Rochelle shrugged. "I feel my new show will have a compelling format for what people are concerned with today. Today, Reebah."

"Yeah, today. It's starting to look kinda grim from where I sit."

The next night, standing at an illuminated podium in a dark auditorium filled with an invited audience who had come to hear her speak, Rochelle turned and caught a glimpse of Reebah standing in the wings. Her arms were folded over her swollen belly, and she watched Rochelle with her face still and pensive, almost— could it be?—wary.

"*L*arry and I don't have sex," Rocky says. "We hold each other and have *cosmic* sex, do you know what I mean?"

Cat nods. Her desk is piled with papers: notes, to-do lists, people to call back, letters to type. Nothing cosmic in *her* days, no sex her in *her* nights; just loneliness and cartoons. Her *Legends* strips have been taking shape on the drawing board, as she scrapes her soul for material every night after dinner ... just as she had planned when she took this job, but with a higher personal price than she had imagined. When she doesn't have energy for interior excavation, she sharpens her pencil on *Max & Min* in which she gleefully dissects Celebrityville. She has learned that humor is wrought of anger and frustration. Crappy trade-off, but artistically effective.

"Nothing can touch that kind of love," Rocky says.

Cat's fingers whiz across the keyboard. She has work to do and speeds up her typing, but Rocky doesn't take the hint.

"Do you know that Andrea Dworkin says intercourse is an act of violence against women?"

Cat stops typing, faces her boss, and asks, "Do you agree?" Personally, she finds the sentiment too stark. She thinks that love cuts just as deeply between the sexes as hatred.

Rocky gets that glazed pop-eyed look—space traveling again. "Larry has guaranteed me multiple orgasms without penetration."

"Well, if it works for you ..." Luckily the phone rings, cutting Cat off just as the clichés really begin to flow. Her hand lurches for the receiver, lifts it, hits the bleeping red button. "Rocky Love's office," she answers in her best melodious greeting.

"Is she there?" That voice; Cat recognizes it immediately.

Holding her hand over the mouthpiece, she whispers, "It's your brother again."

Rocky hurries to take the call in her bedroom. Moments later, her laughter fills the hall.

"Where are you?"

"Somewhere. Here."

"You're in New York, aren't you?"

"That's not why I called."

"Why didn't you leave a number when you called me before?"

"Why are you asking me so many questions?"

"Because I miss you. I want to see you. *Please* don't hang up. Nathan, you're an uncle, did you know that?"

"Leslie and Lisa, a matched set, Uncle Nathan Uncle Nathan! And little Norman, Dokta Little Norman he thinks that's so funny he doesn't know what I mean but he will one day one day he will."

"Yes, you know Robby's kids, of course."

"What does that mean, *of course*?"

"Nothing."

"You been talking to him? Smart sister, so smart."

"No, I haven't. His kids are older, that's what I meant. Nathan, what about Parker, my son?"

"What about him?"

"Aren't you interested in meeting him? He looks just like me."

"Maybe, maybe."

"Would you like to come over for dinner?"

Silence.

"Or I could go to you."

"There's nowhere to go."

"I'll visit you where you live."

"I just want to talk."

"All right, let's talk. Was there something special?"

"No."

"Nathan, don't disappear again, let's stay together—"

"Rock Rock Rock."

"I love you, Nathan. I've always loved you."

"I can't."

"Do you need money?"

More silence.

"Tell me where you are. I'll come to you."

"No!"

"Why did you call me?"

"Because I wanted to talk to you."

"Give me your number so I can call you, too."

"I have to go."

"Nathan, promise to call me again. *Promise.*"

Click. Silence. And the sharpest coil of loneliness she has ever felt.

She throws off her caftan, gets in the shower and prepares for her lunch date with Larry, chanting ROCKY LOVE ROCKY LOVE ROCKY LOVE in the powerbase of her silent mind. Her name empowers her and she begins to feel better. What is this hold Nathan has on her? She must take control; she has to forget. She hopes her date with Larry will help.

An hour later, a traffic jam on Fifth Avenue forces her out of her taxi into the hot afternoon. She walks along 57th Street in her black leather miniskirt and jacket, black fishnets and ankle boots, her bronzy hair wild at her shoulders. A long strand of pearls swings at her strategically revealed cleavage. She lifts her chin and does not even flinch when a nasty beggar approaches her. ROCKY LOVE ROCKY LOVE ROCKY LOVE. They are ghosts, these people, soulless ghosts sent to haunt her. She believes she has been blessed, gifted, protected by the Great Goddess, deliberately coddled, chosen. *The poor*, as she thinks of them, the huddled hungry masses have been likewise deliberately forgotten, and it is neither her fault nor her responsibility to raise them from the near-dead.

She feels sexy in her fishnets and stabs at the pavement with her sharp high heels. Onward. The revolving door of the Russian Tea Room receives her, and she enters the royal red and golden room like a movie queen: chin up, chest forward, proud.

The maitre d', a small neat man, flashes a stock smile when he sees her. He checks the reservation book. "Yes," he says briskly. "Please follow me."

Her heart beats rapidly as he leads her farther from the central area to a small table against the wall.

The bastard. Why has he shunted her off to the side? ROCKY LOVE. Doesn't he know who she is? She waves to a movie director and star seated toward the middle of the room. He raises his chin, acknowledging her. Nearby is a table of five, and Rocky recognizes a journalist who wrote an early rave for her radio show, the *Mad Wife*. He doesn't see her. She adjusts her chair, uncrosses and recrosses her legs.

Larry is late. She hates this. She is hungry and would like to eat a roll, but it will ruin her lipstick. She smiles at a gossip columnist, seated smack dab in the middle of the room at a round table, with the wife of a financier and an interior decorator who is a multimillionaire.

"Get up," Larry says. He's standing next to the table in a navy double-breasted suit with shiny brass buttons. His red tie dances with white polka dots.

"You look like the fourth of July, darling," she says.

"We're being seated over there." He points to a small square table near the gossip columnist.

"No," she whispers. "The bitch will print it."

"She'll print this, too. Come on."

Rocky rises and follows Larry to the other table, center stage. People nod, wave, smile. Rocky does her best celebrity swagger. *Just wait until they read my memoirs, it'll show them who I am, someone to reckon with*. ROCKY LOVE. She can hardly be patient enough to....

"Sit," Larry says. He snaps his fingers by her face. "Rocky, *have a seat*."

Lunch doesn't help, after all, so when he invites her back to his apartment she immediately agrees. How *could* she feel self-affirmed after that scene with the maitre d' and all those people watching her? Maybe this time Larry will be able to have an erection. It doesn't matter, she tells herself. She'll take whatever he can give her, even if it's just a good laugh. Anything to snap her out of this funk.

He lives in a two-bedroom penthouse decorated in bachelor shades of eggplant and maroon. Puckered leather couches and polished walnut tables give the living room a cozy winter feel, even in summer. In his bedroom, a round bed sits beneath a ceiling mirror—*high hopes.* A large window overlooks the East River which today sparkles under a potent noon sun.

They undress without speaking, as is their habit.

Larry sits naked on the bed, crosslegged and stomachy like a balding hairy-chested Buddha. Rocky wears a black lace bodysuit with a split crotch (which she carried with her in her purse, just in case) and dares him to use it though she knows he won't. Can't. She's had him in her mouth for a full minute and still he's limp and small.

He pushes her away and she tumbles to her side.

"I want to tell you a story," he says, "about my childhood. Did you know I was once a child?"

"It's hard to believe," she says. She'd rather hear a story, anyway, than coax him fruitlessly.

"I tell you this in all confidence," he says. "I'm going to write about it some day. It's been on my mind a lot lately. I want to share it with you, as a friend."

"You *know* you have my confidence."

Staring at himself in the ceiling mirror, he beings. "When I was fifteen, I saw my mother one day in her room, alone. My father had a mistress, and we all knew. Mommy was a young woman, thirty-five, and Pop hadn't slept in their bed for a year. I went to ask her a question about my homework one night after dinner. Her bedroom door was closed, but not locked, and I pushed it open without knocking. Mommy was lying on the bed with her housedress on—it was pale blue, with buttons up the front, almost like a uniform—and she was still wearing her flowered apron. She was crying. I stood there and she cried and looked right at me but she didn't say anything. She just kept looking at me. Then she nodded. When she nodded, it meant yes, come in. Her pain excited me. I had an erection. At the time, I thought she sensed my excitement and was inviting me in to...." He stops talking, stares up into his own eyes. "I actually believed my mother *wanted* me. That's when I knew I *wanted* her."

"You're making this up," Rocky says.

Larry shakes his head. "No, it's true. This is my deepest secret and you should be honored I'm telling you."

"I am. Go on."

"Ever since then, in my fantasies, the woman I fuck is my mother."

"Larry! You're shocking *me* and I thought I was shock-proof! What happened to her?"

"She died a year later, on the street. Her appendix burst and she didn't tell anyone about the pain. It was morning. She went out to sweep the sidewalk in front of our house, and dropped. I have always been convinced my fantasies killed her. I have been unable to have ... normal sexual relations ... ever since."

Rocky strokes his limp, hairless hand, which is as fragile and soft as a child's. She joins him in staring at the mirror—staring at herself—appalled, excited, memorizing each detail of his story. So, Larry has fantasized about incest. (*She* has actually experienced it.) What a fool he is, she thinks, sharing his dark secret with a woman he continually fails to satisfy. Is this how he deepens intimacy in a relationship he can't actually consummate? She feels a spasm of jealousy, wondering if he has told this story to other women. The thought makes her grow wet between her legs.

She shifts her gaze to his mirror-eyes. "What did your father do after your mother died?"

"He married his shiksa mistress. And then he cheated on her, too."

They laugh together, buckling into a hug.

It's so nice and quiet when Rocky is gone, a state of solitary independence Cat has begun to appreciate more and more. She feels comfortable, almost serene, in her air-conditioned bubble suspended over the hot city streets. She can see the oily shivering heat in the air, hovering over the treetops, whose deep summer green has turned the park into an oasis. She's getting better at not letting Rocky's angst spill into her. Like this morning, when the long-lost brother called. As Rocky's bellowing laughter turned into shrieks of frustration, Cat remained concealed in her office, half listening, half working, not caring either way. When Rocky streaked past her in a black leather skirt suit, Cat didn't warn her how hot it was outside, knowing that an implication that the outfit was anything but perfect would be followed by a storm of insecurity.

At lunchtime, it's too hot to go out. Cat decides that with Rocky gone it could be relaxing to take a break in the cool indoors. She goes to the kitchen, makes herself a sandwich, pours a glass of orange juice and sets herself up at the oval table with the newspaper. Annie joins her with a glass of iced tea.

After a few minutes, just as Cat is reading the last headline on the front page, Annie whispers, "I seen bruises on her, on the backs of her legs."

"Rocky?"

Annie nods. She wears the grim expression Cat knows is reserved for the most serious topics.

"Does she bruise easily?"

"Well, I never seen bruises like this before."

"I don't understand."

Annie stands, tugs down her yellow sweater. She has a dare look on her face. "When's she comin' home?"

"About four-thirty, for Serena. They have a healing session." Cat lets a grin pull across her face.

"Come on, lemme show you somethin.'"

Cat follows Annie through the living room and down the hall to Rocky's bedroom. "I don't know what to make of this," Annie says, opening the bedroom door. "It scares me, I'll tell you that." Annie goes to Rocky's dresser, and from a tiny lacquered box extracts a key. She bends down and unlocks the padlock on the old trunk on the floor. Dark and heavy, with bands of rusted metal, it looks like something retrieved from a sunken ship. Annie heaves open the top. It is filled with menacing things: black silk, red garters, leather straps, whips, handcuffs.

Cat stares into the chest, stunned. "What is all this?"

Annie's pale blue eyes are wide and bright. "Honey, you tell me."

"She wrote some notes for a lecture on women and masochism, and there was something in there about the extremes of love and sado-masochism, but I never thought—"

"She's been thinkin' about it? Then she's been livin' it." Annie nods her head once, decisively, punctuating her statement.

"But who with?" Cat says. "It couldn't be Larry."

"You work for her long enough, you'll believe anything." Annie lowers the heavy lid and the two women retreat to the dining room. They sit at the table and eat Lorna Doone cookies in silence.

Finally Cat returns to her office, feeling lethargic and confused, and plunks herself down at her desk. She doesn't know how to understand this new information about Rocky. Cat knew her boss was neurotic, compulsive and narcissistic as well as smart, brave and spaced-out. She is full of contradictions and paradoxes: a feminist who loves lingerie and spike heels, a mother who loves her child yet neglects him, a controlling boss who leaves you alone to work, a woman who craves love from men yet distrusts them, who has the means to be independent yet believes she needs a man to survive. Now this: feather boas and leather straps and steel shackles and heavy chains and spiked cuffs and fringed whips. It terrifies Cat to think that Rocky might actually play with these accessories of pain.

Cat cannot focus on her work; her mind has turned to violence.

And she wonders: is Rocky's violence as cosmic as her love? Is it just as much an abstraction, a wish, a hope, a delusion? For a moment she thinks that if Rocky loses hold, she, Cat, will lose her job before she has finished paying her debts, and then she'll be back at square one, alone *and* broke. Then the absurdity of that thought takes her to the next: that she who has so little will be fine no matter what, while Rocky who has so much may not.

Cat feels a headache coming on.

She wishes she could forget what she saw, unlearn what she now knows, chalk it up to a celebrity run amok—nothing a good publicist couldn't solve. But she can't. It's too late. And why won't anyone just tell the truth about what's hidden in our trunks, proverbial and otherwise? Why can't *she*?

She realizes she has a decision to make: whether or not to call John and tell him about her new discovery. It would certainly spice up the book. It's tempting, but she's already told him too much, and once the fun of that dinner wore off she began to feel a little dirty. Maybe it's not too late to redeem her dignity and go back to being neutral. She decides to sleep on it and see what tomorrow brings.

The next morning, Cat arrives at her office to find Rocky standing at the desk, speaking French and laughing into the office phone. When she hangs up, she announces, "Yves is coming! We need to make some plans."

Cat takes a pad and a pen and follows Rocky down the hall, her infamous hungry has-been hips swaying beneath her caftan. When she swings open her study door, Cat is surprised by a big poster that wasn't on the wall yesterday: Rocky Love's smiling face, many years younger, above the bright red legend *The MAD WIFE talks ... and listens*. The poster-face, enlarged and up-close, looks young, on the verge of laughter. The sprightliness of her poster-smile is a striking contrast to the complexity of her expressions now. Cat sits down across from Rocky, who is crosslegged and bloated on the velvet couch, and holds her pen above her pad—speechless, silent, ready.

"I'll need an appointment with Lisa Long for this afternoon, cut and henna. If she can't fit me in today, then Monday. Book a room for Yves at the Paramount Hotel from Tuesday to Friday. No one should know he's coming. Larry cannot know about this. Do you understand?"

Cat nods.

"Tell no one."

"Okay."

"Nothing excites me more than the thought of getting fucked by Yves."

Cat almost notes that, too, but catches herself.

"Last item: call Larry and tell him I love him. Just to throw him off the scent."

Cat pretends to jot down that instruction, but instead doodles an angry gnome with a polka-dot scalp, a limp penis, and a whip. She hugs her pad against her chest to hide the drawing and asks, "Is that all?"

But Rocky has already tuned her out, so she returns to her office to get started.

"So sweet," Yves coos in Rocky's ear, alone in the elevator at the Paramount Hotel. She runs a hand down his belly and whispers, "Let's stay in and order room service, no?"

"Ah, you awe eencwedible. But please to see New Yochk."

"Tomorrow night," she says, stroking the crotch of his pants, feeling him grow and harden. Not-so-smart but always good-to-go, just as she thought when she first spotted him at that cocktail party in Paris. Married, but who cares? He is reliably great in bed, or bath, or boat, or elevator, or anywhere. As she changes his mind about going out to dinner tonight, his lips part, revealing long teeth and a middle gap. He blushes to his hairline.

His hotel room is large, clean and comfortable. They order champagne, gravlocks, caviar, sour cream, pumpernickel bread and *tartes au pommes*, which they eat in the Jacuzzi. Rocky leans back, submerged to her nipples, her large breasts splayed against her ribs and magnified under water. She knows her breasts fascinate Yves; their size has always captured the attention of men. His body is covered with frizzes of curly gray-brown hair that skim the surface of the water as he stretches out beside her. Except for his round belly, his body is pleasantly taut.

Dinner waits on a tray next to the tub. He leans over the edge, prepares a slice of bread and gravlocks and sprays it with juice from a wedge of lemon. She devours it in two big bites. He laughs, then crams a spoonful of caviar into his mouth. They become abandoned, shoving food at each other, half of which drops into the tub. Tiny black curds of caviar bob on the churning water. Capers sink. Sour cream dissipates, turning the water milky white.

In the morning, Yves keeps the appointment that justified, to his wife, this visit to New York. Rocky walks up Madison Avenue in the dazzling blue-skied warmth, stopping to gaze in store windows without really looking. She marvels at how good Yves makes her feel. There is a bounce in her step today and she feels almost young again. It's been too long since the glory days of her youth.

Standing in front of a shoe store, staring at her reflection in the glass, a familiar voice comes from behind.

"Hello there!" Connie's reflection, carrying a large shopping bag, comes into focus beside her own.

"Darling!" Rocky turns around and kisses her friend. "I've been meaning to call you. I've just been so busy."

"Aren't we all? I've been out running errands. Isn't this a gorgeous day?"

"Yves is here."

"Yves from Paris? Last summer Yves?"

Rocky smiles hugely. "That man sure knows how to—"

Connie shushes her. "Rocky, we're in public."

"I wish I could roll Yves and Larry into one man. With Yves's cock and Larry's brain, he'd be the perfect lover."

They walk slowly uptown, as Connie says, "I saw Larry, by the way. Rick took me to an AIDS research fundraiser at the Waldorf, and Larry was there. He has a great stand-up routine."

"He did it for me once, naked," Rocky says. "Was he with someone?"

"I don't know, we only spoke for a minute. He said he'd invited you."

"I told him I was busy wining and dining a producer from L.A." She laughs. Connie shakes her head, and Rocky retaliates for what she regards as the innate judgment in that, with: "How is Rick's wife?"

"It's not the same," Connie says. "They have been married for years, they have children, and I understand why he doesn't want to walk out on her. What's your incentive for stringing poor Larry along? Why not just let him move on?"

"*Poor* Larry? Have you ever known an impotent pervert—"

"Shhh. He's my *friend.*"

"Larry ain't no saint," Rocky says, bouncing along. "I adore him, but let's face it, he can't get it up and I'm horny."

"Please," Connie whispers.

Rocky shouts: "Horny!"

Connie freezes, her face flushes, then she breaks into a spontaneous smile. Rocky believes her friend vicariously enjoys her raunchy pronouncements. Everyone does; it's what turned Rochelle Libbon into Rocky Love and made her a star. She winds her arm through Connie's and pulls her along. "I'm taking you to lunch," she says, "and giving you every filthy detail about last night and tonight."

"Tonight? How could you know about that?"

"Hopes and dreams."

Cat sits in her cool-conditioned office in the sky, wishing it were lunchtime already—she's dying to go out and walk—but Rocky has left her a heap of typing. More raw material for the memoirs. As her fingers play the keyboard, a sensation of recognition pings through her mind. Rocky has sketched an affair with a gnome-like cosmic asexual man, a famous playwright, whose Oedipal fantasies make it impossible to consummate a relationship with a woman. It is obviously Larry Drumm.

After a while, Rocky buzzes the intercom to issue a few directives, ending with, "Did you type my pages?

"I'm almost finished ... but Rocky," Cat blurts out, "is it true about Larry? It seems kind of risky to ask John to put that in your book." As soon as she's said it, she wishes she hadn't. What was the point? Obviously it's a bad idea for Rocky to spill Larry's beans in her memoir.

"Fax John those pages right away," Rocky tells her. "And messenger a copy to Connie. She has excellent judgment."

Meaning that Cat's own judgment is flawed. Well, if Rocky wants to publicize Larry's private angst—with or without Connie's or anyone else's approval—then let her. She'll only hang herself in the end.

An hour later, Cat has finished the typing, faxed the pages, made the copy, called the messenger, typed two letters, made one phone call and answered four.

Rocky appears in the doorway. "Da da! How do I look?"

Cat swivels around in her chair. Rocky is wearing a black silk jumpsuit with a spangled silver belt and black lace-up boots with spike heels. She looks bloated, her skin is ashen and there are dark swaths beneath her eyes.

"Terrific," Cat says, and spins back to face the computer.

"You made the reservation?"

"Yup—Humbert's at seven o'clock."

"Do I look sexy?"

"Yes."

Rocky heads for the kitchen. She thinks Cat's acting sulky and doesn't want her own vibes messed up before she meets Yves later for dinner. She finds Annie in the process of unloading groceries.

"What is Parker having tonight?" Rocky asks.

"Spaghetti."

"Again?"

"That's all he'll eat."

Rocky stares at the older woman. She feels her face go heavy, the feeling that comes just before she spaces out, or travels out-of-body, or whatever it is that happens that gives her that blank, lost sensation like white sound filling her, numbing her mind. She doesn't like the feeling but it's too strong to resist. She tries to conjure up the rod, joining her to earth, to reality, to bolster herself, bring herself back. Annie looks like she's in a dream: her face all crunched and worried, staring.

"Honey, you okay?" Annie asks.

Rocky feels her head nod slowly.

"Hungry? Have a piece of this nice French bread." She slides the loaf out of its long paper bag, breaks off a piece and hands it to Rocky. "Here, honey, eat."

Rocky feels her hand take the bread and lift it to her lips. She hears herself say, "Thanks." She feels her jaw moving and tastes the doughy bread in her mouth.

The ringing phone jolts her back. After a moment, the intercom buzzes and Cat announces, "Rocky, you there? It's Larry."

She takes the call at the kitchen wall phone. "Hello. I'm *wonderful*. How's the sexiest man alive? Oh, darling, I'm booked tonight, one of those dreary cocktail parties for Stan the producer man. Yes, lunch tomorrow, one o'clock. I love you, darling."

She hangs up and sighs. "Isn't he wonderful?"

Annie nods.

Rocky presses the intercom to Cat's office and says, "Make a reservation for lunch tomorrow for one o'clock at The Russian Tea Room, two people. Cat? Hello, Cat?"

Suddenly Cat is standing next to her in the kitchen doorway, having appeared out of nowhere. It gives Rocky the creeps the way that girl seems to see right through you. "Oh! I just buzzed you and asked—"

"I heard," Cat says. "I'll take care of it."

"I wish you wouldn't be everywhere all at once the way you are sometimes. Do you know you can be *too* efficient?"

"Sorry, Rocky."

"And stop being *sorry* all the time." Rocky pushes past. "It's annoying."

Cat follows Rocky through the living room, where she puts on her fur coat— even though it's eighty degrees out—and slings her purse over her shoulder. She catches Cat's eye in the mirror and orders, "After you make the lunch reservation, call Larry to confirm, *pronto*. Got it?"

Cat nods in affirmation, holding a stubborn silence. Rocky has never been quite so plainly *mean* to her. She should quit this job, is what she should do. But if she can stick it out just a little longer, she'll have her debts paid off along with a solid year of experience to put on a resume without much else on it. Unfortunately, *aspiring cartoonist* doesn't cut it in a job interview. And Cat has to eat.

She returns to her office and makes the lunch reservation. Then she calls Larry, for whom she suddenly feels a new camaraderie, as if he has passed over from the other side, Rocky's side, to her own—the side of the bilked.

"Hi, Mr. Drumm, this is Cat Gold from Rocky Love's office."

"Cat, I think at this point you can call me Larry."

"Thanks. So, Rocky asked me to make a reservation for lunch tomorrow, one p.m. at The Russian Tea Room. It's all done and I just wanted to confirm that with you." "Tomorrow, lunch, one o'clock, check." "The reservation's in her name," Cat adds. "Of course it is. Is the madame still in?" "She just left." "Off to see the producer—"

"Yves," Cat says. "That's right. Humbert's at seven o'clock." As soon as she says it—impulsive payback for Rocky's sharp words just before—she feels the satisfying release of a steam pot freed of its lid.

"You mean Stan."

"Right. Stan. My mistake."

"Who is Yves?" Larry asks in a tone that sounds rhetorical. "Isn't he...."

His voice trails off, and Cat lets the silence speak. She imagines that Rocky has told him all about her sexual exploits with her married lover last summer in France. Why not? She told everyone else.

"Well, that's it ... Larry. Goodnight."

"'Night. Thanks."

Next, she calls John. He answers on the fourth ring, "Yes, I'm here!"

"It's Cat. What's wrong?"

"I was on the can. Why does that always happen?"

"You could have let your machine pick up."

"Most people hang up if you don't answer after three rings. I'm a shut-in lately, nothing but work, and I need every call."

"How's the book going?"

"Great. I contacted the people on the list you faxed over and most of them were willing to talk, I mean *really talk*. I was amazed. Thanks."

"How about another interview?"

"Lemme grab a pen. Okay, ready, who?"

"Me, right now, tonight."

"You sound charged-up."

"I am."

"Fantastic. Where should I meet you?"

They make plans to meet at seven-thirty at a bar in the Village. Although she has not completely abandoned her sense of moral dilemma, or made up her mind to tell him everything she knows, she feel an urge to *talk*. And she knows that John will be an eager listener for whatever she decides to tell him.

In the back of Humbert's, in a dimly lit corner, Rocky and Yves sit with their knees interlocked beneath a round table. A small candle between them sends shadows flickering across their faces. Yves has consumed two vodkas-on-ice and some wine. Rocky has also had some wine, which she knows will cost her dearly in guilt and self-reproach. They are waiting for the appetizers, and then will decide on dinner.

She fiddles with a breadstick, picking off each tiny seed with the tips of her long nails. She's thinking of his wife—Princess Paulette is what Rocky calls the woman—and smirks to restrain a bubble of laughter. Yves sees the humor flash across her face, and smiles. Such a sexy smile. His black shirt is buttoned to the neck, and he wears no tie. The black shirt with the white suit is charming, though admittedly she'd rather just have him naked, in bed. This dinner out is for him.

He says, "You 'ave such funny."

Her eyes blink rapidly. "What, darling?"

He reaches across the table and gently strokes her neck. His fingers travel slowly down, to the top of her breasts, and then he withdraws them. "You," he says, "you are a woman of such good amusement."

He is trying to be charming. She laughs. And wonders: *How can such a sexy man be so dumb?*

Halfway through their pumpkin soup, Rocky notices a small man in a black coat and hat sitting at a table near theirs. He has long gray curls falling down the sides of his face and thick round glasses. He looks like a man in disguise, as if he is supposed to be a Hasidic Jew, but somehow, well, isn't. Rocky can see that he has pancake makeup on his face, and a long fake putty-nose and witch's chin. She decides he is either crazy or putting on an act. There is nightly entertainment at Humbert's, a singer or a comedian. Yves twists around to follow Rocky's gaze.

"Ah hah," Yves says. "What beezar."

The man spins around and looks at them. From behind the coke-bottle glasses, his small brown eyes fix on Rocky. Something in the way he stares seizes her attention. She looks at his hands: they are small, finely boned, hairless.

They are Larry's hands.

She drops her spoon in her soup plate, and says, "Let's go."

"But we 'ave not to eat," Yves says.

"*Now.*" She stands.

Larry gets up and waddles over in a ridiculous clownlike walk, stopping in front of their table. Yves laughs. Rocky stands there, frozen.

Larry starts to shake. The top of his hat pops up and out springs a red paper flower. Someone claps. He does not smile. He takes a step closer to Rocky, and she says, "Now, wait a minute," and Yves grins like a child at the circus.

Larry quickly taps his bulbous black shoe until smoke pours from the toe.

People are watching.

Rocky says, "Stop it. You are being stupid and cruel."

Larry smiles. He is wearing big white fake teeth. Yves howls with laughter. Rocky turns bright red. She is about to leave when Larry opens his black coat and *voila* out springs a giant rubber penis attached to his groin over his black slacks. He jerks his hips forward and white liquid squirts out. Diners gasp.

Rocky shouts, "You sick motherfucker!" She grabs her purse from her chair and runs out, with Yves stumbling behind her in confusion.

Rocky and Connie sit at the oval table in front of a plate of crustless sandwiches and a pot of chamomile tea prepared by Annie, who busies herself in the kitchen and keeps an open ear.

Connie's voice is pinched with tension. "Darling, you *can't* use something so personal to Larry in your memoirs."

"Why not?"

"It's *wrong.*"

"It's interesting, and it's true."

"But it's part of *his* life story, not yours. These are *your* memoirs."

"He told me about it."

"You're violating his trust. It isn't *worth* it. And it doesn't add anything to your story."

"He humiliated me in public," Rocky says. "I don't owe him anything."

"But Rocky, that happened *after* you wrote this. This came first. I just don't understand."

"We shared confidences. This is creative license. He would understand that."

"Not this; he would not understand this. This goes way beyond creative license. If I wrote a script based on, well, based on *this*, you don't think Larry would come after me? It's so obviously *him*. And anyway, I'd never do it. He's my *friend*."

Rocky's voice rises. "You've always been jealous of my success."

"Oh, *please*, this isn't one of your shows."

"What did you say?"

"Rocky, I promise I am not jealous of you. The only reason I brought this up, about what you're saying about Larry, is to protect you. It's libelous."

"*You* told him about Yves."

"Oh, please—"

"You had to ruin it for me."

"I did not tell Larry!"

"Liar!"

"I did not tell Larry anything."

"Get out of my house!"

"*Gladly.*"

Cat hovers in her office and listens as the front door slams shut. She feels a kind of thrill. She never anticipated that Connie would bear the brunt of her petty mischief. Had she known it, she would not have slipped the information about Yves to Larry. Or would she? She wonders how much damage she can do without being accountable. And then it strikes her, fleetingly but with impact, that she is becoming as nimble at deceit as Rocky. She is learning from a master. She smiles, standing there alone in her office, just smiles and shakes her head— giddily safe within the eye of a brewing storm.

Chapter 14

The Rise and Fall of Rocky Love

Mother of the Year

People magazine did a cover with Rochelle holding Parker and featured her in an article about working motherhood. Rochelle described her round-the-clock routine, juggling diapers and meals and phones and lectures and celebrity requests. "My plate is full," she was quoted as saying, "but I like to gorge myself."

She won the Mother of the Year award and displayed it on the mantle in the living room. Charlie hooked the network on the idea of *Mother Love* and was about to enter contract negotiations. She felt her life was perfect, balanced. She was the spectacular hub around which the spokes of her life—"my people"— whirled. It was not for her to worry; she could pay others to do that.

Nancy took care of everything, so that Rochelle could come and go and the family was cared for and the household ran smoothly. The lecture circuit loved Rocky Love, and her trips sometimes lasted three or four days. When Jason became uncomfortable with her absences, she reassured him that it was temporary and reminded him that it was all part of her master plan, that as soon as she was back on track with a morning show, she'd be home every evening with him. She swore that by the time Parker was in school, she would be home early enough to meet him and take him home.

Lying side by side in their bed, holding hands, she said, "Picture it. I'll be happier when I'm working again, and we'll have lots more money."

"We have more than enough money now," Jason said.

"You do very well, darling, yes. But Charlie says he can get me a very good contract, we could have ten times the income we have now."

Jason's hand relaxed in hers.

"Won't that be great?"

"Sure, of course it will, Rocky, but we really don't need it."

"Need? No." She knew he was right, yet she felt the desire to forge ahead as a need. She needed to move on, to flourish; she needed to resurrect recognition. She needed something, a wind on her embers, she needed to flare. Jason's resistance to her ambition annoyed her. Their marriage had settled into routines, albeit complex routines, and much as she loved him she was *bored*. Even their sex had grown stale. If he had wanted a passive wife, he should have married someone else.

The next afternoon, Rochelle traveled to Boston to speak at the Cambridge Women's Caucus, on the first evening of her stay, and at Radcliffe on the second. She would return home late the second night. She arrived at the hotel in the afternoon, and because there was to be a party for her after the first lecture, she rested before getting ready to go out again.

She was just drifting off into half-sleep, which was the most she could manage in the afternoon, when the phone rang. She cleared her throat and answered, assuming it must be the woman from the Cambridge group.

But it was a man's voice, which said, "Rock!"

"Hello?"

"Rock 'n roll!"

"Who is this?"

"I saw your face at the checkout. It really blew my mind. I didn't buy it though, don't know what it said."

Yes, she knew this voice; she had always known it was just a matter of time before she heard it again.

"Nathan?"

"Yup, yup."

"Where are you?"

"Don't ask." He laughed.

She heard a new gritty depth in his voice. He was older now. She wondered if he had a family.

He said, "I'm a public, one of those little ants that crawl around and make The Great American Public."

"Do you have a job?"

"J-O-B," he spelled.

"What are you doing?"

"I'm talking to you on the phone. I'm remembering the good times. But they weren't so good for me."

"You sound like a song." She laughed but he didn't; he used to laugh at her jokes. Silence. "Nath?"

"Yup."

"I'm married now. I have a son."

"Mrs. *Dokta*."

"No, no, Jason is a lawyer. Bobby was a doctor, my first husband."

"You marry quick."

"It just didn't work."

"You married a black man." He laughed again. "I saw you on TV a few times."

"What did you think? Did you like the show? Because I'm planning to do another one—"

"Thanks," he said abruptly. "Thanks for hammering the nail in my coffin. Thanks a whole helluva lot."

He hung up quickly with a bulletclick that left Rochelle short of breath. Shot. Stung by the bee that gave her life and was dying for it. She loved Nathan way too much.

After that call, something crashed inside her, as if she had been gliding along a surface that had buckled and she was tumbling into a dark pit. Nathan was her awful truth, the person with the memories that motivated her. She wanted to see him as much as she hoped he would never contact her again.

She wanted to forget everything, but it clung to her memory like dust. The little declarations that Mabel had shouted at Rochelle over the years stuck in her mind with uncomfortable accuracy. *Sick. Bad. Crazy.* Mabel was her worst critic and the one who got farthest with her, who goaded her into denial.

The idea of having to deliver a lecture tonight suddenly made her panic. Something about having spoken with Nathan, unexpectedly after so many years, and particularly since he sounded so strangely detached from reality, caused a rupture in her confidence that went deeper than she had realized was still possible. She had thought she had become more solid than this. But the lines inside were still fuzzy; and they crossed and sizzled and burned now, again. She feels like a murderer who has killed in transgression and attempted to return to normal life, but finds, by dint of some peculiar inclination, that he cannot.

She would never escape Nathan.

But then she realized that she didn't feel guilty as much as tempted; that she had always been most excited and intrigued by the forbidden. It didn't matter how he had found her today. What mattered was that she knew he would find her again, sooner or later.

She called room service and ordered a bottle of Scotch. Later, standing in front of the bathroom mirror, applying a trace of kohl around her eyes, her hand slipped and she realized she was drunk. She wiped away the rogue line and carefully redid it. She brushed her teeth and gargled, and felt confident there was no odor of alcohol on her breath; but the Caucus representative who met her in the hotel lobby quickly developed a look of concern.

She wanted to tell the woman *my husband doesn't want me to have a career* and *my brother-who-I-love called me today* but of course she could never explain. Somehow, she made it through the lecture and the party afterwards. She had never been as relieved to be alone as she was when she returned to her hotel room at nearly midnight.

She slept late the next morning and woke hungover, but somewhere in her dreams her mind had found a point of balance. Family, she thought; her built-in nemesis. An encounter with Nathan had always been enough to pull her out of reality, which was why she knew it was best that he usually kept away from her. She reminded herself that she had accomplished a good life, that she had made strides, gained a voice, found love. Nathan would vanish again, and Jason would grow comfortable with their dual-career life. Everything would be all right.

After a good hot shower, she decided to go out for breakfast. She had noticed a cafe around the corner, and decided to go there. It was a tiny place full of plants, and a brick wall festooned with paintings by local artists. A glass case displayed pastries, and on top of the case were baskets full of handmade bread. She ordered a croissant and a cappuccino, and waited at a small round table for the waitress to bring them over.

There was only one other customer: a young man, blond, clean cut, wearing jeans and a purple T-shirt. He was reading a copy of *Fear of Flying*. When he noticed her watching him, he winked at her. He was very handsome and clearly confident about himself. She wondered if he recognized her. She smiled.

"Have you read it?" he asked, indicating the book.

"Not yet, but I hear it's a brilliant novel."

"Do I know you?" he asked. "That sounds like a line, I know, but I really feel like I know you."

"You may have seen me around." The waitress brought her breakfast. Rochelle stirred a dusting of cinnamon into the frothy milk of the cappuccino. She looked over and the young man smiled. "Do you come here often in the mornings?" she asked.

"Sometimes. I just moved here."

"From where?"

"Seattle. I wanted to be on the east coast. I'm not sure Boston's the last stop, I'm thinking about New York."

"I live in New York."

"Ah, a scenic attraction." Coming from another man, it would have sounded crude; but he was, somehow, charming.

"What do you do?" she asked him.

He crossed the small room, digging a hand into his back pocket, and handed her his business card. It was black with gold lettering that announced TIM CHRISTIANSON/ACTOR, MODEL, VOICE-OVERS. A phone number was printed below his name.

"Well, I should get going." He flashed a white smile. "It was real nice to meet you ...?"

"Rocky Love." She smiled, and waited for a reaction. But he did not appear to recognize her name. "You really don't know who I am?"

"Sorry." He shrugged his shoulders and smiled. "Should I?"

"When exactly were you born?"

"1963."

That put him in junior high about the time she had reigned on morning television. There he stood before her: a full-grown adult who, until this moment, had been unconscious of the existence of Rocky Love. Evidence of her invisibility. Well, that was about to change. Once *Mother Love* was officially picked up by a network, *everyone* would know who she was.

"Nice to meet you," she said, slipping his card into her purse.

"Call me any time," he said, by way of goodbye.

Back in her hotel room, she took him up on his suggestion—and the challenge of his innocence—and called.

Jason sat at the oval glass table as Rochelle prepared two plates with the dinner Nancy had cooked for them earlier: roast chicken, mashed potatoes and Brussels sprouts. She set down two cloth place mats, served the food and poured them both a glass of white wine. Jason had been describing something, a new twist in a case of which he'd kept her apprised since it had started months ago. But she couldn't concentrate;

her mind kept drifting to ocean eyes, sunlight hair, the thrilling arrogance of youthful confidence.

"What is it, Rocky? You aren't listening at all," Jason said.

Rochelle cut a sliver off her chicken breast and raised it to her mouth. "I think we need some time apart, maybe just a weekend." She put the chicken into her mouth and didn't chew, just held it there, with her eyes wide and waiting.

"What's wrong?"

"It's just me, I'm feeling overwhelmed, I guess I need some time alone to get deeper into myself."

Jason nodded thoughtfully. "I don't want to hold you back. But maybe we should take a weekend together?"

"Oh, darling, I love you, but I think what I really need is one little weekend alone."

"I guess I could take Parker to the country for the weekend."

"Yes," she said. "Or you can stay here. I was thinking of going to the islands."

"Islands?"

"Jamaica, maybe."

Jason stared at her for a minute, digesting the idea. "If that's what you need, I guess it's okay. This weekend?"

"Yes, I think so."

"Well, fine. I'll take you to the airport."

"Don't worry, darling, I'll get a car. What I need is just a few days of complete independence. You understand."

On the way to the airport, Rochelle felt a whirl of excitement—and terror. Tim had come to New York earlier in the week to look for an agent for film work. He was to meet her on the plane, and had been instructed that if he saw her at the airport not to even smile. But would he? What if he turned out to be some kind of celebrity basher, marriage breaker, con-man, liar, gigolo? What if he wasn't what she imagined: an easy lover who would slink in and out of her life at her command?

She spotted him sitting alone in the business class lounge, reading a newspaper and drinking a beer. She sat at the other end of the lounge with a glass of wine, looking around casually, trying not to stare at him. He was gorgeous, lean and young and blond in crisp blue jeans and a white shirt in some nappy material that looked like raw silk. His legs were crossed and from time to time he swung one of his black cowboy boots. His golden hair was thick and wavy, his face a perfect smooth canvas. It struck her that he may not have known what he was doing, he may have been too young to understand. Maybe this was a big mistake. Or maybe it was what she needed right now to get her back on track, get her lifeblood flowing, rejuvenate her sense of self. Right or wrong, she decided, she had herself to please.

Rochelle boarded the plane first. Their seats were together and she took the window seat that was assigned to Tim. She looked out the window until she felt the swoosh of someone sitting down next to her.

"Hello." He cracked his whitewashed smile. There was a little cleft at the tip of his nose.

"Hello," she said coolly, as if meeting for the first time.

"I'm Tim."

"Rochelle Libbon."

"For a minute I thought you were Rocky Love," he said, and they shared a laugh.

When they landed, they departed the plane separately. Rochelle got her luggage and wandered out to the front of the small island airport where freelance taxi drivers aggressively sought fares. She declined their offers, and waited. After a few minutes, a little white car pulled up and she got in.

Tim drove the rental car about an hour down the coast to Runaway Bay, before pulling into the gravel driveway of what he had called his "family's old vacation place." Tim had explained that his parents, who lived in Connecticut, had recently lost most of their money but had retained most their properties, a conundrum that had left Tim ill-prepared yet desperate for work.

He parked in front of a salmon pink villa surrounded by palm and acacia trees, and took their bags inside. The house had probably been beautiful once. But now the walls were cracked and peeling, the white wicker furniture was dirty, the floral chintz upholstery was ripped and everything was coated in dust. Nothing, though, neither time nor neglect, could ruin the view.

Rochelle opened all the doors and sunlight rushed in on a cool breeze.

"We used to have live-ins, three of them," Tim told her. He tossed the bags at the foot of the stairs and took off his clothes. "A cook, a maid and a gardener." Rochelle looked beyond the murky pool, at the overgrown lawn strewn with large coconuts. Four tall palms stood at the fence that separated the lawn from the beach. His jeans lay on the floor like an abandoned skin. He wore a tight red bikini. "I always wear my bathing suit under my cloths, so I can jump right in." He dashed through an arched door and across the patio, and plunged into the filthy pool with a magnificent scream.

"I'll join you in a few minutes," she called. She lugged her bags up the stairs and down a long hallway. There were four bedrooms. She found the master bedroom and parked her suitcases there. This had probably been a nice room once, too, before the rattan floor coverings had developed holes, and the white walls had yellowed, and the furniture had lost its polish, and the porcelain in the bathroom had cracked. She rubbed a clean circle on the bathroom mirror and inspected her make-up. It would come off in the water; she hadn't thought of that.

She changed into her black strapless bathing suit. She had recently developed a tenacious fungus on her toenails which made them craggy and yellow, so applied another coat of dark red polish and waited for it to dry.

"Hey," Tim called up. "What are you doing?"

She could hear him splashing around in the pool and went out onto the balcony to look. He was sprinting through the water like a silverfish, submerging himself completely so he became a ghost of flesh and red suit. She felt young all over again: like Rochelle Libbon spilling out her raw thoughts in drag, like a buxom girl in T-shirts whose hair was a mop of weeds and didn't care, like a raw young girl oozing *it. Loveme. Now.*

"Coming!" She slid her feet into her white leather spangled thongs and went to the pool, holding in her stomach, which had flopped out all over the place ever since her pregnancy.

Tim treaded water and watched Rochelle carefully lower herself into the pool from the side ladder. The surface of the water was littered with bugs, but she didn't care. It was cold, and she could feel the soft flesh on her thighs shivering. She plunged all the way in.

Tim's virtues as a lover went beyond his youth. He was potent, able and practiced. His sexual energy was intense and she knew she had finally met her match in bed—or pool, or wherever. She hadn't realized how dissatisfied she had been until now, until Tim. Later, they lay entangled in his parents' bed, half covered in a white sheet, cool air blowing in through the open windows. A bluish light from the sea shimmered in the room. His body glowed taut and discreetly muscled in a knot with her own creamy voluptuous body.

"You're outstanding," she said, like an old man to his juvenile nymph. She loved the reversal of their roles: her power, his youth. "Tell me where you got your experience."

Tim kissed her neck and then moved away. He folded his hands behind his head and began. "When I was thirteen, I slept with my babysitter, Sue. She was twenty. She seduced me. I was tall for my age, I looked like I was fifteen. I took to sex right away. By the time I got to high school, I knew what to do. I had any girl I wanted. Then I went to college for a couple years and I guess I had a kind of reputation, you know, as a stud." His eyes flashed at Rochelle, and she smiled, though admittedly the word had thrown her off a bit. *Stud.* The mad wife would have said it and even liked it, but she herself had always considered herself beyond susceptibility to *studs*. But she wasn't; she had just fallen prey, happily, and loved it. "Well, I dropped out of college, just never liked school, and now I'm a struggling actor." He laughed at himself. So did she: at his beauty, his sex like strong perfume reeking from his pores, the clichés through which he defined his life. *Stud. Struggling actor. Couldn't resist.* Not as innocent as she had assumed (or hoped) but even so—a treasure.

"Do you work much?" she asked.

"Mostly as a model. The acting work tends to be non-paid, modeling brings in some money."

"You do voice-overs, too? Your card said—"

"Oh, yeah. Well, I figured I'd say so, just in case something came along."

Rochelle decided she would have it all: marriage, baby, home, lover. She decided that since the beginning of time powerful men had kept women and she had every right to keep a man. So, back in New York, she met with her accountant to make arrangements.

Steve Nodler, president of Nodler & Co. (accountants to the stars) was a polished man in his middle years, with thick brown hair, a friendly face and a few extra layers of flab which in his case spoke of stability, prosperity and long hours at the office. He was paternal with Rochelle, and she felt comfortable with him. He sat behind his big paper-piled desk and she sat in front of it. She told him that she had some private business to transact that must remain between the two of them. He nodded, unfazed; this was not a new scenario. She said she was renting an apartment on East Tenth Street and taking a credit card in the name of a friend. Steve listened. She said she was opening a checking account for a friend and wanted to maintain a balance of five-hundred dollars. He nodded. She said she wanted to use the interest income from her personal investments but to avoid tapping principal. He nodded. She said she wanted no written reports of these transactions sent to her home. He nodded. When she was through, he tactfully shifted into normal business, reviewing her investment statements and explaining the quarterly financial reports.

For six weeks after Jamaica, Rochelle lived in a frantic daze: watching every expression on Jason's face, trying to be home as much as possible, while spending time with Tim every day. She became well acquainted with the public phone on the corner of Spring and Lafayette Streets. Sometimes she popped in at the Tenth Street apartment for just twenty minutes. Tim accommodated her. She imagined he waited for her, until one day—the day before she was scheduled to leave town to do a lecture in San Diego—she visited the apartment at four in the afternoon and he wasn't there.

So she waited. She didn't particularly like how he had done the place up—in black leather and chrome furniture, with cheaply framed posters on the walls— but he had had the sense to select a big comfortable bed and outfit it with satin sheets. She waited in the main room: living area to the left, dining area to the right. And she waited: plunked into the leather couch, with her stiletto-heeled leather boots on the glass coffee table. Waiting: with the radio blaring rock 'n roll to drown out the anxiety that was ricocheting around in her mind, pacing the apartment, opening drawers, searching for a hidden life, for a clue to his whereabouts. Hours passed, and she knew she should go home. At nearly seven she called: "I'm at Lisa Long's," she told Nancy, who promised to pass the message on to Jason when he got home.

Tim appeared just before nine o'clock and found Rochelle drunk on his couch. Scotch drunk, the bad kind, when you felt mean and acted crazy.

"Where have you been?"

"At an audition." He dropped his red canvas shoulder bag on the floor and removed his brown felt hat. "What's going on?"

She barked laughter. Her makeup had worn off by now and she wasn't even trying to be pleasant. "I've been here all afternoon!"

"I'm sorry, I didn't know you were coming, I would have planned a parade." He went to the kitchen and poured himself a glass of vodka and soda.

"Give me more." She held out her glass.

He sat on the leather chair that matched the couch. "You know where it is."

She threw her glass and it shattered against the wall. "Get it for me!"

Tim's face showed glimmers of disgust and fear; he was not a good enough actor to hide his feelings, to protect his position.

"Don't you understand that I love you?" She wilted into the corner of the couch.

Tim finally took the cue and wrapped his arms around her. "Shouldn't you be home tonight?"

"I wanted to see you before I leave town. Why weren't you here?"

"I didn't know you were coming. I was at an audition for a commercial."

"Come with me," she said. "We'll have a week together. *Please.*"

"Sure, okay baby, whatever you want."

When she arrived home after ten o'clock, she found the table set for two, with candles and a vase spilling red roses. At one setting was a plate of salmon, new potatoes and sautéed green beans. The other plate was empty, smeared, eaten.

Jason was stretched out on the couch, watching TV. Rochelle went straight into the bedroom and shut the door, appalled with herself for not having recognized the degree of her obsession. She had made a big mistake, a Nathan-sized error. She knew exactly what she had to do: dispossess Tim, *now.* He brought out the worst in her. She shouldn't have drunk so much, shouldn't have loved Tim for his beauty, youth, sex. Shouldn't have lost control.

She lifted the receiver of the phone by the bed and dialed Tim. One red button on the row lining the bottom of the phone lit, and she stared at it as toward a beacon of hope, an act of control. She didn't think; she had never called him from home before.

He answered on the second ring.

"Tim," she said.

"Hey, Rocky, are you okay?"

"It's over."

He paused, then said, "I know."

The button remained lit, burning red, for a few moments after she had hung up. She noticed, but in the sweep of her relief she didn't quite understand that Jason had been listening on another extension.

He did not come to bed.

In the morning, when she woke up, he was already dressed. Nancy had taken Parker to school, so when Rocky wandered out in her robe, she and Jason were alone. A suitcase was sitting by the front door and Jason was biding his time with the newspaper, waiting for her.

"Am I traveling today?" Rochelle asked, confused.

"No, I am." Jason stood up. "I already said goodbye to Parker and Nancy."

"Goodbye?" And then she remembered the red light on the phone last night. Her conversation with Tim. Her drunken late-night return home to a cold dinner. "I can explain all that," she said, before he asked her to.

"No need, Rocky. The writing's been on the wall. I thought you were seeing someone else but now I know it."

"So you're storming out? Without even confronting me?"

"I'm not storming. I'm just enacting the inevitable and leaving. Rocky, I'm *tired* of hoping things will change, when they won't, because we are who we are. I think we both know that we want different things out of a marriage. Let's just face it and get this over with sooner rather than later."

"Jason, please—*stay*."

He walked past her and picked up his suitcase. "I'd like to work out a way to see Parker regularly. Once I have my own place, he'll be able to spend weekends with me, which should free you up to do whatever you want to do ... which is what you do anyway."

"What does *that* mean?"

"You'll figure it out."

"The biggest mistake I made," Rochelle told Leo, "was to marry a lawyer."

Leo, nearly forty now, shared a large apartment on West End Avenue at 78th Street with Rich, who supported them both as an investment banker. Leo cooked, kept house, sculpted and arranged their social life. Rochelle sat at Leo's antique table in her white leather pants suit and silver boots. In his domestic role, Leo had taken to old jeans and sweaters in bright colors. The mustache was gone and his hair had grayed at the edges. He held his slender hand over hers. Rosy evening light filtered through two large windows. They drank Beaujolais, and waited for Rich to get home from work.

"The rotten press I'm getting right now is bad enough, but Leo, this isn't living. I can't concentrate on anything. I *can't* go on like this forever."

"You won't. It'll be over sooner or later, and you'll move on."

"The network canceled our meeting last week."

Leo's face was still, concealing expression. Then he said, "They're probably just busy." His voice was soft, and not too convincing. "You're a strong lady, you have everything in your favor."

She lifted a newspaper from a stack on the table, then slapped it back down. FEMINISM'S DOUBLE STANDARD. HAVING IT ALL MEANS MORE THAN YOU THOUGHT. CAN ROCKY LOVE BEAT THE ODDS? "Trash, subhuman garbage. The press is turning this into a witch's trial."

"Honey, all you need to worry about right now is keeping Parker."

Rochelle had loved Jason Barthoff and she couldn't understand why he was being so vengeful. He wanted everything:

the loft, the beach house, Parker. Her affair with Tim had been a transgression, but people wouldn't see it that way and Jason realized that. Steve Nodler had informed her that he was obliged by the court to release her financial records, and so it would all become public knowledge: the secret apartment, credit cards, bank account, Tim, everything.

But it was nothing compared to a marriage.

Now it was being left to a court to decide. Well, you didn't have to look far to see that Jason had been a good husband, a good father and a good provider, even without her money. He had been loyal, and faithful, and there up until the very end. And he had loved her, she was sure of it. She had never dreamed he would use the mad wife against her. But now it all came out: where truth met persona, where what she had done in her life and said on the air collided into fact. She had *become* Rocky Love, more media creation than real woman.

The days were long now, an endless route into loneliness. She resented her dependency on Nancy, who fed her, kept the loft clean and prettied with flowers, and on some days was the only adult with whom she spoke. Parker tooled around, a three-year-old dynamo, with Rochelle's round soft face and a head of wiry black hair. Nancy dressed him in denim overalls, colorful cotton shirts and tiny sneakers. He had a silver Space Invader water-squirting laser gun and if he shot you it was a sign of affection. Even with Rochelle home all day, he zipped around after Nancy, shooting at her with his little gun, talking shyly to his mother if she happened to pass through his secret world.

Rochelle saw the ways in which her celebrated life had divested her—"Don't let this sudden fame hurt you," Norman had said—leaving her null and empty and alone. No one could get through to her. Told she would bounce back, she didn't quite believe it. Told Parker was only going through a phase and that one of these days he would reconnect with her, she knew deep down that they had never made the original connection to begin with.

Drinking helped: white wine in the middle of the day and with dinner, brandy after. The crazy thing was that it wasn't Jason she missed, but her obsession for Tim. He had been an adventure, a dare, a purpose, a charge more electric than drink. But he was gone. She yearned for him, especially at night, and wished they had never met.

Finally, she called her old therapist Dr. Carr for help, and after a few private sessions in which she rambled and spewed confusion, he recommended that she attend his weekly group. Though annoyed at the suggestion, she was desperate enough to try anything.

The group was held on Thursday evenings in Dr. Carr's office. Rochelle didn't like listening to the problems of other people, except for one woman— Connie Wagner—whom she had known superficially, years ago, as a producer at the network where Rochelle had had her first solo television show. It turned out they had more than the network in common: Connie was a veteran recovering alcoholic, and offered to shepherd Rochelle to her own sobriety. She also offered to fix her new friend up with the former husband of a woman she had met at an Alcoholics Anonymous meeting.

"I'm not ready to date," Rochelle said, though unconvincingly.

"I think the question you should ask yourself is if dating is ready for you?" Connie's girlish face, framed by a blond page-boy, tilted back in humor. For the first time, Rochelle laughed at herself. *What the hell*, she thought, *I could use a little fun.*

Mort Gold was a good old fashioned New York dreamer, a man of forty-nine who blew a brass trumpet and made his living as a piano salesman. He was short and balding, with a large hooked nose and soulful brown eyes. He wore fringed silk scarves around his neck and carried a rectangular Italian shoulderbag which he usually forgot at restaurants. He said, "Rochelle, you're a mensch," and pinched her cheek. He took her out for bites-to-eat, and asked her if she thought he was going bald.

"Not at all," she would say.

He grazed his grizzly brown hair with a clean squarish hand that reminded her of a doctor's. "Are you sure? It seems thin on top."

It was thinning, but Rochelle wouldn't want anyone to tell *her* she was going bald, even if she was. "I've never seen such a full head of hair," she said.

Rochelle drove the Mercedes along the Long Island Expressway, through a brilliant whirl of red, orange and yellow leaves spinning down as lightly as feathers. Mort hummed away in the passenger seat. Nancy and Parker sat in back. Parker sang along with Mort's deep voice, in his high squeaky one, and all of a sudden, out of the blue, Rochelle emitted a huge laugh.

Mort said, "I told you it was in there!"

Parker clapped. Nancy smiled.

Mort felt like an old friend, a piece of her past, a good artsy crazy brother with a familiarity she felt was straight out of her childhood; a father-brother-friend with whom she did not have to be famous.

His own divorce had just gone through. "When it's over," he told her, "kaput, it's over. You just have to get through this hard part with your head screwed on right." From his description, his marriage sounded like it had been miserable: twenty-two years of a drunken wife who drove him to other women. "But I was blessed with two wonderful children, Eddie and Cat. Eddie's in law school now."

"And Cat?"

"She just finished college. She studied art. I tell her she's going to have a hard time as an artist but why should she listen to her old man?"

"How old is she?"

"Twenty-one."

"When I was twenty-one I was pretty wild," Rochelle said. "Drove my parents nuts."

"That's how it's supposed to be, isn't it? Unfortunately my kids didn't have the luxury—their parents were too busy being irresponsible children themselves."

Mort sighed. "Twenty-twenty hindsight, as they say. If I could do it over again— " "You'd be the same screw-up of a parent you were before!" Rochelle laughed. "Right?" Mort blushed—in embarrassment or frustration, Rochelle couldn't tell. "My kids have turned out okay, luckily." "I'd love to meet them some time," Rochelle said, surprising herself by actually meaning it.

In the morning, Rochelle woke to a sweet familiar smell. She put on her robe and hurried barefoot down the stairs to the kitchen. Nancy was supervising Parker, who was scribbling crayon masterworks at the table. And Mort was at the stove in Nancy's canvas apron with a big black-and-white cat on the front, holding a spatula poised above a sizzling griddle. Blintzes. Rochelle breathed the heavenly smell. She would have to thank Connie again for this man.

The makeshift family shared a peaceful weekend they all hated to see end. And if Rochelle had known what was waiting for her in the city, she might have extended their stay at the beach.

First thing Monday morning, Mabel called. There was a mystery in her voice as she issued an invitation to meet for lunch. Rochelle reluctantly accepted.

Standing in her closet, trying to decided what to wear and torn between pleasing and offending her mother, Rochelle chose a new white suit with pleats in the skirt and a double-breasted jacket with brass buttons embossed with some kind of fashion crest. She wore the suit without a blouse, and because her better sense told her not to, she put on black lace tights embroidered with cabbage roses and black patent leather pumps with two-and-a-half inch heels. Mabel would think the shoes were sleazy but they were the lowest Rochelle had other than flats, and heels did justice to her legs.

She applied her makeup conservatively, and looking at herself in the mirror she saw Rochelle Libbon trying too hard to win Mommy's approval. So she stroked on a little more blusher and touched up her eyes with kohl, giving them an Asian curve at the outer edges. She bent over, whacked away at her thick hennaed hair with her brush, and flipped up. There, *that* was the woman she was, the one in the mirror with wild wiry hair atop a colorful face, the one with the burning *it*. She tugged her suit jacket to bring up her cleavage.

Rochelle took a taxi a few blocks to Aix, where they had agreed to meet at one. She figured her mother wanted to talk to her about the mess she had made of her life, and all of a sudden didn't want to go in. She paid the driver, got out and stood in front of the restaurant thinking it over.

She stood there, torn, curious about what Mabel had to say and dreading it. At first, the *taptaptap* on glass blended into her thoughts; then she heard it externally, and turned around. There was Mabel, inside Aix, tapping on the glass with her knuckles. She mouthed something that Rochelle couldn't make out; but it didn't matter exactly what the words were, because obviously her mother was telling her to come inside.

The maitre d' greeted her effusively and she smiled her *thankyousomuch of course you know me I'm famous* smile. "I'm lunching with my mother today," she said, and he laughed with her as if mothers were some kind of joke. She told herself to remember to tip this man well.

"Look at you," Mabel said, as soon as Rochelle was close enough to hear. "That could be a very handsome suit."

"It's new."

"So are you going to sit or do you eat standing now?"

Rochelle sat. She tried to smile and could feel the muscles in her face contort into something different, a change in expression, but she wasn't sure what. Mabel looked at her like she was a page full of scribble.

"So, Mom, how are you?"

"It's not me we're here to discuss," she said. "But just for the record, I have arthritis in three joints and I am in pain."

"I'm so sorry, I didn't know."

"Of course you didn't know, I never told you. Why should I worry you now, with all your troubles?"

Rochelle was taken aback by this; her mother had rarely acknowledged that her life wasn't easy despite all the luck she'd had.

"I know what it's like to be a woman almost forty, with children and responsibility," Mabel said. "Though I had to do everything myself."

"Mom—"

"Never mind that. The point is that even though, Rochelle, I do not think you are the best of mothers, you gave birth to that child and you have every right to raise him. He is *my* grandson."

Rochelle felt something almost like warmth from her mother, a diffuse pride loosely aimed at her.

"I'm doing everything I can to get custody. My lawyers are talking to his lawyers and—"

"Listen to me Rochelle. That man who by the way I was just starting to like, that ex-husband of yours, is trying even harder." Her tired brown eyes widened for emphasis.

"What do you mean?"

She snapped open her purse and pulled out an envelope from which she extracted a letter. She unfolded it ceremoniously, her eyes darting to Rochelle so as to gather up her daughter's reaction as she cleared her throat and read: "Dear Mabel, You know how deeply grieved I am over the demise of my marriage to Rochelle, and as you know the details I won't upset you by bringing them up again. My concern now is for my son and his well being. As you yourself have been blessed with an enduring and stable marriage"—Mabel's eyes flitted from the letter to Rochelle—"you may not know the procedure of a divorce filing of one party against the other. In essence, the party suing for divorce has the burden of proof against the other party, and in the case of child custody suits, the burden of proof in the claim against the second party is fully on the shoulders of the first party and everything presented is taken into account by the presiding judge. This is to say, that I must, unfortunately, prove Rochelle's incompetence as a mother. It is an onerous pursuit, but for Parker's sake, and as his loving grandmother I'm sure you will agree, a necessary one. As Rochelle's mother, you perhaps know her better than anyone; and I know you have serious doubts as to her capacity to responsibly raise a child. The issue here is not her ability to hire someone else to raise the child, but her *own capacity to be his primary nurturer* in, let's say, the case she should lose her ability to hire childcare. In our life together, she showed almost no interest in Parker. Your testimony as to her character—your honest appraisal, Mabel—would serve your grandson's present and future well being. Please consider this, and if you choose to, contact my lawyers."

Mabel waved a business card. "This was with the letter. And so what do *you* think *I* your mother would do upon receiving a letter like this?"

Rochelle was speechless; she had no idea.

"What *did* you do, Mom?"

"I phoned you and made this date, that's what."

"Have you responded to that?"

"Why should I? If nothing else, I gave birth to you. That's the easy part. *Raising* a child is the hard part. But what would you know about that? Never mind. I have not even shown this to your father. I will *not* bear witness against my own child—"

"Mom, thank you—"

"—even if I have plenty to say."

After lunch, Rochelle hailed a taxi in front of Aix and left Mabel alone on the curb. She leaned out the window and said, "I'll call you soon, Mom." As the cab pulled into traffic she could hear Mabel's disembodied voice answering, "Don't bother."

At home, Betsy handed her a small pile of pink message slips: two journalists, her lecture agent, her psychic healer, and Mort. Betsy stood there in her tight skirt and knit top, waiting for an order, but Rochelle was too preoccupied. She went to her desk and jotted down a list of all the people she could think of whom Jason might have contacted. Then she marched across the loft to Betsy's workspace and handed her the list.

"Get these people on the phone, then put them through to me. When you see I'm off, call the next person."

Betsy said, "Okay," and flipped through the Rolodex.

Bobby Love was first on the list; his testimony of her non-maternal nature would have found a perfect listener in Jason. Bobby said that yes, he had received such a letter, but no, he had decided not to answer it. "I'm happy now," he said. "I have a wife and two baby girls and I only wish the same happiness for you, Rocky. I have nothing against you. I don't want to get involved in your divorce. I'm sorry it didn't work out."

Next she called her brothers. Even though she doubted they would defame her, she had to be sure. To her surprise, neither Robby nor Leo had received a letter.

Then she spoke with Suzanne, her assistant at the network during her Bobby Love years. It had been a long time and Rochelle tried to be warm, but Suzanne's tone was chilly. She said, "Yes, I did get a letter like that."

"And?"

"I think the lawyer I talked to was named Tannenbaum, Irwin or something Tannenbaum. He asked me some questions and I answered. We talked for about ten, fifteen minutes. Obviously I didn't tell him anything he wanted to hear because he didn't ask for a written statement."

Rochelle thought Suzanne sounded disappointed. "Well," she said, "I'm relieved to hear that. I should have had you sign a nondisclosure form, it's something a celebrity should always require."

"*Had* me sign one?"

"Yes."

"Rocky, you can't just *have* people do whatever you want, even if you're paying them."

Rochelle could see Suzanne in a memory-bubble floating around her mind: a young woman, olive-toned, long black hair, leaning earnestly over her desk for three years, working. She should have known by Suzanne's passivity that she would betray her one day, rise up and scream her angry jealousy at whoever would listen. Rochelle said, "You have a real problem with authority, Suzanne. I treated you well, I tailored the job to your personality. You had a little too much leeway with me and now—"

"Stop it, Rocky."

"Don't you dare talk to my ex-husband's lawyers, or either of my ex-husbands!"

"A person can do whatever they want. *You* taught me that."

Rochelle hung up and wanted to scream.

Immediately, the intercom buzzed and Betsy announced that Scott McNeil was on the line.

He was coy, circumspect, happy (she thought) to finally have one over her. Yes, he had gotten a letter from the lawyers. She asked him if he had responded to it, and he said, "As a matter of fact, I did. I'm glad you called, Rochelle. One of my classes has been discussing the evolution of your persona and there was general agreement that since the early *Mad Women* your style has radically changed, gone from, shall we say, intellectually sharp and edgy to, well, soft, riddled with surprising clichés. Do you think your fame has had a deleterious effect on your ability to seriously confront topical issues? Or perhaps motherhood? Or possibly even both?"

"Scott, I'm in a custody battle here. What did you say about me to my husband's lawyers?"

"Well, sorry, Rochelle, but I really consider that confidential."

She slammed down the phone. A minute later, the intercom buzzed, and without consulting Betsy, Rochelle lifted the receiver and said: "Who is this?"

"Hey, Rocky!"

"Reebah?"

"Honey, you had your assistant call me. How're you doing?"

"Oh, Reebah, it's so good to hear your voice. I'm having such a hard time. You've probably heard about what's going on."

"Actually, no. I'm working or chasing Lil around. She's two and a half now, can you believe it? Did you get the pictures I sent you?"

Rochelle couldn't remember. Betsy may have put some photos on her desk a while back, along with all the other mail she rarely inspected. Betsy always marked the important things and left the rest in a pile that kept growing until she was instructed to throw it away.

"She's a doll," Rochelle said.

"Okay, talk to me. You sound burned out, Rocky. You don't sound good."

Rochelle was struck by this. She was so accustomed to people telling her she looked great, sounded great, was doing great—even in times of trouble, as now— that she was surprised by Reebah's remark. Then she felt relief. Reebah knew what was good in her. Reebah knew the real Rochelle Libbon.

"My husband is suing me for custody of Parker."

"Oh, Jesus. Why?"

Rochelle sighed. She hated telling this story. "He thinks I had an affair."

"Did you?"

"Well, yes."

"Even so, honey, that's not grounds for you to lose custody."

"And I was always busy with my career, so I had a little help around the house, which he interprets as my being disengaged. It's a *conspiracy* against working women, is what it is."

"I'm so sorry, Rocky. Tell me, what can I do to help?"

"He sent letters to people who know me, asking them to be character witnesses. But it sounds like you didn't get one."

"Nah, honey, I didn't get one. And if I did I never would have answered."

"Of course not, I don't know why I thought you would."

"It sounds like you're forgetting who you can trust. It's funny, I thought you sold out, you kinda turned into the enemy—"

"What?"

"What I'm trying to say, Rocky, is that now I can see that the road you chose is more of a mudslide than a road. But it may have been inevitable for you to go that route. It's not your fault. You never even wanted to do that radio show to begin with, I pulled you into it."

"Reebah, what are you saying? Can't you see I'm having some real prob—"

"Yes, I can see that. Honey, we all make mistakes. Listen to me, you keep strong, and don't worry about me hurting you because I won't." She paused. "Okay, Lil just ran into the kitchen by herself, I have to go." She hung up the phone.

Rochelle felt helpless, muddled at the core. How could Reebah question her integrity? She hadn't done anything worse than the average CEO did on a regular basis—she had served herself, thank you very much—and now she would be punished for it. Punished, and held responsible. Was it her fault that the women's movement had suffered a backward slide? How was she to blame for that? She could feel the fabric around the brass buttons on her white suit pulling, almost popping.

Betsy's voice on the intercom announced, "Tad Crawford."

Rochelle didn't want to talk to him, but knew she had to. It had been nearly four years since they exchanged negatives and sex.

She asked him about the letter.

"Yeah, I got one." She could hear the clink of a glass on a hard surface and there was a pause as he swallowed something. He sounded intoxicated. "Blew my mind, I mean, *me* a character witness for *you*. Like I really know you that well."

"So you didn't respond?"

"Well, I don't know what the hell I could have to do with your divorce, but yeah, I called."

"Please tell me what you said."

Another pause, another clink, another swallow. "They wanted to know about Greece, you know, so I told them. It's not like it was some big mystery; everybody knows."

"What else?"

"About last time."

"You told them?"

"They said it was all confidential, no one would find out. Hell, my girlfriend would fucking kill me if she knew."

"What about me, Tad? Did you *think*?"

"What? You weren't married. There's no law against two consenting unmarried adults—"

She slammed down the phone. How could she have predicted that a chance meeting on a plane when she was twenty could create so much fallout later in her life? She pictured Jason's lawyers separating her mistakes, braiding them into one big noose with which to hang her. Court was the big threat they knew she'd try to avoid. If only they thought there was any possibility, *any chance* that Tad Crawford had fathered Parker....

Then it struck her: *Could* Tad have fathered Parker? If a blood test proved it, would Jason have any right to custody?

She buzzed Betsy. "Get me Tad Crawford's address, and tell anyone who calls that I've gone out."

Rochelle taxied to a derelict warehouse building on Laight Street, just yards from a busy intersection where traffic came together in a knot of honking madness. The intercom buttons were so small and close together that she had to use the tip of her long fingernail to press the one next to the names Crawford/Shoenfeld. When there was no answer, she pressed it again, holding it longer.

A window three floors up opened and a male voice shouted, "Who's there?"

"Tad? Is that you?"

"Who is it?"

Rochelle stepped back onto the curb and saw Tad leaning out the window. "I need to talk to you."

He grinned. "Miss me or something?"

"Just one minute, please."

He disappeared briefly then returned with a bunched-up athletic sock. "Here, catch." He threw the sock out the window. "The key's inside. I'm on the third floor." He shut the window.

Rochelle unballed the sock and used the key to let herself in. The hallway was fit to be condemned, there were holes in the walls and flakes of paint hung from the ceiling like bats. She quickly climbed the two filthy flights until she reached the third floor, where within a gaping doorway stood Tad Crawford. His eyes were glazed and the minute he saw her, he laughed. He was drunk.

"Well, well, well," he said.

She pushed her way past him. "Are we alone?"

"Sandra's not here at the moment."

The loft was large and raw, with some old furniture arranged in the corner between two large windows. Far to the left of that was a double bed draped with a nubby white bedspread. Against the opposite wall was a makeshift kitchen. Photographic equipment cluttered the large open spaces.

"Do you actually live here?" Rochelle asked.

He ignored the slight and walked past her, across the loft—and it was then that she saw the swirling cowlick in the back of his dense black hair. It traveled to the right and ended in a clump that was as irrepressible as Parker's. When Tad sat down in a tattered armchair by a dying fichus tree, leaned back, crossed his legs and looked at her, all she could see was a time-warped mirror reflection her son.

"I need you to do something for me," she said. "It's very important and I need it as soon as possible, today if you can."

"I'm working all day today."

"I'll pay you."

"What's the job?"

"I want you to take a blood test. I need to know your blood type."

"It's B positive."

"I need documentation."

Tad leaned forward and propped his elbows on his knees. "Does he look like me?"

She could not bring herself to answer. All she wanted were facts and proof and Parker.

"I'm not sure I'm ready to be a father."

"I only want your blood sample, nothing else. You don't have to meet him. You don't have to do anything. This may be a long shot, but if it pans out, it's worth anything to me."

Tad nodded slowly and continued to look at her. "How much?"

"A hundred dollars."

He laughed.

"A thousand. Two thousand. How much do you want?"

"How about five thousand for the test, ten thousand if it's positive?"

"You're lucky I won't sue you for paternity."

"I'm not so sure I want to do this test."

"Let's say five hundred to take the test, and five thousand if it pans out."

He reached up and picked a sickly yellow leaf off the fichus tree. "Sure, what the hell? But there's more one thing I'll want, besides the money."

"What?"

"If he's mine, I'll want to meet the kid."

Chapter 15

You Look Like Someone

Rocky sits alone on the terrace in the bright summer evening, a glass of white wine in her hand. Just one glass, she promises herself, to help her relax and stave off the loneliness that has begun to invade her these past weeks. No Connie. No Larry. No Yves. And since Annie and Parker left yesterday to spend August at the beach house, the prickly sensation of abandonment has imploded, creating a cavernous void that echoes, echoes, echoes. She sips her wine and gazes out and down at the city streets. She can see Madison Avenue as it reaches up into East Harlem, though from here she can't really see the details that far uptown. What she sees is the march of time, the evolution that laid this city and will someday forget her. She will fade away as if she never existed.

One more glass of wine. The chill, in this heat, is refreshing.

Just as she is beginning to feel safely enveloped in the deepening purple of twilight, the telephone rings. She answers it in the kitchen. When she hears the breathing silence that follows her hello, she knows who it is. Somehow, through the ether of night and loneliness, he has read her signals.

"Nathan, where are you? Come over, I need some company. I'm all alone."

"That's too bad little sister."

"Please, let's be friends."

"Maybe."

"Why are you calling me then?" she shouts.

"Okay, okay, calm down Rock calm down."

"I'm having a bad night. *Please*."

"I've been watching you."

"Where? When?"

"Everywhere, all the time. I've seen your show a million times. I heard you talk on stage. I was there, I saw you."

"You came to one of my lectures? When?"

"Long time ago. You looked good, Rock, real pretty."

"Nathan, can you come over and talk?"

"Now? You mean right this minute?"

"Why not?"

"This is not a good time for me, not a good time."

"When? Pick a time, any day."

"Tomorrow."

"When?"

"Noon."

"Where?"

"Your place."

"Great, I'll give you lunch."

"No, I don't want to come in. I'll meet you outside."

"All right, fine. Nathan, I can't wait. I love you, I miss—"

He hangs up. She stands in her kitchen, surrounded by surfaces she barely knows, and listens to the long drone of the dial tone. Nathan, her Nathan. Tomorrow, seeing him, she will feel so much better.

On Thursday morning, Cat arrives at the penthouse and is struck by the spookily abandoned feeling of the place. She looks into the dining room and kitchen, then proceeds down the hall toward Rocky's suite of rooms. Both doors are closed.

She goes to her office. On her desk is an empty wine glass with lipstick marks along the rim, sitting next to a messy pile of papers Cat had left neatly stacked when she went home the night before. Underneath the glass is a sheet of paper with Rocky's large round script. *Make a reservation for noon at Leonardo's, tomorrow, 2 people.*

Cat sits down, neatens her desk and makes the reservation. Then she goes to the kitchen to deposit the wine glass in the sink and make a pot of coffee. She skims the newspaper headlines while waiting for the pot to fill, then returns to her office with her coffee and her head packed with a variety of news details she will have forgotten by the end of the day. Just after eleven, her intercom buzzes.

"Hello, hello, are you there?"

"Good morning, Rocky, how are you?"

"Exhausted. Could you please bring me coffee?"

"Right away."

Now that Annie is gone for the rest of the summer, Cat has been pressed into minor domestic services. She doesn't really mind, so long as it keeps the peace. In the kitchen, she pours a mug of coffee, prepares it with cream and sugar substitute and carries it to Rocky's bedroom.

Cat knocks lightly and Rocky summons her in. The shades are drawn and the room is dark. Rocky is in bed, propped up against a mountain of pillows.

"Just set it down there."

Cat sets the coffee mug on the night table. "You okay?"

"I didn't sleep well. I have to be ready to go out in less than an hour. You made the reservation?"

"Yes."

"I have to get dressed."

By quarter to twelve, Rocky is on her third outfit, none worse than the next, none better. She runs back and forth, up and down the hallway, seeking Cat's advice. Each time, Cat tells her, "You look terrific." Rocky answers with a silent, worried expression and departs again only to return in something new.

Finally, around noon, Cat decides she has to escape. It's a drill she has down pat. First, she makes herself visibly ready for outside: hair brushed, a touch of lipstick, purse on her shoulder. Then she advances to Rocky's suite, knocks lightly on the bedroom door and pushes it open an inch.

"I have nothing to wear," Rocky says. She is standing at the threshold of her closet door, wearing black lace panties and a necklace of jet beads.

"Rocky? I have to get to the post office before the line gets too long."

"You can't leave yet. I need you. I'm running so late."

"But if I get stuck on line, I'll be out twice as long." Cat knows that Rocky doesn't like her domain to be left unattended, and would rather sacrifice a minute now for an hour later. "Is there anything you need before I go?"

Rocky stares vacantly into her gaping closet. She doesn't answer.

"I'll be back soon," Cat says.

Rocky nods vaguely, and disappears into the closet.

Cat rides down in the elevator and listens to her sneakers squeak on the marble floor as she crosses the lobby. The glass panels that frame the front door reflect the blinding summer light. Angel, the doorman, comes in from outside.

"I ring upstairs and nobody answer. This guy, he's waiting for Rocky."

"Who?"

"This guy out here, he says she's meeting him, but I don't know." He pushes open the door with one hand. Cat sees a man standing under the awning with a knapsack dangling from one hand.

She goes outside and conjures a professional can-I-help-you smile as she approaches the man. He twists around and she thinks she has seen him somewhere before.

He is tall and thin, with thick once-brown salt-and-pepper hair and a long rounded nose. He has a wily been-there face and intense eyes that feel like bullets when they look at her. The eyes are not afraid; they seem to know just who she is, and it frightens her.

"Hi," she says. "I'm Rocky's assistant. Are you waiting for her?"

"You look like someone," he says.

"Well, I am someone. I'm me."

His nostrils flare and his eyes roll.

"I'll call up and tell her you're waiting. You are ...?"

"Tell her Nathan's waiting. Tell her Nathan's been waiting a long time." A bitterly ironic smile fans across his face.

So this is him, the mystery brother.

She goes back in to use Angel's phone, and rings and rings until finally Rocky answers. She promises to be right down. Cat delivers the message, to which Nathan replies, "Sure, like I haven't heard that before." She represses a smile, bids him goodbye and walks away. He's either crazy or he knows his sister well.

When Cat gets back from her errands and is alone in the penthouse, she can't resist spiriting into Rocky's study to look at the Love Wall—the tilted collage of new and old photos, in color and black-and-white, big ones and small ones, publicity photos, family photos, baby snaps, sunsets, winter trees, every image of life Rocky values. She searches and searches and then finds Nathan in a small scallop-edged black-and-white snapshot from a long time ago. A young Rocky stands with him, arm-in-arm, and they both look dazed. Now Cat remembers what she thought when she first saw the picture—that they looked like lovers—and what Rocky said: "No, that's me and my brother Nathan, after he got back from Vietnam." He has the same look on his face, the same bullet eyes.

And she knows, in that instant, that there is something between them, something that has kept them passionately apart all these years. Something that even Rocky Love has been unable, or unwilling, to talk about.

The moment Rocky sees Nathan waiting under the awning she feels euphoric. She can still see the last glimmer of his face, twenty years ago, turning away as he pulled shut the door behind him. She had never imagined they would be apart so long. He looks so much older now, weathered and lined, and his eyes are so brilliant they frighten her. She rushes to him. He stoops to lay his knapsack on the pavement but doesn't have time before she is in his arms.

"Whoa, watch out, you're knocking me down." He staggers backward but manages to keep them both standing. She kisses his cheek. "Hey, hey, lemme go."

Standing back, she looks at him and begins to cry.

"I thought you said lunch, like we'd have lunch. What's all this?"

"Nath, I've just missed you so much."

"Let's eat."

She reaches into her purse, finds her sunglasses and puts them on. Mustering a smile, she leads her brother, her dear long-lost finally-found Nathan, to the corner of Madison Avenue where they turn south. He walks silently at her side. She feels vulnerable, under-clad, in the russet washable silk dress she finally decided to wear. The fabric keeps billowing up, revealing skin. Now and then she receives a glance or a nod from a passerby who recognizes her. She smiles, lifts her chin. After the third time, Nathan says, "Man, it's too much, little Miss Celebrity, ha ha ha!"

"I'm used to it," she says. "You'll get used to it, too, if you hang around long enough, Nathan." *Nathan.* She loves saying his name. She can't believe they are together again.

She takes him into Leonardo's, a small, expensive Italian restaurant, and is led to a table in the middle of the room. She automatically sits facing the door, and then regrets it; this is a private, not a public, moment. But it's too late—Nathan has already planted himself across from her.

"Where are you living?" she asks him.

"Why do you need to know so much?"

"It's an innocent question."

He pauses a moment, and smiles. "Downtown, I have a little place of my own. Took me half an hour on the subway just getting here, you wouldn't believe it."

"I haven't been on the subway for years."

His eyes, embedded in folds of tanned skin, fix on her. She smiles, he does not, and the strange tension hovers until Nathan finally shakes his head. "Man, it costs a buck twenty-five, can you believe it? I would have jumped the turnstile but there was a cop. Buck twenty-five, it isn't right, it's too much."

"It's too much for that stinky subway," she agrees. "You should take taxis, it's much nicer."

A flash of humor brightens his face. "Good idea, sis. I have this great job, pays big, I'm a rich man, you wouldn't believe it."

"Of course I would. I've always known that we were both destined for great things."

Their eyes lock in a silence that is broken only when the waitress appears with two menus that are so large they have to lean back in their seats to hold them.

"The food here is great," Rocky says. "Have whatever you want, lunch is on me."

He scans the menu hungrily.

"So tell me about your job," she says.

His eyes dart from the menu to her face. "Why?"

Rocky squares herself in her chair, faces him directly and folds her hands together on the table. She will scale every obstacle he raises between them. She will not let him defeat her; he will not escape from her again.

"There's so much I don't know about you. Did you ever marry? Have children? Tell me everything, Nathan. I want to know everything about you."

He continues to stare at her. "Oh yeah, I'm married and everything, a coupla kids, the whole bit, and I'm a doctor."

Rocky laughs, fast and loud. "A doctor, huh?"

"Dokta Nathan, that's me."

"No, really, tell me."

"Okay. I'm a building whatever, I wear this uniform, I'm a whadyacallit."

"Security concierge?"

"Maybe."

"Doorman?"

"Right, that's what I do."

Rocky feels her heavy celebrity smile hanging on her face, the one that attaches to her persona like a Halloween mask she is expected to wear and so wears with enthusiasm, the one she hides behind. But she doesn't want to use it on Nathan and tries to yawn it away. "I'm so tired."

"Tell me about it, couldn't sleep, lumpy bed."

"Really, Nath, do you have a family?"

"Big family, great family. You want to meet them?"

"I'd love to."

"Absolutely, you'll meet them. We'll have you over, you and your kid."

"Parker. He's in the country for the summer, but I'm sure we could—"

"You'll meet them. You'll see. They're really something."

The waitress stops to give them a basket of warm bread and a tiny bowl of butter slices. Nathan reaches for a piece of bread, butters it and devours it in two swift bites.

"I'll have linguine primavera," Rocky says.

Nathan butters another piece of bread. The waitress smiles patiently, until finally he notices. "I'll have what she's having."

"You can have whatever you want," Rocky says.

"I don't care. I'll have what you're having. That's what I want." There is a note of anger in his voice, to which the waitress responds by nodding and moving away. He reaches for more bread.

"So, where've you been all these years, Nathan?"

"Been here a long time, long time."

Rocky wants to ask him about California, about wherever else he may have been, but she won't do it. She will have to wait until he tells her. She wishes he would show some interest in her life, ask her some questions, help get the conversation, their future, started.

When the waitress returns with their pasta, Nathan orders a caffeine-free Coke, and Rocky asks for a glass of white wine.

He eats ravenously. She picks at hers, lacking an appetite. She just can't get over the fact that he is here.

The bill comes and she produces a credit card.

He stands, and says, "I have to go."

"Wait!" She gathers her credit card and the receipt and follows him outside into the sticky afternoon. "Where can I find you?"

"I'm standing right here."

"*Nathan.*"

"You're too much, sister." The glint in his eye frightens her in so many ways, for so many reasons. "Gotta go, I'll be late." He hurries off in the direction of Lexington Avenue.

"But Nathan!" she calls after him. "Where can I find you?" Rocky stands there and watches him vanish as inexplicably as he appeared.

Cat spends Saturday morning cartooning at her kitchen table. By early afternoon, she decides to tackle her laundry, despite the inevitable crowd at the laundromat. Maybe, if she has some energy left over, she'll call a friend to meet her later for dinner.

Miraculously, she finds two free machines, loads them up, then decides to take a walk during the hour-long wash cycle. Because she now reflexively avoids St. Mark's Place—where she last saw Teddy and Isabel together, and where Isabel and *Freak* sit like a bunion on Cat's life—she walks quickly in the opposite direction, deep into a neighborhood in which she has grown comfortable. She doubts she ever would have moved to the East Village if not for Teddy. The surface can be frightening, a dragon-eyed tattoo of poverty and drugs and homelessness and hopelessness. But now that she's been here a while and can see beneath the sur-face—the muscles under the skin—she loves it, actually loves it here. She has seen strength and history in the face of the craggy old man staked-out in the tenement doorway, sadness and loss in the pained stoop of the urine-soaked lady with a matted brown wig who lives in a refrigerator box in wintertime, bitterness and disappointment in the green eyes of the young mulatto man beset with the bloat and scabs of heroin addiction, and the energy of hopeful imagination in the children who each season grow bigger and smarter as they pound their turf like warriors demanding, "Gimme change, lady." Sometimes they say please. She has seen their faces enough times to know who they are. Sometimes she gives them change, sometimes she doesn't, depending on her mood. Either way, she doesn't feel guilty down here like she does uptown when she sees street people, because up there the contrast is so much starker with their poverty set against the background of such great wealth. Here, she lives peaceably with the less fortunate, shops and eats and goes to work and launders her clothes. In a funny way she is more comfortable here than uptown in the penthouse, where she has become a sticky combination of helpmeet and undercover spy.

She walks down Third Avenue, browsing in stores, finally heading toward the homemade ice cream parlor on the corner of Bowery and Fourth Street. She comes away with a big dip of chocolate-chip ice cream on a cone. In the heat she has to lick fast to keep the ice cream from dripping to her hand. By the time she looks up from her melting scoop she is nearly at the corner of First Street. She arbitrarily heads east and two blocks later, as she nears Second Avenue, her cone is a little stump. She pops it into her mouth and chews, savoring the final bite of her treat. Then, as her eyes veer left toward the avenue, she is struck by the sight of Nathan Libbon, filthy and agitated, hunched over a garbage can.

She stops and stares. Could it really be him? It's almost impossible to believe, this man whose sister has so much, this man whom she saw only four days ago standing under Rocky's awning. But when she recalls his vivid, haunted face, she *can* believe what she sees now: a broken man who is either poverty-stricken or deranged or both. She can believe, in fact, that he is just like his sister, lost and desperate and unequipped for life, but with less money or possibly no money at all.

She steps back into the doorway of a bodega and watches him. When he gets what he can from the garbage—two soda bottles, a paper cup and a greasy crushed paper bag—he lurches away. She follows him down First Street past First Avenue. Just before the intersection, he turns into a vacant lot.

She waits a minute before approaching it, then walks by slowly enough to look and see what's there: nothing, just a few piles of rubble, an overturned rusted shopping cart, a few split retreaded tires and, against a brick wall at the back, a wire mesh garbage can black from fire and two battered doors leaning against each other in a kind of tepee. Inside is a filthy mattress half-covered in green plastic bags onto which Nathan lowers himself. He lies down on his side and props himself up on his elbow. With his free hand he places the paper cup in front of him, then pours in a little liquid from both soda bottles, a Diet Coke and a Sprite. He opens the paper bag and stares inside a moment before reaching in for the butt-end of a hero sandwich which he promptly eats. He washes it down with the mixture of sodas. Then, in one fierce movement, he swipes away the refuse of his meal. His elbow buckles and he lies down, staring up at the top of his ceiling where the doors meet in a point.

Cat turns around and runs back up First Street. She runs and runs until she is back on Second Avenue and heading uptown. When she can run no more, she stops to catch her breath. She thinks she ought to tell Rocky. But *should* she? There is something so deeply private about Nathan's predicament; she feels as if she has peeped through his window and watched him undress. Suddenly, she remembers her laundry. Over an hour has passed. She hurries back to the laundromat on Sixth Street. Someone has taken her clothes out of the machine and piled them haphazardly into a basket on the floor.

The Legend of My Hunger

The funny thing about instability is that routines can stay the same for years and years and then one day the whole mechanism just breaks down, as if trouble appeared out of nowhere like the Dark Invader.

I lived my life assuming that my family was like every other family: that Daddy was hardly ever home, Mommy was usually drunk or asleep, and brother hated our home life so much that after boarding school he went to college three thousand miles away. It didn't seem strange to me that at the age of eleven I did all the housework. Things needed to get done and no one else took care of them, so I did.

When I was in the sixth grade my best friend was Maddy. She lived two blocks up and one block over. Maddy was little, with a round face and black eyebrows and dark brown hair that her mother braided each morning. We had a deal that if I went with her to church on Sunday mornings, she would keep me company when I did my chores. Maddy did not have to directly participate. I figured it was only fair, since I wasn't Catholic and didn't believe in church but just sat there and waited for it to end.

The Red Apple supermarket was right around the corner from our apartment. Every Saturday morning, we struck out to the store with a big clattering foldup shopping cart. I carried a purse containing only the blank check Dad had made out to Red Apple, the check cashing card and a letter authorizing me to use it. Dad slept late on Saturdays because his band played clubs until four or five in the morning; he crept in around sunrise, and when I got up I usually found him sprawled out on the couch. The TV lived in my room, so when Maddy came over we could shut the door and watch our shows without bothering anyone. If Mom was out of bed when we left to grocery shop she would follow us to the door, apologizing for not going herself and explaining that she was just too tired. Once we were in the elevator, we would break into hysterical giggles and mimic my mother's standard lines: "Oh, thank you, girls" or "I'm just so tired today" or *"You're much better at the dishes than me anyway"* or *Thank god for daughters."*

"You know what it is, though?" Maddy said. Her standard line.

I shrugged. My standard denial.

"My mom says your mom drinks.*"*

"Everybody's parents drink."

"Yeah but—"

"Oh darn, I forgot the coupons."

"So what? You have a check.*"*

We agreed that coupons didn't matter as much if you were paying by check, it was just that Dad always told me to bring them. But a check, being only a piece of paper, was less significant and therefore less valuable than real money, we agreed, and so your purchase was already discounted. In a wave of relief, having passed swiftly through the danger zone of Mom's alcoholism, we swished through the lobby and onto the street, talking and laughing, dragging the shopping cart.

Sometimes after shopping we would take over the kitchen and make box cakes or slice 'n bake cookies. I had a rule that before we ate any of it, I had to dust and vacuum the whole apartment. If Maddy was desperate enough, she would help. Wet work—cleaning the bathroom and washing the kitchen floor—was saved for Sunday afternoons, after church.

Sometimes, for fun, we would shut ourselves into my room and read Zap Comix and MAD. And sometimes I would drag Maddy out to Planet Z Comics on 79th Street. But she didn't like to go because we were always the only girls and she was developing and it made her self-conscious. So after a while I got in the habit of going alone.

There was not a comic book I did not admire. I read, studied, learned them all: their palettes and techniques, their organization, their quests. And I fell in love with every superhero; it was impossible not to. But I never related to the buxom blondes the heroes saved. Those females were different creatures than me. I knew, even then, that I was not the kind of girl who would grow up to be coddled and protected. I already knew too much about independence, and I didn't really trust love (at the time, my parents' love) to make you safe.

I ate TV dinners once or twice a week. Otherwise I would cook hamburgers or spaghetti. But the best meals were when Dad cooked, and then we would have steaks with fancy sauces and complicated potatoes and salads with dressings flavored with mustard or lemon or dill. These special dinners always happened on the spur of the moment. If Dad decided to come home for dinner and wanted to eat well, he simply showed up and said, "Let's go to the store," and off we went on our treasure hunt.

We never went to Red Apple for these special meals, but to Zabar's and Fairway on Broadway. And we didn't take the shopping cart, either; Dad said it made him feel old. Zabar's always had a festive atmosphere. Tables were piled with fancy foods— cheeses and dried fruits and foreign chocolates and handmade breads and jams and pâtés and everything the grocery store didn't have, special vinegars and pastes and all kinds of nuts and fishes and cold cuts and everything, everything, too much almost to choose from. Dad would tell me not to get lost and then he'd charge into the crowd with a plastic shopping basket slung over his forearm. I had to chase him. He pushed through layers of people to get to what he wanted: Indian peppercorns and French mustard and New Jersey cream and Norwegian cheese and German crackers and dark Russian bread. Next we would go to Fairway, whose stalls spilled fruit and vegetables onto Broadway like mounds of colorful poker chips. Dad selected fat purple eggplants and huge naval oranges and shiny apples and long perfect greenbeans and curly red leaf lettuce and the biggest container of cider. He didn't look at prices, not for these special meals.

When we got home, if Mom was awake, she might dress up a little, put on some makeup and do something a little different with her hair—tie it back with a scarf or barrette. We'd turn off the lamps and light candles and Mom wouldn't drink and Dad would act cheerful and I might feel good. It was a starvation diet of happiness but it kept us running for years.

Then I reached puberty, and everything changed. Not because my parents changed, but because my perception shifted, my feelings enlarged and distorted, and my role of caretaker started to make me feel shortchanged. It was amazing how a little blood on my underpants at the age of thirteen suddenly altered everything, but it did. One day, I simply pulled out: stopped taking care of the apartment, stopped filling the cupboards with food, stopped pretending everything was all right or would be.

After a while, dust began to grow so thick in the corners that it was visible from across the room, floors lost their shine and started looking shabby, cupboards emptied without being restocked, sinks and tubs developed a greenish hue.

Mom seemed aware of a change; she would remark that things seemed quiet. One day she told me she was lonely. She told me how much she hated my father, how much she missed Eddie. My presence didn't seem to comfort her at all. She drank earlier and earlier, filling her coffee mug with vodka, convincing herself (and no one else) that it was water. By afternoon her mind was filled with white noise and veils and she was not happy but she was not quite so sad.

It was Dad who looked at the dust and saw dust, not helplessness; to whom a sink full of dirty dishes was a sink full of dirty dishes, not abandonment; who opened a cupboard looking for something to eat, and finding nothing but two old cans of kidney beans and half-a-box of lasagna noodles decided it was time to shop, not give up. So he took the shopping cart to Red Apple and bought what he thought we needed, based on what we normally had in the cupboards. And since the apartment was so dirty he got up on Saturday morning and dusted, vacuumed and scrubbed the bathroom. Then he started coming directly home from work to make sure there would be something for dinner, because even though I had grown into a long stalk of a wisecracking teenager, I was still his little girl and it was his responsibility to see that I ate.

I was very thin and I wore only black, and except for my long light hair I would have been a shadow. I was waiting to get through high school and go away to college, to grow up as fast as possible so I could move out and up and on. I slept at Maddy's whenever I could.

My happiest moment was when I broke the triple digit barrier and weighed in at ninety-nine pounds.

The harder Dad tried to get me to eat, the harder I refused. He cooked and baked up a storm, left out plates of brownies and Tollhouse cookies which he knew I used to love, cooked thick juicy steaks and overfed chickens and doused vegetables in butter. But I wouldn't eat off my diet, which consisted of one hard-boiled egg in the morning, one cup of plain yogurt and one apple at noon, and one bowl of salad, no dressing, and a glass of skim milk in the evening.

Mom's attitude was live and let live; *it had to be, since she was so tired of people telling* her *to stop drinking. So when Dad in despair tried to enlist her in his crusade to fatten me up, she said she couldn't help, it was out of her hands, I would get hungry one day and eat.*

Three years passed.

Eddie lived in Washington, D.C. now, having traveled miles and years from the upstate prep school, to UCLA out west, to law school at George Washington where he was editor of the law review. When he called to announce one of his rare visits, he said he'd be bringing a friend, but only when they walked in one Saturday did our family realize that Eddie was a man and had paired himself with a woman.

Dad made a pot of coffee, which he served in the living room along with a plate heaping with homemade raisin-walnut rugelach, Rose's recipe. Penny, the friend, sat between Eddie and Dad on the couch. Mom sat in the armchair, looking washed-out from all her drinking and not sleeping enough. I sat crosslegged on the floor in my black jeans and black sweater and black pointy-toed boots, all angles and bones like a stick figure, and felt like Eddie was just some faded-out-of-my-life uncle who'd dropped in for the afternoon.

Penny said, in a friendly voice, "Hello, Cat, how are you?" and I knew they had been talking about me. Then, after an awkward silence, Dad asked Penny what she did, and she said, "Me? Well, I'm getting my master's in social work," and Dad and Mom both oohed and ahhed but I just looked at my knee, admiring its sharp bend.

Penny sat on our old sofa like it was something special, in her clean bluejeans and crisp pink blouse. I thought she was too perky and too nice. She was what you would call petite, like a fluttery bird, with brown hair feathered over her forehead and ears. She had that fresh, healthy glow.

Eddie sat next to Penny, looking oddly grownup. Over the ten years since he'd left home, he had visited a total of four times, including now. The first time was after he finished high school, when I was eight years old, and things had not changed that much. He still wore tattered clothes and crazy hair and carried a chip the size of a skyscraper on his shoulder. Then, two years later, he flew out from California for the holidays, and he seemed strangely calm. He had chopped off much of his hair so it was a finger-length golden halo, and he had shaved so his face looked smooth, and his clothes were clean, and he talked about school as if he really liked it. The next visit was before he started law school, when he flew in to New York to interview at Columbia and NYU. He was accepted at both schools, but chose George Washington because, he told me with the old secret glitter in his brown eyes, "Anywhere in New York is too close to home for me." So now here he was again, and it was 1979 and he was twenty-six years old and practically a lawyer and had a steady girlfriend who was so normal it was weird.

Eddie stared at me, which made me uncomfortable because he had turned out so handsome and I felt like such a dumb kid. What I didn't know was that he remembered me better than I remembered him, because he was older and had known more about life during the nearly six years we had lived together, when I was just coming into life. I remembered that he was my big brother, his name was Eddie, and he was the boss. I remembered I had liked it that way. I glanced up and found he was still staring, and smiling now, too.

"You're pretty," he said. "Do you know that?"

I shrugged.

"I mean, I can remember you when you were a little kid. You were really cute. And now you're grown up and you're pretty. And I really like you in black."

Mom watched Eddie with a strange expression as if she didn't know why he was saying those things, because everyone knew I was too thin and it was depressing the way I wore black all the time.

But I smiled. "Really?"

"Oh, yes!" Dad said, and I knew he was faking it, following Eddie's lead in trying to make me feel good, because he lifted the plate of rugelach and practically threw it at me, saying, "Here, have one!"

"No thanks, Dad," I said.

"You know," Penny said, "they really are too fattening. But oh, I'll have one, even though I shouldn't." She picked the biggest one off the top of the heap, and bit half of it.

Something about Penny eating that rugelach and savoring it even though she shouldn't made me want one, too.

Then Penny said, "You know, Cat, I wish I had your discipline. I bet you'd look great in those skinny little dresses they're wearing now. Hey, let's go shopping this afternoon, Eddie's treat." She touched his knee.

A moment of astonishment flashed across Eddie's face, then his expression turned paternal. "Good idea."

"Can I bring Maddy?"

"Sure," Eddie said.

So I called Maddy, who came right over, and off we went to Bloomingdale's. We raided the Casual Dresses department, led by Penny's infectious enthusiasm. Eddie waited outside the dressing room to give opinions when requested. Penny darted in and out in clothes she knew were way too expensive. She looked good in almost everything, and would buy nothing, not today.

Maddy lumbered in and out of the dressing room, whining about how she was too fat in everything, and Eddie told her she looked just fine. She sighed and went back in to change and came out in something else.

When I came out to look at myself, I just stared blankly into the three-way mirror. Everything was too big; I couldn't under-stand why they didn't make clothes small enough to fit. There was only one thing that wasn't loose on me: a red knit dress, size one, that hugged me like a second skin, and told the truth. I looked at myself in this bright color in this bright light, repeated three times, and was surprised to see so many bones. Eddie stood back and surveyed me. He must have seen even more than I did, because he could see my back with its long knobby spine and skin stretched tight over ribs. I must have looked like a fossil, like a refugee from Bangladesh, like an incarcerated Jew. I hadn't realized how small I'd shrunk myself. My control had backfired and gone out of control like an overzealous leader who in his desire to rule becomes a ruthless killer.

I didn't have the courage to turn around and look at Eddie, so I met his eyes in the mirror. His face looked tight, like he was holding something back.

"This fits," I said softly.

And he said, "Hey, Cat, put some meat on those bones."

"Yeah," I mumbled, "all right."

"I mean it." His voice was low yet strident. "This is Eddie talking, you have to listen to me, don't forget that."

When Cat finally turns from the computer, she notices that three hours have passed. Her laundry is still jammed into the bag, probably wrinkled beyond hope. She saves her file on a disk—she doesn't keep anything on Teddy's hard drive in case he comes one day to claim it—and switches off the monitor.

As she folds her clothes into neat piles on her bed, she can't stop thinking of Nathan. Of his filthy tattered clothes, his skin streaked with sweat and grime, his hand shaking as it grasped someone's garbage for his meal. What always strikes her when she sees lost people living on the street is that they were once someone's child. They were once standing on the same ground as everyone else before a chasm opened up and swallowed them.

Cat stops folding her clothes and goes to the kitchen. There must be something here, something better than garbage for Nathan to eat. With all the cooking she's been doing lately, she always has too many leftovers. She fills a plastic container with Mediterranean Chicken Salad, and cuts two fat slices of mocha cake. She packs paper napkins and a fork. She stops at the deli for a loaf of Italian bread and a liter of spring water.

First Street seems like the end of the world, a crack in the city's surface into which half its refuse falls. In a town in which empty lots are gold mines for developers with skyscraper visions, the redundant rubble-filled vacancies on this street feel like broken promises. And just a few miles uptown live some of the richest people in the world. Cat banishes these thoughts and marches on. She is on a mission, a lone person doing what she can.

When she reaches the vacant lot, she finds him lying exactly where she last saw him, prostrate under his makeshift tepee. The plastic bag full of food feels heavy and she wonders why she didn't think to bring other provisions as well—a wet washcloth, bandaids, antiseptic, a clean sheet. Mocha cake? Will he laugh at her? She is just considering putting down the bag and leaving when his head snaps in her direction.

He stares at her, standing on the sidewalk, looking in. Then he twists around to his knees and bolts to his feet. "You?"

"I'm sorry." She takes two steps backwards. "I brought something to eat."

"You're Rock's slave!"

Cat digs her heels into the rubble. "I am *not* her slave."

Nathan laughs with a peculiar mixture of ridicule and empathy. "Yeah, you are. Everyone's her slave. I'm her slave." He shrugs his shoulders and her compassion for him returns. He could be her own brother covered in dirt, if Eddie had not had the good sense, or ability, to grow up and get a grip.

"She didn't send me," Cat says. "I came on my own."

"Bullshit."

"I live nearby. I saw you by accident. Here, I brought you some food."

"Already ate, already ate."

"It's homemade."

"I always wanted to meet a girl who could cook."

His smile is rotten. She should have brought a toothbrush.

"I have my own problems. I just thought you might be hungry, okay? Do you want it or not?"

She stands firm as he approaches her, crossing from his carpet of rubble onto the sidewalk. He reaches for the bag and she gives it to him. His fingers brush hers and she feels an urgency to wash her hands. A symphony of odors fills the air between them. It takes all her might not to run away. He nods his head quickly, for what seems a long time.

"I'd invite you in, but...." His face twists into a cynical mask.

"I have to go." She leaves him behind, standing on the sidewalk, holding the plastic bag. Her feelings are mixed to a froth; she's not sure what she has done or why. But she knows she will go back.

He is not there when she returns the next evening, and she feels relieved, exempted from the challenge of another strange conversation. She walks into the rubbly lot all the way to his tepee and deposits the large brown shopping bag.

Toothbrush, toothpaste, gallon of water, towel, sheet, razor, shaving cream, peanut butter, jelly, a loaf of pre-sliced bread, a pound of homemade Technicolor Bean Salad, a homemade pear-and-apple pie in an aluminum plate, plastic utensils, a roll of paper towels, and a neatly typed list of addresses and phone numbers of emergency services for the homeless. At the bottom of the list she has typed her own phone number, but not her address. She hurries out of the lot, onto the sidewalk and around the corner—away from the bleak avenue.

At home, she serves herself the remaining portion of Technicolor Bean Salad, with some bread and cheese on the side, and pours herself a glass of red wine. It feels perfect to be locked inside her apartment tonight. Alone and lucky. She turns on *60 Minutes* and eats with the plate propped on her knees. When the phone rings, she lets the machine answer.

"Hey good fairy slave. Beans beans they make me fart good for your head good for your heart. You spoil me. Is she paying you for this?"

Cat lunges for the phone. "No, I told you, I'm doing it on my own."

"Were you sitting there the whole time listening to my voice?" She can hear the honking sounds of traffic in the background

"I'm eating dinner."

"You have no sense of humor, that's your problem. I bet she bosses you around. If you had a sense of humor you wouldn't feel so fucking guilty you had to feed the fucking poor."

"Poor? All you have to do is pick up the phone and Rocky'll give you whatever you want."

"Yeah, well."

"Nathan, why don't you ask her? I know she loves you a lot."

"You don't *know* how much she loves me. You don't know how *much* she loves me."

She is silenced.

"Why do you think I'm out here? Why do you think I'm out here, lady?"

"I don't know," Cat says quietly.

"I got two choices, that's why, only two." He slams down the receiver and she is left with a buzz in her ear. One man. Two choices. And a lifelong secret that won't stop resonating in what's left of his mind.

Chapter 16

The Rise and Fall of Rocky Love

Suspended Disbelief

S itting at the table with Parker, while Nancy prepared their breakfast, all Rochelle could see was the swirling cowlick in Parker's thick black hair. She sipped her coffee and stared at her son, her beloved adorable son in his blue pajamas covered in red space ships.

"What're you looking at, Mommy?"

"You need a haircut."

"I'll take him this afternoon, after school." Nancy set a bowl of cereal in front of Parker and a bowl of fruit salad in front of Rochelle.

"No, I'll take him."

"That's all right, it's on the way."

"I'll take him after breakfast."

"But he's got preschool at eight-thirty."

"So he'll be late." Rochelle spooned a kiwi slice into her mouth.

"Yay, a mommy day!"

"Can't it wait, Rocky? They're expecting him." Nancy stepped around to see Rochelle's face. "You won't even be showered and dressed until ten o'clock, at least."

Rochelle separated out a banana slice and ate it. "Delicious fruit salad. May I have some more coffee, please?"

"But—"

Rochelle pushed her half-empty coffee cup toward Nancy, and dug for a grape. Nancy took the mug and returned to the kitchen.

"Why are you taking me, Mommy?"

"Mommies are supposed to take their babies for haircuts."

"I'm not a baby."

"I know you're not, sorry."

"Nancy always gets me candy afterwards at the place."

"Candy's not good for you."

"She always does."

"We'll see."

"She *always* takes me to the place."

"What place?"

"You don't know. You never took me before."

"Then you'll have to show me."

Two hours later, they were on their way out the door. Nancy watched them go, still as a statue, face taut with anger. Rochelle ignored her, took her son by the hand and left.

Parker was clearly happy for the break in his routine. He ran ahead of her down every block, and waited at every corner. Nancy had him well trained. When Rochelle tried to take his hand to cross the street, he objected. "I don't do that anymore, I'm old enough to cross myself." He ran across, hopped onto the curb, and waited. When they got to the barber shop, Parker ran to the door and began to open it.

"Wait," Rochelle said. "We have another stop to make, first."

"But I have to get my hair cut."

"Later. Come with me."

All the way to the doctor's office, Parker asked, "Where are we going, Mommy?" and she answered, "You'll see." When they arrived, he stood by the door and jutted out his bottom lip in rage. "Why did you bring me here?"

"What's wrong, darling? It'll just take a minute."

"I hate Dr. Rabinowitz. I'm not sick. Why didn't you tell me? I want to go to school!"

"You can go after this."

"What about my haircut? And you said you'd take me to the place for candy."

"After the haircut I'll take you to the place and get you as much candy as you want."

"I might want the whole store."

"Fine."

"Really?"

"Anything you want. Just come inside and let Dr. Rabinowitz see you for one minute."

Parker entered the doctor's office reluctantly, but he entered. Five minutes later, they were back on the street heading to the barber for the haircut he didn't need, and to his favorite place where he would buy enough candy to make him sick. But Rochelle was satisfied; she had both blood tests now. She had only to wait for the results.

Four days later, Rochelle went to see Jason at his office. With her was her new lawyer, David Halperin, who carried in his briefcase the results of Tad's and Parker's blood tests. David was as coldly professional as Jason was warm and friendly. Young and slick and ambitious, David didn't care about being liked, he only cared about winning; he was the kind of lawyer Jason hated most. This seemed an asset to Rochelle, because to distract him would be to disarm him. And David, likewise, would be unafraid and uncharmable; he would take his sharp knife and slice directly to the heart.

Jason was waiting. His desk was uncharacteristically neat and he was wearing a gray suit. Rochelle knew what that meant; she had been married to him, after all. It meant he was prepared to fight. He came around to greet them with smiles and handshakes. David shook hands cordially and nodded and did not smile. Jason stiffened slightly, released his hand and retreated behind his desk.

David swung his briefcase onto his knees and flicked open the latches. He withdrew the blood tests, closed his briefcase and set it back on the floor. Then he leaned forward and pushed the blood tests across the desk to Jason.

Rochelle recalled lying in bed with Jason when she was pregnant, the warmth of his hand circling her taut belly. He sang a lullaby to their unborn child. She blinked back the start of tears as she watched him now, reading the documents. Then she sobered up. She was here because he had waged battle against her. She was doing what any mother would. She was fighting for her child.

When he finished reading, Jason looked at David, then at Rochelle. His face seemed to shrink and harden as he processed this new information. This simple biological evidence that the woman he had loved and married had deceived him even more than he had realized. This proof that his son was not his son.

He shook his head, rubbed his eyes, took a deep breath, and handed the papers back to David.

"What about Parker?" Jason asked David.

"Parker loves you as a father. You can have visitation rights, but clearly there is no entitlement to custody."

"Does he know?"

David looked at Rochelle. She said, "I don't see any reason—"

"You tell him." Jason leaned forward, flattened his hands on his neat desktop and lifted himself halfway up. "You tell him who is father is, or I will."

Rochelle had not expected this from Jason. "Are you serious?"

"Completely. You cannot perpetuate this lie on our ... on your son. He'll find out eventually. Tell him now. You tell him. Take responsibility, for a change."

"What do you mean by that?"

"Calm down," David said. "Let's all collect ourselves."

"I'm finished." Jason sat back in his seat. "He's yours, Rocky. And I mean it, if you don't tell him, I will."

"Tell him he can't do that, David."

David's manicured fingers smoothed the top of his slacks. "You just won, Rocky."

"I said tell him he can't talk to Parker about this."

"That's a different matter," David said, "and perhaps it would be best for the boy if someone told him the truth right away."

"No one has the right to tell me how to mother my child."

"Mother your child?" Jason shook his head and tried to laugh; but instead, he began to cry.

Parker didn't really know who his father was these days, with all the men who came and went from the new penthouse. His mother had told him they had to move uptown because "uptown was a state of mind." What had she meant by that?

He sat crosslegged in front of the picture window that overlooked Central Park, wearing a red nylon cape and holding a plastic steering wheel, maneuvering himself through space.

His mother had explained to him that he had many fathers now, which made him a lucky boy. He could tell which one it was by the feel of the hand on his head or shoulder, and by the smell the man brought with him. Mort's hand was warm and firm, and he smelled of cooking, curries and cookies and sometimes puey fish. Tim's hand was light and cool, and he smelled of cologne; it was the scent that reached Parker first, before the hand. His mother called Tim her "new friend" but Parker was sure he'd heard that name before. When he asked her, she said Tim was a friend his real daddy (who he never saw anymore and who he missed *so much*) didn't like but now that Daddy was gone it was okay to see Tim again. And there was another friend, Tad, whose hand was kind of damp and so hairy that it tickled Parker's cheek, and he always smelled of beer. He liked Mort best and Tim worst but it had been made clear to him that he had no choice in the matter. Something funny happened when his real father left. It was like the swoosh of a vacuum sucking up his real life.

His mother had explained that she had to "clear the decks," "root out the betrayers," "cleanse herself of any poisonous mistrust" in her life. Parker hadn't known what she was talking about. He turned the wheel slowly, shifting his universe right.

Then Nancy left, crying and hugging Parker like she didn't want to go. And when he asked his mom why Nancy was leaving, the answer was, "Nancy's not on our side." Funny, 'cause Parker had always thought Nancy loved him.

There was another lady now, Annie, and she was nice, but he wasn't used to her yet. She took him to school and picked him up, fed him, bathed him, clothed him, read him stories, hugged him and all that. But she wasn't Nancy so he had to get adjusted. That was what his mom had said, "Just give it time, you'll adjust."

Rochelle was also trying to adjust to regular life now that the divorce was settled and drifting into the past. It had been hard for her, had challenged her a little too deepdown, had shaken her basic foundation of self-confidence. No one took kindly to the news of Parker's biological paternity. Mabel had disowned her once again, and even Norman seemed distant now. Leo was a rock, or pretended to be; he had been judged too much to presume to judge others. And Jason, well, he had been so stunned by the revelation that he dropped everything, *splat*; what he had loved and wanted and fought for suddenly wasn't his. She had never seen a strong man shift so quickly from euphoric fight to retreat. It was a violent withdrawal, which gave her an initial sense of victory that quickly dissolved into sadness. Now, she felt like a flat tire: empty, squashed, treadless.

And then Charlie called to lower the boom about *Mother Love*. They had been so close to a contract, actually in negotiation. He said, "You didn't think I could finesse *this* one, Rocky honey, did you? Getting you out of this one is not a do-able thing."

"But I had no choice," she pleaded. "Don't they understand that I couldn't lose my son? He's my child! The only way would have been to let Jason have him."

"Rocky, first of all, calm down. Second thing, listen to me, and remember I'm on your side. A little reminder: Jason's lawyers already found out about whatsisname, the kid's real father, so you were cooked no matter what. So don't sweat what you did afterwards. You did what you had to do. The network wasn't gonna sign either way."

"They would have if it had been a man."

"You tellin' me Donahue wouldn't get skewered if it turned out he had another woman and kid behind Marlo's back? Honey, he'd get it, too."

He was right; she had gone too far. She had always managed to bounce back. But like Charlie said, "Not this time, baby. It's kaput." He told her to take a vacation, and get back to him when she had another project in mind, which, he said, "you're gonna."

But she didn't feel even a seed of hope. The difference between this and other times of derailment was that she felt finished, whereas in the past she had always had a mischievous eye cast upon the future.

Twice a week, she was visited by Serena, her psychic healer. Serena said, "*Visualize* your happiness, *draw* it to you with your own good energies. You have power, here," she touched her forehead, "and here," she touched her stomach. Rochelle sat across from Serena on the floor of her study. They had lowered the curtain over the magnificent view, and meditated in shadow.

"Look inward," Serena said, "to flourish outwardly."

Rochelle practiced her affirmations every morning. "I am beautiful, full of power. All good things come to me now. I am healthy, wealthy, wise. I am beautiful and young. Only the positive now manifests in my life." She wanted to throw in something about hexing the no-gooders who had deserted and betrayed her, but Serena said their objective was to create a positive charge in her chakras, and negative thoughtwaves would only weaken her.

Every morning, she meditated and visualized, concentrating on drawing all good forces into the culmination of her perfect existence, and things like that. She had decided to replace Betsy, but instead of firing her and hiring someone new, she used it as a test case for her developing inner powers, and meditated on it, sending out positive thoughtwaves with which to attract the-perfect-assistant-for-her-at-this-moment-in-her-life.   For

Parker, she visualized health, wealth and happiness, created for him a perfect future with the positive thoughtforms she emitted into the universe.

After lunch, she would dress in one of the skirts she had had shortened to meet the new mini fashions. She liked suit jackets that pinched her waist so her figure looked voluptuous, blossoming, not fat. The higher the heel, the better, for high heels lengthened her legs. And more and more, her color was black, not because it was the color of power, authority or fear, but because black slimmed. She would hit the city streets for appointments in the afternoon: hair, nails, fittings at her favorite designers, tea at the Mayfair, drinks at the Polo Lounge. Then, home to see Parker for dinner. Often, she would eat with him at six: plop herself down at the table next to him and wait while Annie served up dinner. And then, when her date arrived, Mort or Tim or sometimes someone else, she would dress herself up and head out for an eight o'clock dinner at a restaurant. And often, after sex, she'd get so hungry she would have to tiptoe out to the kitchen for a snack. If her lover of the evening was Mort, he would join her. If it was Tim, he would languish in bed and smoke a joint.

She saw Tim only in the city; Mort was the one who blended more naturally into the countryside. Tim was too slickly handsome, groomed for the city. Sexually, he was amazing. She thought he had the best penis in the universe and let him do all kinds of things to her with it. She liked to hold onto it, like a handle, while she fell asleep. He'd lie on his side to accommodate her.

She had resumed payment of his rent—he had moved to an apartment just a few blocks from her new penthouse—and filled his wallet with plastic and paper money. He kept them supplied with cocaine.

Connie left messages inviting Rochelle to attend AA meetings. Rochelle stopped returning the calls.

One wintry Sunday in Amagansett, early in December, Rochelle and Mort relaxed together on the long feather couch, sharing the newspaper. Annie sat on the old comfortable armchair, reading a book. Parker played monster war in the dollhouse castle Rochelle had given him early for the holidays, and Tad sat next to the castle, aiming a flashlight at the monsters that Parker maneuvered. The smell of rugelach baking was sweet and rich. First Mort would roll out the dough—which he liked flaky so used lots of butter—then he'd spread it with his own special apple-honey mixture, and then sprinkle it with poppy seeds. Sometimes he dusted it with crushed walnuts. It was an all-purpose rugelach sure to bring back childhood dreams. Rochelle lay back, her feet on Mort's lap. He held her toes loosely, wearing an apron dusted with flour, reading the magazine section.

Rochelle's nose twitched, and she said, suddenly, "We'll market you!"

"What's that, honey?" Annie said.

Rochelle looked at Mort. "Gold Rugelach."

Mort smiled, tilted his balding head back, thought it over. "You mean, start a company?"

"Yes. Mrs. Fields did it with cookies. There's an untapped market in Jewish desserts. Rugelach in different flavors and sizes. You'll make your million, you'll sell the company, and be free to *live* your music."

"That's a mean idea," Tad said.

"You'll photograph the rugelach," Rochelle told Tad. "I'll fund the company, get it going. You'll quit your job, Mort, and direct the bakery."

"What'll I do?" Parker asked.

"You can be the little boy eating rugelach in the ads. Would you like that, sweetie?"

"Yeah, okay."

Annie spread her book face-down across her knee. "Oh Lord, we're gonna have ruggle comin' outta our *ears.*"

The next night, in the city, Rochelle rolled over and whispered to Tim, "I'm going to make you a star!"

He seemed interested, curled his body around her, and said, "How?"

"I'm going to introduce you to everyone I know in Hollywood. You have everything it takes. All you need me for is to open the right doors."

"I need you for more than that." He smiled.

Yes, oh yes, need me *pleaseneedme*. She kissed him, her soft lips pressing his taut mouth, forcing it open. He stroked her body like it was the most glorious one on earth. He pressed his fingers under the black lace of her teddy, and with the other hand reached down for the snaps between her legs and undid all three with a quick tug.

They slept until ten. They did one line of coke each, then headed for the kitchen. Annie was sitting at the table with her tea and the morning paper. She had been up since six, as usual, and had already taken Parker to school.

"May we have some breakfast, please?" Rochelle sat at the table. Tim, wearing only jeans, sat next to her.

"What would you like?"

"I'd *love* a Spanish omelet," Rochelle said, "but don't use any butter on mine."

Annie waited for Tim's order.

"That sounds good to me, but with butter."

"Coffee's on the way." Annie retreated to the kitchen.

"I'll have Tad fill out your portfolio," Rochelle said to Tim. "I'll do your resume myself, and then we'll go to L.A. for a week or so. We'll stay at The Beverly Hills Hotel. I'll introduce you around, take you out, show you off. I guarantee you'll have at least one screen test while we're out there. I can make it happen," she snapped her fingers, "just like that."

Late at night, the sweeping view inverted, and what was green became a well of darkness beyond which loomed a canyon of tall boxy shapes and white lights. Sometimes a reddish light sizzled along the edges of the Westside nightscape, a toxic red glow from New Jersey.

Rochelle and Tim sat crosslegged on the parquet floor, facing the huge plate window. They wore handmade caftans that were a gift from Serena: Tim's was white, Rochelle's black. They sat side by side, holding hands, looking out. With Parker and Annie long asleep, the quiet was exquisite.

"The city has an aura tonight," Rochelle said. "That means that somewhere in this city, tonight, a miracle is happening."

"Yeah, wow," said Tim. "It's so red." He passed her the half-smoked joint.

She drew on it. "This is an aphrodisiac, you know."

"Tell me about it," he said, and disengaged his hand from hers. He ran his hand under her caftan and along the inside of her thigh.

She stared out the window, smiling. "Those fabulous lights."

"Let's turn this one on," he said, lightly touching her clitoris.

Rochelle didn't notice his clichés so much anymore; he was too good a lover, and her mind was too tired from fighting, lookinggood, beingfamous, explaining herself. And between the powder, booze and smoke, an onion skin had formed around her mind; subtleties didn't penetrate like they used to.

She slid slowly down until she was lying on the floor and raised her arms above her head. Her bronze hair fanned out beneath her. Her eyes were wide open, watching the white ceiling, and she concentrated only on the sensations of this seduction. His job was to thrill her and hers was to let him. He sat up on his knees, pulled off his caftan and tossed it aside. His blond hair stood in crazy tufts. His eyes looked small and dim, glistening, faraway. His body was long and straight and tight, and every inch of it was tan, even his genitals. She paid for him to lie under tanning lights at the health club, and to exercise, to keep his body perfect. That was part of his job and he willingly complied. He lifted up her caftan and pulled it over her shoulders and head. She lay there like a rag doll, letting him, accommodating with only the smallest movements. Then, he lowered himself over her, and as he placed his penis almost inside her, he said, "I love you," then slid all the way in.

Her hips jerked up in reaction and she struggled to hold herself back. His was the active role, hers the passive. That was the deal, unspoken but understood. She had *had it* with giving and trying and paying, for nothing; she knew now that she had a special role in the lifeforce of the universe: to be loved, admired, served. There was no need for her to *do* anything in return. Serena had helped her with this. In the past, she had been so burdened with guilt, driven to do, try, strive, struggle, deserve. No more. Now, finally, she was free.

She lay there as Tim slid himself in and out of her body. She could feel him watching her face. She stared at the ceiling, letting her mind do all the work, feel the sensation, not care about pleasing him. He was used to it. He clamped his lips to one of her breasts and sucked like a baby. Her breasts went red. He rode her more furiously until her vaginal muscles clamped around his penis. Only when he felt her coming did he join her in release.

He brought them wine, cold Riesling from the refrigerator. She liked to watch him move around the living room naked, doused in a silver hue from the citylights. She liked to lie on the floor, uninhibited, in front of her window with her legs spread and oozing. She liked to think that maybe someone was watching, yearning, loving her from afar.

Even after sex, Tim's penis was thick and erect, suspended straight out in front of him. He sat on the floor and handed Rochelle one of the glasses. "Cheers."

She flashed him a big smile and clinked his glass.

It was still early, not quite nine, when they finished the wine and went back to the bedroom to dress, leaving their glasses and caftans scattered on the living room floor. Rochelle put on a black silk dress and black pumps. Tim wore a white double-breasted designer suit with baggy pants, and a pair of black and white Italian shoes.

"Hey—let's walk!" Tim said.

Rochelle looked at him, a finger stuck into the back of her shoe, challenged. Her eyes sparkled. "All right, let's do it."

So out they went into the cool autumn night, and instead of taking the usual taxi, they walked the six blocks downtown to the patisserie where they often went for chocolate rum cake and espresso, and to find one of their special friends.

When Annie heard the front door click shut, she lumbered out in her robe and slippers. She always waited up to clean their mess so Parker wouldn't have to see it when he got up early in the morning. There was a fist in her stomach, pre-disgust at what they might have left. Annie had found all variety of underwear, food, drink and whole vegetables scattered on the floor and furniture. She had found magazines with blood and white fluids streaked conspicuously on upholstery. Once, she found urine dripping down the window. But tonight it was not so bad.

She folded the caftans and fluffed the pillows on the couch. She brought the wine glasses to the kitchen, washed them, dried them and put them away. Then she heated herself a cup of hot milk and sat with it in one of the comfortable leather chairs in the soothingly dark dining room. Usually she took her after-dinner snacks to her room, just in case one of them lurched naked toward the kitchen. But tonight, since they were out, she let herself rest a few minutes.

The clunk of bolts turning in the front door lock woke her abruptly. She opened her eyes and sat up straight as the door swung open and Rochelle's throaty laugh poured in. She wanted to say *Quiet, he's sleeping*, but didn't; this was Rochelle's house, she was his mother, her boss.

Annie stood. Rochelle, Tim and two men came in. They were all giddy, excited, overdressed, shiny, arrogant. Annie didn't like the people Rochelle and Tim brought home together. She thought Rochelle didn't try to make real friends but settled for these phonies instead. She had heard Rochelle say as much: "I can't trust anyone; I'm too famous for people to treat me as if I'm real."

Annie would have liked to treat her real, tell her to grow up and take responsibility for herself, her son, her work, her life. She would have liked to slap Rochelle across the face and tell her to pick up her own mess, stop dreaming, stop telling lies, stop making promises she would never keep.

Rochelle saw Annie standing tentatively in the opening between the dining and living rooms, like she wanted to run back to her room unnoticed.

"Hi, Annie," Rochelle said.

Tim turned around, and said, "Hey."

Annie decided to take a grandmotherly stance and greet their friends with civil disinterest. "How are ya?" She did not expect an answer.

One man said, "Good evening."

And the other one, a small skinny man Annie especially disliked, just pressed his lips together and waited for her to disappear. She knew these two from other late night appearances; she knew what they wanted, who they were and what they sold. If she were Rochelle's mother she would have kicked these drug dealers out of the house on the spot and told her to pull her act together. But she kept silent; she was Rochelle's employee, Parker's nanny, and she understood that the best way she could protect him was to make sure she didn't get fired. She was beginning to understand what had happened to the last one.

Not only did the cocaine thin Rochelle but it rejuvenated her mind, or so she thought. Now, in the mornings, she meditated for ten minutes, locked her study door, did a line of magicdust and uncapped her pen. She had decided to begin her memoirs, and watched her script flow onto the blank pages like waves, a brilliant surf.

C h a p t e r 17
Confidential

Rocky goes to her bedroom, locks the door and heaves open the trunk. She kneels in front of it, looking for something special. Cream lace. Red leather. Black fringed whip. Studded wristband. Ankle cuffs. Split-crotch panties. Garters, fishnets, spangled pasties. She particularly likes the split-crotch panties, the whip and ankle cuffs, and pulls these out of the tangle. She tosses the things onto her bed and carefully lowers the lid of the trunk. She peels off her slacks, sweater and silk underpants, and puts on the panties and sheer black teddy that grips her bosom together. She dabs Opium perfume on her neck, armpits and between her legs. Then she goes to her closet to look for something to wear over her costume.

There is a knock at the door. The knob wiggles. Cat's voice says, "Hello? It's locked."

Rocky unlocks the door, swings it open and smiles. She sees the girl's eyes jump from her to the bed, where the whip is coiled like a snake.

"Don't worry, it won't bite you. Neither will I."

Cat stands there in her khaki slacks and lime-green blouse. She has new hot pink laces in her basketball sneakers. The front of her hair is swept back and clipped with a pink plastic butterfly. Rocky can't remember how old Cat is, exactly—twentysomething. She'd like to give the young woman a little fashion advice, and thinks, suddenly, *no wonder that boyfriend of hers dumped her.*

* * *

Cat waits as Rocky belts a gold kimono around her waist, then hands her an envelope that has just arrived by messenger. The return address is that of a lawyer, and a red stamp below the address announces *Confidential*. Rocky rips open the envelope, reads the letter and slaps the stapled pages at the air.

"Larry's suing me! He wants to block my memoirs! Well, he can't do it!" Her eyes—dilated, scared, scary eyes—fix on Cat. "Who told him?"

Cat holds still, offering nothing.

"It must have been Connie." Rocky's tone is fierce. "I'm going to sue that bitch."

Cat leaves, shutting the door behind her. From the hallway she can hear Rocky's voice raving inside her room. Minutes later she charges into Cat's office, transformed from lewd to somber in a black dress and leather sandals.

"I'm meeting with David over dinner tonight. Make a seven o'clock reservation at the Surf Club."

"For two people?"

Rocky stares out the window, suddenly frozen, just gone. She looks perilously close to the endless sky.

"Rocky? You okay?"

"How could they do this to me? Larry and Connie were my friends, I don't understand it." Rocky turns around, anguished. "I don't want anyone to know about this, all right?"

"Of course," Cat says, possibly even meaning it. She is beginning to feel truly sorry for Rocky.

"He's wrong if he thinks I won't fight back. He knows I'm very litigious, he knows that about me. Has he lost his marbles?"

Cat doesn't know what to say. She boots up the computer and watches the start-up commands scroll down the blue screen. Rocky remains at the window, staring out.

After a minute, she turns around. "Well," she says, "when the going gets tough, the tough go shopping." The joke falls flat. "I'm going to Bergdorf. If anyone calls, I'm in a meeting."

Noontime gives way to early afternoon. Without Annie and Parker around, it's way too quiet here. Cat works for a while before feeling overcome by a subversive restlessness, a residue of distraction that seems to linger in the air like one of Nathan's many odors, like Rocky's expensive perfume, like her residual feelings for Teddy. She tries to push the feeling away, but finally gives in to it. She can't concentrate, she can't work. She makes some personal calls that eat up over an hour. Then she kills another hour doodling some new ideas for a cartoon. As the afternoon reaches its groggy middle and Rocky still isn't back, she gives herself permission to leave early. She knows she shouldn't, but her restlessness has grown too strong and she just has to get out of here.

All the way down in the elevator, through the lobby and along the hot August streets, she fears running into Rocky. If she does, she'll pull out the usual explanation about a trip to the post office for priority mail stamps. But it's not necessary. She reaches the subway, descends into the sweltering tunnel—and is safe.

Twenty minutes later, she ascends at Astor Place and heads home, stopping at the corner *don't walk* light. That's when she sees Teddy crossing in her direction. Her heart jumps—at least that's how it feels—twists and lurches and bangs at her chest. She wants to run away but he sees her before she has a chance.

He plants himself in front of her, his blue eyes bright but not happy, and says, simply, "Hi." His hair has grown inches longer in the four months they have been apart.

"Hi," she says.

"How are you, Kitty Cat?"

She loves the sound of her old nickname spoken by Teddy's voice, and against her better judgment, she smiles.

"So, how are you?" he asks again.

"Fine. Working. You?"

He doesn't answer, just shrugs his shoulders as if to indicate that he doesn't know. "I thought about calling you, to say hi, you know.... Bullshit, I *did* call. You weren't home."

"You should have left a message. I would have returned your call."

"Really?"

The answer that pops to mind is *Yes you turd, I was almost the mother of your child, we mixed DNA, I loved you and would have married you if you'd only asked but you lost faith in us, remember?* But what she says is, "Sure, why not?"

"I guess I should have, then."

"How's your dissertation coming?"

"Slowly, but getting there. And your cartoons?"

She shifts her weight from foot to foot. "Haven't done much lately," she lies, "just sketches." The *Legends* are too personal to share with anyone, even Teddy, *especially* Teddy. She wonders if he saw the busted-wedding-cake cartoon she left with Isabel. Hopes not. It was too close to the work she's doing now, too raw, slicing a woman in half like that and showing the inner contradictions.

"Shouldn't you be pushing a little harder right now?" he asks. "You had a golden opportunity handed to you."

"You overestimate yourself, Teddy. *Freak* isn't exactly a golden opportunity."

"Didn't Izzy give you the letter she got from Exit Ramp?"

"Exit Ramp? That gallery?" *The* gallery for emerging cartoonists.

"They're putting together their annual show. They were interested in seeing some of your work."

"What letter?"

"God damned Izzy. I should have known.... Listen, Cat, call her up."

"I asked her to send me the last cartoon I left with her. I never heard back. I didn't feel like dealing with her and I guess I just let it go."

"She published it, didn't you know?"

"She *published* it?"

"I assumed you knew. Izzy and I weren't talking much by then, it was such a mess—"

"Please, spare me." Cat really doesn't want to hear about the two of them. She wants only to think about herself, her plundered cartoon, her missed golden opportunity to be considered by the only real cartoon gallery in the city for their annual show. Everyone goes to that show—all the critics, editors from the big magazines, book editors, film animation people. You can start a career in the annual Exit Ramp *Cartoonworks*.

"Call her," Teddy says. "Ask her about the letter, she probably still has it. Get it from her."

Cat nods, then shakes her head. "No, I won't let her jerk me around. If I call her, she'll bullshit me. I'm going over there right now."

"Go for it." Teddy is smiling now, beaming really.

"I'm on my way. Thanks, I think."

"Good luck." He bends to kiss her cheek and she lets him. His lips feel soft and familiar against her skin. She smells his musky smell, and she misses him. When he pulls away his eyes look as full of emotion as her heart.

She reaches St. Mark's Place, marches up the front stoop and jabs the bell.

Isabel's head pokes through the open window. "Yeah?"

"I want to talk to you!"

Isabel stares down at Cat for a moment, then disappears. The buzzer sounds quickly, but in that brief instant Cat manages to open the door. She walks through the hallway, up the grim tenement stairs, to Isabel's. She knocks. Waits. Finally, the door cracks opens.

"I'm busy," Isabel says.

"I understand you have a letter for me."

They face each other awkwardly, the bleached waif-like Isabel, cigarette burning between two yellowed fingers, and Cat who in comparison feels earthily robust.

"That's it?" Isabel asks. "That's all you want?"

"Just give me the letter, please."

Isabel releases a snort of laughter and swings the door all the way open. Placing her fingers against her lips, she takes the last drag of her cigarette and a long ash flutters to the floor. She goes to her desk where she mashes out her cigarette in an overflowing ashtray and rifles through a pile of papers. Toward the bottom she finds a ripped-open envelope addressed to Catharine Gold c/o *Freak*, and hands it over.

"Who opened this?" Cat asks.

"Who do you think?"

"You had no right to open my mail. And you had no right to publish my cartoon."

"You submitted it to me."

"I wrote you a letter asking for it back."

Isabel grins archly. "Never got it."

"You're a liar."

"Look, I don't care what you call me. I'm a business woman. I survive. You want your so-called career to move along, then you tend to it yourself. Don't expect me to come running after you."

"I never expected that. I only expected the usual courtesy."

"Courtesy? That's a word I don't even know." Isabel crosses the room to a bookshelf crammed with *Freaks*. "Guess I forgot to give you your two copies."

For a second Cat feels like throwing the *Freaks* back at Isabel, but she doesn't—they belong to her. Everything she had the first time she walked into this room still belongs to her: talent, ideas, probably even Teddy's love. She looks at Isabel—the survivor, the fighter, the weathered sage—and feels almost sorry for her. Cat has what she came for; there is nothing else worth saying. Between Rocky this morning and Izzy now, Cat wonders *What is it with these women?* At twenty-five, younger than both of them, she vows never to be so desperate that she will plunder her way through life. Yet already she senses that it will take a magic trick or two to get what she feels she deserves (though she hasn't yet decided exactly what that is) without a struggle.

The minute she gets home, she phones Exit Ramp, but their machine answers with a message that they are closed for the day.

"He couldn't get it up, not once." Rocky crosses her ankles on the leather ottoman and sits back in the matching armchair. She hasn't said anything about Cat's absence yesterday; assumedly she got home after six.

Sunshine dazzles through the big office window. Cat had planned to call Exit Ramp first thing when she got to work, but Rocky was waiting for her, and she's still here. It's almost noon now and she still hasn't dressed, she's still in her caftan and slippers with her hair a royal mess.

Suddenly, Rocky says, "Like making some money!"

Cat looks up from her work. "What?"

"Charlie's going to sell my memoirs for two million dollars."

Cat's fingers fly over the computer keyboard, typing nonsense.

"Call John," Rocky orders Cat.

"And say what?" But before Rocky can answer, the phone rings with a call from her lawyer.

Rocky takes the call standing in front of Cat's desk. "No, I will not change my mind. It has nothing to do with Larry Drumm. He's an egomaniac, that man. No, I will not change a thing on demand." She slams down the phone and tells Cat, "I am creative. I *create*. I don't *confiscate*. I've *never* had a man who hasn't been convinced he was the cause of my success."

Despite everything she herself has done to contribute to this mess, Cat feels sad seeing Rocky so confused. Sad and satisfied and frightened and excited. She feels so many things, watching Rocky unravel.

"And Larry," Rocky says, "is angry at me because he couldn't get an erection. I'll tell you, it's the same old story. Men always blame women in the end." She shakes her head. Then she reaches up and touches her hair. "Will you make an appointment for me at Lisa Long's, please? The works." And she marches out.

Minutes later, Cat's intercom buzzes and Rocky's voice says, "I'm indisposed should anyone call." Then it buzzes again: "Except for the following people...."

"Who?" Cat asks into the intercom. "Except for who?"

Rocky's voice responds, "Whom." Then, after a moment: "I will speak with the following people if they call...." Again, her voice fades to silence.

"Rocky?"

"Yes?"

"Which calls should I put through?"

"Lawyers and lovers," Rocky says, and the static of the intercom snaps off. And then suddenly it buzzes and her voice adds, "And my accountant, I'll talk to Harold. I need money. And Charlie or his secretary. And call John."

Cat puts the call through to John. "Greetings from the loony bin."

"Uh oh."

"Rocky wants to talk to you. Watch out, she's on a roll."

"All right, ready."

"We should talk again soon," Cat says, "there's a lot happening here."

"Excellent. When?"

"Anytime. After work? I have something to show you."

"Want me to meet you there?"

"No, meet me at my apartment at seven o'clock."

"Where are you taking me?"

"You'll see. Nowhere you expect, that's for sure."

She puts the call through to Rocky. Then she reaches under her desk for her purse, and takes out the envelope from Exit Ramp. She unfolds the letter and reads it over one more time before dialing. It is short and friendly, describing the show, which is to open in January, and inviting her to submit some work. The name at the bottom of the letter is Marshall Korn.

When Marshall Korn finally places her name, he sounds surprised but pleased. "I assumed you weren't interested," he says.

"I just got your letter. It got buried under a mountain of paperwork at *Freak*." She knows better than to malign Isabel professionally.

"Well, we're finalizing the show next month. I guess we could look at something if you get it to us soon."

"That's no problem. I can have my portfolio ready in a couple of weeks."

"Good. Give me a call when you're ready and we'll set something up."

"Thank you, I appreciate it. And I'm sorry I was so late getting back to you."

"Don't worry about it. It really won't change our decision."

"Thanks again."

She hangs up the phone, leans back in her chair and re-plays the conversation in her mind. Marshall Korn sounded like a nice man. She believes what he said about her lateness not mattering. If she hadn't left work early and run into Teddy, she never would have found out about the letter. She considers calling Teddy to invite him to dinner over the weekend, cook him a feast. Then she decides she won't. She doesn't owe him anything. Why should she feel so grateful to have been given what was rightfully hers?

That night, promptly at seven, John arrives with a bottle of wine. "Just in case it's BYOB where you're taking me."

"It's definitely BYOB, but alcohol might not be the best idea."

"Where're we going, an AA meeting?"

"Worse."

"Is there food involved, at least? I'm starving."

"I'm bringing food, but it's not for us. You'll see." She hands him the shopping bag she has prepared. "Let's go."

She leads him down to First Street. They continue east beyond First Avenue.

"It's *Mad Max and the Thunderdome* down here," John says. "Ever see that movie? It *made* Mel Gibson's career."

"Nope, don't like post-destruction futurisim. It's depressing."

"I guess you don't need to see it, since you're living in it."

"It's not me who's living it," she says. "But I'll show you who is." She turns into Nathan's vacant lot.

"This is a joke, right?" John stumbles after her. "Hey, Cat, wait a minute."

She heads straight for the shelter, which is strewn with dirty plastic forks and empty containers. "He isn't home." She deposits the bag.

"Who isn't home?"

"Nathan Libbon, Rocky's brother."

"No way!"

"Way."

John stoops to look inside the rickety tepee. "He lives in here?"

"Yup. I've been bringing him food."

"For how long?"

"Since Saturday."

"Does Rocky know?"

"He doesn't seem to want her to."

"You should tell her," John says. "This is really terrible."

"I don't know who's crazier, do you?"

"Good point. What now?"

"I want you to meet him. Let's leave him a note in case he comes back soon."

"We could go back to your place and wait for him."

"I don't think I want him to know where I live."

"Right."

"There's a pizzeria on the corner of Second Street and First Avenue, we'll go there." She takes a pen out of her purse, finds an old receipt, jots a note telling Nathan where he can find them and weighs it down with a stone.

At the pizzeria, Cat and John sit side by side on an orange bench, sipping large waxed cups of soda, waiting for a plain pie. She is watching the street through the grimy window when all of a sudden there is Nathan lurching up the pavement, his thick hair bouncing. She notices he has shaved his face. He sees them through the window, stops walking and stares in. She gestures him to come inside. Finally, he opens the door.

"What is this?" Nathan stares at John.

"John's a friend of mine."

Nathan shakes his head furiously, and then suddenly stops.

John slides out of the booth and thrusts out his hand, smiling a little too hugely to mask his obvious discomfort. "John Paglia, great to meet you."

Nathan wipes his hand on the back of his filthy jeans before shaking. John does not flinch.

"We ordered a pizza. How about something to drink?"

"Coke."

"Coming right up." John goes to the counter.

"No caffeine!"

"Large caffeine-free Coke, please," John orders.

"No caffeine!"

"It's taken care of," John says over his shoulder.

"Have a seat." Cat gestures to the bench opposite hers. "I'm glad you could make it."

"Yeah well like I didn't have any plans tonight." He drums his grimy fingernails on the Formica table. *Nail clippers*, she thinks, *a bar of soap.*

John brings a giant-sized paper cup. "One caffeine-free Coke." He sets it down in front of Nathan along with a straw. Nathan immediately peels the paper off the straw and plunges it into the soda. He hunches protectively over the huge cup and grips it with one veined hand. His lips purse around the straw.

"How long have you been here?" John asks.

Nathan's lips detach from the straw. "About two minutes."

"No, I mean New York."

"Long, long time."

"I understand you fought in the Vietnam War."

"How the fuck did you know that?" A fury rises in Nathan's eyes.

"Rocky told me. I'm writing a book about her."

"A book?" Nathan chuckles; the nascent storm has passed.

"I've interviewed almost everyone in your family."

"Not Earl, he's dead."

"No, not Earl. But I've talked to Rocky's former husbands and her friends. I've had long talks with Leo, and Robby, and both of your parents."

"Mom and Dad!" Nathan releases a sound that is half laugh and half shout.

A bell dings. The pizza is ready. "I'll get it." Cat goes to the counter and retrieves their pizza. When she gets back to the booth, Nathan is talking rapidly to John.

"Dad was never there for us, he was always working, and he left us with Mom, and she wanted us to be just like him, but we didn't know him, he didn't know us, and she didn't know us either, she only saw what she wanted to, and we all had to grow up to be doctors except Rock and she was supposed to marry a doctor, which she did, she did, now look at her, she's all plasticy, Earl's dead, Leo's a fruit, I'm crazy. They cut me off, Dad kicked me out, kicked me right out, sent me to this school you wouldn't believe, it was like a military school and if I told you what it was like there you wouldn't believe it, so I ran away, I had to, and there wasn't any money, but I wrote to Rock, she used it in her articles and it was okay with me but she got rich and I was broke and then I got drafted, and I went, I didn't fight it anymore, I went, and then...."

Cat listens silently to the flood of tortured reminiscence. He sounds more hurt than crazy, more angry than deranged. She wonders if anyone has ever asked him before to tell his side of the story. He goes on and on, weaving the dark fabric of his life, taking the golden threads of his sister's life and weaving them through his own, pulling threads from his parents' stories and weaving them with his own, telling everything, all his truths, all at once, reweaving the stories John has heard from everyone else. Except for one surprise—though it does not surprise Cat.

Twenty years ago, Nathan and Rocky were lovers, just for one night.

She knew it. And now John knows it. Which means that, when all is said and done, so will the entire world.

The next morning, Rocky happens to be standing in front of Cat's desk when the phone rings.

"I'm hungry I'm hungry I'm hungry I'm hungry!"

"You must have the wrong number," Cat says, and hangs up.

"Who was that?"

"Don't know."

The phone rings again.

Cat ignores the first two rings. "It's probably the same person."

"Maybe it's not." Rocky reaches for the receiver but Cat answers first.

"I'm hungry I'm hungry I'm hungry!" This time Nathan is so loud that Cat's ear automatically jerks away, and into the free air sail his words, his unmistakable voice.

Rocky's face freezes, on alert. "Who is that?"

"It's your brother." Without thinking, Cat thrusts the receiver into Rocky's hand.

"Hello? Nathan, it's me. Your waitress? What do you mean?"

Cat watches Rocky's face as she listens to what sounds like a drone of babble. After a while, Rocky says, "I'll tell her." She hangs up the phone.

"He says he's been waiting for his food. What does that mean? He said you were his waitress."

"I don't know. He's kind of off the wall, isn't he?"

Rocky's face pinkens. "No, actually, he's not. Do you know where he is?"

Cat shrugs.

"*Tell me.*"

"I don't want to get involved in this."

"How do you know where he is? I don't even know."

It seems plainly wrong not to give her what she wants. Nathan is her brother, after all, and the charade has gone on long enough. Cat has her *own* brother and her *own* life and her *own* things to worry about. She has to worry about getting out of here, for one thing, preparing her portfolio for Exit Ramp and paving her way out.

"I saw him one day, downtown, in my neighborhood."

"Where exactly?"

"First Street, east of First Avenue."

"I want the exact address."

"That's it. He lives in a vacant lot in this thing he built." Cat presses her fingertips into a tepee.

Rocky pushes herself away from the desk, her gaze heavy on Cat. "Are you saying he lives on the street?"

"I was planning to tell you."

Rocky stalks out of the room. Moments later, Cat hears the front door slam shut.

As soon as Rocky's taxi crosses East 14th Street, she senses that she is in foreign territory. She sits in the back seat, clutching her purse, watching urban scenes flicker past. A strange combination of emotions gives her the feeling of a sickened high. Yet more than anything she feels elated to finally know where to look for Nathan. The taxi careens around the corner of Second Avenue and First Street and speeds east for a block and a half, before slowing down and stopping.

"This it?" the driver asks.

Rocky peers out the window. "I don't know, it doesn't seem right. Will you wait?"

"It adds up, you know."

"I don't care how much it costs." She hesitates before opening the door and stepping out, and hesitates again before walking between two battered parked cars and up onto the sidewalk.

This can't be right.

But there, in front of her, is a vacant lot. And there, pressed against the back wall, is a tepee shelter with a man huddled inside. Rocky turns around to make sure her taxi is still there. It is idling by the curb and the driver is watching her, a gesture of chivalry she finds comforting. She turns around and proceeds into the vacant lot.

As she walks, sharp bits of rubble lodge between the bare soles of her feet and the bottoms of her white leather sandals. She does not want to enter the lot. If she had the power to turn away from Nathan now, she would do it; she would do it in an instant. But she does not, she cannot, because Nathan is herself, her motivation, the seed of inspiration that coaxed her into being. He originated her. He has been inside her body.

She moves carefully toward him until she is about ten feet away. Stopping, she turns around to look at the taxi. Still there, but not watching, fiddling with his radio, getting bored.

"Nathan, wake up. Nathan, it's me."

His eyes open but his body remains still.

"It's me."

He stares at her.

"How are you?" she asks.

Navigating himself into a seated position, he says, "Great, how are you?"

"I want you to come with me."

"Where to?"

"Home. Why didn't you let me know?"

"Maybe this is my life, maybe that's why."

"I can help you."

"This isn't about you. This isn't about being famous. This isn't about being right. This is about me—me me me me." He springs out of the tepee and paces the rubble. "I don't know if I want your help. This is my life. Mine."

"I would take your help," she says. "If I needed it, I would ask for it."

"But you don't need it." He shouts: "DO YOU?"

The force of his voice sends shivers through her. She collects herself. She will overcome this obstacle; she will.

"Yes, I do need your help. Money isn't everything, Nathan. I'm lost, too. My life is falling apart, too. I need you, too. I *need* you. When I saw you last week I thought my ship had finally come in. I did. You can help me. I'm asking. *Help me.*"

He stands by the blackened garbage can, hands poised on his slender hips, body pitching slightly forward. He shakes his head repeatedly, then sighs. "All right. You're full of shit, Rock, full of it, but I'll come. I'm hungry, I stink, I'm tired. Fine, I'll help you, I'll come. Fine. Okay. You got me. I'll come."

She wants to turn back toward the taxi in the expectation that he will follow her, but she can't take that risk. He's right, he does stink. Nathan stinks. This is Nathan. She steps forward and reaches out her hand.

"I'll get my things." He goes to the tepee and digs around behind the mattress for his knapsack, into which he zips his few belongings. When he does not take her hand, but instead walks beside her, she feels relieved.

The taxi driver shakes his head. Through the open window, he says, "No way, lady."

"I'll double the fare."

He considers it. "Triple, maybe."

"Fine, triple. Now let's get going."

Nathan snickers. He opens the back door and gets in. Rocky gets in after him. All the way uptown his foot taps on the floor, tap tap tap. Rocky rarely glances at him. She has one goal in mind: to get him into the shower and wash his clothes. After that, she doesn't know.

Nathan falls asleep directly after his shower. Seeing no alternative, Rocky puts on Annie's rubber gloves, picks up his clothes and dumps them into the washer. She uses two scoops of detergent and sets the machine on heavy duty. She presses the on button, and hears a satisfying whoosh of water. Then she goes back to check on Nathan, clean glistening Nathan who sleeps so soundly, anchored in dreams. She sits on the edge of the bed, then lies down beside him, from to time whispering his name, "Nathan, Nathan," on the chance he might gently wake.

Chapter 18

The Rise and Fall of Rocky Love

Queen of the Dream

*D*rinking and drugging and the deep dark anxiety of waiting-for-Tim-again were trapping Rochelle in a bell jar from which she observed that others appeared terribly distorted, unkind and unfair. But those watching her, looking in, were increasingly troubled by the sad twisted shape of what they saw. Rochelle was heavy and bloated; her expressions had the look of a mask, something hard placed upon her face to hide the truth of her pain. She was trapped in the distortions of an obsessive love, and by the substances she used to sustain the illusion that it was working. It was destroying her.

It wasn't Connie who convinced her she had to change things, saying, "Because I care about you, I have to make some observations. When Tim moved in with you, I thought, *he's a little young, but fine, he turns her on and it's her life*. But when Annie called me that night and I came over and found you strung out on your bedroom floor wearing Tim's clothes, then I didn't think *well that's okay*, I thought, *she's in trouble, it's time to help her*." No, it was not Connie who penetrated Rochelle's mind at first. Nor was it Serena when she said, "Your kundalini is blocked, you aren't focusing, your channels aren't flowing anymore." It hadn't mattered to Rochelle for some time whether or not she had access to her lifeforce. Nor was it Parker, who kept a distance and eyed her with quizzical concern. Even Annie tried, saying, "Honey, you're getting fat again." Not even that fazed Rochelle. What got through to her, finally, was a smell.

It was *CoCo* by Chanel; she would have known it anywhere. And the last place she had ever wanted to smell it was on Tim's undershirt.

Then the other signs appeared: unexpected absences, a sudden interest in auditioning for parts when he hadn't even tried since moving in with her; and phone calls with no one on the other line when Rochelle answered. It was obvious he had another woman, but still, she searched frantically for hard facts. Three months after the smells began, clues surfaced in his credit card bills: hotel rooms, jewelry, clothes, all the cliché other-woman charges. She was appalled, angered, consumed with jealousy. She hated him, yet refused to consider letting him go. It didn't occur to her that he had been destroying her for three years, or that she had used him to destroy herself. All she saw was her man deserting her in stages.

Finally she asked him: "Who is it?"

"Darling?"

He sat on the chair by a window in their bedroom, unlacing his black sneakers. She stood by the bed with her hands planted on her hips.

"With whom have you been sleeping?"

His fingers froze for an instant before continuing to pull at his laces.

"No one," he said, "just you."

"The Plaza, the Waldorf, Bulgari, the River Cafe. How *dare* you spend *my* money on some bimbo!" Her face was hot, burning. She wanted him to deny it, to serve up some delicious explanation, something sugared and spiced enough to hide the ugly scent she had picked up. She wanted him back, wanted him to convince her he'd stay. She felt that without him she would die.

His blond head, face still so young, sunk between his shoulders as they shrugged meekly. "Her name's Lorraine. She has a place downtown. I'm moving in with her."

Laughter burst from Rochelle like a shout.

"I got rid of him," she told Annie. "He was no good for me, I had to let him go." Even though it was a lie, it was a beginning. Annie listened and nodded.

Now everyone moved in on Rochelle like a squad team for mental health: Connie, Serena, Mort, Annie, Leo, Norman, even Parker. She let them all care for her in their own individual ways: Connie, by involving her in Nar-Anon, a twelve-step support group for addictive people; Serena, by upping the ante on her spiritual quest; Mort, by feeding her homemade cakes; Annie, by encouraging her to diet; Leo, by listening to her repetitive tales of love and loss; Norman, by letting him visit her with memories of the family and the past (as if to remind her that, no matter what, she had one—a family and a past); and Parker, by saying "I love you, Mommy" even when she didn't tell him first.

After months of forced sobriety, spirituality and family times, Rochelle decided it was time for a comeback. She would retake her success, rejuvenate it, create a new beginning for the second half of her life. And she would do it with her memoirs. A bestselling tell-it-like-it-is by Rocky Love would give her a tremendous boost. Offers would come to her. She would be back on track. But she hadn't worked on her memoirs for a long time, as long as she had been sidetracked by Tim and cocaine and wine. She had to find the pages Betsy had typed, so went to the office to look.

She had never gotten around to firing Betsy; the girl had left on her own months ago. The office was now a wreck, piled with unopened mail, old pink message slips for calls never returned. In her search, she discovered that instead of filing, Betsy had simply dumped papers into an empty drawer. It was worse than Rochelle had imagined; she would have to hire someone soon.

Finally, she found the paperclipped pages of her memoirs under an old newspaper on top of the credenza. Dust clung around the edges. She blew off as much as she could, sat down in the chair, and began to read.

And what she read shocked her. She had written these pages of her life in a state of inspiration—and they were awful. She had poured herself out, but had failed to tell a story.

She would have to begin again; there was no other way.

Chapter 19
Zap

C at sits at her table with cartoons spread in front of her. It's a rainy Saturday morning and she is ready to organize her portfolio for Exit Ramp. There are so many choices it boggles her mind. She knows she should show her strongest work, which her gut says are the *Legends*: stand-alone cartoons as well as comic strips about alcoholism, ACOAism, anorexia, divorce, loneliness, romantic love, abortion—the dark underside of growing up in a dysfunctional American family. *Her* dark underside, anyway. Or she could show *Man in Tights: The Adventures of a Bisexual in the Age of Aids*, but it's already feeling old to her. Then there are her *Max & Min* strips—they are much more fun than her other work—but Rocky would probably sue her. Ironically, the *Legends* comics are a safer bet, though they will expose every one of her vulnerabilities. And what if, *what if* Marshall Korn hates them? Would she ever overcome such a poignant rejection? While she contemplates the possibilities, she moves the sharpened tip of a pencil in a long slow arc over a sheet of white paper, an act of drawing-and-thinking that has always cleared her mind.

Then *zap*, the doorbell rings, concentration busted.

She gets up, considers her unkempt attire—old ripped jeans, worn slippers, stained white sweatshirt, no bra—then decides not to worry about it. It's probably Con Ed, or some delivery, though she can't imagine what. Possibly something that needs to be left for a neighbor.

But when she opens the door, there is Teddy, rainsoaked, smiling, carrying a flat wet paper bag.

"What are you doing here?" she asks, lamely trying to hide her pleasure at the surprise.

He steps inside and looks around the apartment. "Just about the same," he says.

"I haven't had much time to change things yet."

He nods, looks her over. They both know that her statement was inaccurate, that it isn't time you need to change things, but inclination.

"This is for you." He hands her the wet bag.

She takes it to the kitchen and peels back the sopping brown paper to reveal Matt Groenig's cartoon books, *Love is Hell* and *Work is Hell*. She laughs. "Thanks."

"I saw them and thought of you and, well, of us." He shuts the front door and steps into the kitchen. "Just kidding."

"Come in, why don't you?"

He takes off his dripping wet jacket and hangs it by the hood over the doorknob. He's wearing the green-and-aqua striped shirt she always loved. Bending over, he snaps a pair of rubber galoshes off his wing-tipped leather shoes.

"They're antiques," he says. "Don't want to ruin them."

"You bought them in that old junk shop," she says.

"Touché."

"So, how'd you know you'd find me in?"

"It's Saturday morning. Is there some place else you might be?"

"Sometimes," she says.

"Oh? Where?"

"It's none of your bee's wax. If you want coffee, I'll make some."

"I want," he says, and sees the makings of her portfolio scattered across the table. "You got in touch with Exit Ramp?"

"Isabel had the letter sitting on her desk the whole time." She stops the vitriol from forming into words. Standing in the kitchen doorway, she looks at him hovering over the table, truly interested. She recalls, when they were together, how encouraging his concern for her artistry was. It was one of the many things she had loved about him. She could have gone on loving him forever, the way he came along and changed her life, changed solitude into loneliness, friendship into need. Loving Teddy changed her from a creative mind comfortable in isolation, into a female, body gushing fluids, wanting to please. Life became a banquet of desires, fulfillments, hungers. Loving Teddy changed her. He teased her out of her contentment. Then ran.

She goes into the kitchen and puts some water on to boil. She knows she should not be doing this, loving him secretly in her heart. He hurt her once; won't he do it again?

She brings coffee in for both of them, puts the mugs on the trunk in front of the couch and sits on the blue canvas director's chair. "Actually," she says— because she has to, because this feeling she has for him is too dangerous—"I *am* seeing someone right now." The lie seems insignificant in the broader context.

"Who?"

"You don't know him."

He looks around the apartment. "So, where is he?"

"He isn't here."

"Why not?"

"He just isn't."

"So it isn't exactly serious."

"I'd rather not talk about it."

"You brought it up."

"Tell me about Isabel. What happened?"

"No."

"Fine, Teddy, good. So don't ask me about...."

He grins. "You almost said his name."

She clenches her lips, snorts laughter.

"Hey, Kitty Cat, he doesn't exist, does he?"

"He brought me those flowers." She points to the white roses John gave her.

"Oh, nice—they're dead."

"Well, they're old."

"Okay," Teddy says. "Truce. I'm sorry."

"What for, exactly? I'd like to know."

"For bothering you. For disturbing you. It's just that I was really glad to run into you on the street." He stands up and moves in the direction of his jacket.

"Wait," she says. "Sit. Drink the coffee I went to the trouble to make for you."

He turns around to look at her, his eyes twinkling. "You sound like Grandma Rose."

She takes that as a compliment, and smiles. Teddy had once told her that her grandmother was the loveliest bossy woman he'd ever met, and that he wished he'd had a grandmother like her. Grandma Rose, who had loved filling Teddy up on espresso and baked goods, received the news of their breakup with one of the most dreadful silences Cat had ever experienced.

"Really, Teddy, sit down. Since you're here I want you to know what I've learned these last few months." By *learned*, she also means *endured* and *inflicted*, but she knows better than to lay it on too thick in her introduction.

He drinks his coffee and she proceeds to describe her recent life to him, which mainly consists of stories about work. She holds him captive all morning, beyond noon and into the early afternoon, figuring she owes him some discomfort. She wants him to know the good and the bad, how she has acquired all kinds of new skills and is now an able typist, a good cook and a deceitful in-house spy. How her sorrow over the abortion and her despair at losing him and her loathing of Isabel have created a shell around her heart. How she entered Rocky Love's life to help her, and to help herself, but instead became the final domino poised to make an icon tumble. How she assessed her choices and did not always make the nicest ones. The words *anger* and *strength*, *satisfaction* and *regret* pepper her story. She isn't proud of herself, but she won't lie.

Not a wisp of judgment clouds Teddy's deeply listening expression. Eventually he pleads hunger and begs to take her out to a meal. She agrees. They can see through the windows that the rain has stopped; the black street is glossy and there is a bluish hue in the air. They go to the deli on the corner of Second Avenue and buy two beers to bring to the Indian restaurant which, like most, has no liquor license. Then they come back up the street to their old favorite place called *Taj*.

Inside, it's dark and narrow and crowded with small square tables. The thick molding on the walls is carved with an elaborate design. The air is incense-sweet. A young man in a gray suit and white turban seats them against the wall. Another man brings menus, two glasses and a bottle opener.

Cat can't get over how normal it feels to be with Teddy. But she wants to know, before she gets swept into love again—because she can feel it happening, the deep-down undertow—she wants to know what happened. The truth.

She leans forward, as Teddy sips his frothy beer, and says, "Please tell me about Izzy."

He nods, puts down his glass. The room is dark and sweet. They are in the No Smoking section and so there is no cloudiness, no confusion. This is one of their clearest, cleanest, lightest moments together in months. The truth. The real truth: just what really happened.

The story begins amidst appetizers of meat and vegetable somosas and banana fritters, and continues and ends with lamb curry, chicken tandoori, rice pilaf, mango chutney and poori.

"I knew her before I knew you," Teddy says. "Well, you know that. But we were lovers. She wasn't exactly my girlfriend, and I guess she resented that, and then you came along." He shrugs his shoulders with uncharacteristic timidity.

"Came along?"

"I went out for a slice of pizza," he says, "and things changed."

"Two slices. You had two slices that day."

He smiles, nods. "Right. You had one. That was the last night I saw Izzy for a while."

"You spent the night with her the day we met?"

"Yes."

"Go on."

"The thing is, I never explained what happened. I just stopped going over, and she only called me once, and you answered the phone. Remember? You told me someone hung up."

Cat remembers: it was the morning after their third night together, Teddy was in the shower and the phone rang. When she answered it there was a pause, then a click.

"That was her. I didn't see her again until the night I took you over."

"Don't leave anything out, Teddy. What are you forgetting?"

He stares at her. Thinks. Nods. "Yes, there's something. About three weeks before I met you, she had an abortion. It was her idea, but I completely agreed."

"I know. She told me."

"I guess that shouldn't surprise me."

"When did you start seeing her again, Teddy?"

He thinks a moment, nods, then begins. "She published you in *Freak*, and I was really grateful."

"Grateful?"

"That she helped you, Cat. Not that you didn't deserve it."

"Did I?"

"Yes, you did. She knew it, too. She wouldn't have taken your cartoons as a favor, that's not Isabel. She liked your work."

"But not me."

"I don't know, probably not. But that isn't even the point, is it? She resented you."

"Obviously. Why did you bring me to her in the first place? That's what I can't understand."

"In my mind, it really was to show your work."

"Teddy, it doesn't take a psychiatrist to know there had to be more to it than that. Most people try to avoid having their girlfriend meet their ex."

He grins. "You're right, of course. In perfect hindsight I can see I was planting a bomb. And when it didn't go off on its own, I went back to detonate it."

"Meaning?"

"I went to her apartment one afternoon, to thank her for publishing you. I asked her for copies of *Freak*, and she gave them to me, and she asked me to stay for a drink, and I did. We talked."

"And then?"

"Then—we went to bed."

She reminds herself that she asked him for this. She *hates* hearing it yet it's a relief to know the facts.

"Then?"

"Then we avoided each other, until one day we bumped into each other on the street. It was just before you had your abortion, and things were not good with us. Then it started up, and I got very confused, and when you asked me to move out I felt paralyzed."

Details, she wants *details*. "What happened?"

"You were angry with me and I knew it. She was angry, too, but anger suits her better than you. Know what I mean?"

Cat stares. She does and she doesn't. "Go on."

"I have always been afraid of the commitments involved with having a family. I'd like to have one, believe it or not, some day. I don't know if I can describe the feeling of panic."

"Try."

He pauses, thinks, continues. "It overwhelms me when I think of what it would mean to be responsible for another life, what it would mean to support a family, day in and day out. I can hardly breathe. It terrifies me. And then the feeling is *I have to get out*, whether I want to or not."

"So you called Isabel?"

He smiles, nostrils flare. "From the frying pan into the fire." But Cat isn't in a laughing mood. She waits. And finally, he continues. "Actually, I didn't call her, I just went over. In the end that was what really burned her up. She said she wasn't there for my convenience, that I was using her." He winces. "But I think she was right. I just wandered over one afternoon and there she was and I stayed for hours. I told you I was in the library. She told me I was making a mistake with you, that you were too dependent on me, that I was asking for trouble. She told me I was lucky you were going to have an abortion. She told me that a woman has a 'profound right'—that's what she said—to have the baby if she's pregnant, and the man who impregnated her has a 'moral obligation' to take care of the mother and the kid whether he wants to or not, and that I was lucky you let me off the hook, and I should get out while I still could."

"Izzy said that to you?"

"Yes. And I was confused about what had happened between us, and I listened. But Cat, it was different with you. I was confused because I loved you and I was scared of reaching the next level, of being responsible for loving you. I never loved her. *Never*."

"That's why you left me for her?"

"No. I was scared and restless. She gave me reasons to run away. They were the wrong reasons, but I ran anyway."

"She was in love with you, Teddy. Didn't you know that?"

"No, not really. I mean *no*. Love and Isabel never came together in the same thought. But she is a force, Cat, you have to admit that. She moved me. It was mainly an intellectual thing, and sex."

He is right, Isabel *is* a force, and she influenced Cat, too.

"I saw her for about a couple of months. It was ridiculous. In the end, she was acting more possessive and dependent than you ever did. That's when I knew she had manipulated me with all this jazz about my rights as a man. Love isn't about rights and even-steven and logic. I remember the moment I knew how much I missed you. Izzy was setting type for the issue of *Freak* with your wedding cartoon with the smashed cake and the halved woman. It all came flooding back— that I loved you. And I realized I had made a mistake. Then Izzy started saying I seemed distant and what was going on and she felt like she was being used and for example remember the beginning when I didn't even call, I just came over. She grew up on Long Island, you know. That bohemian thing is just a charade to fool herself into thinking her unhappiness has a purpose. Some time in June, I told her it was over."

"June?"

"I didn't want to call you until I had my head screwed on straight."

"But you didn't call me. You saw me on the street by accident, and today you just showed up."

"236-4079."

"That's my number."

"You had it changed after I moved out, but I got it from Izzy's Rolodex. I memorized it."

Cat insists on paying for her half of the meal, so as to avoid confusion, at least for now.

He walks with her down the block, back to her apartment, formerly theirs. It's dark out and a little chilly and now she knows the truth. She also knows that she is still in love with him. So when he says—standing together in front of the building, both aware that this is a pivotal moment: that she can invite him upstairs, or simply go in alone—when he says, "Believe it or not, I'm really and I mean really sorry about what happened, I mean everything," she believes him. He isn't perfect by a long shot, and never was. But she sees him better now, with his fault lines glaring, and figures that any man would end up looking like a cracked egg after a while.

As soon as that image enters Cat's mind, she thinks of Rocky and her cynical commentary about the limited capacity of men. What about women? Separately, one is probably no better than the other. And isn't it when you put them together that you get all the trouble and all the fun? She could make a stand now and self-righteously reject Teddy for being highly imperfect the first time around. But in her heart, she wants him back.

She thinks of Samuel Johnson's famous assertion that "Marriage is the triumph of imagination over intelligence. Second marriage is the triumph of hope over experience."

Hope over experience. Cat can't argue with the sentiment as she slips her hand into Teddy's, plunging back into a love that, however imperfect, feels too tempting and unfinished to refuse.

Chapter 20

Rise and Fall

*R*ocky sits on the patio, basking in the cool breezes of the late September evening, waiting. It is a transition time of day: Parker finishes his homework, Annie gives him his dinner and then stays with him in his room, Cat finishes her work and leaves, Nathan returns from his mysterious daytime outings. Mostly, she is waiting for Nathan. She feels nestled inside a steely blue calm, the eerily still inside of a storm which feels too good to be true, the eye, where power is so dense it doesn't move. It waits. She waits inside it. The cool winds of the drugs that once swept her through time could not compete with this.

August was a test, she now thinks. Foregoing the pleasures of the beach house and staying in town was dangerous for her, and she did it anyway. She needed to spend some time alone with Nathan. And to work on her memoirs, which finally, today, are finished. As soon as her book is published, she will be back at the top of the list, top of the charts, top of the world. Her comeback will be magnificent, and this, she now understands, is what she had to save her energy for.

The sliding glass doors open and Cat emerges into the heights of sky and air, carrying a thick manuscript. Rocky has been anticipating this moment for days. John had called to say he was almost finished, and that he had reworked everything into a "new and improved" version of her memoirs. The first draft was good; she expects this one to be great. Her life, her magnificent life, her brilliant career.

Cat lays the heavy manuscript in Rocky's lap. "Here you go. Enjoy. I'm on my way home."

"Is John here?"

"No, he messengered the disk. I printed it."

"I'm so excited! I've been waiting for so long for this moment. Cat, do you realize how much things are going to change now? You'll benefit from this, too. We'll all have more money. We'll get lots of attention."

The girl nods and smiles, but routinely, as if she hasn't heard a word.

"You'll see," Rocky says. "Is Nathan home?"

"Haven't seen him." Cat steps back inside and slides the glass doors closed.

Rocky likes it out here, alone under her own tent of sky. She runs her hand over the smooth cover sheet, then looks down and reads the title: *The Rise and Fall of Rocky Love.*

Fall?

She begins to read. And she reads. And she reads.

Once daylight has vanished and the white page blends with the black words, she moves inside. There is Nathan, sitting on the couch, leafing through *New York* magazine.

"How long have you been here?" she asks.

"Long time."

"Why didn't you tell me? You don't know what I've been going through." She drops the manuscript on the coffee table. "I gave him hours of interviews and he spews out these awful lies. He has twisted and mutilated my life. My life, Nathan. *My life.*"

"The book?"

"This is *libel.*"

"So don't publish it." He flips through the magazine, stopping at a full page close-up of Madonna.

"This will never be published. But it doesn't matter. Libel is libel, and *intent* to libel must be a crime. That insolent ghostwriter is going to pay for this. I should have known...." She reels back to the day he rebuffed her overtures. Gay? She doubts it. He must have been planning this all along.

"What a fox!" Nathan says of Madonna in a bustier.

Rocky grabs the magazine and hurls it across the room. "Nathan, do you hear me? Do you understand what is happening here? Nathan!" She grabs a chunk of manuscript and plops it into his lap. "Read this! Just *read* it."

She picks up the second half, where she left off, curls into the corner of the couch and continues to read. Nathan leans back and stretches his legs in front of him, crossing them at the ankles. He lifts the first page and shakes it out before fastening his attention to the story.

It is after midnight when Rocky finishes reading. Nathan, always a slow reader, is only halfway through. He has not rendered an opinion yet, but she doesn't need to hear it. She knows exactly where she stands and what she will do.

She goes to her office, sits at her desk and dials Charlie's home number. When he finally answers, she shouts, "What took you so long?"

"Who is this?"

"Charlie, we have to talk."

"Hey, Rocky, I was sleeping."

"I just finished reading the memoirs. It's outrageous! You should see what that egomaniac ghostwriter has done to my life. I want you to sue him. Call my lawyer and sue the bastard."

"Hold it, Rocky. We've already got one lawsuit flapping in the wind, let's not start another one unless we have to. Can we talk about this in the morning when we can think straight?"

"I am thinking straight right now."

"I'm not. Babe, it's late. You gotta get some sleep. Will you do that for me?"

"I can't sleep, Charlie."

"I'll tell you what. I'll call John right now and we'll all meet at your place first thing in the morning, say nine-thirty, and we'll hash it out. Let's not sling any lawsuits around until we've really talked it over."

"*No.* I want you to sue him, right now!"

"Honey, no one gets sued at midnight. Nine-thirty, okay? Get some sleep. We'll talk it over tomorrow."

Rocky slams down the phone. Sleep? She will never sleep.

"Nathan? Nathan, come here!" She waits for a minute but he doesn't come. So she goes back to the living room. And there he is, sitting on the edge of the couch holding a manuscript page in front of his face, laughing.

By nine-thirty sharp, Charlie, John and Rocky are seated around the dining room table. Charlie seems more interested in the breakfast Annie has laid out than in the really pressing issue of this meeting. For once, Rocky is annoyed by Annie's hostess reflexes; coffee, maybe, but the scones and muffins go too far. John is clearly enjoying his apple-walnut muffin. The nerve. This is the last muffin he will ever eat in her penthouse.

The manuscript, now creased and smudged, sits in a heap of unaligned pages in front of Rocky. She slaps her hand upon it. John's eyes rivet to her face. Charlie quickly drinks some coffee to wash down his mouthful of scone.

"This," she says, "is an outrage! *Totally* unacceptable. Full of lies and slander and libel."

"Libel?" John says.

"You should be a fiction writer," she says.

"It's all based on interviews. I have notes, tapes, transcripts. I talked to almost everyone you know. You were aware of that. You even encouraged me."

"My people did not give you your words. My people did not give you your attitude of ridicule. And where did you get the idea to call it *The Rise and Fall* ...? What fall? No one has fallen. Are you out of your mind?"

"Now hold on, Rocky," Charlie says. "A title can be changed, no problem."

"It's not just the title, Charlie, it's everything. Here." She pushes the bulky manuscript toward him. "Read it."

"All right. But for the purposes of this meeting—"

"Read it."

"I can't read it this very minute." Charlie faces John. "Can you tell me your side of this real quick?"

Rocky snorts and shakes her head. "He has no side. He's a hack. I hired him to work for me. On your advice, Charlie, he came through you."

"Let's just keep calm here. Nothing is undo-able. That's my job, doing and undoing, so let's not forget I know how to do these things. I gotta hear both sides, Rock, just to give me a picture. John?"

"I talked to everyone. I can't change the facts. I didn't live her life—she did. What can I do?"

"You could crawl back under your slimy rock," Rocky says.

"Honey, calm." Charlie tries to pat her hand and she instantly pulls it away.

"I've done an enormous amount of work on this," John says. "I've lived it, breathed it, slept it, ate it. This is my *Citizen Kane*. This book has taken almost a year of my life and I really think I did an excellent job with the material. I gave you what you wanted. Think about it. Think about the angle and the sales potential. You may not see it now, Rocky, but what you have here is a gold mine. This will jump-start your bank account. You'll be set."

"My finances are fine. It's my career I'm worried about."

"What career?" John says. "You haven't worked in years."

Charlie shoots John a pleading look.

"Let's face it," John says, "this book is going to hurl you back into the big time. Somebody's going to snap up the film rights. Picture it, *The Rocky Love Story* on prime time TV. You've never even done prime time. This will put you right in the center. It's beautiful. This is going to work just like you planned."

"I didn't plan this and I don't want this and I won't have this! This garbage will never be published with my name on it or for that matter with your name on it. You're off the book. Charlie, find someone else. Find someone who can write."

"Oh, hon, now? After all this?"

"Now. Do it. *Now*."

"My contract still stands," John says. "I get paid for what I did no matter what. My royalty is written in stone."

"We can't afford this," Charlie says. "Rocky, John can do re-writes. We can work everything out. But we cannot afford to pay him what his contract which is legal—binding, Rocky—says he's gotta get. And we've still got the Larry Drumm lawsuit hanging over our heads like a goddamn guillotine. What are we supposed to do? There's limits. We can't afford to pay John off *and* pay another writer for a full re-write *and* pay off Larry Drumm when this thing hits the stands and his turn comes around. Babe, one thing you could do now is strike out that Larry Drumm chapter, just toss it out, save yourself a bundle."

"Whose side are you on, Charlie? And who is this royal *we* you've been talking about? Nothing is at stake here for you. You're not paying for any of this. This is my story and my life and I won't take orders from you or Larry Drumm or some hack writer."

"No one's saying you should take orders. All I'm saying is think about it. Look at this gorgeous place you live in. Look at it. Well? You get socked from all directions and honey, you'll be forced to sell. Maybe the beach house, too. Then what? Can you see you living in some dump with no view and nowhere to go on weekends? I can't. But that's reality. People are taking the hit every day. These are bad times; everybody's making compromises."

"Not me."

"Think it over, that's all I'm asking. The bit about Larry Drumm? It'll hurt him. He's got a life and a career, too. And that section isn't so good, anyway."

"That's right," John says, "it really isn't. We could cut that easily."

"See? We'll cut it. Save you a million bucks."

Rocky looks at them sitting at her table, evil twins using their agreement to manipulate her as they eat her food and take her money. She wonders where John got so *much* information about her life. It could have come from anyone, possibly even from Charlie. How does this little ghostwriter know so much about her?

"Were you interviewed, too, Charlie?"

"'Course. Everyone was. You gave the green light."

"And what about my staff?"

"I talked to everyone," John says.

"Why didn't you stop this, Charlie? Your job is to protect me."

"I'm trying to protect you, if you'd let me."

"You're in collusion with the enemy."

"Oh, jeez." He shakes his head as if frustrated, but she can see that he's scared; his forehead has clumped into a single expression of worry. He's dangling over a precipice and Rocky feels a sensation of enjoyment in her own power holding him there. It is an excellent feeling, this ability to call the shots. "It's over, Charlie," she says. "You're out."

"But I'm with you, babe. I always have been. Think of what we've been through together, all the years, it's been—"

"It's over. I'll find a new agent. I want you to messenger me all my papers, everything you have of mine."

"You're joking."

"No, I'm not."

"This is too much." He stands. He is shaking. "After everything I've done for you, after spilling my blood and guts for you."

"Goodbye."

"My contract still stands on this book, too, Rocky," Charlie says. "I've steered it all this way and I'm not walking away empty-handed, either."

"This is not going to be the book. Both of you, get out of my house. I don't want to look at you anymore."

"She's out of her mind," John says. "It's true."

She stands, casting her most powerful glare at these two vipers who have just eaten her food, who are trying to rob her, to ruin her. Celebrity rule number ninety-nine: You are safe from no one.

"I'm not changing my mind. All contracts are terminated. I'm clearing the decks, starting fresh, period."

"I'm getting out of here," John says. "You'll hear from my lawyer."

"Sorry, babe, but you'll also be hearing from mine." Charlie follows John out.

Annie hurries out of the kitchen to follow them. Rocky listens to her bid them goodbye with her sweet tone begging forgiveness. For what? What does she have to be ashamed of? Whose side is she on? If Parker didn't need a nanny, Rocky would fire her, too.

Annie comes into the dining room and stands in front of Rocky in another one of her annoying sweatshirts with a faded cartoon whose slogan has been laundered away. "Honey, did you have to do that to those nice boys?"

"Where's Nathan?"

"I haven't seen him today and I was up at seven. He must have gone out early. Rocky, about your brother, I've been thinking—"

"Clear the table!" Rocky stomps away and proceeds down the hallway, *her* hallway. She sees that Cat has come in and is sitting at her desk, *Rocky's* desk, doing something. What? Probably drawing one of her amateur comic strips on paid time. She veers into the office and stands behind Cat, who spins around.

"Morning, Rocky. How are you?"

"What are you doing?"

"Ordering supplies. We're running low."

"We?"

"Well, the office."

"Who is this royal *we*? That's what I'd like to know!"

"What?"

Rocky leaves the office. She does not owe this girl an explanation. She goes straight to her study, sits down at her desk and buzzes Cat.

"Get my lawyer on the phone."

A minute later, Cat's voice returns over the intercom: "David's secretary said he's out of town until tomorrow, but she'll try to get a message to him to call you back."

Rocky does not respond. That isn't good enough. Why can no one pull through when she needs them?

The day passes in an agony of unreturned phone calls and blank stares from Cat and Annie and waiting-for-Nathan who doesn't come home. Rocky feels dizzy, disconnected, disowned. Even Parker seems afraid of Mommy today. She waits until the noises of daytime have passed out of the penthouse, until quiet descends.

The bedroom is dark; the burgundy walls absorb all the fragmented evening light. Why did she let Tim convince her to paint the walls this wine red? It's so dark. She raises her satin slip, opens her legs, closes her eyes and masturbates. But it doesn't work anymore. It used to work, but now she is too aware that she is alone. Once, she could conjure images of love potent enough to soar in her famous bed in her dark room in her penthouse amidst her rich busy life from which she looked out at a world of have-nots and felt strong. Once. Now, tonight, she is as weak as anyone without hope could be, and the difference between now and before is that she knows it. It's over. She can't make it work anymore.

Hours pass and she lies awake, listening to the quiet. At 3:35 a.m. she hears Nathan return and go to his room. At 6:10 the bluish light of daybreak brings the room into focus. Her body feels heavy, exhausted, as she pulls herself out of bed. She gets her silk caftan from the hook on the bathroom door, puts it on and heads out into the just-getting-light apartment. She goes to the kitchen and starts a pot of coffee. Then she sits at the table with Annie's kitchen pad bearing this legend at the top of every page: *GOOD INTENTIONS*.

C h a p t e r 21
Good Intentions

*I*n one whole year, Cat has never seen Rocky so completely enraged. She is almost beautiful this morning, uncharacteristically down-to-earth, without any makeup and with her hair a grizzly mass. Her caftan moves like waves as she rushes back and forth through the penthouse, snapping orders. "Cat!" "Annie!" They respond like soldiers, aiming for the end of the day. Rocky comes in and out of Cat's office, holding a little piece of paper which she recognizes from Annie's *GOOD INTENTIONS* kitchen pad. It is covered with words scrawled in red marker. Rocky looks at it, issues an order and leaves. At one point, she says, "No one can be trusted. There's going to be a complete changing of the guard around here."

A messenger comes with a big package from Charlie Webb's office. Cat opens it and finds copies of letters, notes and contracts dating back years. A short cover letter wishes Rocky good luck finding an agent she'll feel "confident can steer you where you want to go."

When the phone rings with a return call from Rocky's lawyer, David, Cat braces herself and puts it through. Rocky has been waiting for this call all morning. Cat is not surprised by the war cry that emanates from Rocky's study the second the red light on the phone has faded. Feet pound the hallway and suddenly a crazed mass of Rocky is filling the doorway.

"Take a letter!"

Cat spins around and poises her fingers above the keyboard.

"Dear David,

This letter will officially terminate our professional relationship, effective immediately. Your refusal to cooperate with my decisions, and your admitted collusion with my former agent, Charles Webb, with whom you spoke this morning before contacting me, indicates an inappropriate hierarchy of priorities in concern to my best interests. The legitimacy of my dismissal of both Charles Webb and John Paglia should be a matter of faith and trust between you and me, not a forum for discussion. Because you have failed to discharge your professional obligations as my legal servant, I find no alternative but to sever our relationship. Therefore, you are ordered to return to me all papers and files related to me or my business which are currently in your possession.

Sincerely,

Rocky Love Barthoff

RLB:cg

"Messenger that over right away." "Will do." "Where is Nathan?" "He went out." The pupils of Rocky's eyes darken and shrink as they pin themselves accusingly on Cat, as if it's her fault Nathan disappears. "Where?" "I have no idea." Cat twists around to put a piece of letterhead in the printer. "I saw him talking to you before." "He said he was hungry. Maybe he went out for something to eat." "When he gets back, tell him we're going to the country." "Okay." Rocky paces quickly between the window and the door, slowing down occasionally to scan her *GOOD INTENTIONS* list. She stops and faces Cat. "Print out a copy of the memoirs." Cat nods, turns to the computer and pulls up a directory at random. She begins to scroll the cursor up and down the screen, wondering how this will effect John, for whom she feels no small amount of sympathy. Just last night he called her at home to say he was going to sue Rocky. If Rocky goes ahead with this, she'll be breaking their contract. Doesn't she realize that?

"Rocky, maybe that's not such a good idea."

"What?"

"I said—"

"Just *do it.*"

"But he's suing you. You'll only make it harder on yourself."

"How do *you* know that?"

Cat shrugs. "I must have overheard something."

"I'll print it myself, then!"

Rocky rushes over to the desk and tries to sit on the chair with Cat still in it. Cat falls against the edge of the desk, which she grabs in an effort not to fall to the floor. But Rocky's rear end bumps her with such force that, before she can get a good grip, she makes a twisted landing beneath the desk.

"Ouch!" Cat cries, but Rocky ignores her.

Rocky is banging away at the keyboard with her long chipped red fingernails. "How do you work this thing? Where is the print button?"

Cat crawls to the other side and stands. "That hurt."

Nathan appears in the office, knapsack over his shoulder, sucking on a long string of red licorice.

"Tell me how to print!"

Cat eyes her purse underneath the desk next to Rocky's feet. If she could only reach it, she could get out of here—for good.

"Nathan," Rocky says, "do you know how to print?"

"Print?"

"Get packed, we're going to the country."

"Country?"

"Hurry up. We're leaving as soon as I finish this."

He stands behind her, places his large hands on her neck and, licorice dangling between his lips, begins to knead. In a garbled sounding voice, he says, "Hey, sister, relax, relax."

Her jaw clenches as she taps keys at random. The computer beeps repetitively and then the screen flashes to a blank blue slate. She hits the keyboard with a flat palm and the computer instantly reboots itself.

"I said get packed—we're leaving!"

"Don't go," Cat impulsively says to Nathan. "She'll eat you alive."

Rocky pitches forward, in Cat's direction, like a missile aimed for flight. "*Who do you think you are*?"

"No one, Rocky. I'm *no one*." Cat crouches down under the desk and reaches for her purse. Just as she's about to grab the strap, Rocky's foot slams down on it.

As Cat tugs, the strap weaves between Rocky's toes. Her enraged face swings down to look under the desk just as Cat liberates her purse strap.

"You're fired!" Rocky says.

Still on her hands and knees, Cat notices for the first time in her year of service to the great Rocky Love that there are three hardened wads of gum stuck to the undersurface of the desk.

"I said, you're fired!"

"I heard you the first time." Cat crawls backwards, purse in tow, and stands up. Rocky stands and Nathan puts his arms around her in a hug whose obvious motive is to restrain her. He directs a quick wink to Cat.

"I mean it, don't go with her," Cat says to Nathan, hoping her words will reach him, tug him back from the edge of a precipice off which he has fallen before.

"Don't worry about me," he says. "I'm going to the country, to the country. If I don't get out of this city I'll go crazy."

"I order you," Rocky says, "to print the memoir before you leave this room!"

On the verge of refusing, Cat stops herself. Yes, she will stay a little longer, but not to print the manuscript for Rocky. She has a better idea.

"Okay, I will. I'll stay and do it and then I'll leave."

"That's right, you will." Rocky lifts her chin defiantly, conquering windmills.

"Come on, Rock, let's go pack," Nathan says.

"You're the only person I really need," she says to Nathan. "Do you know that?"

"Yup, yup, let's get ready." He pulls her out of the room. Cat stands in place, listening as they travel the hallway and Rocky's bedroom door slams shut.

Cat moves quickly now. She doesn't have time to sift through things carefully, to remove every cartoon she has taped to the walls, to locate loose papers she has set aside to take home. She only has time for this: she flips open the plastic disk case and finds the diskettes John gave her so she could transfer each draft of the memoirs onto the hard disk for revision. When she has accounted for each disk, she calls up the hard disk directory on which she has stored every draft of the memoirs, and systematically deletes them. When every byte of memoirs is erased, she shuts down the computer and slips the floppies into her purse.

At the last minute, she decides to call Teddy to tell him she's been fired and ask him to meet her for lunch. She dials his number and is listening to the answering machine when the office line rings. On reflex, she answers it.

"Hello, Cat, how are you?" It's Rocky's father, Dr. Libbon. Cat has never met him in person but she knows his voice well.

"Fine. You?"

"All right. Is Rocky home?"

"Sure, I'll try her." Cat buzzes Rocky's bedroom, then her study. No answer. "She's busy with...." But no one has divulged the presence of Nathan to his parents. He is Rocky's secret weapon—and Cat's. But why use it? The game is over, and it never had any real purpose, anyway. "I'm sorry, I guess she's not around."

Dr. Libbon sighs. "Is everything okay? I had a distressing call from a reporter this morning. I understand Rocky's put the penthouse up for sale." He hesitates. "This reporter seems to think she told a broker her apartment is haunted. Can you tell me anything about this?"

"No, I hadn't heard. Actually, Dr. Libbon, Rocky has been upset. She's fired everyone, well, except Annie."

"Everyone?"

"Her agent, her lawyer, the man who was helping her write her book, me."

"I see. You don't know where she is?"

Maybe, Cat thinks, maybe there's still time to save Nathan. Maybe, if their father gets to the beach house soon enough, he could help his son before Rocky has a chance to dabble with the poor man's pliant mind, not to mention his body.

"She was going to the country today."

"On a weekday?"

"Actually, she's in pretty bad shape, Dr. Libbon. Maybe it would be a good idea if you talked to her. Maybe in person."

"I'll give it a little time," he says, "and if I don't hear from her, I'll drive out."

Cat hangs up the phone and looks through the window into the lush autumn blaze of Central Park. She has finally come to hate Rocky. She is ready to leave. But she will miss Annie, and she will miss this view. As for the rest of her credit card debt, she's close to paying it off. She'll figure something out; get another job, now that she's got a year's worth of office experience under her belt.

She finds Annie in her room across the hall, sitting quietly on the edge of her bed.

"I'm gonna miss you," are Annie's first words.

"You heard?"

"Everything."

"Are you going to stay?"

"I don't know. I can't walk out that easy; I got Parker to think about."

"Right, that's tough." From down the hall they hear the sound of something crashing against a wall. "I better go. I don't want to be here when they come out."

"I don't blame you, hon. Good luck."

"Tell Parker goodbye for me, okay? Tell him I'll send him some more comic books."

They share a long hug before Cat leaves, the memoir-disks tucked safely away in her purse. With all the gossip Rocky has kicked up in her fury, the media's interest is piqued. Last night on the phone, John said that Charlie was already putting out feelers for a deal.

It is a spectacularly beautiful day for an eastward drive to the sea. Breezes swish gently through the roadside foliage. The sun is brilliant on the windshield and Norman adjusts the visor to block the glare. He peripherally observes the weathered competence of his hands as they grip the steering wheel of their old reliable Volvo wagon. He has had a good life, been a steady husband and a responsible father. And now his daughter needs him. She hasn't answered any of his calls from yesterday or this morning. Mabel advised him not to run to Rocky: "She's a grown woman. She made her own bed—let her lie in it." But she is their daughter and Norman loves her. He can wait it out no longer.

Perhaps his time for action was long ago, when his children were young and he could have offered more guidance. Perhaps it was wrong to wait for a crisis. Perhaps, in the past, if he had listened to his heart first and his wife's advice second, some of the shattering of his family could have been avoided. Perhaps if they had pressured their children less and loved them more, they could have been saved.

Were he to be as honest as his private thoughts, he would have to admit that he blames Mabel. Oh, he blames himself, too, of course, but she made the rules that he followed. He didn't have to follow them, but it seemed easier, it kept the peace. The children must have felt this even more strongly than he did, and with less definition between self and other; they absorbed her messages completely, and eventually they splintered and withdrew. Leo with his double life. Earl, poor Earl, with his need to please. Only Robby became who she wanted them all to be, and chances are he would have chosen medicine and family on his own, either way. But perhaps if Mabel hadn't goaded Rocky into rebellion she might have calmed down, grown up, stabilized. And to think about Nathan, *lost*, breaks Norman's heart.

Norman will never forget the look on Nathan's face when he was told he was being sent away to boarding school. Even Norman thought it was ludicrous. But Mabel was set on it—to "straighten him out" and "teach him responsibility" and perhaps most telling, "get him away from Rocky." Mabel really believed her daughter was being misdirected by Nathan's adolescent angst. Norman argued with her, he remembers it clearly. "It's harmless," he had said. "They'll both grow out of it. Don't worry so much." But Mabel's mind was made up. There was no discussion; he had no voice in their children's lives. He understood that then, that very day, in the ugly slash of Mabel's closed mouth. When it opened, it released a directive and he couldn't bear to challenge her, because to change roles midstream would have been to change the course of their marriage. He had thought if he could just keep the peace. He remembers her words exactly: "Tell him now." And Norman did. Told him. As if he knew what he was doing. He tore Nathan from their home and their lives. They have not seen him since.

There has been too much loss to let Rocky go now, not if he can help her by stretching out a hand in love—not judgment but *love*—to help her back through whatever darkness is swallowing her. He remembers her birth clearly, that little hand reaching. Way back then, he would never have imagined how much that tiny hand would grasp in life, and how desperately it would struggle to hold on, and how self-destructively it would create its own losses. But no matter what has happened, or why, she is still his child. She will always be his baby girl.

He steers the car to the exit ramp and proceeds four miles or so to the house. It has been a long time since he has been here, what with Rocky's and Mabel's feuding, yet he finds that he remembers the route.

There it is: the bleached old house that looks innocuous enough on the outside and inside is a masterpiece of renovation. Norman pulls the car up the gravel drive and parks next to his daughter's green Mustang convertible. The top is up, which probably means the car has not been used today.

The front door of the house is locked. Through the glass panels on either side of the wide door he can see right through the living room, which appears quiet and empty. A picture window on the far wall frames the ocean beyond.

He goes around to the other side and tries a glass door, which slides open easily. Wind chimes tinkle. It is cool inside the house. Were it not for the window being open and the glass doors unlocked, he would have guessed no one was home.

"Hello?" he calls. "Rocky, it's Dad!"

There is no response, so he decides to look around. First, he tries the sun-porch, which is cluttered with newspapers and two coffee mugs. It occurs to him that she might have a guest, and he fears he has intruded. Then he remembers what prompted him to come here: Rocky has been unstable, taking drastic action, waltzing too close to the edge. These are not normal times, he reminds himself, otherwise he would not have come uninvited. He hopes he's overreacting and he'll find her happily entertaining some nice new or old friend. He will apologize, excuse himself and drive home, satisfied, in time for dinner.

He checks the dining room, the kitchen, the laundry room and the downstairs guest room. Nothing. So he heads upstairs.

At the top of the stairs he nearly collides with a tall man who, after a quick moment of surprise, he recognizes as his son, Nathan. He is stark naked. Norman's breath catches in his chest. He feels, briefly, that he will suffocate. Then his breath flows and he steps back in confusion. It has been well over twenty years since he has seen his boy—this man.

Nathan's smile is sudden, like a threat. He too has been taken by surprise. "Dokta Dad!" he bellows, laughing.

"Nathan?" It is Rocky's voice, coming from the master bedroom. "What's going on?" She appears in the bedroom doorway, wearing a black merry widow with garters and black lace stockings. Her large breasts are squeezed together and she wears no underpants. There are vivid bluegreen bruises on her thighs and red welts around her wrists, ankles and neck. Her teased hair looks metallic, unnatural, vulgar. She stands there frozen, staring at her father. Finally she says, "Daddy," softly, just a whisper.

Norman calls upon all the strength of his whole long life to hold back the torrent of grief and regret pushing at his throat. In a low controlled voice he manages to say, "Get dressed, both of you, now."

Chapter 22
Rocky Love

ROCKY LOVE ROCKY LOVE....

Rocky sits with her hands folded together on top of a brand new pad of lined white paper, eyes closed, meditating. It is so quiet and calm here at the hospital, much better than she had thought it would be. So quiet, in fact, it seemed an excellent opportunity to get back to work on her memoirs. But first, it is necessary to create the right state of mind, to renew confidence, to tap into the creative forces. She doesn't know why she allowed Charlie to talk her into hiring a ghostwriter. It is her own story, *hers*.

She can write it herself—and she will. Beginning with page one. *Page one* she writes in the upper left hand corner of the page. She underlines it. And again. Then the tip of her pen anchors itself to the center of the page. *Sunrise of a Star* she writes. Crosses it out. *Rocky Love Live!* Crosses it out. *The Diary of a Mad Wife.* Sounds familiar, crosses it out. She can't think of the right title now; no matter, it will come. She peels away the page and crumbles it into a ball. In the upper left hand corner of a fresh sheet, she writes *Page one*, underlined. Halfway down the page she poises her pen and begins to think. Then she presses pen to paper and writes.

I am a creature from another world, a child of the universe where stars and moon are peaceable neighbors. With the God-given beauty of light we are siblings gazing down upon the earth. I love you, earth, you are mine as I am yours. Now, to the story of how I came to be. Humanity. This form of human life, the flesh of body, was the armor I wore when I was called to the front lines. But when my voice sailed across my country it was free, free, unfettered by the flesh of my hand holding my pen as I write my story. I look at my fingers curled around my pen and wonder how it knows to form the right words. It is a miracle. This perhaps is the most important thing I can tell you about myself, the miracle of how I came to be the woman you know as Rocky Love.

"Rocky, hello? Anyone home?"

Rocky's face swivels to a woman standing in front of her, a little old lady carrying a round tin can decorated with a pear surrounded by script letters announcing SWEETS & TREATS.

"Hello, hello?"

"Yes?"

"I baked you a chocolate babka. It's a little squashed in the can but I thought better that than ants all over the place. You can keep it in your room this way." The little old lady plops the can on top of page one and brushes her soft cheek against Rocky's. The perfume is familiar.

"Mom."

"Do you mind if I sit?" Mabel lowers herself onto one of the unoccupied chairs at Rocky's table. She does not bother to remove her hat and coat.

"Is Dad here?"

"He's talking to the doctor. So, what's new with you?"

"I was just writing my memoirs."

"Parker, he sends you 'a thousand kisses.' His words, not mine."

"How is he?"

"Having the time of his life, what else? He's sleeping in Robby's and Earl's old room. We bought him all the latest toys. You should *see* my grandson now. What a boy!"

"Where's Dad?"

"Didn't I just tell you? He is with the doctor, Rocky, *with the doctor*. He'll be by in a few minutes."

Rocky nods. "I've just been writing my memoirs. Mom, would you like to read the first page?"

Mabel's face suddenly looks as tight as a raisin. "Later, maybe."

"I'm going to explain everything," Rocky says.

Norman walks up behind Mabel. She tugs on his coat sleeve and gives him a long look.

"Hi there, princess." Norman bends to kiss the top of Rocky's head. "How are we feeling?"

"We?"

"The doctor says you're doing well."

"I started writing my memoirs. Do you want to read the first page?"

"Here." Mabel removes the top of the can. "It's pre-cut. Have a piece." She forces out a piece of babka and proffers it to Rocky.

"I'm not hungry."

"Then you eat it." Mabel hands it to Norman.

"Leave this for her. We have plenty to eat at home." He hands it back to Mabel.

"Well, I can't fit it back in there now." Mabel nibbles at the cake. "As good as always. It's my mother's recipe. She was always the best baker. Whenever you're ready for it, Rocky darling, you just let me know." ROCKY LOVE

"Hello, hello? Anybody at home? What's wrong with her?"

"She's tired. We'll go get some lunch and come back later."

"Norman, look at her. Is she sleeping? I can't tell."

"We'll come back." Norman puts his hands on Mabel's shoulders and nudges her up. "We'll find a nice place in town for lunch."

"I'll ask one of the nurses what's good. We don't want to eat just anywhere." They walk down the long clean hallway together in their autumn coats.

When I was a little girl I used to wonder where I came from. I remember when I found out. When I was four and Nathan was nine, we saw something through a hole in the attic. We were playing in our secret place where we played together all the time. There was a window frame with no window, just a loose old board. We heard some loud sounds of banging, bang bang bang, and being children we were drawn to it. It had to be a monster. Nathan wasn't sure so he pulled off the loose board and it came off right away. There was a hole in the wall and it looked down into the bedroom where Daddy and his wife stayed. There was a monster on the bed. I was right. I said Nathan, look, I was right. He was already looking and he started to laugh and he said there was no monster, it was just Daddy and Mommy on the bed with no clothes. The bed kept jumping and Daddy was smothering Mommy and I was glad, then I looked at Nathan. I said if he kills her, will we starve? Nathan pushed me aside and put the board back up. He put his arms around me until we were hugging each other on the floor. He said don't you know where babies come from? Yes! I said. Yes I do! I was born a mineral, a shard of diamond splintered off in the big bang, and when the force of the bang drove me into the earth I multiplied until I was a cave of jewels. They found me and took me home and raised me an orphan in the wrong setting, they did, and I grew as one of them and when my voice sailed across the country it was full of diamonds splintering into the hearts of my audience, and I was free.

C h a p t e r 23
Exit Ramp

*T*he pink bull's-eye appears on the early pregnancy de-
tector wand just six days after Cat is fired, one day after
she files an application for benefits at the Unemployment
Office, and two hours before her appointment to show her
portfolio to Marshall Korn at Exit Ramp. The dot appears instantly, confirming what her swollen breasts have suggested
for days. She is pregnant. Again. Not six months after the first
time—demonstrating her complete irresponsibility as a human being. She had *meant* to see her gynecologist and get her
diaphragm replaced. She really should have. She will have
to explain to Teddy why she didn't, and wonders now if she
unconsciously-deliberately did *not* take care of that…. No! She
shakes herself free of guilt and doubt. She *knew* this could
happen, because it happened once before. She *allowed* this
to happen. It *was* irresponsible of her, and she will take the
blame. But she will also admit to herself and anyone who asks
that she *wants* this baby, even if she shouldn't want it, and she
will *have* this baby, even if technically her life is not in order.
Her decision is made before the pink dot on the pregnancy test
has completely darkened. This time, Teddy will have to make
his own decision, by himself.

She wraps up all the test paraphernalia in the brown paper bag it came in, and buries it deep in the bathroom garbage
can where Teddy will never see it. She will tell him when she's
ready, face to face, and take whatever comes.

She lowers the toilet seat, sits down and thinks. Some
women say they can feel the prick of conception as it happens,

that within minutes they know they are pregnant. Not Cat. But searching back a few weeks, she thinks she can pinpoint the night it happened.

The way it looks, Lucie Gold Foster had the great good fortune and determination to plunge into life on a warm night in early September. Teddy had just finished a big commission for *ArtWorld* magazine, an article on post-pop ultra-minimalist neo-geo painting and its hyper-expressionist roots, and he decided to use his set of keys to greet Cat at her place with a bottle of celebration champagne. When she walked through the door from work, he aimed the bottle above her head and let the cork fly.

"I finished my article today!"

"Congratulations."

"That's three thousand dollars in the bank."

He poured the foaming champagne into two wine glasses he had set on the table. Cat kissed him and he squeezed her into a big hug, rocking her back and forth.

"I'm starving," she said. "I have to eat something first."

"Drink one glass." He smiled his best seductive smile and his blue eyes went steamy. "I love you." His mouth was warm on her neck, which she craned so he could kiss more of her. His kisses were lusciously slow and soft and she could taste the champagne on his tongue. Tiny bubbles flitted through her brain and Teddy touching her, dancing her across the floor, intoxicated her completely.

They moved to the bed. Hovering over her, Teddy unbuttoned her blouse. His eyes were smiling and his mouth was soft and relaxed. She knew the look, when he was in a loving mood, and it thrilled her as much as it always had. They undressed each other slowly. It was like a first night together, but better, because they knew each other's contours so well.

Cat decides it happened that night. It was the night they began to discuss the idea of Teddy moving back in. This would be the story she would tell Lucie, when she grew up: that her parents had separated long enough to know how much they needed each other, and on a night when everything was wonderful they created her out of love.

Cat gathers her portfolio, filled with *Legends* cartoons and comic strips, and makes the short walk over to Exit Ramp. Though it is only nine blocks away, every step feels like a month, every block a year. In this one day, her life could change forever. She is pregnant. She did not destroy her uterus with the abortion. She will not be punished for the rest of her life. She will not be sentenced to solitude forever. She will not starve to death without a job. Maybe she won't even die undiscovered.

When she pulls open the glass front door to the gallery, a little bell dings above her head. A pretty young woman seated behind a reception counter—a curved, comma-like construction—looks up and doesn't smile. She notices Cat with the apparent assumption that she has come to look at art, until she spots the portfolio.

"Can I help you?" the woman says with the defensive superiority of an *art world professional* dreading the bad work of yet another aspirant.

"I have an appointment with Marshall Korn."

"Oh." Now the young woman smiles. "I'll let him know you're here." She disappears behind a wall of glass blocks and Cat takes the opportunity to look at the current show. The front room is all Mary Pini and in the back she sees a few Art Spiegelmans. Excellent company ... if they'll have her.

"Hello!"

She turns around. Marshall Korn is tall, with a halo of brown hair around a bald spot on the top of his head. His skin is mocha and he has striking brown eyes the shape of almonds. She shifts her portfolio to her left hand so she can shake his with her right.

"I appreciate your taking the time so late in the process," she says.

"It's nothing. Shit happens, right? Come on, let's take a look at what you got." He walks around the glass block wall and stands by a big table. Against the opposite wall is a desk, much nicer and more organized than Isabel's, Cat notes. She lays her portfolio case on the table, unzips it and splays it wide. One by one, she shows him her cartoons. He observes each one thoughtfully, without revealing a glimmer of reaction. When she is finished, he asks her to go through them again.

This time he stops her frequently and laughs when something's funny, asks her questions, admires a line. When they reach the end again, he says, "You've got a very strange and quirky sense of humor. It's dark, but what a bite."

After an anxious moment of uncertainty, she recognizes the compliment. "Thanks."

"Can you leave this here for a week or so? We have a committee."

"No problem," Cat says. "My address and phone number are taped inside the portfolio."

"I know where to find you, then." He smiles, and tags on a little chuckle. "Interesting stuff."

They shake hands and she leaves. Solitary but not alone because Lucie is splitting away inside her body. Unemployed but not useless. Free for the rest of the day but not without direction. "Interesting," he had said. Not insipid or self-involved or unaccomplished. *Interesting*.

Word arrives a week later that she has been accepted into the show at Exit Ramp. To celebrate, Teddy takes her out to dinner at one of the nicer local restaurants. The food here is especially good, and normally she would relish the treat while obsessing over her amazing fortune—her first big break—and plotting and planning her cartooning future, but she can think of nothing but the fact that she is pregnant and he doesn't know. She has come to realize that in keeping the truth from him, she is failing the litmus test—*honesty*—she herself had set for the revival of their relationship. She has also come to realize that, despite her initial bravado, she is terrified of losing him again. She needs to feel strong when she tells him because there will be no turning back. And for this strength she considers enlisting none other than her unborn child.

She could wait until Lucie is big enough to resemble a human being, pull out her copy of *Our Bodies Our Selves,* locate the page with the picture of the fetus tucked cozily in its mother's womb and tell Teddy, "This is how big Lucie is now." He'd look at the picture and see a person as tiny as a thimble, sucking her thumb.... *No*, Cat decides, splitting a breadstick in half as Teddy smiles at her across the candlelight, she won't do that. It would be a cheap shot, worse than that idiot-protestor outside the abortion clinic last April, confusing murder with choice. "I've made a decision," she'll calmly explain to him (as soon as she can muster the courage), "a choice I am going to live with. I'll accept whatever choice you make for yourself. So let's just take it from there."

A few days later, Cat receives a call from Leo Libbon, one of Rocky's brothers, asking her to return to work for a few more days. He needs help sorting through his sister's business records so they can be stored indefinitely in the basement of their parents' house in Brooklyn. Cat hesitates a moment. She had thought she would never go back; she certainly has no desire to.

"You'll be paid, of course," Leo says.

"It's not that."

"If you could come, it would be a tremendous help. I already packed up the household things with Annie, lovely woman, but we didn't have a clue about what to do with the office. There are so many papers lying around. Rocky won't be there, by the way."

That is really what Cat wanted to hear. "Where is she now?"

"Upstate, in a private psychiatric institution. Very posh." There is a hint of amusement in Leo's tone.

"Is Nathan there too?"

"No-o-o-o. He's in his own loony bin in New Jersey, not so fancy but decent. Nath doesn't require the same fineries, and I guess Mom and Dad didn't want them in the same state." Leo's amusement ripens into a chuckle, which Cat shares. She likes the sound of this brother.

"I can go tomorrow," she says.

"Great. But she changed the locks so I'll leave a set of keys for you with the doorman. Give me a call when you plan on going over and I'll meet you there."

"Where are Annie and Parker?"

"Annie retired, and was she happy about that! She went to stay with her sister in the Berkshires. Parker's under the dubious auspices of my mother. We all had Sunday dinner yesterday. Sweet kid, but lonesome, like a poor little rich kid, know what I mean?"

"Yeah, I do. It must have been hard for him to say goodbye to Annie. Was there any chance she would stay?"

"I think she would have if we'd pressed her. My mother was set against it, though," Leo says. "She wants to raise him herself."

The penthouse has an awful empty ghostly feeling and Cat can't wait to get the packing over with. She misses Annie; it doesn't feel right here without her. And she misses Parker's sweet after-school visits when hours of office work could be softened by play. The one person she doesn't miss is "Rocky the rocket," as Charlie Webb once called her. Well, that was the understatement of the century. Cat wonders if, a year ago, she was one of the last people alive to still think of the great Rocky Love as a hero. Now she can't imagine why she did. Rocky's time has passed, and what's left of her is a chimera, a bubble that pops on first touch. That, and maybe Cat just grew up enough in a year to recognize that the complexities of being a woman cannot be solved by mere hopefulness, excitement or sloganism. She will not give up on feminism; she will reinvent it, differently, to suit herself, using cartoons as her medium and voice. She will take up the challenge to *have it all*, family and work, and see how it goes. But she won't rely on outsized heroes; if she wants a hero, she'll draw her own.

She moves through her old office to a desk that has devolved to chaos. There is a lot to be done. She begins by sorting through the piles on her desk. From time to time she glances at the picture window and is captivated by the brilliant sky, blue and puffed with clouds, and the colorful treetops of Central Park. It has been a view of mixed emotions, a year of passages, and already she feels nostalgia for the exquisiteness of the view she will never see again, not from exactly this perspective.

Less than an hour into it, the doorbell rings. Leo, no doubt. She goes to the front door, looks through the peephole and sees a thin man with gray-blond hair, miniaturized by the convex coin of glass. He's wearing a red and blue tropical shirt, baggy Bermuda shorts, black sunglasses and bright white hightop sneakers.

She figures he's somewhere in his forties, based on what she knows from the memoirs. Other than Nathan, she has never met any of Rocky's family in person.

She unchains the door and opens it. "Hi, I'm Cat."

"I figured as much." He shakes her hand and smiles warmly. He seems different from Rocky and Nathan, more balanced and grounded. Nicer.

"Want some coffee?" she asks.

"I'm off the stuff, but thanks."

"Well, I already got started in the office."

"Super," he says. "I'm here to help. Do we need more boxes in there?"

"We do."

He leads her to the section of living room wall where flattened cardboard boxes are stacked. "We bought a ton of these things. The movers said they'd buy back whatever we don't use." He grabs a stack and they go down the hall to the office.

"I've always gone searching for boxes when I moved," Cat says. "Nasty roachy boxes from deli basements."

"Well, money breeds all kinds of conveniences, doesn't it?" He drops the boxes in a heap on the office floor and turns toward the window. "What a spectacular view."

"That's one thing I'd like to take with me."

"I had realtors over here all last week, and this view about doubles the price of this place."

"Your sister is a successful woman."

"*Was*. Let's face it." He claps his hands together. "Shall we get started?"

"I thought I'd pack up the files and label them, you know, for posterity."

"She'd love that—*posterity*." His laugh is a quick crescendo. "I'll build the boxes and then you can give me another job to do, how about that?"

"Sounds good."

The afternoon drifts by. Leo's company is comforting, and as they work they talk, gradually spilling out their stories. He tells her things about himself that she already knows from Rocky's memoirs, as well as things she couldn't have known, daily trivia about his life with his boyfriend Rich. They talk and talk, pack files, seal and label boxes. In the late afternoon they order in Chinese food and eat together at the dining room table.

Cat doesn't quite mean to, but somewhere along the line—somewhere in between bites of cold noodles with sesame sauce—her defenses fall away and she tells him, spontaneously, that she is pregnant.

Leo's noodly chopstick suspends over his plate like weeping willows. The expression he turns to her is kind, serious, free of judgment. "Congratulations. Is boyfriend happy?"

"He doesn't know."

"Oh?"

"I'll tell him eventually."

"I see."

"Last time he blew a fuse, then we broke up. I really think it's my choice, and I have to make it alone."

"S'pose so."

"You don't approve?"

"It's your body, but I don't see what you have to lose by telling the man. You may lose more by waiting."

"Lose more?"

"Women are always bitching about being demeaned by us men. Well, lemme tellya somethin', we get demeaned plenty, too. A man doesn't know he's fathered a child until someone tells him. Don't you know straight men live with a knot in their guts just wondering?" He shrugs. "But I'm not you. I don't live in your body. I don't really know how it feels to live your life. You gotta know what's best for you." He twirls the noodles around his chopsticks and takes a hearty bite.

Cat had not even considered that, by withholding the news from Teddy, she is being just as irresponsible toward him as he was toward her during the first pregnancy, and she had resented him for it. Maybe she doesn't really have the right to withhold the news from him. She thinks about it for the rest of the day as the chaos of the office is transformed into orderly rows of boxes. Leo doesn't mention it again. When they part ways for the evening, he kisses her cheek. "Tomorrow, same time, same place?"

"See you then."

It's warm out, almost hot, but there's a breezy dry feel in the air and Cat decides to walk for a while before getting into the subway. She is afraid to tell Teddy, despite her grandiose scheme for living alone, handling it, having her baby, being fine. She is afraid of that moment when it snaps, *over*, and he gets up to leave. But she remembers that she's been through it before and she survived. She will survive this time, too. At 59th Street she descends into the tunnels and rides the number six train downtown.

She arrives home with her tiny-knot-of-cells Lucie multiplying swiftly in her uterus, expecting to find quiet, to march into the study where Teddy would be reading or writing at the desk and stand straight and tall in front of him and tell him.

Instead, she enters a kitchen full of lush cooking smells, and Teddy, in a blue canvas apron, standing at the counter dicing an onion.

"Afternoon, kitten," he says.

"Evening."

"Ah, evening, you're right. Is that maybe why I'm cooking dinner?"

"Glad you're in a good mood." She stands in the doorway between the kitchen and living room and crosses her arms over her chest.

Teddy stops dicing and looks at her. "Okay, I'm listening."

"You won't like it."

He shrugs his shoulders and she begins.

"I just want to say, first of all, that I have no expectations of you whatsoever. That's number one. Secondly, you don't have to tell me that you've made your position clear, because I know that. And last of all, no matter what you may think of me, I am a capable person and I'm responsible for my own decisions."

"I figure we're due in June."

"Excuse me?"

"I know you're a capable and responsible person, but that doesn't make me stupid."

She stares at him, astounded, confused.

"You didn't get your period, and your breasts are definitely bigger than usual." He smiles, thin-lipped and sexy, and his eyes get their greatest dazzle look.

She doesn't like this, not one bit. He wasn't supposed to know her secret; it was supposed to belong only to her. She leaves him in the kitchen, goes to the bedroom and sits on the edge of the bed. He follows her in.

"You don't have much faith in me," he says, sitting down beside her.

She twists around to look at him. "Are you kidding me? After last time?"

"Last time was last time. We've both been through a lot."

"You've got years before you get your degree," she says. "You're in no position to have a family."

"Don't forget it's my kid, too."

"What are you saying, Teddy?"

"We'll stay right here. It'll be a little crowded, but we'll just stay put, do what we have to do. You'll have the baby. We'll manage. I can't afford to buy you an engagement ring, but if you'll take a rain check—"

"Is this some kind of joke?"

"Cartoons are your department. I'm a serious guy." He smiles brilliantly, taking her in his arms.

Feeling the warmth of his body, smelling the salty musk of his neck, she has no idea if love and hope and effort will be enough for them to go on, but she does know that she will try in every possible way to make this work. She realizes now that, despite the hypocritical bloat of the messenger, the heady message of her youth persists inside her. She *does* have enough grist to survive, and hopefully *thrive*, as a complete person all on her own. She doesn't have all the answers yet, sitting here on her bed with her beloved. Her life is a maypole of loose ends. But somehow, sooner or later, she will find a way to make every end meet. And this time, he's going to try with her.

"I don't need an engagement ring," she says. "I don't *want* one."

He seems to understand. Their arms tighten around each other and, face hidden in his neck, Cat cries with relief.

Cat agrees to meet Leo two days later at his parents' house in Brooklyn Heights, to help organize storage. She turns onto a street called Columbia Heights, finds the house number Leo gave her, and stands in awe in front of the corner mansion facing the river and its quintessential bird's-eye view of Manhattan. Before ringing the bell, she gives in to a temptation to walk around the house and stand on the Promenade for a minute.

There it is, the island of Manhattan, looking bigger and better from afar. This is the view they all use, the photographers and filmmakers, when they want to steer your imagination to the heart of the metropolis. They stand right here, in front of the Libbon house or one of its neighbors, and allow their wide angle lenses to drink in the river as it flows beneath the Brooklyn Bridge and up toward the Empire State Building, and as it curls southward around the twin monoliths of the World Trade Center, to the left of which the Statue of Liberty bears her torch. It is all here, everything you need to build dreams, just beyond Rochelle Libbon's first window.

Leo greets her at the door. She feels a small thrill at the thought of entering the house she knows only through John Paglia's descriptions. The real house is cozier than she had imagined—old and grand, full of bright polished wood, Oriental rugs and thick draperies. A wide staircase curves up from the spacious entry hall on either side of which are a set of French doors leading respectively to living room and dining room. A rich, sweet smell lingers in the air.

"Mom's baking one of her things." Leo rolls his eyes. "Come on, Parker's in the kitchen. He's been waiting for you."

Leo maneuvers Cat through a dining room surrounded by windows covered in white lace curtains which partially obscure the magnificent view. The kitchen is large and renovated with modern appliances and wooden cabinets. At a central butcher block island, on a high stool, sits Parker with a large piece of paper and a set of colored markers. A small woman with short gray hair stands at one of the counters, cracking eggs into the bowl of a mixer.

"Mom, this is Rock's assistant, Cat Gold."

"So you're the girl on the phone," Mabel says.

"Nice to finally meet you, Mrs. Libbon."

"Hi, Cat!" A loose front tooth dangles in Parker's smile.

"Hey there." She goes over to look at his picture of a tooth fairy depositing a box of riches by his bedside. "Nice drawing. Did you get the comics I sent you?"

Beaming, he smiles and nods. She ruffles her fingers through his hair.

"If I give you my address," she says, "will you send me your drawings sometimes?"

"Yes! Will you send me more comic books?"

"You got it."

Parker throws his arms around her, and they hug.

"You know," Cat tells Mabel, "if you ever need to go out, I'd be happy to babysit."

"What?" Mabel says, tugging her apron belt and squaring her shoulders. "Me. Go *out*? I'm not so sure the world's ready for such a shock." She breaks into a smile crowded with tea-yellowed teeth John failed to mention in the memoirs.

Cat laughs. "Leo's got my number. Call anytime."

"Okay," Leo says. "Lovefest's over. We've got work to do in the basement."

"Not so fast, young man. She's our guest. Maybe she'd like a bite to eat."

"Hungry?" Leo asks Cat.

"No, thanks. I had lunch before I came."

"All right, fine," Mabel says. "You don't look so well-fed to me, but anyway— " She shrugs her shoulders with so much expression that the bitter and controlling memoir-Mabel comes to life in Cat's mind. And yet the real-life woman seems, well, so much more than a caricature.

"Can I come?" Parker asks.

"Sure, kiddo." Leo squeezes Parker's shoulder.

They take the staircase from the pantry that leads down into the basement. "I cleared some space over there." Leo indicates the far wall in front of which is a wide open area. Nestled into the left corner is a jumble of bicycles and skis and baseball bats and dusty toys. "I moved all that stuff over there this morning."

"Wow." Parker heads into the pile. "This is so great! Can I have some of this stuff?"

"Whatever you want," Leo says. "It hasn't been used in years."

"Cool, a bike!"

"Don't you have one?"

"Mommy won't let me." Parker weeds through the pile until he has unearthed a red stingray with leather tassels on the handlebars.

"That was your Uncle Earl's."

"I don't have an Uncle Earl."

"Didn't your mommy tell you about Earl?"

Parker shakes his head as he drags the bike to a piece of open floor.

"Earl was your mommy's and my older brother," Leo says. "He looked a lot like Uncle Robby."

Parker tries to spin the wheels but they are so rusted they barely move. "This doesn't go."

"Well, we could get you a new one, how would that be?"

"I like this one."

"Then we'll get it fixed up for you."

Parker sits on the long banana seat and makes a revving sound. "Here I come, Uncle Earl, ready or not!"

Leo looks at Cat. "Nothing ever dies, as they say. Did you know that Earl actually enlisted in the Vietnam War?"

Cat nods; she knows that, and so much else, about this family she has only just now met.

"Uncle Leo, when can we get it fixed?"

"How about tomorrow?"

Parker dismounts and tosses the bike on the floor. He goes running up the steps, calling, "Grandma, guess what?"

Leo looks at Cat and smiles.

"I took your advice," Cat says. "I told Teddy."

"It wasn't advice, really."

"I took it anyway."

"And?"

"He already knew."

"Well, it just goes to show."

"Show what?"

"We ain't as dumb as we look." He winks. "I've already planned the wedding invitations, decorated with cherubs and shotguns."

"Gee, thanks. But we haven't gotten that far."

"Keep me informed; I'm a sucker for gossip."

"I will." "And I'm a good listener, too. You've got my number.... Call me anytime." "I just might." They get to work, piling boxes against the wall with the oldest files on the bottom and the newest on top. Everything is labeled in thick black marker. If Rocky Love should come back to her senses and back to life, and decide to recreate herself again, she will know exactly where to find her paper trail.

Chapter 24

Rocky, babe, this one's for you!

*T*here is an early snow the second week of November, a force of nature that slows Cat down now that her breasts are heavy with milk and her mind is foggy from sleeplessness. Leaving the gym, she is ill-prepared for this frozen deluge. Wetness seeps through her sneakers and into the loose arms of her coat sleeves. Cold bites at the tops of her ears. Her aching muscles carry her home in what feels like slow motion, slower and stranger for the eerie purple twilight of this unexpected storm. But even in the best of weather, she is not fond of her thrice weekly visits to the gym; she is simply determined to pull her body back into shape. She is deliriously happy. This morning, Lucie looked her straight in the eyes and smiled.

Tonight will represent another first. After five months of being held prisoner by their beloved screaming infant, Cat and Teddy are going out. The event is a book party launching *The Rise and Fall of Rocky Love* by Rocky Love with John Paglia.

Cat feels excited and nervous about stepping back into that world again. Of all the people involved, she has kept in touch only with John, who has apprised her of each major hurdle as it was vaulted: the successful maneuvering of lawsuits against Rocky by both Charlie Webb and John, the negotiation with Larry Drumm resulting in the removal of the offending material and resulting in the dropping of his lawsuit, Rocky's surprising move transferring power of attorney to her father, the book auction of John's final version of the memoirs, a sale for a shocking amount of money, and all the subsequent subsidiary contracts which have convinced John he is now a mini mogul. Recently, pre-publicity for the book has been showing up everywhere—newspapers, magazines, radio, television talk shows, the works.

Notably absent from all the hype has been Rocky, whose deranged withdrawal has spawned a kind of Howard Hughes myth. Ironically, she seems to be missing her own comeback. Cat has actually wondered if Rocky is saner than ever, pretending insanity to enhance her fame, waiting it out in her posh upstate asylum until the time is ripe for a highly public return. In any case, Cat's theory that celebrity has a life of its own is being proven by this book's ability to thrive without the involvement of its subject.

When Cat arrives home, she finds Teddy pacing back and forth, holding a restless Lucie in his arms. From birth, their daughter has insisted on being rocked frequently and fast, and if you slow down her face screws up as her personality transforms from angel to gremlin. Her cries have the power to reach into the core of your being. And her smiles can toss you high onto a cloud.

"If she wasn't so cute, I'd—" Teddy passes Lucie into Cat's arms before she is out of her coat.

"Don't say that, Teddy. Here, just give me one minute." She returns Lucie to him and begins to peel off her wet things.

"I didn't say it, I *almost* said it but I didn't actually say it."

Teddy sits at his desk, bobbing Lucie on his knee, and gazes blankly at an open book. She instantly protests with a peal of crying. He stands up, paces and rocks, and she simmers down.

"I'll nurse her now, then I'll get ready, then I'll nurse her again right before we go," Cat says. "I have to decide what to wear; I don't know if I'll fit into anything."

"She just had a bottle so you could get dressed now if you want." He kisses Lucie's cheek, and again.

Cat rifles through clothes so squashed into her half of the closet that she can barely tell what they are. She hasn't worn most of them for over a year and they probably won't fit, anyway, as her body has shape-shifted along with her life. She wishes she had splurged on a new outfit, but money has been tight and she has yet to receive the first check, meager though it will be, for her contribution to a book of new cartoonists Marshall Korn parlayed out of a series of Exit Ramp shows.

Teddy carries Lucie into the bedroom and lays her down on the bed. As soon as her face begins to screw up, he tickles her. He hovers close enough for her eyes to focus on him and recognize her father, smiling and cooing until she cannot help but smile back. "You love your daddy," he says. "Yes, I know you do, yes I know."

These small moments are Cat's evidence that she did the right thing by Teddy. Slowly, over the days and weeks and months, he has undeniably fallen in love not just with the idea of Lucie but with every bit of her, every smell, every sound, every silence. She is every inch his daughter. He often takes her out on walks, and Cat suspects his motive is not so much to give her fresh air as to be the man behind the stroller in which sits the most beautiful baby alive.

"What about you?" Cat asks. "What'll you wear?"

"That's easy. My tweed jacket and my zigzag tie."

In the end, Cat puts on a black dress, black fishnet tights and leather boots. She wears the dangling crystal earrings Teddy gave her on their first and only wedding anniversary.

By the time Lucie has been fed and Janet has arrived to babysit, it is well past the hour when the party was to begin. They rush out in a hurry, hail a taxi and in fifteen minutes are standing in an elevator traveling thirty floors up to the 57th Street penthouse party space which has been rented for the night.

The elevator doors scroll open and they are greeted by the face of Rocky Love, a huge photographic blowup of a young woman laughing. The picture, which Cat recognizes as an early *Mad Wife* publicity shot from the Love Wall, is propped on an easel in a white gallery-like foyer. The same picture fills the cover of the book, which is stacked on a table near the easel. A banner across the top of the book jacket boasts *#1 New York Times Bestseller*. Cat and Teddy both pick up a copy.

Cat leafs through the book, which in its final form seems so simple—the neat, sharp tip of an iceberg. She turns to the back flap to look at the author photo. There are two. The first, in the top position, is a head shot of Rocky as she looks today, her face made-up, her hair hennaed and teased. Beneath is a more candid photo of John, wearing jeans and a leather jacket, on what must be the Brooklyn Heights Promenade with the dramatic backdrop of Manhattan looming behind him. Cat flips to the front pages until she finds the acknowledgements; she has wondered if her contributions would be noted. The writing style of the acknowledgement page is lively and terse, uniquely John's. There, in the middle of a long run-on sentence studded with names, is hers. Gratified, she closes the book and replaces it on the table.

They follow the sounds of high spirits through a wide doorway, and enter an enormous room crowded with clusters of people talking, laughing, holding glass tulips of champagne. To the right is a long bar covered in white linen and manned by four servers wearing tuxedos. And to the left are a series of doors which lead to a patio beyond which is a dark vastness sprinkled with stars. The view is grand and mysterious and seductive. Teddy begins to steer her in its direction.

"We should say hi first." She pulls him away from the view and into the crowd, searching for familiar faces.

The first one they see is recognizable only by association. "Look, that's Reebah Jameson." Cat directs Teddy's attention across the room to a group of people huddled together in a far corner. They are listening to a woman in a gold dress with a swath of colorful African cloth tied around her short hair. Except for a pair of hoop earrings, she wears no jewelry or makeup. She speaks with a seriousness and warmth that seems to emanate naturally from her face and is visible even from afar.

"She's so beautiful," Cat says. "She looks better in person than in pictures. I think that's Rocky's dad on her left."

"Want to go say hi?"

"Not yet. I'd love to find Leo, though."

But on the search for Leo, they find John instead.

He appears uncharacteristically polished and urbane in an expensive suit and tie, an effect that dissipates as soon as he opens his mouth. "You made it!" He envelops Cat in a hug from which he manages to reach out to shake Teddy's hand. Pulling away, he asks her, "How's the mommy doing?"

"Great," she says. "Exhausted, as usual, but we're having fun."

"Still running a sleep deprivation experiment in your apartment?"

"You can say that again," Teddy says.

"So, have you checked out the crowd? Do you have any idea who is in this room at this very moment? Are you aware of the power collected right here? You wouldn't believe the business cards I've got in my pocket, it's on fire."

"We saw Reebah Jameson."

"She's going to make the toast. Okay, now keep calm, look around the room."

Cat and Teddy begin to look. Within moments they make sightings of Oprah, Rosie, Diane Sawyer, Barbara Walters, Candace Bergen, and even Jerry Seinfeld. "It's an entertainment Hall of Fame," John says.

Teddy laughs. "Look, it's Geraldo."

"I talked to him," John says, "and he's much more intellectual than you'd think."

"Amazing," Cat says. "This whole thing is just incredible."

"And those are just the faces you recognize," John says. "The presidents of all three networks are here, all three, the *presidents*. And there are William Morris and ICM people crawling all over the place. I must have had seven agents come up to me and give me their card. Charlie thinks this celebrity bio is gonna top *Iacocca*."

"What's George Stephanopoulos doing here?" Teddy asks.

"Who knows? But he's here, and that's what counts," John says.

"My God, he's talking to Leo!" Cat says. "We have to go over there."

John is first out of the starting gate, cutting a path through the bodies with smiles and nods and hand shakes. Cat and Teddy trail close behind. When they get into earshot, they can hear that George and Leo are chatting amiably about the current Broadway theater season.

John pumps George's hand a little too hard and a little too long, but George hangs in there like a trooper. "*Good* to meet you," John says. "*Good* to have you here."

"My pleasure," George says.

Leo weaves an arm through Cat's and tugs her close to him. "How are ya?"

"Excellent," she says. "How are you?"

"Just terrific."

"And?" He widens his eyes and nods, waiting for news. Despite good intentions to keep in touch, they haven't spoken at all since the day Cat finished helping him organize Rocky's stuff in the Libbon basement.

"The baby was born on June 19th, and she's wonderful."

"Healthy? Cute? Brilliant?"

"All of the above. This is my husband, Teddy Foster."

Leo and Teddy shake hands. "Congratulations on *everything*," Leo says. "I won't hold it against you that you didn't invite me to the wedding."

"Hey, they didn't invite me, either," John says.

"We eloped," Cat says. "City Hall for fifteen dollars, then we went out to dinner with my brother and his wife."

"I saw the cartoon show last winter," Leo says. "I liked your stuff a lot."

"You did? Really?"

"Rich and I *both* did. So, are there cartoons in your future?"

"Probably just Saturday morning cartoons."

"Insecurity is ugly," John says. "Projecting success is half the battle."

"Thanks for the tip." Cat screws her face into a sarcastic smile; but he's right and she knows it. "Actually, one of my comic strips is going into a book of new cartoonists. I'm pretty excited about it."

"She's in good company, too," Teddy says. "It's going to be an important collection of established and emerging animation artists."

"*Important.*" Cat laughs. "You sound like a critic."

"I am a critic."

Though she *is* hopeful and excited about her cartooning prospects, she doesn't want to talk about it tonight. "Leo," she asks, "is Annie here?"

"No, couldn't make it. She's in Florida."

"I don't suppose Parker's here."

"He's home with Mom."

"Your mother didn't come?"

Leo shakes his head. "Mom was never the greatest supporter of Rocky's career. Dad came alone."

"Well, the book looks pretty snazzy," Cat says. "Do we rate a complimentary copy?"

"No need to ask," John says. "Just steal one on your way out."

"Here's something I've always wondered," Teddy says. "How can a book that hasn't even been published yet become a bestseller?"

"Charlie fixed it," John says. "He got the distributor to push advance sales, and he got the number one slot at the Book of the Month Club. The first printing sold out last week, it's already in its second printing, every bookstore on earth has copies, we've got displays in all the big stores. Rocky's dad gave permission for me to go on a national book tour on her behalf. I think I'll be a good salesman, don't you?"

"Definitely," Cat says. "But don't you wonder why Rocky gave up so much power? It's totally uncharacteristic."

"She couldn't make the decisions that were coming up," Leo says. "The family had to talk it over. We all felt she couldn't, well, concentrate, and there have been a lot of legal decisions to make. Dad would try to talk to her and she'd start throwing fits. Finally he asked for power of attorney and she gave it to him, just like that. We needed the money to pay for her hospital and Parker's going to need an education." He shrugs his shoulders. "Do you know, she's still writing her own version of the memoirs? We've kept her totally up to date on the book, every step of the way, but she just keeps on writing her own. Dad didn't think it was a good idea to give her a copy of the real book."

"Yet," John says

"Yet," Leo echoes. "Eventually we will, I suppose."

"It's her story," John says. "She's got top billing."

Suddenly the room is filled with an amplified patter. Attention swivels to a podium at the back of the room, where Charlie Webb stands, tapping on a microphone.

"Ladies and gentlemen," he says. "May I have your attention, please?" He waits for silence, and continues. "Thank you. I'm Charlie Webb of Webb Associates, and I've had the honor of representing Rocky Love for the last fifteen years." A murmur and a splatter of applause. "Before I introduce our keynote speaker, Reebah Jameson, I want to thank everyone in this room who made Rocky's book possible, and to say how sorry we all are that she isn't here to join us." He looks down to address a video camera pointed at the podium, and lifts a glass of champagne. "Rocky, babe, this one's for you!" Cheers erupt throughout the room. The camera swerves to record a communal raising of glasses. When the roar has died down, Charlie continues. "We love you, Rocky Love!" More cheers. "Now, to introduce Reebah Jameson, the co-author of *The Rise and Fall of Rocky Love* ... John Paglia."

John weaves through the crowd and stands at the podium. "Thank you, thank you. Let me briefly say what an honor and pleasure it was to work with the infamous Rocky Love, a woman who is anything if not unique." Cheers and laughter. "Who is Rocky Love? What drove her? What inspired her? What troubled her? It's all in the book. Rocky and I worked closely together to make her book the most accurate record it could be. In fact, the last time we met, she told me how pleased she was that the book had captured her voice. She really feels as if she wrote this book herself, which tells me that I did my job. After you read her story, I promise you, you will never forget the inimitable woman who is ... Rocky Love!" Applause. "Reebah Jameson has known Rocky Love since college, and has herself gone on to become one of the most celebrated writers and activists of our time. If anyone understands Rocky Love, it is Reebah Jameson. And so, I am proud to introduce ... Reebah Jameson!" He steps away from the podium.

Reebah moves behind the podium with queenlike confidence. She smiles and surveys the crowd a moment. Cat feels a chill of excitement and takes Teddy's hand.

"I don't know if anyone really understands Rocky," Reebah begins. "When I first knew her, at Bennington, there was no Rocky Love. There was just this smart, confident, full-of-life young woman named Rochelle Libbon. I mean, she was proud, she spoke out, she fought, she did what she wanted to. She was one of the first active feminists of our generation. She came to life in those times, and she brought those times to life. The sexual revolution. The rebirth of the feminist move-ment. The Vietnam War. The times were manifested in her and she also helped to manifest those times. I never knew anyone quite like Rocky. I never saw a woman take such magnificent flight in a revolution that was partly of her own making. Every movement needs a voice, a symbol. And at a time when we needed one, it was Rocky. She came to being at my side, on the radio. She invented herself on the air. She never knew what she was gonna say, oh no, but when she said it, it was thrilling. She didn't study or take notes or draft programs. She just up and shouted and got the message out. The girl I knew, Rochelle, she was a force, no doubt about it. Rocky Love got born on the radio. And Rocky Love got born some more on television. She is one of the lucky few of us who manage to find our perfect venue. She was television. She moved us, didn't she? Didn't she?" Applause and cheers. "Yes, she did. But in her heyday, she was more than a television personality. More than she even realized, she gave us courage. She dared us to confront ourselves. She infused America with an infectious spirit that never would have reached so far into the heartland of our country without her. She was brilliant. And her courage and her brilliance and even, later, her psychosis were all rolled up into one person, one voice, who was bigger than life and more than anything else was there when we needed her. Our horizon is brighter for having known her. She's not here now because she's had a fall. We all take falls, and then we get back up. And so will Rocky Love. We will see her again, to be sure." Loud applause. "And in the meantime, let's keep looking out beyond ourselves and remember that the red edge of the sunshine we're basking in tonight is the blood of Rocky Love."

There is a rupture of applause and a sea of tiny match flames rise above the heads. Someone turns off the overhead lights and a hush falls, and in the dark and silent room the dancing flames seem to burn so much more brightly.

The reverent mood evaporates as soon as the lights consume the candlelit darkness. Speeches over, the party is back in swing.

"Let's check out the view," Teddy says.

They navigate through the bodies until they reach one of the doors leading onto the patio. Stepping into the chilly air, they stand in awe of the night sky, dark and vast, speckled with stars. Among the other people who have drifted outside, they see Leo and Norman Libbon leaning against the railing. It is time at last to meet the father, in person.

Arms linked, Teddy and Cat approach. Leo turns around and smiles. "Is this gorgeous or is this gorgeous?"

"It's gorgeous," Cat says. "Dr. Libbon? I'm Cat. I was Rocky's assistant. This is my husband, Teddy."

"Good to meet you." They all shake hands. "Isn't this phenomenal?" Norman glances toward the party. "She isn't even here and, well, look at it."

"She'll be back in action before you know it," Cat says.

"I almost wish she wouldn't." Norman shakes his head. "What I mean is, I wish she would have a nice life and be happy."

"That's not Rock," Leo says.

"No, it's not, is it?" Norman takes a deep breath of the chilly air. "All this time, Cat, I've been wondering.... Did you know Nathan was with her at the beach house that day?"

Against the open night sky, Norman looks vulnerable, uncertain, as if he could take one step backward and tumble down. But she has to tell him the truth.

"Yes."

"So you knew I would find them together?"

"I thought if you got there sooner, there might be time for Nathan."

Leo puts his arm around his father's shoulder. "Dad, you couldn't have gotten there soon enough."

"That's right, I can see that now." Cat anchors herself by holding Teddy's hand. "I'm sorry."

"It's not your fault, dear." Norman reaches out a hand and squeezes her forearm. "I can only blame myself." He smiles, and the lines on his face reveal a map of experience. For an instant she sees a shadow of Grandpa Ben in the folds around the eyes, and affection rises in her heart.

"My grandparents have been married for sixty-three years," Cat says, "and they can't be held responsible for everything that happened in our family."

"That's right." Leo pats his father's shoulder. "Chalk it up to the mysteries."

"It's cold out here," Teddy says.

"Go on inside and warm up," Leo says. "We'll say goodbye later."

As they walk to the nearest door, Cat turns and glances over her shoulder to see that Norman is watching her. He tries to smile but instead his mask drops off and his face gives way to sorrow. His eyes sparkle with tears. For a moment Cat stops; she is staggered by this lovely man's pain. Only when Leo nods and waves does she muster the courage to follow Teddy back into the party.

She finds him standing next to a pyramid of cheese cubes, skimming the book, and peeks over his shoulder to read with him.

ABOUT THE AUTHOR

Katia Lief is an international bestselling novelist. She teaches fiction writing at The New School in Manhattan and lives in Brooklyn. Learn more at katialief.com